Finding
Georgina

Books by Colleen Faulkner

JUST LIKE OTHER DAUGHTERS

AS CLOSE AS SISTERS

JULIA'S DAUGHTERS

WHAT MAKES A FAMILY

FINDING GEORGINA

Published by Kensington Publishing Corporation

Finding Georgina

COLLEEN FAULKNER

KENSINGTON BOOKS
www.kensingtonbooks.com

KENSINGTON BOOKS are published by

Kensington Publishing Corp.
119 West 40th Street
New York, NY 10018

All Kensington titles, imprints, and distributed lines are available at special quantity discounts for bulk purchases for sales promotion, premiums, fund-raising, educational, or institutional use.

Special book excerpts or customized printings can also be created to fit specific needs. For details, write or phone the office of the Kensington Sales Manager: Kensington Publishing Corp., 119 West 40th Street, New York, NY 10018. Attn. Sales Department. Phone: 1-800-221-2647.

Kensington and the K logo Reg. U.S. Pat. & TM Off.

eISBN-13: 978-1-4967-1156-4
eISBN-10: 1-4967-1156-4
First Kensington Electronic Edition: March 2018

ISBN-13: 978-1-4967-1155-7
ISBN-10: 1-4967-1155-6
First Kensington Trade Paperback Printing: March 2018

10 9 8 7 6 5 4 3 2 1

Printed in the United States of America

Finding Georgina

1

Harper

I always thought I would see Georgina again. In heaven. What I *didn't* expect was to walk into my favorite coffee shop, fourteen years after my daughter was kidnapped, to find her making a cappuccino.

The New Orleans police never came right out and said so, but from the beginning, they assumed my little girl was dead. I heard their whispering. I saw the heartrending looks on their faces. They thought my Georgina had been sexually assaulted. Murdered. Her body buried in the bayou. The police went through the motions of the investigation, but with no leads, it wasn't much of an investigation. Georgina was just there one moment and gone the next.

People used to ask me, back in the days when people still spoke of Georgina, how I managed to go on after she was taken from us. They would ask how I managed to get up each morning and get through the day, not knowing what had happened to her. Realizing I would probably never know. The simple truth is, I tried not to think about it. I tried not to think about the things that happen to little girls who are abducted from their strollers and never seen again.

So for all these years I prayed that my Georgina's death, if she really was dead, was quick. Painless. I prayed she wasn't afraid in the last moments of her life. But I knew she had to have been. What two-year-old wouldn't be afraid when she's taken from her mother by a stranger?

But I also prayed, prayed fervently when I wasn't praying that her death was quick, that she was safe and happy, living life in another city, another state, cared for by parents who, while not her birth parents, loved her. I think a part of me never really believed Georgina was dead. A part of my mother's heart.

My head swims and I grab the doorjamb, afraid I'm going to pass out. I used to do it all the time, back when Georgina was first taken. I couldn't drive. I couldn't work. I couldn't carry my newborn baby across the living room for fear I'd fall. A defense mechanism my family physician diagnosed. When my brain couldn't handle the heartbreak that had become my life anymore, it would just shut down, taking my body with it. I couldn't be left alone. My mother had to move in with us. I had to take a leave of absence from my veterinary practice.

I feel dizzy, but I manage to keep myself upright. I walk into the coffee shop and let the door with the Christmas wreath on it swing shut behind me. It's January. Why do they still have a wreath up? The bells jingle overhead, reminding me of the bell on the Christmas tree in *It's a Wonderful Life*. When a bell rings, another angel gets her wings, that's what the little Bailey girl says. I always loved that movie. Remy and I used to watch it every Christmas Eve before we went to midnight Mass. In happier days, before our marriage and my heart were shattered by our tragedy.

We always read or hear in movies about hearts being torn in half, but when my Georgina was taken from me, it felt as if my heart had been shattered with a ball-peen hammer. And later, when time had passed and we all knew our Georgina would never come home to us, no matter how hard I tried to pick up the ruins of my heart and glue them back together, I couldn't do it. I couldn't be the wife Remy deserved. And for a long time, I couldn't be the mother our daughter Jojo needed. I think I'm a decent mom now, but if you get too close to me, if you listen carefully, you'll hear the splinters of my heart crunch beneath your shoes. You'll see it like stardust in a halo around my head.

I manage to make it to a table in the center of the neighborhood coffee shop near my office and ease into a chair. I slide my bag off my shoulder, onto the table. I'm going to be late for my afternoon appointments; I just ran in for a pick-me-up Americano. I need to call our receptionist and tell her. But I'm afraid to look away long enough to fish my phone out of my bag. I'm afraid if I blink, Georgina will be gone again.

She's a pretty girl. This Georgina. My height, no, she's taller. Slender, with Remy's dark eyes, his dark, thick hair. Her hair is long and piled high on top of her head in the messy, bird's-nest way her sister wears hers. Only Jojo's hair is blond with red undertones, like mine. Jojo's fair-skinned, too. Not like Remy and Georgina. Georgina has his skin. They look perpetually tanned. His family has been here in New Orleans since Louisiana was settled by the French in the seventeenth century. There's Creole in his blood; the darker skin, according to his grandmother, came from the years when Spain controlled the colony.

I watch Georgina, under the tutelage of one of the baristas, add frothed milk to the cappuccino she's making. She's so beautiful, my Georgina. She looks so grown-up that it's hard to wrap my head around the notion. Obviously I know she'd be older now, look older, but for some reason, I always see the toddler in my head when I think of her.

The barista, Sabine, hands Georgina a serving tray. I can't hear what they're saying; I want desperately to hear her voice. I watch my daughter set the cappuccino and a plate with a chocolate croissant on it on a tray. Georgina carries it to a waiting customer at a table at the far end of the room from me. She walks awkwardly. I'm mesmerized. I try to take in every detail: her lanky gait, the uncertainty on her face, the wisp of hair that falls over one eye.

What do I do? Panic flutters in my chest and I fight the darkness that creeps around the edges of my consciousness. It's just a shortage of oxygen; I breathe deeply.

I don't know what to do. What do I do? Do I call the police? Do I call Detective Marin? No . . . not the police. Not Marin, who thinks I'm a nut job. With facts that might support that notion.

Remy. That's who I call. Remy, my hero. Remy, always my champion.

Without taking my eyes off Georgina, I fumble in my bag for my phone. It's supposed to go in the side pocket of the wine-colored suede hobo. It's not there, of course, which means I have to delve into the abyss. I feel my wallet, my sunglasses case, my readers' case, a pen, and bits of paper. And something I can't identify. A fork wrapped in plastic? My panic rises. What if I left my phone in the car? How will I call Remy? I can't just get up and walk out to the car. What if Georgina leaves?

If she leaves, I'll never see her again.

Again the flutter of panic. If she leaves, how will I ever find her? Where will I look for her? The local schools? The churches? Will I drive through the local neighborhoods?

But the fear is illogical. I know that. She works here. The owners of the coffee shop must have contact information for her. They have her Social Security number, her home address, for heaven's sake . . . But they can't have her Social Security number, can they? Not her real one, because I have her Social Security card in the fire safe at the house. It was issued when she was born. Remy thought we should turn the Social Security number in, but we never had her declared dead, so why would we?

Sweat beads on my forehead, despite the cool weather of early January. Cool, at least, for Louisiana. Maybe it's just another hot flash coming on. I keep thinking I'm too young for hot flashes. Who has hot flashes at forty-four?

Lots of women, says my gynecologist. Perimenopause.

As I watch Georgina walk behind the counter, my fingertips touch the familiar edge of my cell phone and I pull it out of my bag with an audible sigh of relief. Keeping her in my peripheral vision, I choose Remy's name from my "favorites" in my contacts and lift the phone to my ear.

Four rings and it goes to voice mail.

I disconnect and redial.

"Pick up, pick up," I murmur under my breath. "Come on, Remy."

Voice mail again.

I end the call. This is not the kind of thing you leave a message about.

Sabine is walking toward me.

My finger hovers over Remy's name. I tap it.

"Can I get you something?" Sabine asks me. She looks concerned. She's cute; early twenties, short-cropped hair, and skin as smooth as a baby's. I'm jealous of her perfect complexion. My teenage acne has recently resurfaced.

"No, I'm—" The phone is ringing in my ear. Remy isn't answering. Why isn't he answering? He knows the signal for an emergency. Three calls in rapid succession. I hang up when it goes to voice mail. He'll call me back. He has to call me back. "Um . . . yeah . . . yes. A medium Americano?"

"For here or to go?"

I lower the phone. Where the hell is Remy? What if Jojo is sick, or hurt? What if she's been kidnapped? Remy's gently reminded me hundreds of times, maybe thousands, over the years, that the odds of having two children kidnapped, in two separate incidents, is astronomical. But it *could* happen. Like the guy who survived two commercial airline crashes, seven years apart. I always remind him of that.

"I was just asking because it's Thursday," Sabine says. "You have evening hours, right? You usually take it to go."

She's still looking at me with concern. As if I'm acting a little crazy. Weird, at the very least.

"I . . . um. To go is fine, I just . . ." I grip the phone, looking past Sabine to my daughter behind the counter. She's staring at the cash register, trying to figure out how to ring up a customer who has a bag of pastries in his hand. "The new girl. The . . ." I touch my hair. "Brunette. She . . . just started?"

Sabine glances over her shoulder, then back at me. "Lilla? Yeah. This week. Tuesday, I think. After school. I'm training her."

"Tuesday," I echo. I was here Tuesday, Tuesday morning. I got an Americano for myself and a latte and bear claw for Samantha. She owns the veterinary practice where I work as a veterinarian. We used to be partners; she bought me out after the kidnapping. I work Mondays and Tuesdays nine to six. But Thursdays I work evening hours. Which means I was here Tuesday and Georgina came in later. What if I hadn't come in today? What if I had missed my daughter? What if our paths had never crossed again?

But that seems impossible because seeing her here, now, means God always meant for me to have my daughter again. I just know it.

"Lilla," I repeat, testing the sound of the name. It never occurred to me that the people who kidnapped her would have given her another name. Of course they would have. Georgina was so little and just beginning to talk; even if she tried to tell someone her name, they may not have been able to understand her.

My impulse is to tell Sabine that that isn't her name. That her name is Georgina, Georgina Elise Broussard, and that she's my daughter. Fortunately I have enough sense not to say it. "Just the Americano." I force a smile. "And a scone, cranberry walnut. If you have any left."

"Sure do."

As Sabine walks away, my phone vibrates in my lap.

"Remy!" I say quietly into the phone, my gaze on Georgina again.

"I was in a meeting." He sounds annoyed, bordering on pissed. "What's wrong?"

"She's here. At Perfect Cup." My eyes flood with tears and, for a moment, I can't speak. All the pain, all the fear, all the abject sorrow of the last fourteen years lodges in my throat. "Remy, I found her," I choke.

There's a long pause on the other end of the phone. Long enough for me to say, "Remy, I know what you're going to say, but I'm telling you, it's her. It's Georgina. I'm sure of it."

Still, he doesn't say anything.

"Remy?"

He exhales. "Harper . . ."

"I know, I know," I say quickly. I close my eyes for an instant, then open them. She's still there. My Georgina is still there behind the counter. She's not a figment of my imagination. Not part of a dream that seems so real that I can still smell her baby hair when I startle awake in the middle of the night and reach for a Xanax.

I watch my daughter carry a little stainless-steel milk pitcher to the sink. "But it's her, Remy."

He takes his time before responding. "Harper, I can't talk right now. I'm in with the assistant dean." He suddenly sounds tired. Tired of me, I suspect.

"Remy—"

"Baby, I . . . I can't do this, at all," he says. "Not again. I told you that the last time. I just can't."

I can hear the pain in his voice and the tears well in my eyes again. Sometimes it's so easy to get wrapped up in my own loss that I forget she was his baby, too. "Remy, please."

"I have to go."

I press my lips together. Sabine is watching me from behind the counter. "Remy, you have to listen to me." I go on faster than before. I'm bordering on manic. "I know . . . I know I've told you I've seen her before."

"You've called the police before, Harper. You've accused people of kidnapping our child. You've had Child Protective Services interview . . . *disrupt* families. That girl in Jojo's gymnastics class. Remember? You wanted to get our attorney to file a motion for a maternity test."

I close my eyes. "I know," I whisper, "but this is different, Remy." I open my eyes again. "I swear to you"—my voice catches in my throat—"this is our Georgina."

He exhales, or sighs, or maybe it's a groan. "I have to go, baby," he says. "They're waiting on me."

The phone goes dead and for a moment I stare at it. He hung up on me? My husband hung up on me?

Okay, ex-husband. Which I suppose makes it more likely.

I glance at Georgina. Sabine is talking to her as she retrieves my scone and puts it in a bag. Georgina's nodding as she wipes up a spill from the counter. She seems to be a serious girl. Which makes sense. She was a serious toddler, too . . . as toddlers go. Not that she didn't laugh; she was just never as carefree as Jojo was.

I stare at her for a long moment. Is Remy right? Is this just another false alarm? But false alarms are thinking you left the stove on, only to go back into the house to find it off. Or . . . thinking you're pregnant when you're just late. Those are *false alarms*. Seeing your missing child on playgrounds, in grocery stores, on the streetcar. That's different, isn't it?

But is Remy right? Am I mistaken again? Do I want to see Georgina so badly, even after fourteen years, that I imagine her? What if I'm wrong?

Sabine brings me my coffee in a to-go cup, my scone in a bag. I pay her and include a tip. I know how much I owe her because I get the same thing all the time.

"Thanks." Sabine flashes me a smile.

I look at Georgina again. I try to study her without allowing my emotions to take over. Is Remy right? Does she just look like what I have imagined she must look like now? Except that when I saw her, I was surprised by how much older she looks than I had imagined.

And I'm right. And Remy is wrong. The girl behind the counter is our daughter.

I pick up my phone and attempt to do something our fourteen-year-old Jojo does all the time. I pretend to take a selfie while actually focusing the camera on someone or something across the room. Usually Jojo is taking pics of a dog in a stormtrooper costume or a granny in leather pants and a sequined crop top.

I pretend to fuss with my bangs while centering the shot on Georgina's face. I wonder how obvious it is what I'm doing.

I don't care.

I zoom in on her face and take three pics in rapid succession. I look at one after the other.

It's her. I know it's her. Tears fill my eyes again. I message the photo to Remy.

Two minutes later, before my coffee is even cool enough to sip, I get a text from Remy.

Be there in fifteen minutes.

2

Lilla

I slice off two pieces of bread from an English muffin loaf with a serrated blade from my mom's knife roll. Some chefs freak out if someone touches their personal knives, but not my mom. At least not with me. If someone picked up one of her knives at work without asking, I don't think she'd cut them or anything, but she probably wouldn't like it. Knives are personal for chefs.

I carefully wipe off the blade with a hand towel and, stepping over a cardboard box, return it to the leather roll on the center island. We still haven't unpacked, even though we moved to New Orleans three months ago. There are boxes everywhere. Except in my room; I unpacked my stuff the weekend we got here. I don't mind the kitchen and living room being a mess, but my bedroom where I sleep and do my homework has to be tidy. As dumb as it sounds, things are so disordered in my sixteen-year-old head that I need some order somewhere.

I like the house we rented in Bayou St. John near City Park in New Orleans. It's called a single shotgun. You have to walk through one room to get to the next. No hallways. They call it a shotgun because you can stand at the front door and shoot through the back without hitting the walls, because the rooms are lined up, one after the other. I Googled it. I don't know anything about guns, but I guess you could throw a chef's knife from the front door through the back if you wanted to. If you were good at throwing knives.

I wrap up the bread and take my slices to the toaster oven. While I wait, I slide onto a stool at the island and flip open my statistics book. Quiz, third block. I already know the material, but I look over it anyway because I'm a nerd and that's what nerds do. They study even when they're already going to get an A.

I check the time on my phone on the counter. I have to leave in ten minutes. I can walk to school, which is nice because Mom works late most nights. When I was little it was hard on her, working until one or two in the morning, then only getting a few hours' sleep before she had to get me up for school. But even though she's always worked nights, she never let any of my babysitters make my breakfast or take me to school. That was her job, she always said. And even now that I'm old enough to get myself off to school, she still gets up a lot of mornings and makes me breakfast. Sometimes she makes fancy Challah bread French toast, or chocolate waffles with peanut butter sauce, but other mornings she makes my favorite. What I used to call "dippy egg" when I was little. Actually I still call it that, but I made up the name when I was little. It's an egg fried soft in the center of a piece of toast that has a circle cut out for the egg. Mom says a good chef knows how to recognize a good meal, even when it's simple.

The toaster oven dings and I slide off the stool to get my English muffin toast. Mom and I found a cool bakery that makes amazing donuts and these loaves of English muffin bread. I put the hot slices on a plate, glass not paper. We may do cardboard boxes, but we don't do paper plates. Negates a good meal, Mom says. I get Irish butter out of the refrigerator and grab a butter knife on the way back to the counter. We haven't found the silverware or the plates and bowls and stuff yet because Mom mislabeled all the boxes. I found my hair stuff and tampons in the box labeled "coat closet." We bought two place settings of silverware and dishware at a flea market. They're antiques so that's cool. And dishes don't pile up in the sink, so I'm fine with not unpacking the dishware that's probably labeled "underwear."

I'm scraping the tiniest bit of butter across my toast, because that's the way I like it, when Mom walks into the kitchen in her robe. Her hair is all messy and her eyes puffy from only a few hours of sleep. But she's smiling. At me. Because I'm the center of her world. And as uncool as it is, she's the center of mine.

She sleeps in the bedroom behind the kitchen and I have the back bedroom. Which means I have to walk through her bedroom to get to the bathroom, kitchen, or living room from my room. When we moved in, she insisted I take the back room. She said a sixteen-year-old girl needed privacy. I teased her that having the front bedroom was going to get in the way of her love life and we both laughed. Mom doesn't date. Never has. Well, I guess she did at some point because she got knocked up with me. My dad was a one-night stand. Another chef. It used to upset me that that was the way I came into the world, by a busted condom or whatever, but I'm over it. I'm old enough now to realize how lucky I am to have a parent like mine. The kind of mom who, after I was born, decided her priority was being my mother. She said she didn't have the time or the energy to work and be a mother and someone's girlfriend at the same time.

"Did I wake you?" I ask. I make a face. "Sorry."

She shakes her head. She's wearing the bathrobe I gave her for Mother's Day last year. It's bright yellow and has Tweety Birds all over it. She's into old-school cartoon memorabilia.

"You didn't wake me." As she walks past me, she kisses my shoulder. I'm taller than she is now. Taller and a lot skinnier. Mom's kind of short and round.

"Thought I'd work on unpacking for a few hours. Time this house started looking like a home." She goes to the counter and pours coffee beans from a Mason jar into the grinder. Hits the button to grind the beans.

I wait for the whine to stop. "Go back to bed. You didn't get home until two thirty in the morning."

"*Oy vey iz mir.* Fresh fish order wasn't right again. They've got a great menu, but their organization is a disaster." She sighs as she dumps the ground coffee into a press. Then she takes the electric kettle to fill it with water from the faucet. "You working this afternoon?"

"Till seven." I take a bite of my English muffin toast and tap my phone to check the time. I hate that I have to head to school. I'd rather sit here and have coffee with Mom. I'd even rather unpack boxes with her. It seems like we never have enough time together, not with her working nights and weekends. But her new job is a good one, at one of the fancy restaurants in the Warehouse District. I assumed she would want to work in the French Quarter, but she likes the Warehouse District. She says the clientele is better. I was born here, but we moved when I was two, so I don't remember it. But I'm excited about getting to know my birth city.

"We talked about you working and going to school, *bubbeleh*." Mom comes to lean on the counter next to me. She smells good. Like her Calvin Klein perfume and sweet potato biscuits.

I push one of my slices of toast across the counter to her. She takes it.

"You don't need a job," she says, taking a bite.

I guess my mom's not pretty by contemporary standards. Of course, who is, what with the Kardashians plastered all over the Internet? My mom's got dark, curly hair and dark eyes and kind of a big nose. I didn't get her nose. I really don't look much like her at all, really, except my hair is dark and my skin is the same color as hers. We're not white white, but we're not "people of color," either. She says our skin tone comes from ancestors in Hungary. We're Jews.

"We're going to be fine, financially," Mom says. "I'm making quite a bit more than I was in Baton Rouge."

"But rent's higher here," I counter.

The electric kettle clicks off. "I still don't like the idea of you working." She turns away, munching on the toast. "You've got your whole life ahead of you to work."

I close my statistics book. "Right, but I need to save for college."

She laughs, which hurts my feelings a little bit. Sometimes she teases me that she doesn't know where my geekiness comes from. I guess when she was younger, she was kind of wild. Got expelled from school a couple of times. Was promiscuous. *Obviously.* She has tattoos.

"Well, I do." I get off the stool. "Do you know what tuition is at Tulane, even in state?"

She pours boiling water into the French press. "Coffee?"

"Can't. Gotta go." I push my book into my old blue backpack that I've had since I was in middle school. Mom keeps offering to buy me a new one, but I like this one. It's kind of my security blanket.

The front doorbell rings and I look at her. "Who's that at seven forty in the morning?"

"I don't know." She shakes her head. "I called the landlord about the toilet running, but she said she'd call before she sent someone over." She tightens the tie on her robe. "I'll get it."

"I'm on my way out. I'll get it. Kisses." I make a smacking sound with my lips as I throw my backpack over my shoulder.

"Ring me after school," she calls after me. "Good luck on the calculus test."

"Statistics," I correct her as the doorbell rings again. "Frequency distributions." I walk out of the kitchen. "Love you, Mama Bear."

"Love you, Baby Bear."

I peek out the sidelight of the door before I open it because that's what my mom taught me to do. Another notch in my geek belt. There are two police officers standing on our step. Wrong house? There's a whole row of shotguns on our street. But ours is the only mint-green one. I open the door. "Hi."

"Lilla Kohen?" the woman asks. Her skin is so dark that it's shiny, and she has a distinct accent. British maybe?

"Yes?" I frown again because this is totally weird. Cops have never come to our door before. Not anywhere we've lived, and we've lived lots of places. The life of a chef.

"Are your parents home?" There's a white guy with her. He looks like what you think a city cop ought to look like: older; beer belly; stern, wrinkly face. But the woman seems to be in charge.

"Um . . ." I step back, feeling uncomfortable, and I'm not sure why. "No dad. Just my mom."

"Can we come in?" As she says it, she steps into the living room, forcing me to back up.

"Sure." My tone is a little sarcastic. "Mom?" I call, taking another step back.

Mom is just walking into the living room. "I'm Sharon Kohen. Can I help you?"

The guy cop is just coming in the door behind the woman. His radio crackles and there's a voice, but I don't catch what's being said. I'm mildly embarrassed to have the cops see our house in such disarray. I push a cardboard box with the toe of my white Converse to make room for him to come all the way in. It's labeled "books," which might mean the missing silverware is inside.

The woman cop looks at me and then at my mom. "Could we speak with you privately, Mrs. Kohen?"

I wonder if there's been a robbery at the new restaurant. At one of the places where my mom worked in Baton Rouge, a busboy or dishwasher or someone helped himself to the cash drawer one night and my mom was interviewed by the police.

"I'm gonna be late if I don't get going," I tell my mom, looking to her.

She nods.

But the cops don't move out of my way to let me pass.

"Actually," the woman cop says, "we'll need to speak to Lilla, too. But we want to speak with you first, Mrs. Kohen. Separately."

I'm surprised my mom doesn't correct her on the "Mrs." She usually does. She's never been embarrassed by the fact that she was never married to my dad. Or didn't even know his middle name. But there's something about the cop's tone of voice that seems to worry my mother. All of a sudden she's got this odd look on her face. She's holding both ends of the tie to her bathrobe. But she's gripping them really tightly.

"You want me to go into the kitchen?" I ask my mom.

"I think you should leave."

For a second, I think my mom's talking to me. But then I realize she's talking to the cops. There's something wrong with her. Her voice is all wrong. And suddenly I have this horrible, sickening feeling in the pit of my stomach. Like when I'm watching a scary movie and I know the girl is about to be killed by the guy with the ax.

"Mrs. Kohen." It's the guy cop, now.

"Leave. Leave us alone," Mom says in a voice I've never heard. It's like she's scared and pissed and . . . a little bit bat-shit crazy.

The cops look at each other.

"Mrs. Kohen," the woman repeats in what is definitely a British accent.

The guy is speaking quietly into the radio thingy on his shoulder, but either I don't hear what he says or my brain can't process it because the woman is saying, "Is Lilla your daughter, Mrs. Kohen?"

At that moment, time seems to move at two speeds. In a way, it seems as if it takes forever for my mom to respond, yet the moment is over in a nanosecond. My life is over in a nanosecond. Hers too.

Because my mom doesn't say anything. She just falls to her knees in her Tweety Bird robe.

"Mom!" I say, my voice not sounding like my own in my head. Now I'm scared. "Mom, what's wrong?" I drop my backpack on top of the box. I'm moving toward her when the woman cop takes my arm. Not roughly, but enough to make me stop where I am.

"Mrs. Kohen, we had a report filed yesterday stating that Lilla might be the missing daughter of—"

I don't hear what the cop says because my mother makes a sound that I've never heard a human make before. I guess it's what you would call a keen. It's this cry that's more animal than human. The kind of sound that wraps around your heart and pulls it up to your throat so you can't breathe.

"Mom!" I tear away from the cop and throw myself onto the floor in front of her. I don't remember starting to cry, but tears are stinging my eyes. "Mom, what are they talking about?" I say in that voice that's not mine. "Mom, tell them it's not true. Tell them . . ." I reach for her, but she doesn't reach for me.

She lowers her head to the floor, cradling it in her arms, a sobbing pile of yellow fleece and Tweety Birds. And she keeps making those sounds. Sounds that scare me enough to make me pull away. "*Mom?*"

The woman cop is behind me. "Lilla," she says, her voice gentle, as if I'm an abandoned kitten she found in a gutter on Bourbon Street. But her hands are firm on my shoulders. "Lilla, I need you to stand up."

"Mom," I squeak as I get to my feet. "*Mom,*" I sob as the cop pulls me toward the front door. "What are they talking about? Mom, tell them I'm your daughter," I beg, half shouting.

I feel myself being propelled backward, as if I'm being sucked into a black hole. And in a way, I am. In a way, I'll learn, it *will* be, for a very long time. And when I emerge, I won't even be in the same universe.

3

Jojo

"What do you mean they might have found your sister?"

I glance at my best friend, Makayla. We're standing on the corner of State and Freret, waiting for the light to change. We're walking to school together, just like we have since elementary school, only now we actually get to walk alone, without our parents. We're both fourteen.

She wrinkles her nose. Makayla might be the prettiest fourteen-year-old ever. She's biracial. Her dad is Haitian. Her mom's white. Makayla has her mother's blue eyes, her dad's dark hair, and skin that's somewhere between the two of them. I tease my dad all the time about wishing he was Haitian. I mean I'm pretty, sure, but I'll never be beautiful like Makayla.

"I thought some perv decapitated her and buried her in the bayou," Makayla says. "You said he buried her head in one hole and her body somewhere else so no one could ever identify her." The traffic light changes and she looks both ways before we step off the curb.

We wait for a car that runs the red light and then start across. "I never said that."

Makayla doesn't respond, even though I probably *did* tell her that. People don't argue with you about your dead sister. Not even best friends. It's amazing the stuff you can get away with when people realize you're the girl whose sister was kidnapped at a Mardi Gras parade.

I walk beside Makayla in the crosswalk. There's a cute guy on a scooter with a red lunchbox on the back stopped at the light. I make eye contact, smile, and then look at the street in front of me. I'm just learning the whole flirting thing. Sometimes it feels really good, but sometimes I just feel like an idiot. It's an idiot kind of morning, I guess. "That's just what we always thought happened," I tell Makayla. "It's what the police think happened."

"But your mom never thought she was dead." She glances at me. "Didn't she go to a medium or something and try to talk to her, and the voodoo lady said Georgina wasn't dead and that was why she couldn't be contacted?"

I make a face at her. "Now you're just making stuff up. There's no way my mom went to a voodoo lady." I probably told her that, too. I don't remember. I know Makayla's mom has been to a psychic. "Mom goes to Mass, like, three times a week. She doesn't believe in voodoo or magic or even fate. She believes in the *Holy Trinity*." I do the quotations thing with my fingers, then tug on the hem of my skirt; I've had another growth spurt. If my skirt gets any shorter, you'll see Christmas. That's what my grandmother used to say when she meant lady parts. Of course I never quite understood that because I always wear panties. I can't ask her because she died two years ago. Cancer in her Christmas.

I glance at Makayla. We're dressed identically: a skirt, white collared shirt, and navy blazer with the Ursuline Academy emblem over our hearts. Pink Jelly Donut lip gloss and Kerouac Black eyeliner. Just a little eyeliner, not enough for any of our teachers to call us on it. *"This is what my eyes look like, Miss Gerard. They're the eyes the Holy Father blessed me with."*

I stop at Makayla's house every morning to put on makeup because her mom doesn't mind. She just says she's not getting into it between me and Mom, which is totally letting me get away with it. Mom would notice if I was wearing lip gloss and eyeliner. She'd see it. She'd smell it. She notices when I roll my socks instead of folding them. She knows when I have a religion quiz. She knows when I'm getting my period before I know it. The term "helicopter mom" was invented to describe Harper Louise Broussard.

"Your mom always thought she *wasn't* dead is my point." Makayla steps up on the curb on the other side of the street. "Remember that time when we were at Rouses and she left the grocery cart full of groceries with ice cream and everything in it and made us get in the car? We had to follow that guy and his daughter all the way to Kenner because your mom thought she was Georgina."

I don't say anything because I don't remember it. Not that I'm saying it didn't happen. It's happened more times than I can count. At least she didn't call the police that time. That I would have remembered because I would have died of embarrassment. Because *that* has happened to me before, too.

"Mom says she found Georgina in a coffee shop in Mid-City," I say, keeping any emotion out of my voice. Mostly because I know that the things I'm feeling aren't what I'm supposed to be feeling. I'm supposed to be thrilled, ecstatic, overjoyed. I'm none of that. Mostly I'm just annoyed. And I don't believe it. Not for one sec. It's just my whacked-out mom being whacked-out. "Near her office."

"Did you see her?"

I don't answer.

Makayla pulls on the sleeve of my blazer. "Jojo, did you see her?" I guess she's all excited for me. "Do you really think it could be Georgina?"

"Mom took a picture of her with her phone."

"Does it look like her?"

I make a face like that's the stupidest thing I've ever heard, because it is. "I was, like . . . three months old when she was kidnapped." I pick up the pace. "How would I know what she *looks* like?"

"You know what I mean. Does she look like you? Like your mom?"

There are other girls on the sidewalk ahead of us. Ursuline students. I spot Ainsley Royce and seriously think about crossing the street. I can't deal with her bitchiness this morning. We used to be good friends but she got mad because I wouldn't work on some lame science project with her last year and now she doesn't talk to me. It used to upset me that she doesn't want to be my friend, but I'm over it. Dad says this kind of thing happens as you get older; friends come and go as you find your place in the world. Of course he's never been a teenage girl and he's never attended a Catholic school for girls, but I try to cut him a break once in a while.

"Does she?" Makayla is being pushy, which is weird because she's usually pretty good at reading my moods.

"I don't know!" Ainsley glances over her shoulder at us and I lower my voice. I really don't want to talk about this with Makayla for about a hundred reasons. But I know she won't leave me alone until I tell her everything she wants to know. Or at least something. "Not really. I mean . . ." I exhale. I don't want to talk about Georgina. I don't want to think about her. People have been talking about Georgina my whole life. Everything in my house, with my mom in particular, it all revolves around Georgina.

"I guess she kind of looks like me. A little," I confess, "but with Dad's hair. It was hard to tell. Mom's not that good at taking pics with her phone."

I have my mom's looks; we're blond with green eyes. Dad has dark hair, dark eyes, and he's not super white, like Mom and me. The Broussards have been here since the whites ran the Choctaw Indians out and made this city on the banks of the Muddy. There's this old song I like that calls the Mississippi "the Great Big Muddy."

"So what's going to happen now?"

I slow down so we don't run right up under Ainsley's skirt. Which is definitely shorter than it's supposed to be. Shorter than mine. I hope Miss Gerard catches her. Mrs. Blocker is always nice about it, but Miss Gerard is pretty sure that a uniform skirt half an inch too short will get a virgin pregnant before lunch. I smile to myself, thinking Ainsley's probably going to get an after-school detention. She's with these two girls that are the biggest snobs in the ninth grade, Suzanne and Carly. Makayla says they deserve each other.

"I don't know what's going to happen," I tell Makayla. "A DNA test, I guess. To see if my mom popped her out or not."

"Wait." Makayla stops and grabs my arm. "This is for real."

I look at her blankly. "No, it's for fake."

"Your *sister?*" She almost whispers the word.

I start walking again. "We're going to be late."

"We're not going to be late." She catches up with me. "Jojo, this is the most amazing thing I've ever heard in my life. You might have a sister. You know how much I've always wanted a sister?"

"You can have her."

"Jojo, don't you—" Makayla cuts herself off.

I don't know what she was going to say. I don't want to know. But I doubt she was going to say how sorry she was that my life, as I know it, could be about to end. We walk in silence for another block. We're almost to school. The street is busy. Cars dropping off girls and the usual morning traffic.

When Makayla speaks, her tone is gentle. And kind. She's a way better person than I am. "Jojo, I know you're scared."

"I'm not *scared*. It's just that . . . I have a perfectly good life as an only child. What's going to happen if it really is her? I mean, it's not, but what if it is? Am I going to have to share my bathroom? Because I'm not sharing my bathroom."

"Jojo, your mom still cries for her at night. Your parents divorced because—"

"My parents divorced because my mom wouldn't stop acting crazy in grocery stores." We're in front of the school now. It's a big brick monstrosity that takes up a whole block. It's, like, the oldest girls' school in the country. Dad's mom went here. Georgina was going to start nursery school here the year she disappeared. I never had the choice to go anywhere else when Dad said Mom couldn't keep homeschooling me. I mean, it's okay, but because of her, I didn't even get a choice. A lot of things in my house are the way they are because Georgina got herself kidnapped.

"When will the results come back?" Makayla asks me.

"What results? Can I copy your English homework? I didn't do it."

"The DNA test. When will you know if this girl your mom saw in a coffee shop is Georgina?"

I roll my eyes. "I don't know. Mom got a call from the police this morning saying that the girl she saw at the coffee shop might be her." I shift my backpack on my shoulder. If we don't hurry up, I'm not going to have time to copy her homework in the bathroom and I'm going to be in so much trouble with Miss Gerard. She not only checks skirt lengths, but she checks homework, too. Every single freakin' day. "The cops told her it takes twenty-four to forty-eight hours for the test to come back from the lab. But it depends when they get the blood or spit or whatever to the lab and then the weekend is coming up, so . . ." I stop and look at her. "So, I guess I've got at least through the weekend before this potential sister comes and ruins my life that she's already ruined."

Makayla laughs. "You're such a drama queen. Come on, let's get your homework done."

She walks past me and I just stand there for a minute. For some crazy reason my throat is tight, like I might cry. Because Makayla is right: I *am* scared. What if the coffee shop girl really is Georgina? She's so much a part of my life, of Mom and Dad's life, dead. If she really is alive, will that make me dead?

4

Harper

"Monday? They can't tell us anything until *Monday?*" I'm pacing my tiled kitchen floor. Pacing and gesturing. And I'm sounding a bit manic, as if I need a Xanax. Honestly, I'd probably take one right now if I had one. Which is why I don't keep them in the house. I went down that road after Georgina disappeared. It was a road too often taken by women like me, neither grassy nor wanting wear. And a bad choice. "And they say that would be the earliest." I go on with my rant. "It may be Tuesday. Possibly even Wednesday."

"Why so long?" Ann's tone is patient. She's always patient, particularly with me. Saint Ann I like to call her.

Ann's my best friend. Who am I kidding? One of my only friends. I'm too sad for friends. Too intense. Too neurotic. I'm just . . . too much. Not that I blame anyone; I'm too much for myself sometimes. Ann's lived down the street for years. She and I were in a birthing class together when we were pregnant with Jojo and her Makayla. That's where we met. She's the only person I still see regularly, other than Rebecca at the office, who knew me when I was the mother of two. I'd argue that I'll always be the mother of two, even if my Georgina really is dead. So I suppose I just mean she knew me when I was whole.

"The police picked up Georgina from the house where she was . . ." I take a deep breath. "Being held."

I don't allow my mind to go in the direction of what that could potentially mean. I don't think about Jaycee Dugard or Elizabeth Smart and the hell they endured as female captives. On January first, I started a fifty-four-day rosary novena as I do every year, praying for the return of my Georgina. I used to pray to keep her safe and bring her home, but over the years, my prayers changed. I'm not even sure if this year I was praying she come home alive, or if I just wanted closure, even in the form of remains. Now that I'm realizing my prayers may have been answered, I'll take her any way I can get her. Whatever trauma she's suffered, we'll deal with once she's home.

"They picked her up an hour ago," I continue. "They didn't give me details, but I got the feeling . . ." I halt in front of her. Ann's seated on the other side of the granite island, sipping coffee from a blue mug. Mine's green. I reach for it. It's my fourth or fifth cup, so I'm wired. Though maybe it was being up all night that's wired me. "Ann . . . I think the police might have gotten some kind of confession."

"From Georgina?" She's got milk foam above her upper lip. She comes to my house most mornings that I don't have to work, after the girls have gone to school, to have a cup of coffee. She teases me that she comes more for the fancy coffee from my fancy coffeemaker than for the company.

I touch my lip. Our signal. She reaches for a napkin and wipes her mouth.

"I don't think so." I try to recall what the police officer who called said. It's all a blur. It was a woman who called. She told me her name, but I was so excited, so scared. I don't remember who she said she was, only that she was with the New Orleans Police. And she had a British accent. I remember that because you don't hear it every day. "If Georgina knew she'd been kidnapped, wouldn't she have told someone before this?" I think aloud. "A sixteen-year-old girl who's allowed to work in a coffee shop would have had the opportunity to tell someone. And she goes to school. She was on her way to school when the cops picked her up. She was living in Bayou St. John. I don't think the police-woman was supposed to tell me that, but she was almost as excited as I was when we spoke on the phone."

Ann adjusts a chandelier earring. One she's made herself. An intricate copper-and-bead sculpture. She's an artist and works with whatever medium strikes her fancy. She paints, she sculpts, you name it. And while she does make money on the sale of her artwork in its various forms, she doesn't do it for a living. She says she has no problem being a kept woman. It's every woman's dream, according to her. And man's. "Did the police say who had her? Was he the man who kidnapped her?"

"I don't know."

"*Any* details?"

"The police said they couldn't tell me anything because nothing has been confirmed yet. Even that she's really Georgina." My hand shakes a little as I set down my mug. "But it's her, Ann." My eyes fill with tears. "I know it's her." I look down at my hands on the counter. Artist's hands, Remy used to say. He always thought I should have been an artist. The fact that I have no artistic ability never seemed to bother him. "It's her," I whisper.

"Okay, so where is she now? Will they let you see her?"

"She was taken to . . ." I push the damp hair out of my eyes. I jumped in the shower as soon as Jojo left for school. After I stood on the front porch and watched her turn the corner onto St. Charles to Makayla and Ann's. She's supposed to text me when she gets there. The four minutes she's out of my sight before she texts me are the longest four minutes of my day. I'd prefer to walk or drive her to Ursuline where she goes to school, but there was a big brouhaha when she started high school in the fall. An intervention of sorts. Jojo, Remy, Ann, her husband George, and Makayla all ganged up on me and insisted it was time the girls were allowed to walk to school together alone. It's been one of the hardest things I've had to do. To let Jojo out of my sight in a public place.

I meet Ann's gaze. "I think she's been put in some type of temporary foster care. We're not allowed to see her. Not until the DNA test comes back, but the sample hadn't even been taken yet when the police called. There needs to be a court order or something. Which they said they can get today, but . . . Apparently there are rules set in place for how this is done. To protect the kidnapper's rights, I'm sure."

She ignores my sarcasm. "Where's the guy who had her?"

"Hell, I hope." I pick up my mug, but don't drink from it. I begin pacing again. "Or the gallows." I whip around to face her. "Did you know we used to have public hangings here? I don't remember if it was when we were under French or Spanish rule."

"We also had public lynchings," Ann, always the politically correct one, points out. "That doesn't mean it's okay."

I worry at my lower lip, which is already puffy from me gnawing on it. "Okay, so Guantanamo?"

She doesn't answer.

I go back to pacing; the hand-painted tile is cool on my bare feet. It's the first week of January and the Louisiana heat has finally let up. I look up to see Ann watching me.

"You okay?" she asks.

I nod, stopping to lean on the island again. I turn my coffee mug in my hands, feeling the weight and warmth of it.

"You're okay?" she repeats. "You're sure?"

"They might have found her." I choke up. My gaze meets hers. "Ann, my baby might be coming home. My Georgina is coming home."

She reaches out and squeezes my hand. She's tearing up, too. "You need to prepare yourself, you know," she says softly. "In case it isn't her."

"It's her."

"But if it isn't . . . Harper . . ." She says my name in an exhalation.

I try to let myself go to that place. Just for a second. A place where the girl from the coffee shop isn't my missing baby. But I can't do it. Mostly because I know it will be my undoing. If the girl called Lilla isn't my Georgina, my family will be visiting me on the psych floor at Tulane Medical Center, or maybe in some quiet, private place in the country.

But that girl *was* my daughter. She *is* my daughter. I'd bet my life on it. She's my daughter and she's coming home to me. *Please, God, bring her home to me. Lord, hear my prayer.* I brush my fingertips over the tiny platinum crucifix I always wear. A gift from my grandmother on my first communion, which was a gift from her grandmother.

I wonder if Georgina has had her first communion. Which, of course, is ridiculous. Who kidnaps a child and then makes sure she has a sound religious education? As soon as Georgina is home, I'll make arrangements for her to start preparing for her first communion. Because of her age and circumstances, I know I can convince Father Paul to tutor her privately. And I'll give her Grandmama's crucifix when she walks down the aisle in her white dress.

I meet Ann's gaze as I pull my hand away that she's holding tightly. She's still staring at me. Weighing the odds of me stepping over the edge, right here in front of her before she's finished her first cup of morning coffee.

"I'm okay," I repeat. I open my arms as if that's proof. Raise my voice. "I'm okay, Ann."

"Where's Remy?"

"Work. Of course."

"That's not fair, Harper." She reaches for her coffee. "Your ex-husband is more attentive to you than any husband I know. More attentive than my husband."

I point at her. "George is a good man. A good husband and a good father."

"He is." She raises her mug to take a sip. "But Remy goes above and beyond. And you know it. Divorced, you're more married than most couples I know."

I glance away. She's right. I know she's right, but I'm being stingy with my Remy points right now. "He said he'd be over as soon as he could. He had something to do at work first. The comptroller position is going to be open sometime in the next few months and he's paranoid he isn't going to get the job. Even though he's clearly the best candidate. Internally, at least." He's been the assistant comptroller for years. And for all those years, he's worked toward taking over the comptroller position at Tulane University when his boss retires.

"You going to work?"

"I'm on the schedule for a half day. I'm supposed to go in at one. Last appointment is six," I say. I don't always work Fridays, but business has been brisk and with Jojo so busy all the time, I've started filling up my empty hours with work. It's what people do as their children get older, Remy explained to me.

"You should go." Ann gets up, taking her mug with her.

I watch her make herself another cup. "I don't know . . . I don't know if I can . . ." What? Think? Breathe? Care for my patients the way they deserve to be cared for?

"It's going to be a long weekend, Harper. You stay home for the next three or four days drinking coffee and pacing, you won't just make yourself crazy, you'll make us crazy, too." She leans against the counter as the coffee machine warms up with a steady hum.

"Need more milk?" I ask.

"I can get my own if I do. I'm not going to let you redirect. I'm serious. Go to work. The girls have basketball after school. I'll pick them up afterward, get Thai. Come for Jojo at our house after your last appointment. Have dinner with us."

I hear the back door open. I never heard Remy's scooter. He walks into the kitchen from the laundry room and I hurl myself at him. He catches me in his arms and holds me tightly. I can't breathe. But the only place it seems like I *can* ever breathe is in his arms.

"How you doing?" he asks me, his voice muffled by my shoulder. He's holding on to me as tightly as I'm holding on to him. Losing a child is such an awful way to bring two people closer. But it pulls you apart, too. Sometimes I think we divorced because we could manage to deal with our own pain, but not each other's.

I nod, not trusting my voice yet.

He gives me another moment. Another squeeze. Then he kisses the top of my head and lets go of me. I step back, wiping my nose with the back of my hand. When I look up at him, at my handsome, kind rock of an ex-husband, I see that his eyes are teary. I immediately tear up.

"Yeah?" he asks me, his gaze searching mine.

I nod again. Sniff. Turn away, reaching for a paper towel to blow my nose. "Ann's been keeping me company."

He walks over and kisses Ann's cheek. The two of them have had this weird, platonic love affair going on for years. Since Ann and I met, both of us with big bellies. They're the best of buddies. She always says she would have married Remy instead of George if she'd met him first. The funny thing is that her George always says thank goodness he found her first.

"Coffee?" Ann asks Remy, running her hand down his arm.

"Please." He walks over to the sink, takes one look at the dirty dishes piled there, and opens the dishwasher.

I watch him begin to unload the clean dishes.

"Did the police think the DNA testing would take place today?" he asks me, sounding very matter-of-fact. At least to someone who doesn't know him. I know he's as scared and excited as I am; he just doesn't wear his heart on his sleeve like I do.

"They're going to try. She . . . Georgina was taken to a foster home."

"Twenty-four to seventy-two hours for results." Ann pushes the button on the coffee machine and waits for his cup to fill. "You're not going to hear anything over the weekend."

"I knew they wouldn't just bring her here." He's stacking bowls in the glass-front antique cupboard.

I get the idea he thinks I thought that was what was going to happen. That the police would just pick up Georgina, on our say-so, and bring her home. I never said that. I never thought it. I wished it, of course. I hold my tongue. Both of us are too brittle right now for me to be picking a fight with him over something like this. At a time like this.

I watch Remy put away the clean dishes. I feel better with him here in my kitchen. *His* kitchen, technically. He grew up in this house on the edge of Audubon Park, and his father before him. These are his cupboards, his hand-painted floor tiles. When we made the decision to divorce three years ago, he was the one who insisted Jojo and I stay here. We see him almost as much as we did when he lived here. He has an apartment eight blocks away. He rides his scooter to work at Tulane University, which is nearby. People think our relationship is odd, Remy's and mine, but it's been a long time since I cared about what people think about me. That happens when your two-year-old is kidnapped from her stroller while your husband has walked to a friend's house to use the bathroom and you're watching the Krewe of Rex floats go by.

"You going to work?" Remy asks me.

I study him for a moment, seeing him the way others see him. He's tall, six two. Slender, but not lanky. He wears his dark, silky hair that's just beginning to gray at the temples in a kind of man-bob that falls to earlobe length. And he has a short-cropped beard that I've always loved, even in the days before it was in. Today he's wearing army-green cargo pants and a short-sleeved white polo with the university's crest embroidered on the breast pocket. Boat shoes. He rarely wears a suit, and then reluctantly. This casual look works well for him. Looks good on him.

"I told her to go." Ann sets his coffee on the counter next to the sink.

"You should, baby." He looks at me with that steady, dark-eyed gaze that's my heaven. And sometimes my hell.

"I don't know," I say. "I don't know if I can focus enough to diagnose an obstruction in a Chihuahua right now." I reach for my coffee mug and then pull back my hand. "I keep thinking about her, Remy. How scared she must be. Alone."

"The police have social workers to deal with these kinds of situations." With the clean dishes all put away, he starts rinsing dirty dishes and loading them in the dishwasher. "I'm sure she's not alone."

5

Lilla

"I want to be alone," I say from between my gritted teeth.

I cross my arms, turning my back to her so she doesn't see that I'm shaking. I know it's childish, but I can't help it. A tear rolls down my cheek but I don't wipe it away. I've cried more in the last three hours than I think I have my whole life. Mom says I was never a crier, not even when I was a baby. She said I did a lot of staring her down. Was that because she wasn't really my mom? I feel as if I'm going to throw up for a second, but I fight it.

It can't be true. It can't be true.

Even if Mom said she kidnapped me from some lady, I know it can't be true. Can it?

"Lie-la," the woman standing at the bedroom door says.

"It's *Lilla*. No long *i*. It's like Lilly, only with an *a* instead of a *y*. It's Hebrew and means oath of God. *Lilla*," I repeat as if to remind myself that's who I really am. That this is all a mistake. Because I can't be this Georgina the police are talking about. Who would name a baby *Georgina?* That sounds like somebody's toothless grandma.

"Lilla." She says my name again, only this time correctly. She's like the housemother or foster mother or whatever of this place. A social worker brought me after the police took me away in a police car. After they told my mother she was under arrest. She wouldn't look at me. Not even when I asked her to. Begged her. Another tear runs down my cheek. *Why wouldn't my mom look at me?*

"I know you're scared," the woman goes on.

Someone said her name was Gina. The woman from Child Protective Services who "escorted" me here from the police station, maybe? Everything's a little bit of a blur.

"And this has got to be very confusing—"

"I want to be alone," I interrupt. I'm not usually rude to people, but manners aren't high on my priority list right now. I'm kind of having a moment. The type that resembles a shattering universe. "Can I be alone or am I on some kind of suicide watch or something?" It comes out pretty snarky. I can be snarky with people. Well, not so much with people as with Mom. Sometimes. When she irritates me. Especially when she's right about something and I'm wrong.

"Do you have thoughts of suicide?" Gina asks me.

I exhale loudly. "No, *Gina*, I don't have *thoughts of suicide.*" I want to add *but I might if you don't leave me the hell alone,* but I don't say it. Mom wouldn't like that, either. This isn't Gina's fault. I know that. It's Mom's fault. For telling the police she kidnapped me. It's a lie, of course. Mom didn't kidnap me. There's no way I'm not her daughter. It's not possible. We're so much alike, two peas in a pod, *compadres.* We both like . . . English muffin bread and M. Night Shyamalan movies. And . . . and we look alike.

Now I feel light-headed. Because the thing is . . . we *don't* really look alike. A shard of a memory comes suddenly to me. I'm little, like third or fourth grade, and I'm looking in a mirror at Mom and me and I tell her I don't look like her. I ask her if I'm adopted, mostly because I had a friend in school who was adopted and I thought that was cool. Mom got the weirdest look on her face and she kind of snapped at me, "No, you're not adopted!" Then she walked away. Later she made up for her mean tone by taking me to the bookstore to get a book I'd been wanting. I still have the book. *Hatchet* by Gary Paulsen. I could find it right now on one of my bookshelves in my bedroom. If I was home. If I was in my bedroom.

What if I never see my bedroom again? What will happen to my stuff? What will happen to me?

I take a deep breath. Oxygen to the brain. That's what I need. "I'm sorry," I say softly to Gina. I walk over to the window and pull back the curtain, thinking that if I can see the sky, if I can just see that I'm still on earth, that I'm alive and awake, I can . . . I can wrap my head around what's happening here.

When I pull back the pink curtain, and I hate the color pink, the first thing I see is bars on the window. Well . . . a black wrought-iron grate covering it. I spin around. "Am I in jail?" I demand. "Is this some kind of . . . jail foster home or something?"

Gina smiles, but it's a patronizing smile. She's average height, brown hair, not skinny, not fat. She's not someone you would remember after you met her. "You're not in jail, sweetie. They're there for your protection."

"Bars on the windows are going to protect me from killing myself?" I ask, arching my eyebrows dramatically. The rude tone is back.

Again, a smile. Patience of Job, that's what my mom would say. Job's this guy in the Old Testament. He somehow got in the middle of a pissing contest between God and Satan. All kinds of horrible things happened to Job: He lost his money, his family died, he got some kind of gross disease. But he just put up with it because he loved God and whatever.

"We had a break-in last year," Gina tells me. "Someone stole our TV, my laptop, and some jewelry. My sister was afraid after that. And she worried about the safety of girls who stay with us."

Gina and her sister live here. They're the foster parents or whatever they're called. It's not a woman and her husband, which kind of makes good sense. I mean, if you're going to have teenage girls you don't know staying in your house, not having some potentially creepy man around is actually smart. I don't say that, of course. I'm not really in a complimenting mood.

I turn my back to her to look out the barred window again. I can see the sky, even through the bars. It's a pretty day out: blue sky, fluffy white clouds. It looks like such an ordinary, nice, sunny day. But how can that be? Shouldn't the sky be falling? Or at least a little rain?

I don't say anything. Gina doesn't say anything. We both just stand there for what seems like eons; then I hear her start to back out of the room. "How about if I just leave you here to get settled?" she says. "I'll be in the kitchen if you need anything. There's a care package for you there on your bed: toothbrush and paste, hairbrush, stuff you might—"

"I missed my statistics quiz," I say, talking over her.

"I'm sorry?"

I turn to look at her. "School. I'm supposed to be in school right now."

"Oh, you don't have to go to school today." She says it like she just handed me some sort of door prize.

"But . . . I *want* to go to school. I *like* school." I say it deliberately, as if she's a slow learner or whatever you're supposed to call people with below-average IQs these days. It seems like the politically correct words are always changing.

Gina presses her lips together, shaking her head. "I'm sorry, sweetie. You can't go to school. Not until this is straightened out."

I turn my back to her again. *This* meaning my life. I close my eyes, choking on my tears.

How could you do this, Mom? How could you do this to me?

6

Harper

"I can't miss school tomorrow," Jojo announces from the doorway of the parlor where Remy and I are sitting.

Remy came over after work and made dinner while I was still at work. He ate with us when I got home and helped clean up. We came into the parlor to have a glass of wine and talk. We even lit the old limestone fireplace. It's gas now, but when Remy was little, it was wood burning. He has fond memories of sitting in this parlor, playing chess with his grandmother and listening to his father and grandfather argue politics.

"You have to stay home tomorrow." I reach for my wineglass. "Your sister is coming home." The words sound dreamlike because I know this can't really be happening. After all these years, all the prayers, all the tears, Georgina really is coming home.

Jojo plants one hand on her hip in one of her preeminent "obstinate teenager" poses. She's wearing pink plaid booty shorts, which she is absolutely not allowed to wear outside the house and if I catch her in them again, they're going in the trash can. And an Ursuline Academy basketball sweatshirt that's two sizes too big. It's an interesting juxtaposition, the tiny skin-baring shorts and the enormous gray sweatshirt that seems to be wearing her more than she's wearing it.

"You said you didn't know what time the social worker was bringing her over," Jojo whines. "You said it could be anytime tomorrow. I have to go to school. I can't miss English again. I have no idea what's going on in *Fahrenheit 451*. It's the stupidest book I've ever read. *Tried* to read," she adds.

I take a sip of my pinot noir, delaying my response. It's a technique I'm working on, on Remy's advice. He tells me that nothing bad can happen if I wait a beat or two before responding to Jojo, but all kinds of bad things can happen if I speak before I think.

I don't know what the wine is; I didn't even look at the label when Remy showed it to me before opening the bottle to let it breathe before he poured. He's a bit of a wine connoisseur. He has a small wine cellar downstairs. I don't know a thing about wine and I don't have a palate for it, not really. I just know what tastes good to me and what doesn't and it rarely has anything to do with the price sticker. I think he said this bottle was from Argentina. Or maybe Chile. I'm not always a good listener when Remy is talking wine.

"*Fahrenheit 451* is a great book." Remy's input to the conversation. He's also delaying responding to the subject at hand. "I love that book. It cautions us as individuals and a nation against suppressing dissenting ideas. That's why they burn all the books in the story. So no one can express an opinion beyond the ruling opinion."

We get an eye roll from our beautiful daughter.

I squint. I wear contacts, but by the end of the day, my distance vision isn't great. Of course my up-close vision isn't, either. I've been known to put on a pair of readers while wearing another pair around my neck and a third on my head. "Are you wearing *eyeliner*, Josephine?"

She makes a face and takes a step back. "No." She says it as if I've mortally wounded her, making such a foul accusation. I know she wears it to school sometimes, but usually she's smart enough to take it off before arriving home. Georgina's return has us all off our game.

Jojo crosses her arms over her chest. "I'm going to school to-morrow. It's taco day."

"You're not going." I take another sip of wine. It's my second glass and I'm finally starting to unwind a little. All day, since I got the call this morning saying that someone from the state would be bringing Georgina home tomorrow, I've been wound tighter than one of the springs in the Broussard family heirloom clock on the mantel. I begged the social worker to let me see Georgina today; I even called Remy's little sister, our attorney, but everyone seemed to think that if I had waited fourteen years, I could wait one more day. They wouldn't even tell me where they were holding her. As if I'd try to somehow sneak in and see her. Which I probably would have.

The whole last week has been a blur. It really is a wonder I'm not on that psychiatric ward. Tuesday the maternity test came back positive. I was angry they didn't bring her home immediately. A judge had to approve Georgina's *release* to us. The same woman who took Georgina from her stroller, apparently had her right here in New Orleans all this time. How did I never see her? How could my baby have been right here all this time and I didn't know it? I can't even begin to process that information.

I'm relieved, of course; a woman kidnapped her, not a man. The social worker said there seemed to be no evidence of sexual abuse or any abuse, based on interviews with the woman and Georgina. She said Georgina was well cared for. I hope it's true. I pray it is, but right now I can't begin to think about that woman who stole my baby. I just can't.

I shift my gaze to Remy, who's sitting on the leather couch beside me. The old piece of furniture should have been replaced years ago, but neither Remy nor I could bear to send it to the dump. Or even have it reupholstered. It belonged to Remy's father and his father before him and sat in their Carondelet Street law offices Remy's whole childhood. The leather is creased and faded but it still smells so good. Some of my best memories of Georgina are of us sitting on this couch. I have an adorable photo in the hall upstairs of one-year-old Georgina on this couch.

I stare into my wineglass. "Tell her she's staying home," I say to Remy.

"Dad, tell her I'm not."

Remy gets up, raising his hands, palms out, as if he's being held up at gunpoint. Which he is, in a way. "Ladies, I'm not doing this. You know I don't do this. I'm neither judge nor referee with you two." He turns his attention to our daughter. "Don't you want to be here when Georgina arrives?"

"Why?" she deadpans. "Isn't she staying?"

Jojo's tone plucks a nerve in me and I start to come off the couch, but Remy catches my eye—a warning—and I ease back down. I take another sip of wine. He's so good with Jojo. So much better than I am. I'm too controlling, too . . . too wrapped up in every aspect of her life.

Remy tells me all the time that I need to take a step back and a deep breath. He says we've raised an amazing girl who will become an amazing woman, if we'll just give her the chance. But I worry so much about her. I only want what's best for her, and the world is such a terrible place. No one cares about Jojo like I do. No one wants to protect her the way I do. Not even Remy. It pisses him off when I say that, but I know it's true. I think it's true of all women. I carried Jojo in my womb. Her body was an extension of mine, like my leg or my arm, before she was born. And she'll always be an extension of me. Just as I knew Georgina always would be, even if she never came home.

"Jojo," Remy says, "I know you're nervous about meeting your—"

"She's not *meeting* her," I interject. "Georgina's not a stranger. She's Jojo's *sister.*"

Again, I get a look from Remy. Again, he turns back to Jojo. I stick my nose back in my wineglass.

"She *is* a stranger," Jojo says softly. She's looking at her dad like she's going to burst into tears and suddenly I feel guilty. I've been so caught up in my own feelings that I haven't taken the time to think about Jojo's. She's got to be so excited. And maybe

Remy's right, maybe she *is* scared. She must be worried Georgina won't like her. All teenage girls worry about being liked.

I take a breath. *Compromise.* I know I should compromise with Jojo sometimes, that I can't always get my own way. Which I disagree with because I'm the parent, right? But I decide to go with it. I don't want to make waves tonight, not on the eve of the biggest day of our lives. "How about if you go to school in the morning, and your dad can pick you up early if Georgina is coming before the end of the school day? The social worker said she'd text me in the morning with an ETA."

Jojo looks at Remy, ignoring me. "I have a makeup quiz after school."

I snap my head around to look at her still in the wide doorway, framed by the white molding like a picture frame. "What quiz did you miss? You haven't been absent in weeks."

"I think you better take the deal on this one," Remy tells our daughter. Now they're both ignoring me. "I think it's the best you're going to get."

Jojo exhales loudly. "Fine." She turns on her toes, a prima ballerina for an instant, and retreats down the hallway.

Remy runs one hand through his hair that should by all rights be thinning because mine is, but isn't. "She's fourteen, hon. This is a lot to take in for a fourteen-year-old."

"It's a lot to take in for a forty-four-year-old." I raise my glass in a toast and take a drink.

He smiles at me and I feel like I'm melting a little. It's the smile I fell in love with when we met at Tulane as undergrads. It's the smile I still love. I pat the place beside me. "Sit. I want to talk to you about something."

"Sure. We need to go over logistics. My family is dying to come over tomorrow and visit and I know you want to take Georgina by to see your dad. And of course Ann and George and Makayla want to stop by, but I think it should just be us tomorrow."

I nod. "Absolutely. I already told Ann I'd call her when I think Georgina, *we're* up to visitors. But that isn't what I wanted to talk about." I pat the place beside me on the couch again.

"Okay." He sounds suspicious. He slides onto the couch.

I take a breath, turning to him, pulling one leg up so that my knee touches his thigh. I changed into sweatpants after work. I never wear my scrubs in the house; they're too gross with animal byproducts. "Now, I want you to hear me out because I know this is going to sound crazy." I glance at the fire in the fireplace. "Because let's face it, a lot of things I say do sound crazy."

"Harper," he murmurs, taking my hand. It's the gentlest of reprimands. I'm not supposed to say things like that about myself. Or so Ann . . . and Remy tell me.

"Remy . . ." I meet his gaze. "I think you should move back in." I say it in a rush as if I don't get it out quickly, I won't be able to say it at all. I set my glass down so I can take his hand between mine. "When Georgina was taken, we were married. That's the mommy and daddy she knows. You and I loved each other and that . . . that was why our girls were so happy. So well adjusted. You always said that was true. Georgina was a happy little girl."

"She *was* a happy little girl," he says carefully

I let go of his hand and run my fingers down his arm. He has nice biceps; he always has. He does lift weights some, and he runs, but he's never been obsessive about exercise. He just has good genes. His dad had been an attractive, muscular man until his death of a heart attack a few months before Georgina was abducted. "Remy," I say softly. "We've talked about this before, about . . ." I look into his dark eyes and my own cloud with tears. "About . . . trying again. You know I'm not happy without you. I—"

"Didn't you just tell me last week that you were thinking about going out for a drink," he interrupts, pointing a finger at me, "with that drug rep who's been asking you out for a year?"

I look down. I'm still holding his arm. "But everything's changed." I lift my gaze and search his dark eyes and remember that those are Georgina's eyes. "Everything is going to be different now. We have our miracle." I choke on my happiness. "Remy, it's going to be so wonderful. Our baby is coming home and we're going to be a family again. You should be here for that. Don't you want to be here for Georgina? For all of us?" I lean into him and he rests his forehead on mine. I close my eyes. He breathes and I breathe with him. His soft beard brushes my cheek. "I miss you, Remy," I say, holding back my tears because if I start to cry I'm not sure how I'll stop. "I miss you at night so much. I feel so alone in our bed by myself."

He's quiet for a long moment and I'm afraid I've gone too far, that I've pushed him too far. But he kisses my temple and sits up, looking into my eyes. Connecting with me in a way I don't think we've connected in a very long time. "I want to be here, I just . . ." His brows draw together. "What if it doesn't work? Jojo is so okay with our arrangement. I'm sure Georgina would be, too. She's sixteen; she must have friends whose parents are divorced."

"But I want you here." I tighten my grip on his arm. "Don't you want to be here with us?" I know I sound a little bit like I'm begging, but I don't care. I'm willing to beg him to make our family whole again. Truly whole.

Now his eyes are teary. "I *do* want to be here."

"With me?" I whisper. "Do you still want to *be* with me?"

With his thumb, he wipes away the tear on one of my cheeks. "Harper, sex between us has always been good." He smiles, a sadness but also an underlying joy in his voice. "Even after we divorced."

I laugh and sniff and reach for my wineglass. I wasn't exactly talking about sex, but I suppose, in a way, I am. Our relationship is odd in every sense of the word. I know that. We still love each other deeply. We're still best friends. I admire him more than anyone I know. And he loves me, even in my craziness. And we do still occasionally have sex. I honestly think that the reason he moved out was because he just couldn't live with my pain anymore. And I couldn't live with his.

He leans back on the couch. He's considering my proposal. I can see it in his face.

"I know. It's a terrible idea," I admit, wondering why I ever thought, for a moment, he would go for it. Losing Georgina was awful, but what I put my husband through in the years following her kidnapping may very well have been worse. At times, I was *such* a nut job.

"Harper—"

"Just say it. It's a terrible idea." I take another breath and exhale. "I'm sorry. I don't mean to ruin the evening."

"Harper—"

"I don't mean to ruin Georgina's homecoming."

"Harper, let me finish," he says, catching my hand and threading his fingers through mine. "I think it's a good idea."

I look up at him and I'm melting again. Tears spring from my eyes. "Yeah?"

"I can't make any promises, but . . ." He exhales. "I'm willing to give it a try."

"For the girls," I say.

He leans and presses his lips to mine and I feel a little thrill that's more than just a physical reaction; I feel it in my heart. "For us," he murmurs against my lips.

I lift my gaze. Our noses are touching. "Are we talking with benefits?" My tone is teasing and dare I say just a little bit sexy. At least sexy for a forty-four-year-old woman who is perimenopausal and has been having sex with the same man since her sophomore year in college. Albeit sporadically the last couple of years.

"Oh, we're talking benefits." He definitely sounds sexy. He slips his hand around my waist. "I assumed that's what you were offering."

I laugh and he laughs with me and kisses me again and then sits back. For a moment we just sit there looking at each other, pleased with ourselves. I can't believe we're doing this. But we're doing it.

"I'll go home and get some things."

I nod. "I'll talk to Jojo about the plan. Unless . . . you think you should? I don't think we should . . . Georgina doesn't need to know right off, does she?" I pick up both glasses of wine and hand him his. I'm feeling a little flushed. Maybe it's the tannins in the wine, or the fire in the fireplace that's made the parlor warm. Or maybe it's my ex-husband. I feel giddy. Georgina and Remy are coming home. *Thank you, God. Thank you, Mary, Mother of Jesus.*

"No, I don't think so. I don't want to overwhelm her," he says.

He touches his glass to mine; it makes a delightful sound in the old parlor and for a moment I think about how many times that sound has echoed in this room. The house was built in 1909 by his great-grandfather. Four generations of Broussards have celebrated life in this room: weddings, births, financial and professional accomplishments. But no one has ever celebrated the return of a child thought dead, I'm sure of that.

"I'll talk to her. I'll just tell her . . . we're not making any promises, that . . . that we're going to see how things go."

He nods. "And remind her that we love her. Whether you and I are living together or not, we love her and we love Georgina."

He holds up the bottle. I nod and he pours me a half a glass more, finishing off the bottle.

"I think we need to take things one day at a time." He sets the dead soldier on the antique coffee table. "This isn't going to be easy."

I lift my gaze to meet his as I reach for my glass. In all my excitement, my disbelief that Georgina really is coming home to us, I haven't really thought much about the adjustment. I wanted to redecorate her bedroom but Jojo nixed that idea. She said no sixteen-year-old girl wants her mother decorating her room, or even being in it. So I've had to be content with removing all the storage boxes I've dumped in there over the last ten years, and the garbage bags of donations I haven't had a chance to take down to Goodwill. The only thing I've bought so far for Georgina is a mattress and box spring for the queen-sized bed Remy helped me bring down from the attic. And some sheets. Pink, because every teenage girl likes pink, doesn't she? The idea of shopping with Georgina excites me. I've never been much of a shopper, but the idea of seeing what my daughter likes and being able to buy it for her thrills me. What sixteen-year-old doesn't like to shop?

"I should get going." Remy rises from the couch. "If I'm going to pack some things and come back tonight."

"Oh, you're coming back tonight." I get up, and grab a handful of his shirt and kiss him, feeling a little unsteady on my feet. More overwhelmed by the situation than the wine.

"You could come with me." Remy slips one arm around my waist, pulls me against him, and kisses me again, this time teasing my upper lip with the tip of his tongue.

His kiss sets my perimenopausal, far-sighted body thrumming. I close my eyes, tempted. Sorely tempted. "Jojo," I say.

"Not invited."

I groan. "I can't leave her here alone. At night."

"We won't be long. Come on," he cajoles. "A little celebration?" His breath is warm in my ear.

"I don't like to leave her home alone." I lean against him, my cheek to his chest so I can feel his heart beating. "You know that."

"She's fourteen years old. She can stay home alone for an hour." He kisses my temple. "We'll tell her to lock the doors. Set the alarm system. She's got her cell phone. We have ours."

I groan again and pull away from him. "I don't like to leave her. Especially now without a dog." Our dog died more than a year ago, but I haven't been ready to do the puppy thing again yet.

"But you need to learn to be able to leave her," Remy says, an edge to his voice.

I look up at him. "I know. I'm trying. I'll try harder," I add, not wanting to anger him. Wanting to go with him and make love with him on his double bed in his sparse apartment. "Just not tonight, Remy. Okay?"

He kisses me on top of my head. It's the chaste kiss of an ex-husband, not a lover. I hope I haven't killed the mood. "I'll be back in an hour." He heads for the door, pointing at the coffee table. "Save the wineglasses. We'll open another bottle."

I wrap my arms around myself, watching him go. Thinking I'll take a shower and maybe even dig something out of my drawer to wear to bed besides a baggy man's white T-shirt and a pair of cotton boy-short panties. And I'll make love to my husband and sleep with him tonight and tomorrow Georgina will come home and life will be perfect again.

7

Lilla

I lean against the door of the minivan, staring out the passenger-side window. The sun is shining. I don't know how. It should be raining. Dark, overcast. Maybe even thundering. That's the way it always is in movies when life for the protagonist has taken a tragic turn. But that's in movies and this is real. This is really happening to me. It's not a dream. I feel as if it is though because I don't feel like myself. It's almost as if I'm watching this happen to me. Like in a dream. But I can't wake up.

I know I'm not going to wake up. Not ever.

The police, the social worker, the foster lady all gave me the same story. I still don't know if I completely believe it, but they all said more or less the same thing, which means they either seriously coordinated their stories, or it's true. Or at least some version of it is true.

They say Sharon Kohen kidnapped me from my birth mother on a parade route during Mardi Gras here in New Orleans when I was two and a half. From my stroller. My birth mother was carrying a baby in one of those front pack things. The birth dad was with the family, but he wasn't right there when it happened.

My supposed family lives right here, just off St. Charles near the big park that Mom and I have driven by a couple of times. Audubon Park. Mom and I talked about going there some Saturday or Sunday; they have a zoo and a path to walk or bike. My mom and I like to do stuff like that, go to parks. And museums. I'm more into natural history and she's into art, but we've both learned to appreciate what the other is into.

I feel a lump rising in my throat, a little bit like I'm going to throw up. It's a physical response having to do with an increase in cortisol. I Googled it on my laptop after someone brought it to me when they dropped some of my stuff from home off at the house with bars on the windows *for my protection*. I was curious about the whole chemical thing in my brain because I've never been a crier. Unlike my mom, who will cry over a commercial on TV or a mean comment someone makes to her about her hollandaise sauce. I feel as if I've done nothing but cry for a week. And sleep. I've slept a lot. They wouldn't let me go to school. Is that even legal? I didn't want to watch TV or *help in the kitchen* so I hid in the room I had to share with some girl with this crazy story about her mother's boyfriend wanting to date her.

"We're almost there," the social worker says to me. Her name is Katrina. Like the hurricane. When I met her last week, I made a comment about how unfortunate that was, living in New Orleans with that name, but I didn't get anything more than a polite smile. I did some research on Katrina—the hurricane, not the social worker who needs to dye her roots—when Mom told me she got a job here. I was four years old when it hit New Orleans. Mom and I were living in Jackson, Mississippi. At least I think I was four. My birthday is August 14. *Was* August 14. If my mom stole me, that has to be made up. So who knows exactly how old I am? Guess I'll find out.

I don't respond to the lady with the hurricane name. I'm pissed at her. Pissed at her because she won't tell me what's going on with my mom except that the police took her to jail. Hurricane Social Worker said my mom confessed to kidnapping me. I'm pissed at her and all the *authorities* because they wouldn't let me talk to Mom or even tell me where she is so I could write her a snail mail letter. You can't get e-mails in jail. Inmates in the Louisiana prison system have *limited access to the Internet*. You

have to write letters to prisoners and somebody reads them before the prisoner gets it. Google. If I can't talk to Mom, I should
at least be able to write her, shouldn't I? I mean, I'm not the one
in prison. I didn't do anything wrong.

So why do I feel like I did?

I slip my fingers into the latch on the van door, feeling the cool
metal beneath my fingertips. I don't know why I'm messing with
it. I already tried it when we got in. Child safety locks. Which basically means I can't get out unless Cyclone lets me out. Like at
the foster home, I'm in prison. Just no one is admitting it.

"Your parents and sister are so excited," Gale-Force Wind is
saying. She glances my way.

The baby the mother was holding the day I got kidnapped was
a girl. A sister. I never wanted a little sister. Or a little brother. I
wasn't one of those kids always asking my mom for a sibling. I
liked that it was just the two of us. We were always a team. A
good team.

I take my hand off the door. I don't know where I'd go if I
could get away. I guess I could go to our cute little green shotgun
in Bayou St. John. My house key is still in my backpack. But the
police would know to look for me there. They'd come for me as
soon as the birth parents turned me in. I toy with the idea of
going home anyway, to get some stuff, and just taking off. But
who would do that with no money and no family? Where would I
go? I guess I could go to one of my friends' houses in Baton
Rouge, but the police would look there, too, sooner or later. So
I'd have to be homeless. There are a lot of homeless people in
New Orleans. I see them in the French Quarter and under the
bridges. I don't think I'd make a very good homeless teenager.
I'd be too scared. Besides, homeless teenage girls end up being
prostitutes and drug addicts. I've seen it on TV. Documentaries.
I'm too chicken for that. So instead, I'm going to these people's
house. Strangers who say they're my family.

The cortisol in my brain kicks in again. The lump is back in
my throat, threatening to bring up the half a frozen waffle I
gagged down this morning. It didn't even taste like a waffle. My

mom makes the best waffles. And not just Belgian or strawberry; she makes savory waffles like Gouda and BLT, too.

My eyes sting with tears. I refuse to give in to them. I can't spend the rest of my life crying.

"I don't know them," I say quietly.

"No, but you'll get to know them." Category Five says it in a voice that is way too cheerful for my tragedy unfolding here. "They're good people. And they've missed you so much."

I look out the window again. We're on St. Charles Avenue. The green streetcar rattles by, going in the opposite direction we are. I like the streetcar. I've ridden it quite a bit since we moved to New Orleans, first with my mom, then by myself. One day I rode from near our place along Canal Street and then picked up the St. Charles line and rode all the way to the end of the line up-town and then back home again. Just for the fun of it. Mom said I was ready to do it alone.

Mom. My lips move, saying it, but I don't let the word out of my mouth.

I know I should be pissed at her. Doing this to me. I mean, did she really think she would get away with abducting somebody else's kid? Who would do such a thing? The woman I know, my mom, never would, but obviously she's not who I think she is. Or at least she's a lot more. Or a lot less. But I can't even be angry with her. Not yet. Because I've only got room for so much emotion and I'm already filled right to the top of my head with sadness. I'm hurt. And scared. I just want to see her. I just want to hug her. If I can just see my mom, I know I'll be okay. I mean, not *okay* okay, but . . . I think I can keep on living. If I can just see her in her Tweety Bird bathrobe one more time.

"These are big houses," I observe aloud, watching the houses go by as we zip up St. Charles. "Are these people rich?"

"Your parents? I don't think they're rich, but I think they're comfortable. Your mom is a veterinarian. Your dad works at Tulane."

"A professor?"

"An administrator."

A veterinarian. That piques my interest. Just a little bit. I like animals. I've been asking for a dog for years, but Mom says our life is not conducive to having a dog. They're too much work. They eat too much, they poop too much, and they have fleas. We used to have a cat. We found him behind our apartment complex in Atlanta. The last time we lived there. I named him Elie after the guy who wrote this amazing book about his survival during the Holocaust. Because the cat looked like he was starving to death when we brought him home. Mom and I discussed if it was disrespectful to name a cat after an amazing man like Elie Wiesel, but she let me name him that anyway. Eliezer Wiesel died a couple of years ago. The man. I wrote an obituary for him for my school newspaper. I doubt anyone read it except my mom and my English teacher, who gave me extra credit for submitting it to the paper, but it was still kind of cool.

Elie the cat got flattened by a taxi.

I wonder if the Broussards have a dog. That's their name. My name. Broussard. I looked it up on the Internet. It's a French surname, an old Louisiana name. My dad's family is a bunch of lawyers at a ritzy address here in New Orleans. I wonder why he's not a lawyer. I hope he's not the dumb one of the bunch.

But I'm fairly smart. So he can't be too dumb. Unless I take after my mom. You have to be smart to be a veterinarian.

"The house is right down there." The social worker with the unfortunate name slows down, pointing across the streetcar tracks to the other side of the road. "The one with the two-story balcony on the front."

I don't want to look, but I can't help myself.

"We just have to make a U-turn." She gets in the left lane and darts across the streetcar tracks. Driving in New Orleans is tricky and on St. Charles you have to navigate cars and the streetcar.

"They have a house at the park?" I hear myself say. "But there's no road."

"The address is Exhibition Drive. That's the little road that runs in front of the houses, but you can't drive on it here. There's also a road that runs behind the houses."

"Damnnn." I don't curse a lot because Mom says there are plenty of good words out there that won't offend anyone. That doesn't mean she doesn't cuss when she slams her hand in the car door. The social worker doesn't respond. I guess she's heard a lot worse from sixteen-year-olds. "You sure they're not rich?"

She just smiles and turns on a little side street off St. Charles. Calhoun. We pull into a driveway behind the big house that's kind of olive green with white trim. It's one of those old New Orleans houses with a big front porch and a balcony above it. I have to keep my mouth shut not to say wow.

Hurricane cuts the engine and turns in her seat to look at me. She really does need to dye her hair. "You ready?"

I don't say anything. I just look straight ahead.

"Lilla, it's going to be okay." She reaches out to touch my hand but I yank it away. I want to scream at her, "You don't know me! You don't have a right to do this to me!"

I hear her open her door. Get out.

I just sit there. I contemplate sliding over into the driver's seat and speeding away. But she didn't leave the keys. And I can't legally drive yet without an adult.

A red Vespa parked in the driveway catches my eye. There's also a green Subaru Outback. So I guess they aren't rich, otherwise they'd have a big Range Rover or a BMW. I've always wanted to ride a motor scooter. Mom and I actually talked about getting one after I got my full license, for us to share. New Orleans is a good place for motor scooters. Mom once had a motorcycle. In her *younger, wilder days*. I wonder who rides the Vespa. The sister is fourteen. It can't be her. It has to belong to the parents. I think about riding the red Vespa down St. Charles. I bet it would be fun.

My door opens, startling me. It's Category Five. Now she's opening the sliding door. Getting my stuff. I don't know if she went to our house or someone else did. They put it all in a tall, cylindrical canvas laundry basket that had been in our bathroom. In it are some clothes and toiletries someone just randomly chose for me. Supposedly *arrangements* will be made to get the rest of my stuff. I don't know what will happen to our house. I guess we'll lose the lease and our deposit. I wonder what they'll do with our belongings: our books and pots and pans and what about Mom's knives? I bet they're still sitting right there on the counter.

"Come on, Lilla."

I feel myself get out of the van. I grab my backpack that was at my feet and I hold it tightly in my hands like it's somehow going to save me. I think about Hurricane Katrina and the devastation it caused. I wonder if the people in the Lower Ninth Ward felt the way I feel right now when they knew the levees were breaking and there was nothing they could do about it.

The social worker doesn't go to the back door. Carrying my canvas laundry container that's almost too big for her, she takes a sidewalk that runs along the south side of the house. There's a small courtyard garden there with a stone fountain with running water. The center of the fountain is three baby cherub guys standing with their backs to one another. The water comes up between them into a little bowl, and the bowl overflows, pouring water around the naked babies like a circular waterfall. I want to stop and look at it, but I keep walking.

I follow Katrina up onto the porch that has rocking chairs and houseplants in big colorful pots. The porch faces the park and from here I can see the big live oaks with Spanish moss hanging from them. The social worker sets the laundry container down and removes her sunglasses. She reaches for the doorbell, but before she can ring it, the big front door opens. And there she is. I know it's her by the way she's looking at me. The mother.

My mother.

8

Harper

Tears run down my cheeks as I wrap my arms around my baby. My baby who isn't a baby anymore. Who doesn't look like my baby. But when I hug her, when I kiss her forehead, she *smells* like my baby. "Georgina," I breathe, knowing that if God wanted to call me home right now, I'd be content. All I've wanted for so many years is this moment. To have my baby girl home again.

"Harper . . ."

I don't know how much time has passed since Georgina walked in the door. Could be fourteen seconds or fourteen years.

"*Harper.*" Remy squeezes my shoulder and murmurs in my ear. "Let go of her, hon. You're making her uncomfortable."

I take a step back, not wanting to let go of my Georgina. Not ever again. As I release her, I realize she didn't hug me back. She's just standing there stiffly, holding an old blue backpack. And she's not looking at me. She's not looking at any of us. She's just staring at the entryway floor. "Sorry." I laugh and sniff.

"I'm Remy," he says to Georgina. "Your dad." His voice cracks when he says it and I'm afraid I'm going to start bawling. But he doesn't hug her. He just stands there looking at her and she lifts her gaze to meet his. And just for a second I'm a little, tiny bit jealous.

"And . . . that's Josephine. Jojo," he says, continuing the introductions. "Your little sister."

Neither of our daughters says anything to each other. Jojo, standing at the bottom of the staircase, her arms wrapped around her waist, is staring at Georgina. Jojo's still in her school uniform. Ann ended up running over to Ursuline to pick her up for me when Jojo changed her pickup time twice. Ann only dropped her off five minutes ago. Jojo almost missed Georgina's homecoming with her nonsense.

"Sorry, Katrina, right?" Remy offers his hand. "We spoke on the phone. Remy Broussard, and Harper and Jojo." He shakes her hand.

"I can't tell you how nice it is to meet you," the social worker says. "It's so amazing to be a part of this." Her voice fills with emotion. "We don't get to see a lot of happy endings in my line of work."

Remy smiles kindly. "No, I don't suppose you do."

I can't stop staring at Georgina. She's so tall and so beautiful and so . . . grown-up looking.

"Um . . . hi." I offer my hand to the social worker. "Sorry." I laugh and she laughs. "I just can't . . ." I wipe my tears from under my eyes with both my hands and hope I don't look like a raccoon. I actually put on mascara this morning. "I'm so overwhelmed. So happy. I still can't believe this is really happening." I clasp my hands together to keep from grabbing Georgina for another hug. "Thank you so much, Katrina. I still can't believe you"—my voice catches in my throat—"they found her," I manage. I wipe at my tears again. "We made lunch." I gesture toward the dining room. We hardly ever use it. Not with just Jojo and me. Not even when Remy comes over. The funny thing is, when we first moved into the house, when Georgina was born, we ate here all the time. Of course Remy's dad was still alive then. He lived here with us. We lived here with him.

"Lunch sounds nice. A nice . . . icebreaker," Katrina says. "Oh." She points over her shoulder to a gray canvas container on the porch. "Some of Lilla—Georgina's things. Arrangements will be made to . . ." She stops and starts again. "Someone will go to the house and get whatever else she wants. You'll be contacted."

I want to say that it's okay, she doesn't need anything from that woman, that life, but I don't. Instead, I say, "Great," and look at Georgina. "You hungry?"

"Not really." She speaks so quietly that I can barely hear her.

I smile, not sure what to say, and look to the social worker. I don't know what I was expecting, but this isn't it. I feel so awkward. Clearly we all do. I guess I was expecting a big reunion scene, maybe not with Georgina throwing herself into my arms, but things are certainly chillier in the front hall than I anticipated.

"Let's have some lunch, Lilla," the social worker says, touching Georgina on the shoulder, ushering her forward.

Hearing Katrina call our daughter Lilla, the name the woman who stole her from us gave her, grates on my nerves, but I don't correct her. "Um . . . we just made sandwiches, Remy's version of muffalettas, and there are chips and grapes and sweet tea." I take a step back to lead them to the dining room. "But . . . if you don't eat meat, you can just pull it off. Or we can make you something else. Do you eat meat, Georgina? Are you a vegetarian? Jojo was a vegetarian for a while, until she realized she couldn't really eat shrimp po'boys if she was vegetarian."

"Mom," Jojo groans from behind me.

"I'm not a vegetarian." Again, just a whisper from my eldest daughter.

"Oh, good, okay. I mean . . . not *good*. I don't have anything against vegetarians. My patients like them. I'm a vet." I hear myself laugh and I'm afraid I sound like a complete moron. I don't want Georgina to think I'm a moron. This is so much harder than I thought it was going to be. How did I not know this was going to be hard?

The social worker smiles kindly. I can tell she's feeling my pain.

"You can leave your backpack there, Georgina." I indicate the foot of the front staircase where Jojo is parked.

Georgina takes a hesitant step toward the stairs and Jojo sidesteps out of her way. I want to shake Jojo, but I've never shaken my daughter in my life. Either of them. I want to blurt out, "She doesn't have the plague." Instead, I lead the way to the dining room, which is just off the hallway that runs through the center of the house.

"This is such a beautiful home," Katrina remarks, glancing up the staircase at the huge oil portraits on the wall. All men, all Remy's family: judges and lawyers. "I love historic homes."

"It's been in the family, Remy's, since it was built over a hundred years ago." I eye Georgina. She's set her backpack down and is slowly walking our way.

Remy brings up the rear. "You girls want to help me carry lunch into the dining room?" he asks casually. He doesn't look at either of them as he walks past them, following the hall instead of cutting through the dining room.

Jojo huffs but follows her dad. Georgina doesn't say anything. But she goes with them.

I lead Katrina into the dining room, watching Georgina disappear from my view. I close my eyes for a moment. I know I can't watch her every moment of the day for the rest of my life, but she's only been here five minutes. After fourteen years, I feel as if I have the right to want to get a good look at her.

"It's going to be all right," I hear Katrina say. She takes my hand.

I open my eyes, surprised to find her so close. "I know," I say, trying to get a grip on myself.

"It's going to take her a little time," she continues.

I nod.

Katrina smiles kindly as she lets go of me. "And it's going to take you a little time, all of you, to adjust to this new family dynamic."

I exhale slowly. "Right. Of course. I just—" Against my will, tears fill my eyes. I've got to stop crying. I can't be the mom who cries. What will Georgina think of me? "I've waited so long for her to come home. Everyone said she was dead. I thought she was dead." My last words come out as a whisper.

I get another kind smile and Katrina glances at a large oil painting over the antique maple serving buffet. It's a pastoral painting of sugar cane fields rolling down to the Mississippi in the days before the levees. I've always liked it, despite its semi-gaudy, ornate, gilded frame. Another Broussard family treasure. I hear Remy chatting in the kitchen. Nothing from Georgina or Jojo. "Remy's great-great-aunt was an artist," I say. "The house in the background is the Broussard home, in Evangeline Parish where they owned land. It was called *Maison Douce*," I say, taking pride in the fact that my French is decent. "I think it's about . . . 1887."

She studies the painting and I study her. She's a small woman, my age, maybe a little older. Her face is weathered; she looks like a smoker, though I didn't smell cigarettes on her. Her brown hair is cut in a bob. She needs a touch-up at the roots, but she's an attractive woman for her age. Our age. I wonder what made her want to be a social worker. For the state. I can't fathom why anyone would want to deal with other people's suffering all day long. See the things she must see in the city. I can barely deal with a dog in pain. It's a calling, I suppose. Thank God someone has the calling, otherwise, who would bring little girls home to their mothers?

Katrina turns to me. When she speaks, her voice is soft; she glances through the doorway that leads to the kitchen. Obviously she doesn't want Georgina to hear us. "She's had a rough few days. She had no idea she'd been kidnapped as a baby. She thought Ms. Kohen was her mother."

"No idea at all?" I ask. It's a question I've been asking myself since the day I saw her in the coffee shop when I first thought there might be the slightest chance she was coming home to us.

Katrina shakes her head. "Definitely not. It's important that she be allowed to have her feelings."

"Of course," I say.

"This has all been quite a shock. As I know the police told you, she was well cared for." She hesitates. "She was loved," she says without smiling.

"*Loved?*" I whisper. "That woman abducted my baby." My ire rises out of nowhere, but I force myself to remain calm. Georgina is only twenty-five feet from me. I want her homecoming to be perfect. Getting into an argument with her social worker wouldn't be the way to go. "The first days she was gone . . . I thought I was losing my grip on my sanity. I considered committing suicide," I continue. What I don't say is that the only reason I think I didn't do it was because of the church. As scary as it is to think about, even now, I really could have killed myself. "Because of that woman," I say from between clenched teeth.

"I hear what you're saying," Katrina says softly. "Just keep in mind, your daughter had nothing to do with the kidnapping. It isn't her fault it happened. And it isn't her fault that the woman who took her really did love her. It's only natural for a child to love the person who cares for her and loves her."

When I wasn't imagining my daughter buried in the bayou somewhere, her face covered in mud, I was dreaming she was in a happy home. Well cared for, even loved. Now I'm having a hard time dealing with the idea that the monster who took my baby loved her. Worse, that Georgina loved her in return.

I stare at my boots on my feet. I must have dressed and re-dressed half a dozen times. What does a person wear to be re-united with their daughter who's been missing for fourteen years? Jeans, ankle boots, and a white oxford shirt, I decided in the end. Casual but not sloppy. "Do you know why she did it?"

"The kidnapper?" We're whispering again.

I nod. The police told me her name. Sharon Kohen. Our daughter has been living as Lilla Kohen. They have not been in New Orleans for fourteen years. They only moved here three months ago, from Baton Rouge. Apparently they moved a lot, typical for someone who had a secret to hide, according to the police. If you keep moving, it's more difficult for people to get to know you, more difficult to rouse suspicions.

The social worker takes her time to respond to me. She's probably debating how much to tell me. We have an appointment with the police next week. We're supposed to get more information then.

"She lost a two-year-old to Tay-Sachs disease," Katrina explains.

"So she stole my daughter?" As the words come out of my mouth, I realize how cold they sound. How lacking in sympathy. I can't help it. I thought my baby had been murdered. Sexually abused and murdered. I know I was taught better, but I'm a little short on sympathy today.

"The mind is a strange thing. People respond to the same events in very different ways. Some women, when they lose a child, commit suicide." Katrina meets my gaze. "Others kidnap a child, substituting one for the other, not just in their life but their mind. I didn't interview Ms. Kohen myself, but I read the initial psych evaluation. Most of the time, she thought your Georgina *was* her Lilla."

"If I hadn't seen Georgina in that coffee shop . . ." I hesitate, trying not to go there, not able to hold myself back. "I might never have known she was alive."

"It's a lot to take in. A lot to process. As we discussed on the phone, we think it's important that Georgina get counseling. I gave you a couple of names. What we didn't discuss is that we recommend the same for you and your husband and daughter."

"Remy? Counseling?" My smile is thin. "He's not going to go for it. I used to see a therapist regularly. I can see him if I feel the need."

"Bring it into the dining room," Remy says loudly, walking from the kitchen toward us.

Our cue to stop whispering.

He enters the dining room carrying a tray of sandwiches. Jojo has the pitcher of sweet tea. Georgina brings up the rear carrying a plate of grapes in one hand, a bowl of chips in the other. I still haven't heard her say more than a few words at once. She's walking with her head down, her gorgeous dark hair covering much of her face. I meet Remy's gaze. He offers a tight-lipped smile. He's warning me to *chill*. I'm trying.

"Sit anywhere you like," I say, sounding a little bit as if I'm a cruise director. Of course, how would I know? I've never been on a cruise. Remy tried to get me to go on one several times, back when we were trying to *make things work*, before he moved out. I wanted to go. I wanted to make him happy, but I just couldn't bring myself to leave Jojo for a week, not even with Ann.

I watch Georgina set the food down and gaze at the table. Then at the dining room. And I realize she may be a little intimidated by the house. Ann, who lives in a cute double shotgun, says our place looks like a museum: the big, balconied exterior, the antique furniture, the portrait of Remy's three-greats-back grandmother Marie, looking down on us from above the marble fireplace here in the dining room. For us, it's just home. But from Georgina's perspective, it could be overwhelming.

But wouldn't she remember *something?* We brought her here, home from the hospital. Wouldn't something in the house look familiar? Wouldn't *we* look familiar, even if she didn't remember us?

We're all still standing around the table. Remy, the voice and action of reason, takes the chair at the end of the Victorian-era flame mahogany table that seats eight with the leaves out. He looks to Georgina and she slowly takes the chair to his left. Katrina sits to his right. I stand there for a second, debating whether or not to walk around the table to sit beside Georgina. Would I rather be able to look at her or touch her? Because I'm pretty certain she doesn't want me touching her just yet, I take the chair closest to Katrina.

"Can I skip lunch?" Jojo asks. "I ate at school."

"Right. Tacos." Remy points at the table.

With a huff, Jojo takes a chair, but not the one beside Georgina;

she sits on the very end so she's facing her father. As I pick up my napkin I meet Remy's gaze. We silently agree to let it go.

Remy picks up the platter of mini muffalettas, takes two, and passes it to Georgina. She puts one on her plate and turns to Jojo. Jojo doesn't say anything, she just points at me. Georgina hands the plate across the table to me, which is a reach. I have to come partway up from my chair to take it. Georgina doesn't make eye contact. The grapes and chips go around. Georgina takes grapes, no potato chips. Everyone, including my sulking daughter on the end, accepts a glass of sweet tea. I may have grown up in Philadelphia, but my mother was born and bred in Louisiana. I know how to make sweet tea.

The conversation, as we eat, is awkward. Mostly it's Katrina asking us questions: what Remy does at Tulane, where Jojo goes to school, where my office is. Georgina doesn't say a word, except when asked a direct question. I haven't asked her any of the questions I want to ask because Remy made me promise not to grill her, at least not in the first hour after she arrives home. His thought is that we'll have the rest of our lives to talk about the years she was gone from us. I understand what he's saying, but there's so much I want to know. Need to know. But we agreed we'd start on the easy questions: which subjects she likes in school, what her favorite color is, if she plays a sport. Her responses are monosyllables, for the most part. Her favorite class is statistics—I can't imagine why. She doesn't play a sport and she likes gray. What sixteen-year-old likes gray? The more time that passes over lunch . . . drags, the more worried I become. Adjusting to our new family is going to be hard on everyone.

"Any plans for this afternoon?" Katrina asks cheerfully. We've finished lunch and we're edging toward the time when the social worker will leave us.

I look to Remy, who's just getting to his feet to clear the table. "We were thinking we'd take a walk through the park. How's that sound, Georgina?"

She stares at me across the table. Doesn't smile. In fact, I haven't seen her smile yet.

"Or . . . we could do something else." I sound more upbeat than I feel. "What would you like to do, Georgina? Anything. You name it."

I meet my daughter's gaze and her eyes that are my Remy's eyes fill suddenly with tears. "I want to go home. I want my mother."

9

Jojo

I push open the bathroom door without knocking. It's open a little, so I figure the privacy rules don't apply. Right? You only have to knock and wait for somebody to say "Come in" if the door's closed. I cross my arms. I have to look up at her because she's taller than I am. A couple of inches taller. She's going to be tall like Dad, I guess. I got Mom's short gene, apparently.

"I take a shower at six thirty in the morning," I say. I don't even try to say it nice. "So . . . I guess you'll have to get up earlier or use the downstairs shower or whatever tomorrow. This is my bathroom. *Was*."

She doesn't turn to look at me. Instead, she looks into the mirror at me. She's holding a toothbrush. She's wearing a pair of ratty gym shorts and a T-shirt that says "Tulane" that looks new. I wonder if Dad got it for her. He didn't bring me anything today.

"You take a shower at six thirty in the morning on *Saturdays?*" she asks. Like I'm stupid.

I forgot tomorrow is Saturday. Saturdays, I don't shower at all, unless I'm going somewhere. Now I *feel* stupid. "I'm just telling you."

She keeps looking at me by way of the mirror. She's really pretty. Not blond pretty like me, but she's got shiny dark hair like Dad's. Longer than mine. And her skin is so perfect it's disgusting. I have to go to a dermatologist. Zits everywhere if I don't use my special soap and stay away from dairy.

We just keep looking at each other, like we're both frozen. I wouldn't have known she was my sister if I'd gone into that coffee shop. I can't help thinking, *Too bad it wasn't me instead of Mom.* I know that's not the right thing to think, but from the look on her face, I get the idea she's wishing right now it was me instead of Mom, too.

She finally stops looking at me. She turns the water on and runs her toothbrush under it. I still stand there trying to think what to say. Dad says she's definitely my sister . . . *our Georgina.* DNA testing. I wonder if that's true. I was planning on binge watching a couple of episodes of *Buffy the Vampire Slayer* or maybe *The Vampire Diaries* on Netflix, but maybe I'll do a quick Google search. I mean, what if someone *did* make a mistake? It could happen.

"You hurt Mom's feelings today, you know." The words are out of my mouth before I realize it. "At lunch."

She's still running the water over her toothbrush. She turns it off. She's looking at me again and it occurs to me that she looks a lot like Elena in *The Vampire Diaries*, which sucks because Elena is so beautiful. That's why both of the vampire brothers are in love with her, of course. Her dark beauty. I wonder if Georgina has a boyfriend. Had. She was going to a public school. I'm sure Mom's not going to let her have a boyfriend. Ursuline girls don't have boyfriends. That's what Miss Gerard says.

"About wanting to go home," I say, my voice turning mean. "To your *mother.* Because that woman who stole you, she was your kidnapper. She's not your mother."

She presses her lips together like maybe she's going to cry. But she doesn't.

"All she's wanted, for as long as I can remember," I say, now feeling as if I'm the one who's going to cry, "is for you to come home."

She looks down at the sink. Puts her toothbrush down, even though she hasn't brushed her teeth, and walks out of the bathroom. Right past me. She goes down the hall, into her room, and closes the door. She doesn't slam it. She closes it very quietly. Which seems louder in my ears than any slammed door.

10

Harper

"Do you think I should check on her?" I shut off the light beside the bed and roll over to face Remy.

He wraps his arm around my waist, pulling me closer. "You shouldn't check on her again." He leans in and gives me a peck on the lips. "You said good night. Then you went back and said good night again. You told her to let you know if she needs anything. She's sixteen years old. She'll let you know if she needs something."

I tuck my head under his chin, press my hand to his bare chest, and breathe in his scent that's burgundy wine, warmth, and French-milled soap. I used to think it was weird that he used the same soap his mother always used when he was a child. Now it's part of his identity to me. You have to love a man who likes girly, *nice* soap.

It feels so good to have him in bed with me again. Not just for sex. But to have him here all night. After he moved out, he rarely stayed the night anymore, and when he did, he slipped out very early in the morning. I don't know if Jojo knew we were still sleeping together occasionally or not. She never mentioned it, so I don't think so. It was Remy who didn't think he should stay the night. He was afraid it would confuse Jojo. She took the fact that he was moved back in so nonchalantly that, thinking back, I doubt she would have cared. Remy doesn't like it when I say things like this, but I think Jojo's too wrapped up in herself to care. He doesn't get that when I say things like that about her, I'm not being critical. She and I get along well most of the time. We've been a team since Remy left. I love her as she is, but as her mother and a female, I think I see her more realistically than he does.

"I think today went okay." I snuggle against him. "It went okay, right? She seemed to enjoy walking in the park. She liked that dog. Do you think we should get a dog? We've been talking about it." I look up at him even though it's so dark I can't really see his face. "You think we should get a dog?"

"I think we should go to sleep." He kisses the top of my head.

I close my eyes. Breathe deeply. I washed the sheets yesterday and they smell divine. "I think things went okay," I repeat.

He doesn't say anything.

I'm quiet for a moment, but my thoughts are going in so many directions that I can't stay quiet. "I was thinking we'd go shopping tomorrow. The girls and I. She didn't bring much with her. Katrina said someone would be getting more of her things for her from her house, but maybe she doesn't want those things. I don't know if I would, if I were her."

Remy doesn't say anything. He's not asleep yet, but he's close. I've never seen anyone who can fall asleep as quickly as he can. I find it annoying. I sometimes lie awake for hours, unable to relax, replaying things I said, did, during the day. "Remy?"

He exhales and rolls onto his back. I follow him, lying on my stomach, resting my head on his chest. "What do you think? Should I take them shopping? Get her some clothes? She'll need shoes to go with her uniform. Maybe do lunch somewhere fun? What's the name of that courtyard restaurant in the Quarter Jojo likes?"

"Harper."

"The one with the fountain. Jojo likes their crab cake sliders. I don't know if Georgina eats crab. Maybe we should go there? You want to meet us?" I run my hand over his chest that is just hairy enough to be masculine without being too hairy. "I know you don't want to go shopping, but you could meet us for lunch. You said you have to go into the office for a couple of hours, but maybe you could meet us for a late lunch?"

"You can't take it personally, Harper."

"I'm trying to figure out when to take her to see Daddy. I know he won't remember her, but he'll want to see her. He still remembers when she was born. But that might be a lot for Georgina. We should probably hold off on the nursing home visit."

"Did you hear what I said?" His tone is gentle, but he's not going to let it go. "Harper?"

I know what he's talking about. And he knows I know. You don't marry a man, have two children with him, lose a child, divorce, reconcile, and have your child miraculously returned to you fourteen years later and not know each other intimately.

And the tears come again. I roll onto my back to lie beside him. "I'm her mother," I whisper. "And you're her father."

"Biologically, yes."

"She's my child." I pull my arms across my body, almost as if I can cradle her to my breast again.

"Harper." He rolls onto his side, propping himself up on his elbow. He puts his other arm around me. "Can you imagine what it must have been like for her to have the police show up at her door and ask her mother if she kidnapped her? Have her mother admit right in front of her that she wasn't her child? That she, the woman Georgina loves more than anyone in the world, abducted her when she was a baby?"

I close my eyes. I don't want to think about it. "She's our daughter," I repeat.

"She was our daughter. And she will be again. But right now . . ."

He doesn't finish the sentence. He doesn't have to.

I press my lips together trying to fight the wave of panic rising in my chest. This afternoon, when I asked Georgina what she wanted, she said she wanted to go home. She wanted her mother. That woman. That monster. Not me.

"I love her so much," I whisper.

"I know you do," he says in my ear. "And I love her, too. But Katrina is right. This is overwhelming for all of us. And . . . I know you might not want to hear this, but I think maybe it's more overwhelming for her on several levels. She never knew we existed until last week. We've been loving her all these years, Harper. Even when she was gone and we thought she would never come back to us. But she didn't know about us."

I squeeze my eyes shut and I say a little prayer to the Holy Mother. I ask for her blessing. For her guidance. A little extra to go with the fifty-four-day novena that I might just start again as soon as I've completed this one.

Remy rests his head on my breast and strokes my arm.

We're quiet for a long time, but I can tell by the way he's breathing that he's not asleep yet. "Remy?"

"Mm?"

"Do you think this is going to work out? Not with Georgina. I mean with us. With you and me."

"Baby, I don't know," he murmurs, just on the edge of sleep.

It's not the answer I was hoping for, but tonight I'll take it.

11

Lilla

I didn't think I'd sleep in the bed with the ugly pink sheets. After my bathroom chat with my little sister, whose middle name might be B I T C H, I seriously considered climbing out the window of the second-story bedroom. The bedroom they say I slept in when I was a baby.

I thought maybe I could swing from the window ledge onto the parents' balcony and use the vines to climb down. But it's a jump from my window to the balcony. And even if I make it, I don't know if the vines would hold me. I don't know what they are; I'm not much of a gardener. Then there's the issue of where I would go. And the fact that I'm a coward and am afraid I'd break my neck going from the window to the balcony or the balcony to the ground. And it would be my luck I wouldn't die. That would be too easy. Instead, I'd damage my spine and end up in one of those wheelchairs like Stephen Hawking. And the mother would feed me Jell-O through a straw and call me *Georgina* a hundred times a day. And cry a lot.

But after I gave up on the idea of running away, at least for the moment, and got in bed, I fell asleep almost immediately. I had crazy dreams. I dreamed Mom came to the Broussards' pretty front porch off St. Charles and knocked on the pretty front door.

The mother answered and Mom said she was here to pick me up. The mother handed me my backpack and waved and told me to have a good day at school. Then, all of a sudden, the way nonsensical things happen in dreams, we were in jail. It was like the kind of jail in *Orange Is the New Black*, where inmates were wandering around and guards were standing around chatting. Mom and I were both wearing orange jumpsuits and I was doing my homework on this cafeteria table while she mopped the floor. My backpack was there and I was doing my statistics homework. I was doing this crazy stem and leaf chart that had something to do with Mom's signature Southern dishes. She and I were laughing about something and she started making coffee for us. Grinding coffee beans. I could *smell* the coffee.

I woke up sad because I don't know if Mom and I will ever laugh together again. I don't even know if I'll ever see her again. I don't know how long you have to stay in prison when you kidnap somebody's baby and ruin a whole bunch of people's lives.

It's barely light out, but I get up. With everyone still asleep, I'm hoping I can sneak downstairs and make myself a cup of coffee. The parents have one of those fancy coffee machines that grinds the beans, boils the water, and it even has a little hose to suck up milk, heat it, and spew it into your cup. I saw it on the counter yesterday. It will make a macchiato, a cappuccino, or an espresso just by pushing a button.

Last week, when the police arrested Mom and my life imploded, I called the coffee shop where I'd just started working and told them I couldn't come in because I was having a family emergency. I told the manager I'd call back. But I didn't. My story would have been too crazy. She would never have believed me. So much for my first job.

I put on clean underwear and yesterday's jeans. I don't bother with a bra. I don't really need one. I leave on the green Tulane T-shirt I slept in. The dad gave it to me last night. I wanted to say, *No thank you,* but that seemed rude. Since he works there and all. And it was nice of him. I wonder if someone told him I want to go to Tulane. Who would know that, though?

There's an alarm clock on the nightstand. It's seven twenty. The house is quiet.

I think about checking my phone, just in case Mom tried to call, but I don't because I want to save the battery and I already checked last night. I don't have the charger to charge it. I used some girl's at the foster home, but I haven't been anywhere where I could buy one for myself. I wonder how long it will work anyway. When Mom doesn't pay the bill, the phone company will turn it off.

I called her cell phone a couple of times over the last few days. She didn't answer, of course. I listened to her voice, to her say, *Leave a message.* It was stupid and it made me cry. I bet her phone is still plugged in, charging next to her bed. I'm sure the cops didn't let her take it with her. I don't know if they even let her get dressed before they took her to jail. I wonder if when I lose service, my photos will all be gone. I need to send them all to my laptop. I don't want to lose my photos, especially not the ones of Mom. Girls my age say their whole life is in their phone. Mine really is now.

I try to walk quietly down the hall, but my leather flip-flops make that *slap, slap* sound that sort of echoes. The house is kind of cool . . . in a creepy way. It reminds me of a museum or an old house you pay to tour, like one Mom and I went to see in Atlanta once. We lived in Atlanta before we moved to Baton Rouge. Everything is so big here. The ceilings are high and the doors are ginormous. There's dark woodwork everywhere that has a beautiful patina. I took a summer art appreciation class at my school in Atlanta and we talked about patinas on metal, but also on wood. There are old-fashioned lights with colored glass hanging in the hallway. I think they might be real stained glass.

I go down the fancy, wide staircase. More dark, stained wood.

There are big portraits of men with white hair looking down on me. Watching me. I wonder who they are and why they're here. Then I see a little brass nameplate. It's the last name that gets my attention. *Broussard.* They're all Broussards. My name. My family.

The idea is so crazy that I still can't wrap my head around it. If I wrote a short story for English class about a girl who thinks she's one person, but she's really another, I'd probably get a bad grade. No one would think that was conceivable.

But here I am.

At the bottom of the stairs, I peek into the room the mom calls the parlor. It sounds kind of snotty to me. Who has a *parlor?* People who have more than one living room, I guess. The living room here is off the main hall toward the back of the house where the TV is. But the parlor *is* kind of pretty. I like the marble fireplace. There are fireplaces in all the main rooms downstairs.

I get all the way to the kitchen doorway before I realize there's a light on. Someone else is already up. I stop where I am and contemplate going back upstairs. Back to the room where the baby named Georgina slept. I could go out the window. In the daylight, I might have a chance.

I listen. Someone is making something. I hear what sounds like a whisk hitting a glass bowl. Someone who knows how to use a whisk. My mother taught me how to use one. I can make whipped cream from heavy cream with a whisk. A lot of people use an electric mixer.

I'm still standing there in the hall with all the white-haired guys watching me from the staircase, debating what to do, when I hear the dad's voice.

"Morning."

He must have heard me on the staircase.

I consider running. But then I think about my mom and about a conversation we had a few weeks ago about bravery. About what it means. She said that when people think of the word, they think about superheroes, or American soldiers in Afghanistan, but when she thought about bravery, she thought about the everyday bravery she saw in people. The ex-con dishwasher who has the guts to apply eight times to be a prep cook before he finally gets hired. The mom who walks out on her boyfriend and goes to a shelter to protect her kids. The new kid in the class who raises her hand. Mom says bravery shows its face a hundred times a day in front of us. We just have to see it. And sometimes we have to be it.

I walk into the kitchen and just stand there. He glances at me, then back at the bowl in his hand. He goes back to whisking.

"Sleep okay?" he asks.

He's not looking at me so I can't just nod. "Fine." My voice sounds weird. I don't sound brave. I don't feel brave.

"Good. Harper wanted to go out and buy a bedspread and stuff like that, but Jojo and I thought maybe you'd like to pick things out for yourself. Make your room your own."

I realize he didn't say "your mother" and I'm so appreciative of that that I almost smile. Almost.

I smell coffee. See he's made himself a cup. I glance at the coffeemaker on the black-and-gray granite counter. The whole kitchen is white cabinets floor to ceiling with gray and black floor tiles and the swirly granite. Whoever picked out the cabinets and flooring and stuff has good taste. I wonder which one of the parents it was, her or him.

The smell of the coffee makes me think of Mom and, all of a sudden, I'm afraid I'm going to cry. But I don't. Instead, I find my voice that hasn't seemed like my own since the cops showed up at the house a week ago. "Okay if I make myself a cup?"

He looks up again. "Coffee? Sure." He points to the coffeemaker and goes back to whisking. I can't see what's in the bowl. "Mugs are in the cabinet over the coffeemaker."

I notice that he doesn't give me direction. He assumes either I know how to use the coffeemaker, that I'll figure it out, or that I'll ask. Yesterday, the mom kept telling me things like she thought I was stupid. She told me how to get ice out of the ice-maker on the door of the refrigerator.

I walk across the kitchen, which is big and fancy and very modern compared to the rest of the house. I wonder how they get stuff on the top shelves of the huge glass-front cabinets. A stool, I guess.

I open the cabinet and look at the mugs. They're all different: different colors, different styles, different sizes. But they're not the kind like you see in stores. None of them say, "I ♥ NOLA" or "My Norwegian Elkhound is my best friend." They all look handmade. I choose one of medium size that's all white with lit-tle raised dots.

I study the coffeemaker. I like flat whites, but I don't know how to make one with the machine. I choose a cappuccino. While the coffee machine makes noises, I look over at the dad. I see he's got an electric Belgian waffle maker on the counter. He's making waffles. He must be putting egg whites in them.

"Like waffles?" he asks me.

I turn back to watch the hot milk spurt into my cup. Then the coffee. "Sometimes." There's a little bowl of brownish sugar cubes on the counter. Raw sugar. And a cup of little spoons. I put one sugar cube in and get a spoon. I turn around and try to decide where to go. Do I take my coffee up to baby Georgina's bed-room?

"I'll make you one if you like," he says.

But he doesn't seem to really care if I eat one or not. Last night at dinner, I wasn't very hungry. The lasagna the mom made was fine, but when I said I didn't want any, she kept offering differ-ent things she could make me. Like she thought I was going to starve if I didn't eat the lasagna. I'm not fat, but I'm not super skinny, either. Clearly, I'm not going to starve if I skip a plate of lasagna. I had some salad and a piece of bread.

Instead of making a run for the bedroom that seems more foreign than this kitchen, I walk around the island and try to be brave. I climb up onto one of the stools on the far side of the island where he's now mixing dry ingredients in a separate bowl.

"Harper has big plans for you all today. Shopping. To get you some things. Then lunch in the Quarter."

I blow on the coffee, my head down. He goes on with his waffle making. I search for my voice. "Not you?" That sounds stupid. "Shopping. I mean . . . you're not going?" I peek up at him over the rim of the mug.

He makes a face. He's a nice-looking guy. I mean for a dad. He doesn't have a beer gut like a lot of dads his age. Whatever age he is. Old enough to have me, I guess. I do the math. Undergrad degree by twenty-two. Two years of graduate school, probably. Then marriage. A year or two of goofing around, then a baby. I bet he's forty-four, maybe forty-five.

"I'm not much of a shopper," he says. He's mixing the wet and the dry together now.

I sip my coffee. It's good. French roast, which I like. Some people think it's bitter. "Me either."

He doesn't say anything so I don't know if he heard me. Or maybe he gets it. It's not that I don't like clothes. I'm just not into random wandering through stores. I like to buy clothes online. I'd rather wander randomly through an antiques flea market, or a park, or a museum, or even a library.

"I have to go to work for a while. I like to go on Saturday mornings when things are quiet. Weekdays, it seems like my office has a revolving door."

I nod like I understand. But I don't really. Mom never had an office. "What . . . what do you do?" I ask. "At Tulane."

"I'm the assistant comptroller."

"A numbers guy."

"Yup."

I blow on my coffee. "I like numbers," I say softly.

We're both quiet for a minute. I watch him fold the egg whites into the batter. He does it right. You have to have a gentle touch, otherwise the whites will collapse. The batter won't be as fluffy and the end product can seem tough. He pours batter into the heated waffle iron before he speaks again.

"Listen, Georg—" He looks at me and I realize he's as uncomfortable as I am. We're both just pretending we're not.

"I don't know what to call you. All these years, you've been our Georgina," he says, "but . . ."

"Lilla," I murmur, looking down at my coffee. Tears well in my eyes and I'm embarrassed. "I like . . . Lilla."

Again, he's quiet. And I like that. I like that he thinks about what to say before he says it. And this crazy thought goes through my head. *My mom would like him.*

"I don't know if Harper's going to go for that. Calling you Lilla. But . . ." He exhales and runs his hand across his mouth. He's got a nice beard; it's short, but it doesn't look like he forgot to shave. "She's been a wreck all these years. Since you were taken. She loved you so much and now that you're home . . ." He exhales again and reaches for his cup of coffee. "I think we just need to agree now, Lilla, that this is hard. Hard for you and for us. So . . . maybe you could help us out and we can help you? Maybe we can figure this out together?"

He's not telling me. He's asking me.

"I really miss my mom," I whisper. I don't even try not to cry. I just stare into my coffee cup as the tears run down my cheeks.

"Oh, Lilla," he sighs. "I can't say that I understand what you're feeling, because there's no way I can." He hands me a paper towel.

I sniff. I like that he doesn't try to hug me or anything creepy like that. I don't like it when strangers try to hug me. Not even ones with my DNA.

"But I do love you," he says. "I love the little girl you were and even though I don't know you yet, I love the young woman you've become. Because of how strong you obviously are. And smart."

I wipe my eyes and then my nose with the paper towel. "How do you know I'm smart?"

The waffle iron beeps and he opens it. The waffle smells good. "School records. We had them transferred to Ursuline, but we took a peek. That's where you'll be going to school. It's just a few blocks from here."

"I know where it is." My tone is a little snarky. "What if I don't want to go to school there?"

"It's where your sister goes." He sets the round waffle on a white plate.

"It's a Catholic school," I say. "Just girls."

"It is."

"That's going to be a problem." I take a big sip of coffee, turning up the snark. "Because, *Remy* . . . I'm Jewish."

12

Harper

"What do you mean she's *Jewish?*" I stick my head out the bathroom door. I'm standing in my bra and panties, brushing my teeth.

"Harper."

"She's not *Jewish*. She was baptized Catholic at St. Louis Cathedral, like you were. Like all the Broussards." My voice squeaks. "You held her in your arms, Remy, when the priest—"

"Harper, she doesn't remember any of that." He's sitting on the edge of the bed in his boxer briefs. He lowers his head to his hands.

I stand for a moment in the doorway. It's been a really long day and I feel as if I'm on the verge of tears. I step back into the bathroom and spit into the sink. Today, our first whole day as a family again didn't go anything like I thought it would. Nothing like I dreamed it would be on the days I wasn't planning for the funeral we would have at St. Louis Cathedral when someone found Georgina's remains.

I run the water. Rinse out my mouth. As I swish my toothbrush through the stream of water, I stare at myself in the mirror over the sink. She hates me. My daughter. Actually, as of today, both of my daughters hate me.

I started out this morning so hopeful. I came downstairs to find Remy and Georgina at the kitchen counter sitting side by side, drinking coffee and eating waffles. It was one of the million family scenes I'd imagined. He was reading the newspaper; she was reading a *Smithsonian Magazine*. When I asked Georgina about the article she was reading, she actually answered me in multiple syllables. Apparently my daughter likes to cook and likes to read about the history of foods. I didn't even know that was a thing. She told me that she'd read how the General Tso's chicken dish originated in an expensive restaurant in Taiwan. The chef was originally from Hunan province and supervised banquets for the Chinese Nationalist government. When the Communists took over in the late forties, he, like many Nationalists, fled, and he wound up in a restaurant in Taipei. He created the dish there.

I sat down to join them with my coffee. That was when things started going downhill. Georgina told me she didn't like shopping. I was immediately annoyed with Remy for telling her my plans. Georgina announced she wanted to stay home for the day while Remy went to work and Jojo and I went shopping. She avoided calling me "Mom" or Remy "Dad." Jojo was the only one she referred to by name. Of course there was no way I was letting her stay here alone. Not after she told us at lunch yesterday that she wanted to go *home*. What if Georgina ran away?

When the social worker was leaving yesterday, she said, privately, that I shouldn't be too worried about Georgina running away. She said Georgina was a smart girl; she knew there was nowhere for her to go. She said it was actually good that Georgina could express wanting to see the woman she'd thought was her mother and her anger about what had happened to her. I knew I should listen to Katrina. She is, after all, the expert. That doesn't mean I have to like it. Or leave Georgina home alone so she can get lost or kidnapped again.

In the end, it was Remy who basically told Georgina she had

to go shopping with us. So she went. But Jojo didn't want to go, either, so she spent the day texting on her phone, and when she wasn't texting, she was sulking. I wish Georgina had sulked. Instead, she walked around like a zombie all day. We bought almost nothing. Georgina refused to try on any clothes. The only thing she bought all day was a little leather notebook and she insisted on using her own money to buy it. The trip ended up being as painful for me as it apparently was for the girls. No one ate their lunch, their expensive lunch. And later, when we got home, dinner conversation was stilted and no one ate then, either. I drank two glasses of wine and pushed my stir-fry around my plate.

I look at myself in the mirror again. I look tired. And old. With the makeup washed off my face, my eyebrows are almost nonexistent. No one looks good without eyebrows.

"What are we doing about Mass in the morning?" I return my toothbrush to the drawer in the vanity.

Remy doesn't say anything.

"I think we should all go to Mass together." I stare at my eyebrowless face and wonder if I should look into the cost of having my eyebrows tattooed on. Ann had her lips tattooed last year. They're a gorgeous shade of natural-looking mauve. She says it's the best eight hundred dollars she ever spent in her life.

"Remy?" I grab the door frame and lean out the door. He's still sitting there with his head in his hands. I've always been amazed by how much time he can spend doing absolutely nothing.

Slowly he sits up. Exhales, as if I'm annoying him. "Maybe you and Jojo should go. I'll stay here with Lilla."

I flinch when he calls her that. But we've already had that argument once today so I decide not to revisit it. Not tonight. His reasoning is that we can't hit her like a brick wall, that we have to help her ease into her new life. And she's only ever known the name Lilla. I don't care how logical it is. I can't call my daughter by the name that woman who'd better spend the rest of her life in prison gave her.

"We go to Mass on Sunday mornings. That's what our family does."

"I don't go every Sunday," he says. "And neither do you," he adds.

With one last glance in the mirror, I tuck a lock of hair behind my ear and shut off the light. I walk into our bedroom. "It's part of who we are, Remy. We're Catholic. Our faith is what's gotten us through this nightmare. And . . . and she's a part of this family now and we need to do things together that define us as a family."

"But she's Jewish, Harper." He says it quietly.

"She's not!" I snap. "Stop saying that."

He looks up at me. His dark eyes are pleading. He wants me to let it go. "But she *thinks* she's Jewish," he says. "It's the way she's been raised."

Of course I can't let it go. I can never let things go. It's why we ended up in his sister's office signing divorce papers. "She was *raised?*" I point as if I could possibly know where Sharon Kohen is right now. "That woman took her, Remy! She—"

"Lower your voice."

I press my lips together. He means so Georgina doesn't hear me.

I stand in front of him, looking down at him. I'm trying not to cry.

After a long moment, he grabs my hand and pulls me down to sit beside him. His olive branch. He slips his arm around me, resting his hand on my hip, below the hem of my long-sleeved T-shirt, above my panty line. We just sit there.

"I had an awful day," I finally say. "She hates me."

"She doesn't hate you."

"You heard her yesterday. She doesn't want me. She doesn't think I'm her mother. She wants *that woman*."

"She understands that's not going to happen."

"But she wouldn't even talk to me today, Remy. The most I

got out of her was what she told me about a Chinese chicken dish." I rest my cheek on his shoulder. "Did she talk to you? This morning?"

"Not really." He leans his head against mine. "A little."

"What did she say?"

He's slow to reply. "She asked me what I do at Tulane. She likes numbers, too. Maybe she got that from me."

I smile at the thought and then murmur, "What are we going to do?"

"What do you mean? We're going to love our daughter. That's what we're going to do."

I close my eyes. "I mean about the Jewish part. About the she-wants-to-see-that-woman part. About the fact that she doesn't want to go to Ursuline. She doesn't like my lasagna or my stir-fry."

My husband— technically, my ex—sniggers.

I lift my head from his shoulder, fully intending to be annoyed with him. He's not taking any of this seriously enough. But then I can't help myself. The sound I make is more like a snort than a laugh. But then he starts to laugh and I can't help it. It's probably just that I'd rather laugh than cry.

I grab him by the shoulders and push him back onto the bed, laughing with him. "I'm serious," I say, but I'm still laughing.

The back of his head hits the mattress and bounces up a little. He kisses me, a quick peck, and lets his head fall back again.

"Remy," I say, leaning over him, my hair falling over my face. "I don't know what to do. I don't know how to help her."

"I'm pretty sure there's no guidebook for this." He looks up at me. "We're just going to have to figure it out as we go."

I lie on my back, beside him. "I think she should go to Mass with us tomorrow."

"And I think you're expecting way too much, way too soon." He looks at me. We're serious again.

I turn my head to stare at the punched-tin ceiling. "And what about school? She thinks she should be allowed to go to the school she was attending. A public school. I'm not driving her to Bayou St. John every day. That's the one thing she did tell me today. She said she would take the streetcar across town and then walk to school."

"What did you say?"

"Something about over my dead body," I answer, realizing it wasn't one of my best parenting moments.

"I think she's a pretty independent girl. Single mother who worked long hours. Makes sense," he says thoughtfully.

I choose to ignore his reference to that monster as a mother. "Georgina is not riding the streetcar. Not alone. Absolutely not. And it doesn't make sense for her not to go to school where Jojo goes." I gesture. "It's down the street, for heaven's sake."

"So we'll tell her that. We're her parents. We have the final say."

I look at him. "You'll tell her?" I feel like a coward saying it, but right now, I don't want to be the mean parent. I know it's selfish of me, but if he's willing to be the bearer of bad news, I'm willing to let him.

"I'll talk to her tomorrow," he agrees, turning his gaze to the ceiling.

"But I don't think she should go this week." I'm staring at the ceiling again, too. It needs painting. In a house this old, something always needs work. I want to paint Georgina's bedroom, too. It's still the pale lavender I painted it before she was born. "I took off from work," I go on. "And I told Elaine at choir I'm going to take some time off."

"I don't know that that's a good idea, baby. I think we need to go on with our lives and let her find her place in them."

"I thought we could do some things together," I say, ignoring his suggestion. "She and I. While you're at work and Jojo's at school. Get to know each other."

He sits up on the edge of the bed. Stands. "Okay. She can start next week at Ursuline." He walks toward the bathroom. "But I don't think we should make her go to Mass. Religion isn't something you force on people."

"My parents forced it on me," I call after him. "Yours certainly forced it on you."

He goes into the bathroom and I know that conversation is over. Whether I want it to be or not.

13

Jojo

"Wait." I hold up my hand like I'm one of those crosswalk guard ladies. "So I have to go to school . . . and Lilla doesn't?"

"Last week when I wanted you to stay home, you wanted to go to school." Mom gives me one of her looks from across the kitchen island. She's sitting on a stool, drinking coffee. She's wearing mascara and has pulled her hair back in a little stubby ponytail. Usually I like it that way, but I'm in a bad mood this morning. I don't like anything.

"And please don't call her that," she says so quietly that I can barely hear her. But I hear her, all right.

"Why can't I call her Lilla?" I walk to the fridge and get the OJ out. "That's what she wants to be called. I asked her." Which isn't true. But I overheard Mom and Dad discussing it yesterday. She *does* want to be called Lilla. Dad's calling her Lilla and Mom is pissed about it. Typical.

Mom's staring into her cup like she's reading tea leaves. Or maybe coffee grounds. "Her name is Georgina."

I get a bee glass from the cupboard and pour myself some OJ. Mom's got weird taste about some things but I love our bee glasses. They're French cut glass and there's a medallion on each one with a bee on it. "You named her that, but that lady who shanghaied her called her Lilla." I turn around to look at her.

"Mom, you can't just change her name. It would be like if I came down this morning and you started calling me Tiffany."

"Her name's Georgina. Named after my father's grandmother."

Mom does this all the time. She states her case by just repeating what she's already said. She'd make a crappy lawyer. I want to be a lawyer. To carry on the Broussard name. Dad's little brother, my Uncle Beau, says I could totally be a lawyer and work in his office downtown. The Broussards have been practicing law since the Confederate days. I don't know if he really thinks I'm smart enough to go to law school, but it's nice that he would say that. I like Uncle Beau. He gives great birthday and Christmas gifts.

I walk over to the counter with my glass. "Dad calls her Lilla."

"Put the orange juice away, please."

That's another thing Mom does. If she doesn't like the question, or the stated evidence, she just doesn't respond. I glance over my shoulder at the juice container I left on the counter. I take another sip from my glass before I stick the carton in the fridge. "I gotta go. Makayla needs help with her math."

Mom's eyebrows go up. "You're helping Makayla? That's nice."

What she means is that she's surprised. Because Makayla's so smart and I'm so dumb. Apparently, Georgina-Lilla's smart, too. Yesterday afternoon, Mom made us all watch a movie together. It was this old movie about this British dude who was good at math and helped win the war. I think it was World War I. Maybe II. Dad and Georgina-Lilla were talking about the machine he and his guys built that was like a computer before we had computers. The movie was kind of boring, even though Hunky Cumberbatch was in it. That's what Makayla calls him. I don't think he's that hot.

"I help Makayla sometimes," I argue. I actually want to go early so I can copy *her* algebra homework. Makayla's way smarter than me. "You picking me up after basketball or is Aunt Annie?"

"I don't know. I haven't talked to her. One of us will be there." She gets off the stool, taking her coffee with her. "Put your glass in the sink." She points at my orange juice glass on the counter. "And rinse it out."

"Fine," I huff.

"We're going to walk to Ann's with you." She takes another swig of coffee before she sets her mug in the sink and runs water in it.

"Who?" I look at her, making a face. "*Why?*"

"Georgina and I. I thought it would be nice if we had coffee with Ann. Then Georgina and I are going to the hardware store to pick out paint for her room. We're going to paint it together. A little project."

I've been asking Mom for, like, the last year if I can paint my room and she keeps saying we'll talk about it. It's still the same peachy color I picked out when I was, like, ten. I look at her in her jeans and sneakers. "Aren't you going to work?"

"I took some time off. To help Georgina get settled. Get your sister and I'll meet you out front in a minute. I just have to run upstairs."

I watch her walk out of the kitchen. "Where is she?" I call after her. Like I'm supposed to be keeping track of her now? She's the big sister. Shouldn't it be the other way around?

"Front porch."

I groan and walk across the kitchen to grab my backpack from where I left it on the floor in the doorway. I seriously think about just sneaking out the back and walking to Makayla's by myself. But then Mom will holler at me. Or worse, cry. And tonight Dad will pull me aside and talk all quiet and calm about how if I want to be treated like an adult, I need to act like one. How I need to be more sensitive to other people's feelings and blah, blah, blah.

Out in the front hall I grab my scarf off the banister and check my phone. It's only fifty-two degrees outside. I think about running back upstairs for my coat. It'll be chilly walking in my skirt and blazer this morning, though it will warm up as the day goes on. But Mom's upstairs. I wrap my scarf around my neck and wonder if you can pull a scarf tight enough to, like, strangle yourself. I'd be pretty important then, more important than my sister. At least until the paramedics carried my dead body out of the house. But then everything would be about Georgina again. Because she's smart.

And she'd still be alive.

I walk out onto the front porch. Georgina-Lilla is sitting in one of the chairs, drinking coffee. I can smell it. I don't like coffee. She's wearing an oversized Tulane hoodie sweatshirt. I think it's Dad's. It's usually hanging in the laundry room. I don't know what's with her and all the Tulane gear.

I close the front door, stalling. Maybe Mom will come down and I won't have to say anything to Georgina-Lilla. But she looks up at me like she expects me to say something.

"Um . . ." Just standing here next to her makes me feel stupid. She even *looks* smart. "Mom says she'll be done in a second. I guess . . ." I drag the toe of my dorky uniform shoe across the porch floor. "I guess you guys are walking up to Aunt Annie's. She's my best friend Makayla's mom. She's not really my . . . our aunt or anything. I just call her that because she and Mom are . . . best friends or whatever. They met before I was born. When you were a baby." I don't know why I say all that. It sounds stupid.

She's looking at me. At my uniform, I think. Judging. The plaid skirt is ugly.

"I have to wear this. We . . . everybody at Ursuline wears a uniform. You'll have to wear one, too," I add.

She looks away. She's mad that she has to go to Ursuline. Which I guess I kind of get. I don't really like it there, but if Mom and Dad all of a sudden said I had to go somewhere else, leave my friends . . . there's no way.

"We didn't have to wear uniforms at my school," she says. She talks quiet. But smart. She just *sounds* so smart.

We both look straight ahead. The park is our front lawn. It's one of the coolest things about our house. We've got big trees that are really pretty. They're called live oaks. When I was little, Mom used to take me and Makayla over to play under the trees. We'd try to climb them but we never could because the trunks are too big and the branches were too high. Sometimes we'd have picnics and stuff there. Mom would pack a whole basket of stuff, with real dishes. We'd eat little sandwiches on a blanket. Sometimes Mom would put a plate out for Georgina, too. It sounds weird now, but when I was little, I didn't think so. It was just what we did.

I glance at Georgina-Lilla. She looks really sad and I feel bad for her. I don't really want to. But I do anyway. I can't imagine what it must be like to have something like this happen to you. "Did you really think she was your mom? The one who kidnapped you?" The words are out of my mouth before I can stop them. Mom's gonna kill me when Georgina-Lilla tells her what I said.

She's quiet long enough for me to wonder if she didn't hear me or she's just not going to answer me. But then she looks at me with those big, sad Dad eyes. "I thought she was my mother. You've never questioned if your mom is really your mom, have you?"

I make a face. "Yeah, but, she *is* my mom."

"But what if she wasn't? Isn't?" She speaks slowly, enunciating each word. Dad talks that way, too. Maybe that's what makes them sound smart.

What if Mom wasn't my mom? I think about that for a minute and it kind of makes me dizzy the way I feel dizzy when I think about how the earth is just one planet in our solar system, in our galaxy, but there are lots of galaxies in the universe. I love my mom more than anyone in the world, even Dad. I mean, I hate her of course. Sometimes. But I love her. I'd never leave her. I don't even want to go to college out of state. Broussards go to Tulane. I want to go to Tulane. If I can get in.

"Where is she?" I ask. I talk quiet so if Mom sneaks up on us, she won't hear me. She told me I wasn't allowed to ask Georgina questions about before she got here. But that seems crazy because Mom also said she wants me to get to know her. How can I get to know her without asking questions about who she was when she was Lilla? "Your . . . what was her name? The lady who took you?"

"Sharon," she says.

She takes a drink of her coffee and when she does it, she looks like Mom. I mean, she looks like Dad, face-wise, but there's something about the way she moves, the way she holds her mouth when she drinks from the mug.

"Her name is Sharon. She's a chef."

"What happened to her when the cops found out she kidnapped you? Did they throw her in jail, or in a nut house?" I slide my backpack to the floor. "You'd have to be crazy to steal somebody's baby at Mardi Gras, wouldn't you?"

"I don't know." She looks up at me. "I guess they took her to jail, but no one will tell me anything. The social worker said it would be up to Remy and Harper what I'm told."

"You going to call them that? Remy and Harper?"

She shrugs.

I guess it must be weird for her to have called that woman Mom and now have our mom saying that's what she should call her. I can see why Georgina-Lilla wouldn't want to, but there's no way Mom's going to go for her calling her Harper.

I check the time on my phone. We need to go if I'm going to have time to copy Makayla's homework. I open the front door and yell, "Mom! I'm gonna be late!" I close the door. "I'm going to be late if we don't go." I pick up my backpack and head for the steps. "You wanna go with me, or you wanna wait for her? I meet Makayla at her house and then we walk together to school. I'm not allowed to walk alone."

"Why? It's just a couple of blocks, right?"

"Mom's paranoid." I go down the steps. "Until last year, an adult had to walk me to and from school. She's afraid I'll get kidnapped like you did and then she'd be down two kids," I say over my shoulder. Then I head for the street.

I hear Georgina-Lilla come down the steps behind me. I slow down a little bit. She catches up. We walk past our property, toward St. Charles.

"I don't remember anything," she says in this weird, airy voice. "I don't remember you."

I smile, glancing up at her. She's tall. "Well, I sure don't remember you." I shrug. "But I was a baby when you got snatched."

She's quiet for a couple of steps and then she says, "But you knew *about* me."

"Did I ever." We hit the sidewalk on St. Charles and turn right. "As long as I can remember, I've known I had a sister. Well . . . a dead sister."

"You thought I was dead?" She's looking at me.

I make a face. "Don't you read stuff on the Internet? Pervs kidnap little girls and do gross stuff to them and then they kill them. That's what the cops thought happened to you."

"Your mom and dad, they thought I was dead, too?" She sounds like she doesn't believe me.

"Sure. How could they have known that crazy Sharon the chef took you and pretended you were her little girl who died?"

She stops on the sidewalk, grabbing my arm. "What?"

"They didn't tell you?" I know I should shut my mouth now. Mom's going to be pissed if she finds out I told. But the girl has a right to know, doesn't she?

"No one's told me anything," she says. When she looks at me she seems all serious. And almost a little scared. I can't imagine what it would be like to be her right now, which makes me glad Sharon the chef kidnapped her instead of me. Which would have been impossible, of course, because Mom was carrying me in one of those front pack things, so the weirdo couldn't get her hands on me.

"Jojo! Georgina!" I hear Mom behind us.

"I heard Mom and Dad talking," I say, looking up at Georgina-Lilla. This feels so weird. I mean, she's a complete stranger, but I feel this weird . . . I don't know. Connection to her. That's what Aunt Annie would call it. A connection. "That's what the cops told them." I talk quickly because any minute now, Mom will catch up with us and she'll give us crap about leaving the front porch without her. "Sharon's baby died and she was at the parade and you kind of looked like her." I shrug. "So she took you. And then she pretended you were her kid. She called you the kid's name, gave you her Social Security number and everything."

Georgina starts walking again. I walk beside her. It's chilly. I wonder if she has a coat. She didn't bring much stuff with her. Maybe that's why she's wearing Dad's hoodie. I guess someone is supposed to go to the house where she used to live and get her stuff.

"And no one she knew noticed one day her daughter was dead and the next day she had her again?" Georgina asks. "Only she didn't look the same?"

I make a face. "Sounds bat-shit crazy to me, too."

"But we moved when I was two." Georgina says it like she's thinking. Then she looks at me. "Or that's at least what she told me. Sharon. She told me I was born here in New Orleans, but we moved away when I was two to Mobile."

I don't know what to say because all of a sudden I feel like I might cry, I feel so bad for Georgina. Or Lilla, or whatever the hell her name is. This just sucks. It *so* sucks. "But . . . but she was nice to you, right? She didn't, like . . . lock you in the closet or . . . like, make you her boyfriend's sex slave. I've read stuff like that on the Internet," I add. In case she thinks I'm just making this kind of stuff up.

Georgina-Lilla almost smiles, like she thinks I'm funny. But maybe she thinks I'm stupid. I can't tell. "She never locked me in a closet. She never had a boyfriend."

"Where did she say your dad was?"

"She said I never had a dad. He was just a sperm donor. She told me he was a chef."

"Josephine!" my mother hollers.

I look over my shoulder.

She's behind us on the sidewalk, doing her fast-walk thing. "Wait for me," she yells.

"She loved me," Georgina says, acting like she doesn't even hear Mom hollering at us. "I loved her."

I look at my sister. "I'm really sorry this happened to you," I whisper.

Her eyes fill up with tears and she walks past me. "Me too."

14

Harper

I knock on Georgina's bedroom door that's half open and give it a push. "Hey."

"Hey." My daughter doesn't turn around to look at me. I can just see the top of her head, over her bed. That's been made, I note. As if she's a guest. Jojo hasn't made her bed in . . . Jojo has never made her bed in her life, to my knowledge.

Georgina's on the floor on the far side of the room, cutting in with a paintbrush around one of her two windows. Last night, she and Remy pushed the bed to the center of the room. After leaving the paint she picked out to sit in the hallway for two days, apparently she decided that today she'd paint. She made it pretty clear she didn't want any help. Which hurt my feelings because I thought this would be a good thing for us to do together. Remy seems to have good luck getting her to talk to him when they're doing something. Like cleaning up the dinner dishes. Last night they cut up potatoes to make baked fries and talked about malaria.

We're on day six of the first days of the rest of our lives and I don't feel as if I've made any progress with Georgina at all. She responds when spoken to, but still in as few words as possible. She's so polite that I wish she had a little of Jojo's mouth. Sass, I could deal with. Or even anger. But whatever feelings Georgina has, she's not sharing them with me. With any of us.

I stand there in the doorway, trying to think of something to say. Which makes me feel inadequate as a mother. As a human being. I want so badly to connect with my daughter, who's clearly hurting, but I can't seem to find my way. "The color . . . I think it's going to be pretty," I stumble. "Especially with the white trim."

She picked out gray for the walls. What teenager chooses gray for her bedroom walls? For anything? And the only reason she's not painting the baseboard and crown molding black is because I suggested painting the trim would be too big a project right now. She didn't argue with me. I wish she had. Had she put up one word of protest, I'd probably have let her paint the one-hundred-year-plus walls black and put down sod over the hardwood floor.

"You sure you don't want any help?" I ask. "I'm pretty good with a paintbrush." Not exactly true, but desperate times . . .

"I'm fine." Georgina's tone is flat.

A lump rises in my throat and I look down at my ballet flats. I thought my crying days were over when we found her. Since she arrived, I've been fighting a feeling of something that can't be defined by any word but *disappointment* and it's making me miserable. Feeling this way, not wanting to, is awful. What kind of mother am I to be disappointed when I've gotten what I prayed for all these years? What kind of human being does that make me? I keep telling myself that I didn't expect Georgina to come running into my arms, but on some level, did I?

"I . . . I need to go into the office," I say. "To . . . I have to make a couple of phone calls about lab work that came back and . . . note a couple of things in some records."

She doesn't say anything. She just keeps painting. It's so quiet that I can hear the sound of her brushstrokes. And a lawn mower outside. I've been in Louisiana more than twenty years and it still seems odd to hear the occasional lawn mower in the middle of the winter. "I was thinking . . . you want to come with me? We could get lunch after. Maybe see if your dad can get away for lunch?" I throw that in, because like it or not, he seems to be the one she gravitates to. And I'm not above bribery. I wouldn't even be above coercion if I could find some leverage to use with her.

Again, the sound of brushstrokes.

Then she surprises me by speaking up of her own volition. "You're working this week? Remy said you weren't."

I cringe when she calls him by his first name. *Pick your battles*, I tell myself. Remy's advice. "Um . . . no, no, I took some time off. To be with you," I add quickly. "I just . . . I have those phone calls to make."

"I'd prefer to stay here." She sounds so adult.

I exhale and walk into her room. Now that we've cleaned all the boxes and junk out of it, there's almost nothing here. Georgina doesn't own anything. I tried to buy her some things when we went shopping the other day, but there was nothing she wanted. At least nothing she would tell me she wanted. I suppose she's waiting for her belongings from the other house. The police are supposed to let us know when and how we can collect them. I've been half hoping she wouldn't want any of that stuff. Every time I look at her backpack, I have this irrational urge to throw it in the trash. I suppose it's a representation of that woman. The woman who seems to still have a hold on Georgina, even though she's in prison now.

Remy's hoodie is lying on Georgina's bed, thrown over her backpack. She's been wearing it almost nonstop. I pick it up, lift it to my face, and smell it. It smells like him, but also . . . I breathe deeply, closing my eyes. *Her*, I think. Georgina. It's not the baby smell I remember, but it's definitely her. I lay it back on the bed.

"I'll be fine here," Georgina says. She still isn't looking at me. "You won't be gone long. Right?"

"No, not long." I speak before I have time to think about what I'm saying. I'm just so excited that we're having an exchange of words. Any words. Any thoughts. "An hour maybe."

"I'll just stay here and paint."

I bite down on my lower lip. Remy says I need to give Georgina some space. That she needs some time and space to acclimate to her new world. He'd probably leave her alone for an hour, but I honestly don't know if I can do it.

I watch her paint. Her strokes are long and controlled. Confident. And she's precise. Like Remy. If Jojo and I were painting in here, we'd have the hardwood floor covered with a tarp and everything would have to be taped before we picked up a brush. I can't help wondering if she's done this before. In other bedrooms. Other cities. I think a lot about where she's been all these years. What she's been doing.

Last night, Georgina asked Remy again about that woman. She called her Sharon, at least. Not "Mom" like she had the day she arrived. She asked Remy if he knew where she was. He told her he didn't know, which, fortunately for us, is true. Maybe the police will tell us Friday. If there aren't privacy issues, which would be absurd, of course, considering the circumstances. Considering the fact that *Sharon* held our baby captive for fourteen years.

But Georgina pressed Remy. She's a smart one, this girl. And she knows people. I can't say she's manipulative; that's too harsh a word. But she knows how to handle people. How to get what she wants. She asked him if he could try to find out where she was. He responded by asking her if she thought that was a good idea.

He should have been a psychologist or a psychiatrist. He seems to intuitively know the questions to ask. It was one of the things that attracted me to him in our early days of dating. Georgina answered that she didn't know if it was a good idea. Which later, when we were talking after the girls went to bed, he told me he found fascinating. And heartbreaking. Our conversation got a little tense after that. I told him there was no way in hell we were telling Georgina where Sharon was. Ever. That there was no need for her to know because she was never, *ever* going to see her again. Never have any contact with her again.

At that point, Remy lay back in bed, fully clothed, and closed his eyes. He said I need to think long and hard about that. That *we* needed to think about it.

Falling back on my old ways, I went into the bathroom and closed the door.

My gaze shifts to Georgina again. She's still painting. A part of me wants to tell her to get up and get ready to go because she's going with me. No argument. I'm the parent, here. But a part of me wants to give her what she wants. To give her anything she wants, say anything she wants so she'll love me. Or at least look at me.

"I don't know, Georgina," I stall. "I don't know if I'm comfortable leaving you here alone."

She turns around to look at me. I can see that she's been crying; her eyes are red and puffy. Her skin is splotchy. Which makes me want to cry.

"I'm sixteen," she says softly. "I used to stay home alone all the time when M—Sharon worked. I'll be fine."

Her gaze is mesmerizing. And she's right. She's sixteen years old, I tell myself. Sixteen-year-olds stay home alone all the time. They babysit children. Hell, some sixteen-year-olds have children of their own. "It would just be an hour," I hear myself say. "And then . . . maybe I could help you paint?"

She nods. Then she dips the brush carefully into the gray paint, turns her back to me, and returns to what she was doing.

I back out of the room, slipping my cell phone out of my jeans pocket.

Walking down the hall, toward the staircase, I dial Remy. It goes to voice mail. I don't leave a message. As I go down the stairs, I glance up at the gray-haired, gray-bearded men watching me. Men I never knew. Men Remy never even knew, except his grandfather. What would the Broussard men do? Would they leave their great-granddaughter alone in the house after everything that's happened? Would they trust that God would protect her?

When I reach the bottom of the stairs, I autodial Ann. She picks up on the first ring.

"Hey."

"Hey," I say quietly. I don't want Georgina to hear me. "I have to run to the office."

"Okay?"

I hear what sounds like dishes rattling and, lower in the background, music. Jazz. "Georgina wants to stay here," I tell Ann.

"But you don't want her to?"

"No." It comes out in a whoosh of breath. "How can I leave her here? How can I ever leave her anywhere ever again?"

"She's sixteen years old."

I sit down on the bottom step of the staircase. The wood is worn from a hundred years of footsteps. I find that comforting; it's one of the reasons I love this house. "That's what she said."

The dish clatter stops. "She wasn't kidnapped because you left her alone," Ann says gently.

"I know that."

"It just happened, Harper. And it wasn't your fault. It wasn't Remy's fault because he had to pee."

My throat tightens. "I know," I manage.

"It wasn't anyone's fault. Bad things happen sometimes."

"I know."

"Georgina's your daughter."

Ann's quiet for a moment, then, but I can tell from the inflection in her voice that she wants to say something else. I wait for it.

"She's your daughter," she says. "Not your prisoner."

I close my eyes. "I called Remy to ask him what he thought. I'll only be gone an hour. He didn't pick up."

"Remy would leave her," Ann says. "What's she doing?"

I open my eyes. Lift my head. "Painting. Her room."

"Gray."

"Gray," I echo.

Ann sighs. I hear the dishes again.

"Harper, if you want Georgina to be a normal teenager, I think you need to treat her like one. Normal sixteen-year-old teenagers stay home alone. Of course, normal teenagers are at school on a Thursday at ten thirty in the morning," she adds.

An incoming text beeps in my ear. I lower the phone long enough to see that it's Jojo and then lift it again. She forgot a check for a field trip. She wants me to drop it off. "She's going to school next week. I thought she should stay home another week, but . . . she wants to go. She's worried about missing classes. She's an academic, this one." I smile at the thought. I was that way in high school, too. I never missed a day, not even when I was sick.

"And she's okay about transferring to Ursuline?"

I get to my feet. "No, but Remy told her we made the decision she'd go to school with Jojo and it wasn't really up for discussion. It just makes sense for her to go here instead of across town."

"Absolutely," Ann agrees.

I face the staircase, glancing up. "So you'd leave her here?"

"I would. But if you can't do it yet, Harper, you can't do it. I'd offer to come over and stay with her, but I have a dental appointment. You know how it is with an appointment with a hygienist."

I start up the stairs. "You cancel and it will be six months before you can get another appointment."

"Exactly."

Halfway up, I stop. "You think she'll be okay?"

"She'll be fine," Ann assures me, sounding far more confident than I feel. "She wants to stay, right?"

"Right," I agree. "And I'll just be an hour." I exhale. "Thanks, Ann."

"Anytime, sweetie."

I go to Georgina's bedroom. She's moved to the second window. I just stand there in the doorway for a moment. My anxiety is almost overwhelming. I feel short of breath and my armpits are damp. This is so hard. Why is this so hard? God brought my baby back to me. Why can't I trust Him to keep an eye on her for an hour while I'm gone? I touch the tiny crucifix under my T-shirt. "So . . . I'm going to go to the office now."

She turns around. "You are?" She sounds surprised that I'm actually going to leave her.

Not any more surprised than I am. "I'll be an hour. Let me give you my cell phone number."

"My cell phone died," she says. Again, the flat voice. She chews on her cuticle on her thumb. "I don't have the charger. I left it—" She doesn't finish the sentence. She doesn't have to.

"Oh . . . well . . . I can leave you the number on the kitchen counter. If you need anything you can call me from the house phone." I think for a moment. It had never even occurred to me that she has a cell phone. Of course she does. Sharon would have bought her one. Most teenage girls have one. Certainly every one I know. "It's probably going to get turned off, you know," I say. "The plan will be cancelled for nonpayment and they'll disconnect your number."

She turns back to the window. Dips her brush in the paint.

"We'll get you another cell phone. I think the new iPhone is out."

"It doesn't have to be a new one," she says, barely above a whisper.

Again, my heart is breaking for her. The sound of her voice, she sounds so . . . wounded. Now, suddenly, I don't want to go. What I really want to do is take her in my arms and hug her. But she hasn't let me touch her since the day she arrived. And then, looking back, I realize she only let me hug her because I ambushed her.

"Okay," I say, taking a step back. "So, I'll be as quick as I can. Is there something you'd like for dinner? Something you'd like to make, maybe?" I add because that seems to be the one thing I know she's interested in. I choose not to think about the fact that it's probably because it was something she and Sharon, a chef, did together. "I could stop and get the ingredients."

She shrugs. "Whatever."

"Okay. I'll be back in an hour. Hour and a half, tops." I step back, into the hall, fighting the feeling that I'm stepping backward off a cliff.

15

Lilla

From my window, I watch her pull out of the driveway. I feel a little guilty. I wouldn't consider myself a sneaky person. I never lied to my mom about where I was going or where I'd been. Mostly because my life was never interesting enough to have to lie. I've been to a couple parties where people were drinking or smoking weed. I'm not like all judgy about those choices. It's just not my thing.

Jeez, I sound like some old Jew lady.

I almost smile. I sound like my mom.

I slide down, my back against the wall to sit, being careful not to touch the wet paint. Tears well up in my eyes. I wonder how much one person can cry. If you get dehydrated enough, does that stop the tears? I'll have to Google it.

I miss my mom so much that my skin hurts. I've never been away from her for longer than a sleepover at a friend's house and now it's been more than a week.

Today is her birthday. We were going out for dinner tonight to some seafood place outside the city on Lake Pontchartrain. I don't know where. I wipe my eyes. I wish I knew where we were going. I'd go there tonight. I don't know how I'd get there. I only have eleven dollars in my backpack. I doubt I could take a cab to the restaurant and back for that and you have to have a credit card to Uber.

If I did have money for a taxi, I think I'd save it to go see Mom in prison. When I figure out where she is. I think Remy will tell me. Once he finds out. The mom doesn't want me to know. She doesn't want to ever have anything to do with my Sharon mom again. I heard her and Remy talking about it last night when I went to the bathroom. So I guess I've become a sneaky person; I never used to eavesdrop before.

The thing is, the Harper mom doesn't understand that even though she gave birth to me, that only means something to her. It doesn't mean anything to me. I don't know her. I don't even know if I want to know her. And I sure don't need a spoiled, snotty sister like Jojo. Jury's out on the dad. I've never had a dad. But the family's a package deal. It's not like I can pick from an à la carte menu.

I stand up and peek out the window. The car's still gone. She won't be back for an hour. So if I am going to be a sneak, I need to get moving.

I know I can't go see Mom in prison, not yet, at least. Not without a plan, which includes knowing where she is. But there's one place I can go to feel closer to her. And I want to get my phone charger, anyway; the battery was dead this morning. Everyone here has an iPhone. Their cords won't charge my old Samsung.

I walk over to the bed that Remy and I put in the middle of the room so I could paint. I pull his Tulane hoodie over my head. I've commandeered it; that's what he said. I like the word. I unzip the front pocket of my backpack, take out the money, including the quarters, and stick it in the front pocket of my jeans. I'll need the cash for the streetcar. Exact change. If my phone was work-ing, I could use the app that's connected to Mom's credit card and I wouldn't have to use cash. I don't know when her credit card payment is due, so for all I know, it might already be shut off.

As I go out my bedroom door, I look back at where I painted around the windows. It occurs to me that the paint will dry on the brush if I just leave it on the can there. I set my backpack on the floor and go downstairs. I only have to open two drawers to find plastic wrap. I tear off a big piece and go to the refrigerator. I grab a bottle of water and an apple. It feels weird to go into a stranger's refrigerator and take something, but I guess it's supposed to be my refrigerator now.

Back upstairs, I cover the paint can with the lid and tap it down with my heel. I don't want to take the time to look for a hammer. I know there are tools in a drawer in the laundry room. I saw Remy get a screwdriver out of one, but if I'm going to go, I need to get out of here. In case the mom changes her mind and comes back.

I wrap up the brush and set it on the paint can. I turn off the light when I leave the bedroom, swinging my backpack with the apple and the water over my shoulder. The old guys watch me as I go down the steps. One of them reminds me of this grandpa rabbi at the temple where we used to go once in a while when we lived in Shreveport. Mom was never a super Jew or anything like that. She'd get on a kick and we'd go to temple a couple of weeks in a row, but it never lasted long. Organized religion was never her thing. She used to tell me that to her, being a Jew was more about history and her ancestors than about religion.

I feel as if the grandpa rabbi is watching me as I go down the stairs. And making me feel guilty for what I'm doing. Remy will be worried about me when he finds out I'm gone. And he'll find out as soon as the Harper mom walks in and finds out I'm not here. She'll lose her shit. She'll cry. She might call the police. She'll definitely call Remy, and maybe Aunt Annie, too. I hope she doesn't call the police. I don't think they can arrest me for going for a walk without permission from parents who have been my parents for all of a week. But I don't know how an arrest record affects college applications. I don't want to not get into Tulane because I took a ride on a streetcar.

At the bottom of the staircase, I think about leaving a note on the piece of paper where the mom left her cell phone number. I wonder if it's the grandpa rabbi's idea. But what would I say? I'm sure not going to tell her where I'm going. Saying "Don't worry

about me" seems silly. Clearly the Harper mom has got some serious anxiety issues concerning me. And Jojo, too, but mostly me.
Obviously because I was the one who was kidnapped.

I ignore the grandpa rabbi's advice.

I go out the front door and walk along the little road that runs
beside the park. It's a pretty, sunny day and only a little bit chilly.
I walk out to St. Charles. There's a stop in the downtown direction at Law Road. I can't take the St. Charles streetcar all the way
to Bayou St. John. I'll have to switch lines. It will take a while; it's
not fast transportation, but that's okay. I like to ride the streetcar.

I spot the familiar green streetcar coming my way. Green is the
St. Charles line. I'll catch the red cars to Mid-City. I smile.

Correction. I *love* to ride the streetcar.

16

Harper

"Remy!" I rush into his office, my bag bouncing against my hip. "She's gone."

He looks up from his desk, over his thick, black Wayfarer-style reading glasses, but he doesn't move.

"Georgina!" I sniff and wipe my nose with the back of my hand. I've already had one good cry. I'm fighting off the next.

I got home seventy-two minutes after I left. I could have been home in sixty-two minutes, but I had to swing by Ursuline and leave the check so Jojo could go on her field trip. When I walked into the house, Georgina didn't answer me when I called her. I told myself not to panic. She's probably just in the bathroom. But she wasn't. I went to her room. The paint can was closed and the brush was wrapped in plastic wrap. It looked as if she didn't do any more painting after I left. I walked all over the house, calling her name. Then I went outside to check the front porch, the garden, and the walkway in front of the house. No Georgina. I went back into the house and checked the notepad on the counter, thinking maybe she'd left me a note. Maybe she'd just gone for a walk in the park. It seems to be one of the things she actually enjoys doing.

I kept telling myself over and over again not to freak out, even though my heart was pounding and I felt as if I wanted to vomit. I kept telling myself she wasn't gone. That this was nothing like what happened before. It couldn't happen again. It was a mathematical improbability of infinite proportion.

I searched the whole house again. I even checked the walk-up attic. I called Remy and he didn't answer. Then I called Ann. She didn't answer. Then I called Remy again. When he still didn't pick up, I drove to his office. I didn't know what else to do. I'm parked in a no parking zone in front of his building. I'll probably get towed.

"She's gone, Remy," I say, standing in front of his desk, my arms at my sides. "I've lost her again." As soon as the words come out of my mouth, I realize how ridiculous the thought is. It doesn't make me feel any better.

He takes off his reading glasses. "Tell me what happened."

"We have to look for her." I bring my hands to my head, trying to force myself to breathe. I'm not going to let myself become the person I was after Georgina was taken. That irrational, overly emotional, hollow ghost of a woman. I take another breath. "I tried to call you."

"I had meetings this morning." He still hasn't gotten out of his leather chair behind the big antique desk we bought off someone's front lawn in Alabama. We got it on one of our weekend trips when we were still trying to pick up the pieces of our marriage. Before we admitted defeat. Before the divorce.

"I had to go to the office. I had to make some calls. Some lab reports came back and I wanted to call from the office so I would have the records in front of me. I . . ." I press the heel of my hand to my forehead. Just one hand, though. I'm calmer. I know Georgina hasn't been kidnapped. She's a teenager. And a smart one at that. She wouldn't get in a car with a stranger. "She didn't want to go with me. I thought . . . I talked to Ann and—" I meet his gaze, fighting my tears, afraid he'll judge me, even though I know he won't. Not for leaving her, at least. "She wanted to stay home, Remy. I was only going to be gone an hour."

"Harper."

"Ann thought it would be fine. I knew you would say it was fine."

He gets up from his desk. "Harper."

"I was trying to give her some space." My voice cracks. "I . . . I was trying to—"

"Baby." He comes around the desk and puts his arms around me. "She's okay. It's going to be fine. It was the right thing to do, to leave her home. Sixteen-year-old girls stay at home without their parents for an hour. We'll find her."

I rest my head on his chest. He's wearing a green polo with an embroidered Tulane crest and I feel the roughness of the piqué against my cheek. "Should we call the police?" I look up at him. "We should call the police, shouldn't we? But what if they call the social worker? What if people start questioning if we're fit parents?"

He smiles his sad smile and I know deep inside that I'm the one responsible for that sadness. More than the kidnapping. More than the loss of our child. It's a guilt I'll live with the rest of my life. We Catholics, even the bad ones, are good at guilt.

He smoothes my hair. Kisses my forehead and then steps back, taking hold of my shoulders. "We shouldn't call the police. Not yet. And no one is getting the social worker involved. Lilla's our daughter; she's not on loan. She probably went for a walk. In the park."

I close my eyes for a second. He keeps calling her by that name. I press my lips together. *Pick your battles. Pick your battles.*

I open my eyes. "You really think she just went for a walk? She was upset this morning about something." I close my eyes again, realizing that sounds ridiculous. Of course she's upset. She's been upset since she arrived. In her teenage mind, *we* kidnapped her. Not that woman. I'm beginning to see that now. Feel it. It's the accusation I've seen in her eyes since she came home.

I look up at him again. "She was upset about something specific. She was painting her room. She'd been crying."

"I'm telling you, I bet she went for a walk. She's gone for a walk and then she'll come home."

"We should have gotten her a cell phone." I shake my head. "Why didn't we think about getting her a phone? How could she call us if she was in trouble?"

He chuckles, which makes me angry. This isn't funny. None of this is funny. How can he laugh at a time like this?

"Harper, you haven't let her get more than thirty feet from you since she arrived. Why would she need a cell phone?"

"She's going to school next week. She needs a phone."

"I agree. She needs a phone." He puts his hand on my shoulder and steers me toward the door. "Let's go find our daughter. She'll probably be at home by the time we get there."

But she isn't. I search the whole house while Remy makes himself a sandwich. Upstairs in her room, I pick up the paintbrush that had been in her hand this morning. I close my eyes and try to feel her touch. After she was kidnapped, I did this for weeks. Months. I smelled her blankets. I laid my head on her little pillow in her toddler bed. I touched her toys over and over again. I kept a spoon she had used that morning, not caring that there was dried cereal and milk on it. Remy and I had a huge blow-up when he washed the spoon, knowing I didn't want her touch washed off it.

I take a breath and put the paintbrush back where I found it. I glance around her room. It's easy to tell what's missing because she doesn't have much. The canvas laundry container with a few pieces of clothing in it that she brought with her is still by the door. But the blue backpack is gone. And Remy's Tulane hoodie. So maybe she *did* just go for a walk. If she'd run away, wouldn't she have taken the clothes?

I go back downstairs, to the kitchen. Remy is sitting at the counter, eating a chicken salad sandwich on rye, a strange combination, and staring into space.

"She's not here," I say.

"I'll check the park."

"It's too big." I throw up my hands and let them fall. "What are the chances you'll run into her?"

He lifts his gaze to meet mine. He's trying to be patient with me. "She'll be back. I think we just need to wait for her."

I turn away from him and begin to pace.

"You want me to make you a sandwich? I made the chicken salad with pimentos the way you like it. And a little fresh garlic. Lilla's contribution."

"I don't want anything to eat," I say from between clenched teeth. At the refrigerator, I turn and walk back, my arms crossed over my chest. I'm seriously thinking about calling the police, with or without Remy's say-so. What if Georgina ran away? The police said she and the woman lived in a lot of places. What if Georgina took off for Baton Rouge, or Atlanta, or God knew where? A sixteen-year-old walking through a park alone was one thing, hitchhiking I-10 was another. "And I wish you wouldn't call her that," I snap. "Her name is Georgina. We named her Georgina. She was baptized Georgina. She's our child and her name is *Georgina*." The last words stick in my throat. Choke me.

Remy puts down his sandwich, half eaten. He takes a sip from his glass of water. "You stay here. Call me if she shows up."

"Where are you going?" I suddenly feel terrible for speaking like that to him. I know that tone of voice is one of the reasons he left. I don't want to be that woman anymore. I don't want to use that tone of voice with him. With anyone. I lower my head. "Sorry," I murmur. "I'm just . . . scared."

"I know." He kisses my cheek as he walks by me. "I'll have my phone."

I watch him walk for the back door.

"But where are you going to look for her?" I call after him.

"Don't call the police," he says. And then he's gone.

17

Lilla

I sit on the front step trying not to cry, chewing on little bits of dry cuticle. It took me longer to get here than I thought it would. I took the St. Charles streetcar line all the way to Canal. Then I got on the Canal Street line and got off at City Park. I walked to our shotgun from there.

It was such a nice ride on the streetcars. They weren't packed like they are some days. I listened to the dinging whenever a car pulled across the tracks in front of us, and I waved at some little boys standing with their mom on the street. I hung my head out the window and felt the breeze on my face as the streetcar rattled down the tracks. Some old lady asked me to shut the window because she was cold, but after she got off, I put it down again.

Riding the streetcar, I pretended Mom was sitting beside me. Like she did when we first got here. We had a whole Saturday together that day. She explained to me the layout of the city. She told me which way the major highways ran. Where the French Quarter sat in relationship to the rest of the city. She explained to me how the Mississippi River ran through the city and what the deal with the levees was when Katrina hit and they broke. And why places like the Ninth Ward went underwater and the Quarter didn't. My mom is really smart.

Well . . . I guess she isn't *that* smart. Otherwise she wouldn't have thought she could get away with kidnapping somebody's kid and pretending she was her own. And then there was the confession, also not a smart move. If she hadn't admitted to the cops that she stole me, maybe none of this would have happened.

No. If I hadn't taken that stupid job in the coffee shop, *then* she wouldn't have gotten caught. Harper Mom never would have seen me. So if I'm going to start pointing fingers, it's totally *my* fault Sharon got caught.

I keep thinking about how Harper Mom knew it was me. Wondering. It's kind of amazing. I've seen the pictures in the living room of me when I was a baby. Babies don't look like people. I wouldn't have known those pictures of that girl were me except that Jojo told me.

That's not true. I would have known, or at least been suspicious. The little girl in the Georgina pictures looks like the little girl in the Lilla pictures.

I wonder where those baby Lilla pictures are. In one of the moving boxes, I guess. Mom never put them in picture albums, but she had little photo boxes to protect them. I kind of want to find them and compare a picture of baby Lilla to baby Georgina.

Because maybe it's not true? Maybe they're not the same kid? Maybe there was a mistake with the DNA test they ran when they swabbed my mouth?

I hang my head, fighting another wave of tears. It doesn't matter how much I want it to be true, I know it's not. Mom . . . Sharon told the police that she kidnapped me at a parade on St. Charles. She knew too many details. She knew the date and the time. She was telling the truth.

I really am Georgina Elise Broussard.

I frown. Who names a little baby a ridiculous name like that? It's too big for a baby. Too pretentious. *Pretentious* was a word Mom liked. She used to use it all the time when she talked about the customers at the restaurants where she worked.

A lady walks past me on the sidewalk and I watch her. She's

carrying groceries and she's on her cell. She smiles at me as she passes, then goes on with her life as if nothing has happened. As if I'm not living in the *upside down,* like the place in that TV show *Stranger Things.* Mom and I watched it on Netflix. In the show, these kids find a dimension on Earth parallel to the one humans live in. I guess word hasn't gotten through the neighborhood. I guess no one knows about the crazy woman who used to live here who kidnapped a baby.

And suddenly it makes sense to me now why Sharon was never friendly with our neighbors. She never had friends who came to the house or that she met for a drink. We always rented, often moved twice a year.

If you kidnap a kid, you wouldn't want anyone to get too close to you.

The weird thing is that, looking back, I realize that Mom didn't really encourage me to have friends, either. I mean, she didn't *discourage* it, but she always made me feel like she was my best friend. The only best friend I needed.

I guess that lady who just walked by, and is now going into her own shotgun house, doesn't know that the landlord changed the lock on our door.

My house key didn't work.

I panicked when I found out I couldn't get inside the house. I was afraid all of our stuff was gone: the pictures of the toddler who didn't know she'd been kidnapped, my phone charger, Mom's knives.

I ran around to every window, trying to look in. I couldn't see in the front windows because there are accordion blinds. They were here when we moved in and Mom said they were nice ones. That they provided decent privacy. But in the back of the house, I could see through the back door window. It's covered with a curtain . . . well, a dish towel I hung over it. But through a little crack, I could see into my bedroom. I could see my bed, made, just like I left it. I could see my wooden cigar box on my nightstand where I was keeping the tips I earned at the coffee shop.

We bought the box at a garage sale the weekend we moved in. I didn't know what I was going to put in it. I just liked it because it said "Queen of Cuba." I thought that was funny for the name of a cigar company. It was only five bucks, so Mom bought it for me.

So our stuff is still here. The landlord hasn't sold it all or thrown it in a Dumpster. But I can't get to it. I can't get inside.

I look up and watch a car drive by. I don't know what to do now. I really, *really* wanted to go inside. I mean, I know I can't stay here. I know I have to go back to my *upside down*. I have to figure out how to be their Georgina. And maybe still be me. But I just want to walk through the rooms one more time. Because even knowing what I know now about Sharon, I know I had a good life with her. I know I was happy. That was real, even if the part about how I became Sharon's daughter wasn't.

Supposedly someone is coming to the house to get some of my things. The social worker with the unfortunate name, maybe. But I don't think anyone has any intention of letting me back in the house. Shoot. If the cops or the social worker or whoever don't move fast, I bet the landlord *will* sell our stuff. He'll sell my mom's knives; they were expensive. Like hundreds of dollars apiece.

I guess the cops told the landlord that Sharon and her daughter, who wasn't her daughter, wouldn't be coming back. Why he changed the lock, I don't know. Obviously Mom isn't getting out of jail anytime soon.

I watch another car go by.

I should probably walk to the streetcar and head back to the fancy house on the fancy street where I live now. I don't know what time it is, but I bet it's sometime after three. Harper Mom probably lost her shit when she came home and found out I was gone. I wonder if she called the cops. Of course there's no way they'd do anything about a teenager missing for a couple of hours, but still . . .

Now I feel bad. I should have left a note. Told them I'd be back. Because where am I going to go? It's not like—

"Hey."

A man's voice startles me and I look up. It's Remy. I come up off the step, suddenly scared and I don't even know why. It's not like he's a scary guy.

He looks at me and I look at him. He comes over and sits down on the step of our pretty mint-green shotgun where I'll never get to live now. He takes his cell out of his pocket and texts something. Texting Harper, I'm sure. He puts his phone back in his pocket before he says anything else.

"We were worried about you." He doesn't sound angry. Or even particularly upset. He pats the place beside him on the wooden step.

I sit down again. Stare at my backpack at my feet. "I'm sorry."

"You can't just take off like this, Lilla. You have to tell us where you're going. It's what you do when you're part of a family. We let each other know where we're going to be. So no one worries. And that goes for the adults in the family, not just the teenagers. If you're expecting me home for dinner and I have to work late, I'll text one of you."

I bite down on my lower lip. Am I being a baby about this? A part of me wants to lie down on the little grassy patch in front of my green shotgun and cry. A part of me wants to run out into the street and scream. I'm just not sure who I would scream at. I know this is Sharon's fault, but it's Harper's, too. If she'd just walked out of the coffee shop and not said anything to anyone, nothing would have had to change. Sharon wouldn't be in jail and I wouldn't be sitting next to a stranger who's my dad on the steps of my house, locked out. Locked out of my old house, locked out of my old life.

When I speak, I don't sound like me. My voice is shaky. "She wouldn't have let me come if I'd told her."

He's quiet for a minute. Then he says, "You're right." He looks at me. "But we could have figured something out. We could have talked about it. Together."

"I'm old enough to ride the streetcar in the middle of the day," I argue. As if that's an excuse for leaving the way I did. Because I know it was wrong. What Remy is saying about families is true. I know that because Sharon and I had the same deal. She'd text or call and let me know when she was heading home at night, when she was stopping at the market, or whatever. And I would let her know when I got home from school. When I left work at the coffee shop. When I was on the streetcar, joyriding. That's what she used to call it. "I like to ride the streetcar. My mom . . . Sharon, used to let me ride by myself."

A couple on bicycles go by. He's wearing a pink helmet. She's wearing a black one. I wonder if they accidentally got the wrong helmets or if it's some kind of private joke. Mom and I talked about getting bikes. I wanted to ride to school, but she wasn't sure if it was a good idea. She said biking in a city could be dangerous. She thought I was safer on the sidewalk, but she said we'd revisit the conversation. Remy is watching the bicyclists, too. So we sit there in silence. There's a breeze. The leaves on the bush between us and the next house are rustling. The temperature is starting to drop. It's actually getting a little chilly.

"So what's going on?" he says. "Harper said you were upset this morning."

I want to say, "Upset? No, duh. I'm upset about this whole fiasco. Who says a kid who was kidnapped but never knew it should be returned to her birth parents when she's sixteen years old? Who decides that? Why didn't anyone ask me?" But that would definitely be childish. And just dumb because I know you can't let a kidnapper keep the kid, no matter how nice she was to her or how much she loved her.

"It's her birthday," I say.

He looks at me. "Sharon's?"

I nod, looking straight ahead, not at him, because I'm afraid I'll start to cry. "She . . . we were going to go out to dinner tonight. Some restaurant she wanted to try."

"You came here to feel closer to her."

"I guess." I hesitate. "I wanted to go inside. I have a key. I wanted my . . . my phone died. I don't have the charger. I wanted to charge my phone in case—" My voice catches in my throat and I fight the tears because I don't want to cry. I'm tired of crying. "In case she tries to call me," I whisper.

He exhales. "Ah, Lilla. I'm sorry," he whispers.

"Why didn't she call me?" I hear myself say. I wipe at my eyes. "Maybe they won't let her use a phone? In jail?"

"Maybe," he says.

Then he's looking at me again and I feel like he wants me to look at him. Slowly I turn my head. His eyes are teary. I didn't know guys cried. "Maybe she doesn't know what to say to you. Or maybe—"

He keeps looking at me, and for some reason it makes me feel better to see that he's sad, too. That he gets why I'm sad. And I think to myself that maybe it might be nice to have a dad. Sharon always said I didn't need one. But what if she was wrong?

"Maybe she thought it would be better for you if she didn't contact you," he says.

I look down at my backpack. "I need to talk to her. Why won't you tell me where she is? I want to talk to her."

"As I said, I don't know where she is. As for you having contact with her, I think we're going to have to talk about that."

"You mean you won't let me. Harper doesn't want me to ever see her again."

"I mean we'll have to talk about it. After you get to school. After things settle down. Right now we're all pretty overwhelmed. It's been hard for me to keep this private and out of the news. It's the kind of story people love to read about. Hear about."

It had never occurred to me that my picture could have been on the front page of a newspaper. Or Sharon's. Or both. I can't think about that now. I already feel like my head is going to explode.

We sit there without saying anything. I feel he's waiting on me.

"I wanted her knives," I finally blurt out.

"Her knives?"

"Her knife roll. She always carried her knives to work with her and brought them home at the end of her shift. Good chefs carry their own knives. I just . . . I wanted her knives. Before somebody throws all of our stuff in a Dumpster."

"No one is going to throw out your things, Lilla. The social worker said you could have whatever you wanted from here."

"I don't know if I want any of my stuff." I grind my sneaker into the sidewalk in front of the steps. Little bits of sidewalk are coming off. It needs repairing. The next tenant's problem. "It's Lilla's stuff," I say softly. "Not Georgina's. Now I'm supposed to be Georgina."

He doesn't say anything so we both sit there for a couple of minutes. I watch the cars go by. Someone else passes us on the sidewalk in front of the house. Then Remy looks at me.

"You want the knives?"

I nod.

"Okay." He gets up.

"But the house is locked." I get to my feet, too. "My key won't work. I guess somebody changed the lock."

He's looking up at the house. "You check the back door?"

I nod. "We didn't have a key to it. It's . . . was my bedroom."

He's still staring at the house. "You check the windows?"

Again, I nod.

"Okay." He pushes his hands into the pockets of his khaki pants and walks away, headed around the side of the house.

I grab my backpack and follow him. We walk around the side of the house and to the back. Our trash can is laying on its side. I see the bag of garbage I took out the night before everything went down. I bet it stinks now.

He goes to the back door and stands there. There's an old step leading up to the door but it's broken. He looks around. Then he picks up a rock from next to the house. Someone must have tried to make a flowerbed once. Sharon and I had talked about cleaning up the little yard and growing some herbs here.

"Step back," Remy says.

I watch him, fascinated and shocked at the same time as he breaks the window with the rock. He doesn't seem to be the kind of guy who would break a window. You can get arrested for something like this. The old glass shatters. He looks around and so do I. We don't see anyone. He reaches through the hole.

I cringe, afraid he's going to hurt himself. I want to tell him not to worry about it. That I don't care about the knives, but it's too late. He's already guilty of breaking and entering. He's already committed a crime for me.

He turns the lock on the doorknob and tries to push open the door. It doesn't budge. I remember that there's one of those slide bolt things at the top of the door. "Up top," I say. "It's locked at the top."

He feels around and I hear the sound of metal scraping metal. Then he turns the knob again and this time the door moves.

"There's a little bookcase there," I say. Mom and I didn't use the door. Mom said it was okay if I put the bookcase there. She said that if there was a fire we'd be smart enough to move the bookcase to get out.

He pushes the door and I hear the bookcase slide. Things hit the floor. Books.

"There we go," he says.

I think he's going to walk in, but he takes a big step back. He gestures with his hand, meaning I should go inside. "You want me to wait out here while you get what you want?" he asks.

I still can't believe he would break a window so I could get in. I can't believe he'd take the chance of getting arrested for me. I don't know much about a comptroller's job, but I would guess that Tulane University doesn't like their employees getting arrested on felony charges.

I walk up crumbling cement steps, thinking I'll just run in and get the knives. But then all of a sudden I'm a little afraid to go inside. Afraid and I don't know why. I don't believe in ghosts, but I'm afraid the house is haunted.

By Sharon.

By me.

By all the things I thought were true when we moved in. Things that were lies. Sharon's lies. "You can come in," I tell him. Because I'm afraid to go in alone.

I step into my bedroom and over the books that have fallen. It takes a second for my eyes to adjust. Then I move to the center of the room. He follows me inside.

"My bedroom."

He looks around. Smiles. But the smile is kind of sad. I wonder why, but I don't ask. Too caught up in my own sadness, I guess. I just stand there and look around. I was so happy when we moved here. I didn't even care that I had to leave my old school for a new one.

"Katrina said you could have your things. We can put what will fit in the car now, but it will probably take more than one trip."

I stand there looking at the stuff that I know is mine, but it doesn't feel like mine now. Because Sharon bought it all? Sharon, who was pretending I was her kid. Only I wasn't. How could she have done this to me? She said she loved me, but how could she have loved me and done this?

"I don't want it," I say, grabbing my phone charger and practically ripping it out of the wall.

He watches me. "You might feel differently later, Lilla. I can box it all up. Put it in our attic. Then you don't have to decide now."

I don't answer because I don't know how I feel about that idea. Instead, I stuff the charger into my backpack. I don't know why because I don't even want my phone now. I walk out of my bedroom and into hers. Her bed is unmade. The Tweety bathrobe is lying on the floor. I guess they let her get dressed before they hauled her off to the slammer. I walk right through the room because suddenly I'm pissed. I'm so pissed at her that I'm glad she didn't call. I'm glad the phone company is going to shut off our phone service.

Remy follows me.

I walk into the kitchen. Sharon's coffee is still sitting in the coffee press. Only there's green mold around the top of it. I look at the counter. The knife roll is sitting right there where I left it two weeks ago. I could almost swear I smell the English muffin toast I made that morning.

I'm not even sure I want her knives now. But would it seem ungrateful if I told Remy I didn't want them? Now that he broke the law and all to get me in here.

I snatch the knife roll off the counter and turn around. "I'm done."

"You don't want anything else?"

I shake my head.

He glances around at the moving boxes we never unpacked, then back at me. I meet his gaze and I realize I have his eyes. He's looking at me with my eyes. Of course, technically, it's the other way around.

"Okay, then. I suppose we need to get back. Harper's got to be having kittens."

I nod. Walk past him, past the bathroom, through Sharon's bedroom. As I walk past her bed, a framed photo on the nightstand catches my eye. It's me. I'm little. Two and a half, three maybe? I'm sitting on a tricycle, grinning like it's the best thing that ever happened to me in my life. Mom is in the picture; I have no idea who took it. It had to have been taken not too long after she stole me.

I walk into my room, then step back through the doorway, snatch the framed photo off her nightstand, and stick it in my bag. I walk out the back door.

Remy follows me. He closes the door behind him and relocks it.

Out front, he nods in the direction of the next block. "I'm parked right down there." He's facing me. Looking down at me.

"We can't take the streetcar back?" I ask hopefully.

"Nope," he says. Then he walks away.

And I follow him.

18

Jojo

I stand in the kitchen doorway. "Wait, Mom." I know I'm being obnoxious, but sometimes I can't help myself. "So now you're saying I *can't* go?"

Dad is messing with a hinge on one of the doors to the pantry cabinet. He's got a screwdriver and some stuff in a little can. It's the cabinet door that squeaks when you open it. Mom and I both told him months ago it was squeaking. He never did anything about it, but that was before he and Mom got all lovey-dovey again. Before Georgina showed up and Dad moved back in. I never cared that Dad spent the night once in a while. He always left before I got up, like I wasn't going to notice Mom's door closed when I went to the bathroom. Like I wasn't going to hear the sounds coming from Mom's room, the kind of sounds no teenager wants to hear coming from her parents.

It kind of pisses me off though that Dad didn't want to live here with Mom and me anymore, but now Georgina is here, all of a sudden he wants to be with us. Obviously he wants to be with *her*. Not me and Mom.

It's never going to work. Him and Mom. I could tell them that, if anyone asked my opinion. They'll play married again for a while, but he'll leave. Mom's too crazy for him to stay. Too much . . . Granddad used to have some saying about water and a bridge.

I cross my arms over my chest. "I already said I was going."

"You can send her a birthday card."

"*Mom*, I already told you a hundred times. It's not her birthday!" I'm so pissed I could scream. This was planned weeks ago. She told me weeks ago that I could go. I followed all of her silly rules about providing the information, including a phone number for Megan's mom, who I know Mom called before she said I could go. "How can you not remember? This is, like, the biggest party I've ever been invited to. Megan's having a whole bunch of people over. Girls and boys. Everybody's going. It's a big deal."

"I'm sorry, Jojo. I know you were looking forward to this party, but having your sister home is a big deal, too." She's sitting at the counter, writing something on a notepad. Plans to ruin my life, probably. "We're going to see Granddad, as a family, so he can meet Georgina. Then—"

"He can't *meet* her," I interrupt. "That makes no sense. He knows her. Knew her. You can't *meet* somebody you already know. She's his granddaughter. Of course he won't remember. He probably won't even remember that she got kidnapped." I throw up my arms. "So this whole big family trip to the nursing home is a waste of time. I can go to the party. Georgina can go with you to the nursing home and you guys can act like she's always been around."

Even that doesn't get a rise out of Mom. Which is weird, because after yesterday's hullabaloo when she thought Georgina got kidnapped again or ran away or whatever, I figured she'd still be riding the edge. It's like things push her and push her and then she can't get back to normal again for a while. Normal for her. That's the way things used to be with her. She'd get upset about something and stay upset, long after it was over. But since Georgina got home, I've noticed she's not quite so crazy like that.

Mom taps her pen on the counter. "We're going out to eat after we see Granddad. Your dad made reservations at Cochon. You love their macaroni and cheese."

"Dad?" I huff. "Isn't the deal that if you commit to something, you do it? I committed to going to Megan's party."

"I'm sorry you're going to miss your party, hon." He pushes his knee against the cabinet door. I can't tell if he's taking the screw out of the hinge or putting it in. "I know things are crazy right now, but everything will settle down. Georgina is going to school next week and—"

"Is Mom going back to work?" I turn to her. Mom's better when she works. And I like it when she works because that gives her fewer hours in a day to obsess about me. I bet as soon as Georgina figures that out, she'll be on board, too.

"Not next week, for sure. I want to be able to take Georgina to school. Be there to pick you both up after school."

"I have basketball." I groan. "Remember?" I can't believe she's doing this to me. Weeks ago I picked out what I was wearing to Megan's. This guy, Wills, who lives down the street from Makayla, is coming. Everybody says he likes me. I really want to hang out with Wills. "If you pick her up after school, then you have to come back for me. And Tuesday we have a game in Slidell," I throw in. "What? Now you're not coming to my game?" I say it like she always comes to my games, which she doesn't. Which is fine with me. Better than fine.

She doesn't look worried. In fact, she almost looks happy. Which, again, is a pretty big bounce back after the Georgina-is-missing episode. Mom's been in a good mood since I got home from school today. Apparently she and Dad met with the police about that crazy bitch who took Georgina. Georgina didn't get to go; she went with Aunt Annie to get school uniforms. Nobody really said what happened at the meeting, but Mom seemed pleased with whatever went down. I bet Sharon got a hundred years in prison. I don't know a lot about prison sentencing, but I would think she'd get at least a hundred years for what she did.

"Please, Mom?" I know I'm whining like a spoiled brat, but I really, *really* want to go to this party. "Please?"

"We're done talking about this, Jojo. There's some of Ann's

pie left. I'm going to get us a piece. Go see if Georgina wants one. We're going to have a family meeting in a little while."

"A *family meeting?*" I want to say, "What the hell is that?" but I don't want to hear a lecture on why I shouldn't curse. "What's a family meeting?" I make a face.

"It's when a family gets together and they talk about anything that needs to be discussed. Your dad and I thought we might try having family meetings once a week, so we're all on the same page."

I just stand there, staring at Mom. That's got to be one of the stupidest things I've ever heard.

She looks up from her notepad. "Please, Jojo," she says quietly. "Go ask your sister if she wants pie and tell her we're going to have a family meeting in a little while."

I can't argue with her anymore. Not when she uses that sad tone of voice that sounds like she's almost begging me. It reminds me of how things were when Dad first left. Mom was so sad. Even sadder than her usual somebody-kidnapped-and-killed-Georgina sadness. But that's when she and I really became a team. After Dad left. She took care of me and I took care of her. I think that's mostly why I'm upset about Georgina being here now. It's one thing for your mom to be obsessed with your ghost sister; it's a whole other deal when the sister comes back to life. And suddenly everything is about her. I mean, I thought everything was about her when she was dead, but now everything really *is* about her.

And it's just not fair. I was the one here all this time, not Georgina. I was the one who slept in bed with Mom. I made her tea. I told her about all the things that were going on with my friends that I knew they didn't want me to tell. Just to have something to talk about with her. To make her feel like I needed or wanted her advice. So she wouldn't be so sad.

I walk out of the kitchen. I think about just going up to my room. But I don't. I go down the hall. Georgina is in the living room. She's sitting on one end of the couch. She's looking at a photo album on her lap.

"Mom wants to know if you want pie," I tell her, standing in the doorway. "It's pecan. Aunt Annie made it."

She looks up at me. She doesn't smile. "I'm good."

"I don't want any, either," I say. "It tastes good, but it's kind of sweet. Makes my teeth hurt."

She looks down at the album again.

I glance around the living room, then back at her. We haven't said more than a dozen words to each other today and they were about passing something at the table and me saying "sorry" when I bumped into her getting out of the car. I keep thinking that sisters are supposed to talk to each other. Sisters talk, don't they?

"Your room looks good," I hear myself say. "You're a good painter." The second the words come out of my mouth, I realize how stupid I must sound. Childish and stupid to her. Or worse, I sound like Mom, all fakey positive and upbeat.

Georgina makes me feel like a little girl. A dumb little girl. She's only two years older than I am but she's seen so much. Done so much. Thursday, when Mom thought she'd been kidnapped from her bedroom, Georgina had ridden the streetcar all the way to City Park by herself. She just got on the streetcar and went. She even changed lines downtown. I've never ridden the Canal line, but I looked it up on the Internet last night. It goes all the way to the cemeteries in Mid-City. I've been there; we got my bike from a shop in Mid-City. But I've only been there in the car. We don't ride the streetcar often. I don't know why; not safe for some reason, I'm sure.

I chew on my bottom lip, trying to think of something else to say. Maybe about her trip to Mid-City. Maybe I could ask her a question about that.

"Is this me or you?" Georgina lifts up the album, turning it to face me. She's pointing at a photo of a baby. It looks like it's taken at the Audubon Zoo.

I walk into the living room. "Me?" I stare at the photo and

frown because I'm not sure. "Maybe." I sit down on the couch beside her. "Are there dates?"

"On some pictures. Not this one. I found it on the bookshelf. The picture album." She glances up at me. "I hope nobody cares if I look at it."

"Nobody cares. Nobody even looks at them." I study the picture again. "I can't tell what color the hair is." I squint. "Not a lot of hair." I shrug. "Maybe it's you."

"I found these." She flips back to a page.

There are two pictures, side by side, of babies in the same white gown. The first is labeled "Georgina, seven weeks." The second says, "Josephine, ten weeks." The dress is long and white and fancy with lace and ruffles and stuff. Mom had the dress framed. It's on a wall in her bedroom.

I stare at the pictures. "We both wore the same christening gown." I shrug. "Or baptism gown or whatever you call it."

She looks at me like she doesn't know what I'm talking about.

"You know, the dress you wear when the priest puts holy water on your head and your parents promise to raise you in the Catholic Church and whatever. It's one of the holy sacraments."

"Sharon was Jewish," my sister says.

"Right," I say. "But you were baptized, so no big deal."

She seems to think about that for a second and then she turns the page. "This is definitely you." She points at a photo of me walking across the front porch. I look maybe two. "You can tell by the date," she says.

She turns another page and I look at her while she looks at the photographs. She's really pretty. I still can't believe she's here. I can't believe she isn't dead. I mean, who ever heard of something like this happening? I bet Mom and Dad could get some money if they sold our story to TV. I bet they'd make a ton of money. But they don't want people to know Georgina was found. We told our family and friends, of course. Everyone at church knows. People acted crazy Sunday when Mom and I went to Mass. It was kind of fun because since Georgina didn't come, everyone made a fuss over me. But Mom and Dad don't want strangers to know. They don't want anything in the newspapers or on the Internet.

"We look a lot alike, even though our hair is a different color."

I shake my head. "You look like Dad. I look like Mom."

She reaches down between her and the edge of the couch and she pulls out a photo. She places it beside the photo of me on the porch. It's a little girl about the same age. She's on a tricycle.

"That's me," Georgina says softly.

The two little girls do look alike, mostly because neither have a lot of hair. I'm definitely blond in my picture, though, and the little girl in the picture my sister is holding definitely has dark hair. There's a woman in the photo, leaning over the girl, smiling.

Georgina flips over the photo. There's a date on the back. I do the math in my head. It was taken about three months after Georgina was kidnapped.

I look up at her. I know my eyes are big and my mouth is probably hanging open.

She turns the photo over again so I can see. We both just stare at it.

"We do look a little alike," I hear myself say. Then I can't help myself. I have to ask. I point at the woman who's laughing in the photo. "Is that her? Your . . . the woman who . . ." I don't know a nice way to say it and I don't want to be mean so I just let it go.

"Yeah, that's Sharon. Sharon Kohen."

We both stare at the photo for a long minute and then she slides it back down between her and the couch. And both of us just stare at the picture of me.

I glance at Georgina. "Did you get in a lot of trouble for taking the streetcar to your old house?" I ask quietly so Mom and Dad don't hear us. Mom is still saying I shouldn't ask Georgina questions. That she'll tell us stuff when she's ready. But so far, Georgina doesn't say anything unless you ask her something. And then you don't get more than a yes or a no.

Georgina meets my gaze. "Not really. Remy . . . your dad—"

"He's your dad, too," I say.

"Right. Um . . . Dad just . . . he said I couldn't go places without telling them. So they don't worry."

"So you're allowed to ride the streetcar whenever you want?" I ask, annoyed. Why is she going to be allowed to go places alone and I'm not?

She looks at me with her brown eyes. Dad's eyes. "I . . . don't know. We didn't really talk about that."

"I would love to just get on the streetcar and go wherever," I say. "I'm not really into the streetcars," I add quickly. "But I never get to do anything without *adult supervision*. Mom never lets me do anything. I just started walking alone to school in the fall. And not alone. With Makayla, and if she doesn't go to school, Mom walks me, or Dad or Aunt Annie, or someone drives me."

She nods. She's looking at the photo again. Of me on the porch.

"Hey," I say. "You want me to call you Lilla?" I know Mom's going to kill me, but I don't care.

"I don't think she would like it," Georgina says quietly.

"Mom? Definitely not. But . . . that's what people have been calling you as long as you can remember."

"That would be nice," she says quietly. "But I don't want you to get in trouble because of me."

"Oh, I'm always in trouble for something." I shrug. "I don't mind. Sometimes I think I do some things just so Mom has to holler at me and lecture me and she doesn't have time to think about how you got—" I stop before I finish the sentence.

Georgina looks at me again. We both just stare at each other.

I sit there for a second trying to think of something else to say. When I can't think of anything, I get up. "We're going to see Granddad at the old folks' home tomorrow."

"I heard."

"I don't know what Mom's told you, but he has dementia. So . . . he might not know who you are, even after you tell him. Sometimes, when we go, he thinks I'm his little sister. Her name was Annabelle. Mom said he wanted her to name me Annabelle."

Georgina looks up. "That's a pretty awful name," she whispers. Then she smiles.

"*Right.*" I say it like the girls at school, turning the word into two syllables. It always sounds so cool. As I walk out of the room, I remember I was supposed to tell Georgina about the family meeting. I decide to just let it be a surprise.

19

Harper

"That's nice to hear." I point in the direction of the hallway.

"What's that?" Remy glances at me. He's putting some WD-40 in the hinges of the pantry doors. One of the screws was loose and the whole door was off-kilter and he's done some sort of magic with a screwdriver and his snake oil to fix it.

"The girls." I point toward the living room. "They're talking." I keep my voice down.

I can't hear what they're saying. I resist the urge to tiptoe into the hallway. I want so badly for them to get along. Not that they're *not* getting along, I just . . . I want them to be best friends. At least good friends. I never had a sister and my brother and I aren't close. I always wished I had a sister. When Jojo was born, several people made comments about how maybe next time it would be a boy, but I was thrilled that we'd had a second daughter. With the girls only two years apart, they were bound to be friends, weren't they?

Remy comes to the center island, carrying the screwdriver and a little can. "So, family meeting, huh?"

I look at him. "We discussed this. You think it's a bad idea?" I go on without giving him time to respond. "A lot of families have family meetings. It's a way to connect and make sure everyone is

on the same page. It's a way to bring up potential problems before they become problems."

Remy doesn't say anything, but he doesn't like the idea. I can
see it on his face.

"If you think it's a bad idea, say so."

"I'm not saying that talking about things, as a family, is a bad
idea." He sits down on the stool beside me. "I'm just saying that
making it this official thing might not be the best way to approach it."

"It's not '*official*.'" I make air quotes with my fingers and get
off the stool. We'll need plates and forks for the pie.

He exhales the way he does when he's making up his mind
whether he wants to argue with me or not.

I go to the cupboard to get the plates. "She's got to start talking to us, Remy."

"She's been here a week."

"That whole thing with her taking the streetcar. Without us
knowing where she was." I gesture with a dessert plate. "Unac-
ceptable."

"And she and I talked about that. She understands."

I take three more plates from the shelf. My back is to him.
"You two talked about it. But *we* didn't talk about it. Georgina
and I."

"I don't think we can gang up on her."

"Who's *ganging up* on her? Our girls have two parents. We both
have a right, an obligation, to have certain expectations of our
children. That's what being a parent is." I watch him get up, take
a glass from the cupboard, and get water from the refrigerator
door. "Agree or disagree?" I try to control my tone.

He takes a sip of water. He's wearing sweatpants and an old
T-shirt with one sleeve that's ripped. His favorite flag football
tee; he plays on a rec team on Saturday mornings.

I make myself wait for his response. One of the things I
learned when I was getting counseling, before and after Remy
left, was that I needed to learn to be a better listener. Me barrel-

ing through this conversation the way I am is not being a good listener.

He knows I'm waiting for him to speak. He makes me wait. I take the plates to the counter, set them down, and go back for the forks.

"Agree. All I'm saying is that the girls may not be receptive to putting labels on this kind of thing. Maybe we can just . . ." He takes another sip of water. "I don't know. Talk to them."

Easy for you to say, I want to say. It's always come so easy for Remy. Everyone likes him. People open up to him. He's good at getting people to talk about how they feel. I'm not. But I'm working on it. I'm trying. And having a family meeting is a way that I feel I can be a better listener, to Remy and the girls.

I take my time at the silverware drawer removing four forks.

"What do you want to talk about?" Remy asks.

"Sorry?"

He turns to face me. "This family meeting. What do you want to talk about?"

I take the forks to the center island. I see Jojo walk by in the hall, her head down. Texting. I don't call her in because I want to finish this with Remy first. I want us to be on the same page.

"I made a list." I set down the forks. When he doesn't say anything, I look up. He's got this look on his face, as if he thinks I'm being ridiculous. "What? There are some things I want to talk about. I wrote them down. And we're not going to just talk about what I want to talk about. I only did this for me."

He just stands there looking at me.

"You think the list is a stupid idea."

"I didn't say that."

"It's so I don't forget anything." I indicate the legal-size yellow notepad on the counter. "Lots of people use lists so they don't forget things. I make lists all day at work. Don't make fun of me."

He takes another sip of water. "I'm not making fun of you, Harper."

But it feels like he is.

I get the pie and set it on the island. Then I go back for a knife. "Could you call the girls? I thought we'd sit here. We can each have a turn to bring up whatever. I'll get the calendar. It'll be a good time to lay out our plans for the week. I know everyone has things going on, but I think it's important that we make time for each other right now. Together."

He walks out of the kitchen and goes down the hallway to the living room where Georgina is. I don't know what she's doing. Reading, maybe. She reads a lot. She told Remy she likes books about history, but also with a story. After dinner he gave her the first book in Ken Follett's historical trilogy centered around a cathedral. It's an enormous hardback. The size didn't seem to concern her.

I listen to Remy's voice and the softer timbre of our Georgina's. I can't hear what they're saying. Tears spring to my eyes. I still can't stop thanking God for returning her to us. As I cut the pie, I hear Remy go the other way in the hall. He calls up to Jojo, from the bottom of the staircase, I'm sure.

"Jojo! Family meeting!" he hollers.

With four slices cut, I push the pecan pie to the center of the granite island and wait. Then I remember the calendar. I get it from the wall near the back door.

Remy returns to the kitchen.

"She coming?" I ask.

"She?" He reaches for his water glass. "We have two shes. Besides you."

I can't figure out if he's being an ass or I am. Both of us, probably. "Georgina."

"She's coming." He takes one of the stools.

I'm standing on the other side of the island where we prep food. There aren't any stools on this side. "You think we should move to the dining room?" I ask him. "Or is this okay?"

"I think this is fine."

Georgina enters the kitchen first. She's carrying the book Remy gave her.

"Pie?" I ask her. "Aunt Annie made it."

"No thanks." She doesn't look at me when she speaks. She takes the stool beside Remy.

She's not eating much. I'm trying not to worry. Different people react to stress in different ways, regarding food. I think I eat more when I'm stressed. But Ann can't eat a bit when she has a fight with Makayla or George. Once, when she was waiting for a breast tissue biopsy result, she didn't eat for days. Thankfully it came back benign.

"You want something else?" I ask. "Some kind of snack? There's hummus in the refrigerator. Veggies and crackers."

She lifts her head slowly to look at me across the counter. "No thanks. I'm good."

"Well, you have to eat. There's a grocery list on the refrigerator," I tell her. "Write down anything you want. I'll get it for you." I lift one shoulder and let it fall. "I don't know what you like to eat. I usually go to the market on Saturday mornings. Usually to Rouses and sometimes to Trader Joe's. But if there's something you like that's only at Whole Foods, I can get it." I stop and then go on. "What do you like for breakfast? For before school?" I make myself say it. "What did you eat in the morning?"

She hesitates, then says, "I like English muffin bread. Toasted."

I grin. "We can do that." I look at Remy, tickled with my little triumph.

"It comes from a bakery," Georgina continues. "We . . . on the street with all the shops. It runs parallel to St. Charles. Closer to the river."

"Magazine." I look at Remy. "It's probably Magazine. We'll find it."

"It's fine if you . . . can't," Georgina says.

I turn to Remy. "Is Jojo coming?"

"She said she'd be down in a minute."

I wait a few seconds, then go out of the kitchen. At the bottom of the staircase, I holler, "Josephine!"

"Coming!" she screams.

I go back to the kitchen and wait in silence. I'm ready to go call Jojo again when she walks into the kitchen. She just stands in the doorway. Texting.

"Jojo," I say.

"Yup." She goes on texting.

I glance at my list. "New phone for Georgina." I look up at her. "I thought maybe we could go tomorrow. You can pick out a phone," I tell her.

Jojo doesn't look up from texting. "I thought I was getting a new phone next."

"You have the newest phone on our plan. I have your old phone. And Georgina needs a phone on our plan," I say delicately. "Now put away your phone before I confiscate it."

"I'm telling Makayla I can't go tomorrow night. She's probably not going either, then. She won't go without me. So basically, you're keeping both of us from going to the party."

"Tell Makayla you'll talk to her later," I say sharply.

Jojo huffs and slips the phone into her back pocket. She takes the stool on the end, leaving the one beside Georgina open. I stay where I am, standing.

"So, family meeting . . ." I say, jumping in. "You guys probably think this is a bad idea, and it may be, but I thought we could give it a try."

Jojo sighs loudly and rests her chin on her hand, her elbow on the countertop.

"The idea is to come together at least once a week and talk about whatever we need to talk about. Not just what I want to talk about, or your dad, but what you girls want to discuss, too."

"Like you telling me I could go to a party and now saying I can't?" Jojo demands. "Is that something we can talk about?"

I nod. "Yes. Except in that instance, we already had that discussion. You're not going to the party, Jojo. We're all going to see Granddad together."

I meet Remy's gaze. "You want to start?"

"Nope. What's on your list?" But he doesn't say it in a mean way.

I glance down. "Granddad tomorrow night and dinner. Cell

phone for Georgina." I look up. "I can take her." I glance at Jojo. "Do you have basketball practice in the morning?"

"Attendance not required. It's extra, if we feel like we need it. I barely get off the bench, so no need for me to go."

It's on the tip of my tongue to suggest that's an excellent reason to attend an extra practice, but I keep it to myself. She's a decent basketball player, but certainly not one of the best on the freshman team. It was her choice to play. I think the physical exercise and team dynamics are good for her. I'm content if she's content.

"You playing flag tomorrow morning?" I ask Remy.

"If it doesn't rain."

I check off the phone and Dad's visit on the notepad. "Have some pie." I push the pie plate toward them. "Okay . . . next. I know you're all going to hate this, Remy most of all, but . . ." I look up. "We need to discuss making an appointment for family counseling."

Jojo drops her face into her hands on the counter.

Remy cracks a smile.

Georgina just sits there as if she's in her own glass cubicle and can't see or hear us.

I'm beginning to think the family meeting *was* a bad idea, but I forge on. "The social worker strongly advised counseling. We could all go to individual appointments, I suppose, but I thought that maybe we should try something together. To see if someone can help us figure out how to communicate more effectively."

"I—want—to—go—to—the—party—at—Megan's," Jojo says. She looks up at me, her head still on the counter. "How's that for *communication?*"

"Enough, Jojo," Remy says. "Apologize, please."

Jojo groans and sits up. "Sorry, Mom."

I suddenly just want to give up on this whole thing. At least for tonight. I want to pour a glass of wine, crawl into bed, and watch something silly on the BBC on my laptop. I don't even care if Remy comes to bed with me. "Thanks, Jojo," I murmur. Who was I kidding when I thought I could be a good parent? I'm a terrible parent. I love my girls more than anything, but I'm a terrible parent.

"So, moving on," Remy says. "Harper, you see what you can find out about family counseling and then we'll talk about it." He glances at the girls, then back at me. "Anything else, baby?"

"No," I'm relieved to say.

"My turn, then." He turns on his stool to face the girls. "I want to talk about a plan to start giving these two more freedom."

"Yes!" Jojo says, slapping her hand on the countertop.

He looks to me. "Once Georgina gets her phone, how about if we let her figure out where that bakery is on Magazine and let her go get the bread. She can tell us where she's going and how long she'll be gone. She can take the streetcar to the right cross street and then walk to Magazine." He turns to our eldest. "Would you like to try that?"

She meets Remy's gaze. "I would."

I don't want her to try that. I don't want her out of my sight, but I know Remy's right. When I was Georgina's age, I was driving a car. I had a part-time job. And Georgina's clearly every bit as mature as I was. Probably more mature.

I keep my gaze fixed on the legal pad and doodle with the pen. "Okay. Once she gets a phone."

"Can I go get coffee after practice with the girls?" Jojo asks excitedly.

She's been asking to go since the beginning of the school year. A group of girls get coffee and pastries somewhere every Wednesday after school or sometimes after school events. It's usually near the school, but they don't even go to the same place every week. Jojo wanted to walk with the girls and then just call me and let me know where to pick her up, but she's not always reliable about that. In December, she was supposed to call me to pick her up when her CPR class was over. I waited and waited. Then I texted her, then I called her. One of the older girls dropped her off. She didn't have permission to get a ride home and she certainly didn't have permission to ride with a teenager. I grounded her for the weekend for that one.

I glance at Remy. *Great,* I want to say. *Now you've started a revolution.* Instead, I say, "Let's see what Aunt Ann says. Maybe Makayla wants to go, too. Next item on the agenda?"

Remy opens his arms. "That's all I have."

"Georgina?"

"How about if we talk about Megan's party?" Jojo. Like a dog with a bone. "Maybe I could go see Granddad with you and *then* go to the party?"

Remy meets my gaze. He thinks I should consider it. What he doesn't realize is that I didn't really want Jojo going to Megan's party anyway. One of her classmates' mothers was telling me after Mass last week that she had heard that there was alcohol at Megan's last party. Supplied by an older sister.

"Georgina's got the floor," I say.

"So I'm last. What?" Jojo demands. "Because I'm the youngest?"

"Yup," Remy tells her. "Today you go last. Next family meeting, you're first." He takes the biggest slice of pecan pie from the pan and puts it on a plate.

I pass him a fork. We're all waiting for Georgina and I say a little prayer to God and the Virgin Mary, just in case she's listening. *Please let her speak,* I pray. Please let Georgina have something to say to us. What I really want is for her to have something to say to me. Something just for me, but I don't pray for that.

"I want to go to Shabbat," Georgina says, her voice surprisingly strong.

I look at Remy.

"There's a temple right down the street. They have a service on Saturday mornings." She is staring me down with those Remy eyes of hers. "Nine thirty," she adds.

I look back at Remy. I didn't see this coming.

"Okay . . ." he says slowly.

I want to say no, of course. Didn't we already cover this? We're Catholic. I'm Catholic. Catholics don't send their little girls to temple for Shabbat. But he holds my gaze and I swallow hard.

"Is this important to you?" Remy shifts his gaze to Georgina.

Jojo is suddenly interested in our family meeting.

"I always go to Shabbat on Saturday mornings. I don't think you have the right to keep me from going," Georgina says, her voice taking on a stubborn tone.

Her eyes get teary. Then I tear up. I don't know what to do with these feelings. It never, *ever* occurred to me in all these years that when . . . *if* Georgina was ever returned to us, something like this would be an issue. How could she come back to us believing in a different religion? Why would God do such a thing?

I shift my gaze back to Remy. He's watching me. Waiting for my reaction. Afraid I'll flip out, I imagine.

"You can go," he says, slowly moving his attention from me to Georgina. "Okay if I go, too? I've never been to temple. I'm curious."

Georgina hesitates, then shrugs. "Okay. I guess."

I exhale. I hadn't realized I was holding my breath.

"My turn to speak now?" Jojo pipes up.

"One more thing," Georgina says, her voice stronger than it had been a moment ago. "Two."

We all look at her.

"School. I don't want to go to a Catholic school. There was nothing wrong with my school in my old neighborhood. I liked it there. A Catholic school . . . they make you take religion class and go to Mass. Is that even legal?" She's looking directly at me.

"I think that, legally, we can do what we want, as far as education, because you're our child." Remy.

Georgina stares at the counter.

"I think you should give Ursuline a try. If you don't like it there . . . we'll revisit the subject next semester. For convenience's sake, it's just easier for all of us if you go to Ursuline." He's still holding his fork. "What else did you want to talk about?"

"Sharon," Georgina says. "I'd like to know where she is. If she's okay." She's just staring straight ahead now, but not at me, across the counter from her. Not at anything. "You talked to the police today. I know they told you what's going on with her."

He sets down his fork. "She has an attorney. A public defender. She had a psych evaluation and—"

"She wasn't mentally unstable," Georgina interrupts.

I want to argue that clearly she was unstable, otherwise she wouldn't have kidnapped someone's baby and ruined so many lives. Or at least altered them in ways no one's life should ever be altered. But I keep my mouth shut and I let Remy speak.

"And," Remy goes on, "the conclusion was that she is fit to face the judicial system."

"There's no trial if you confess to the crime."

"True," Remy agrees. "But her attorney will advise her of the best way to proceed. If she does take a plea, the attorney will help to ensure that her sentence is fair. And that she gets any mental health care she might need."

"Is she in jail now?"

"She is. But it's some sort of holding facility. I don't know where. Eventually she'll be moved to a women's prison."

I glance at my other daughter. Her eyes are wide. She's looking from Remy to Georgina and back to Remy again.

This is not how I was hoping our first family meeting would go.

"I want to see her," Georgina says, getting off her stool. "I lived with her for fourteen years. I thought she was my mother for *fourteen* years. I think I have a right to see her."

She sounds as if she's going to burst into tears. But she also sounds angry. So angry. And I feel as if all of her anger is directed at me. Why me? Why not Remy? He agreed with me that she should go to Ursuline. And he also agreed that Georgina shouldn't have contact with Sharon Kohen. At least not right now.

"I understand that you want to see her. And I understand why," Remy says diplomatically. And I love him for that. I'd marry him all over again for his ability to negotiate waters I just can't keep my head above.

"And I'm not saying no," he continues. "I'm just saying not yet. Okay?"

They stare at each other for a moment.

"Okay?" he repeats.

"Okay," she whispers.

I let out my breath. "Anything else, Georgina?" I ask.

She shakes her head. Apparently she's had enough of the family meeting, too.

I turn slowly to Jojo. I dread it, but I know I have to give her a turn. "Anything you'd like to talk about? Other than Megan's party?" I revise.

Jojo shakes her head, easing off her stool. Her eyes are still wide with the spectacle of our first family meeting. "Nope." She holds up her hands, palms out. "I'm good here."

I want to throw my arms around her and give her a big hug.

20

Lilla

I stand in the hall, waiting for Jojo to come out of the bathroom. She's been in there forever.

"We're leaving in twenty minutes," Harper Mom announces loudly as she comes down the hallway. "Jojo?" she asks me, pointing at the closed bathroom door.

I nod.

"Out of the bathroom, Jojo!" she shouts. "Downstairs in fifteen minutes!"

I watch the mom go into her bedroom and close the door. Remy's already in there. He gave us the thirty-minute warning bell on his way to take a shower.

It's crazy how two more people in a house can cause such chaos. It's a little overwhelming. People talking all the time. Coming and going. Disagreeing. Jojo will argue about the color of the sky with her parents. I guess teenagers are supposed to be that way. I had friends at school who argued with their parents over everything. It's not been my experience. Growing up, our house was never like this. It was just the two of us. And no one ever shouted. Or even disagreed, really. I was thinking that the number of people in a house affected the overall confusion, but I imagine it's more complicated than that.

Leaning against the wall, I knock lightly on the bathroom door. No answer.

I'm wearing my favorite jeans and a sweater that Harper Mom insisted she buy me. After we got the cell phone this morning. After Remy and I went to temple. Temple was boring. I felt a little silly making a fuss about going, acting like my faith was a big deal, like Sharon Mom and I went all the time. But it was kind of good to sit there. It felt a little bit like my old life. And Remy was nice about it. We hardly talked walking there and back and then it was only about the fact that he skipped playing flag football to go with me. He seemed to sense I wanted to be left alone.

So, all in all, it's been a good day. This afternoon I painted. The walls are almost done. Harper Mom wants to buy me furniture. She offered to take me to IKEA, even though it's hours and hours from here—Houston, I think. I wanted to ask her if I seemed like an IKEA person to her, but I didn't because that's kind of smart-assy. And a little mean. She was just trying to be nice. If she really wants to buy me a dresser and whatever, what I'd really like is to go to some stores that sell old stuff. Not expensive antiques, just . . . interesting furniture.

I knock on the bathroom door again. "Come on, Jojo. I need to use the bathroom."

She jerks open the door. "There's a bathroom downstairs," she tells me.

"But my toothbrush is in here." I watch her prance down the hall. She's dressed kind of weird for a visit to a nursing home. She's wearing a short, tight, black skirt; a T-shirt; and ankle boots. And makeup.

"Mom and Dad in their room?" she asks.

"Getting ready." I watch her go down the hall to her room. A minute later, I hear her come out of her room and close the door. She passes the bathroom door that I've left open while I brush my teeth. I watch her in the mirror. She's got half of her hair up in a ponytail and half down. She's carrying a little black crop sweater. I step out of the bathroom as she goes down the stairs.

I'm halfway to my bedroom to get my shoes when I realize

why she's dressed like that. I sit on the edge of my bed that's still in the middle of the room. There's a bag with sheets in it, gray and white. To replace the ugly pink ones. We bought them today. Also some underwear and a new pair of shoes. Black loafers. For the school uniform. Aunt Annie and I went to the school store and got a sweater, two gray plaid skirts, two white oxford shirts. We had to order some things, too. I have to wear a blazer sometimes. The uniform is kind of dorky, but whatever. I've gone to schools where I had to wear a uniform before. The good thing about it is everyone looks just as dorky as you do.

I grab my new jacket that we bought today. So I didn't have to go to dinner wearing Remy's hoodie. My jean jacket is hanging in my closet in the green shotgun. The new jacket is one of those fleece North Face ones like everyone wears. I've always secretly wanted one. We found it on sale. In gray. Harper Mom said it was obviously meant to be mine.

I flip off my bedroom light and go down the hall. Remy and Harper's door is still shut. Just as I get to the bottom of the staircase, I hear the back door close. I stand there for a minute, debating what to do. My first impulse is that this is none of my business.

But it kind of is because it doesn't matter whether I like it or not, these people are my family. And Remy and Harper really are trying to help me make sense of it all, make it work. Don't I owe it to them to keep Jojo out of trouble? If nothing else, to cut down on the drama in the car ride to the nursing home?

Annoyed that Jojo would put me in this position, I go out the front door. I catch her in the backyard, just heading for the little alley that runs between our property and the one next door. "Where are you going?"

She spins around, startled.

"They said you couldn't go to the party."

She makes a face at me. "Who died and left you in charge? Wait. You died. But then you came back. I still don't think that makes you my boss."

I shake my head. I know fourteen-year-old girls act like idiots sometimes; shoot, I know sixteen-year-old girls who act like idiots, but I don't think it has to be that way. "Think about this for a minute. It's not like you're going to get away with it," I tell her.

"You got away with going to your old house without telling anyone."

"Special circumstances," I say.

She just stands there looking at me. Pissed.

It's starting to rain. It's cold and I'm glad I have the new jacket. I should thank Harper Mom for it again. I glance away, then at Jojo again. If the parents come downstairs, they're going to wonder what we're doing out here in the rain. Especially with Jojo dressed the way she is.

I pull up my hood. I would rather have had the jacket without the hood but it was the only one they had. Harper Mom said it was the perfect coat for NOLA winters. I should tell her she was right. Sharon used to tell me we're always big on telling people what they do wrong. She said that was okay, but it was important to tell people when they did things right, too.

I look at Jojo standing there, shivering, in her shortie skirt, ankle boots, bare legs, and crop sweater. "If you go to the party, they're going to drive over to Megan's and embarrass you in front of your friends. Harper will walk right into the house and tell you to get your butt in the car. You know she will," I say before Jojo can interrupt me.

She hugs herself, glancing in the direction of the house. "I really wanted to go to the party," she says, all pouty. "If you weren't here, I could go."

I know she says it to hurt my feelings, but it doesn't. Maybe because it's a dumb thing to say, or maybe because I don't care what she thinks. I guess I should care, but I don't. "You think I wanted this to happen?" I ask. I don't say it mean or even angry. Though I am starting to get angry. Because I'm standing in the rain having this conversation with her. "Don't you get it, Jojo? I was happy where I was. I was happy with the life I had."

"But Sharon kidnapped you," she blurts out.

"Yup. She did. But she took good care of me." Tears fill my eyes and I look away because I don't want to cry in front of Jojo. I don't want her to think she can make me cry. "And I could have lived the rest of my life thinking she was my mom. So don't act like I did this on purpose. Grow up, Jojo. Stop being so selfish. Stop thinking everything is about you. Because you know what? I don't want this, either." I say it louder than I mean to, and then I'm quiet for a second. She's staring at her boots. "But this is how it is. For me and for you." I shrug. "So just get over it, Jojo."

I start to walk back toward the house, leaving her standing there. I don't even care if she goes to the stupid party. But I don't think she's going. I look back over my shoulder. "Just get in the car."

I'm halfway back to the house when Remy appears at the back door. He holds it open for me. He's wearing jeans and a sweater and a blazer that makes him look like a professor. "What's up?" he says as I walk into the laundry room.

"Forgot something. Jojo's in the car." I don't look at him. I don't know what he saw from the back door.

"Okay. We're going in a sec."

"I'll be right down," I say. I take the narrow, steep back staircase that was probably used for servants back in the day. I run into Harper Mom in the hallway. She looks nice. And I swear she looks younger than she did the day I arrived here. She's wearing black jeans and boots and a pretty blue sweater. She's got beautiful blond hair. Jojo, too. And I'm a little envious. Brown hair's so boring.

"Forgot something," I say, walking past her. I go into my room. She's still standing there in the hallway. Now what do I do? What could I have forgotten? The little cross-body bag I use for a purse is at home hanging on the end of my bed. My wallet's in my backpack, but it seems dumb to bring that. They're buying dinner. Why would I need my wallet?

I hear Harper Mom walking down the hall. But slowly. She's waiting for me. I pick up the book I just started reading off the nightstand and go back out into the hall.

"Your book?"

"In case we have to wait for a table," I say. I make a face to myself. The book is huge. I used to read on my phone a lot, but I like real books, too. But I don't usually walk around carrying huge books like some kind of dork.

I zip in front of her and down the stairs. I make a beeline for the back door, walking past Remy, who's standing in the kitchen. I run out the door and get into the Subaru. Jojo's waiting in the backseat. I shut the door and put on my seat belt.

"You tell them where I was going?"

"You better wipe some of that makeup off your face," I say. Then I open my book and pretend I'm reading.

21

Harper

"You look nice," Remy tells me when I walk into the kitchen. He leans forward to kiss me.

"Thanks." Our lips meet but don't linger. "Where are the girls?" I like saying that. *The girls*. I *love* saying it.

"Waiting for us in the car."

I look at him suspiciously. "Why?"

He shrugs and cuts his eyes at me. "Excited to see their grandfather?"

I grab my bag off the counter, scowling. "Not hardly. Certainly not Jojo. What are they up to?"

He shrugs again. "I gave up trying to figure you ladies out a long time ago. Women are made to be loved, not understood."

"Is that a Remy quote or someone else's?" I sling my bag over my shoulder. My raincoat is hanging in the laundry room. I'll grab it as I go out.

"Oscar Wilde."

I laugh and kiss him again. This time it moves beyond platonic. "I love that you're an accountant and you can quote Oscar Wilde," I say against his lips.

"Is that right?" He kisses me again, wrapping his arms around my waist. "I can quote Shakespeare, too. Wanna hear? 'Neither a borrower nor a lender be; for loan oft loses both itself and friend, and borrowing dulls the edge of husbandry.' "

I laugh and try to pull away, but he won't let go of me. "What does that have to do with the girls in the car?" I ask. "What does it have to do with anything?"

He's laughing with me. "*Hamlet*, Act I." He closes his eyes, then opens them. "I can't remember what scene. No, it doesn't pertain to us at this moment, but it was the only quote this accountant could come up with."

"I love you." I kiss him again and pull away. I realize I've forgotten my lipstick and I dig in my bag for it. The shape is so easy to distinguish from other objects; I don't know why it's always so difficult to find. "How did Shabbat at temple go? You didn't say."

"It was fine. It was good."

"Yeah?" My fingertips touch the little silver king cake baby I carry with me. I don't know if it was ever baked in a cake. My grandmother gave it to me when I was a teenager. It's sort of a talisman, a good luck charm or whatever. "Did she seem like she liked it?"

He looks at me as if I've said something ridiculous. "Does anyone *like* Mass?"

I'm tempted to say that people do, but I can't give an example. I don't necessarily like Mass when I'm there. Later, I like that I've gone. And I do like the ritual of it, going through the same motions Sunday after Sunday, year after year. I like the idea that people long dead followed these rituals, and those who follow me will. I finally find my lipstick and pull it from my bag. I remove the lid and twist it up a little. "Does she want to go again?"

"Didn't say." He steps into the hall and flips off the light overhead, then flips on the front hall light.

I apply the lipstick to my top lip. "You didn't ask her?"

He comes back into the kitchen. "I didn't ask her. She didn't seem as if she wanted to talk."

"You walked all the way home and didn't talk about the service?"

"No."

"I don't know how I feel about letting her go to Shabbat every week. I don't know what the point is." I press my lips together. "Because . . . I know I've said this before." I hold up my hand as if to bear witness. "She's Catholic."

He crosses the kitchen. "We should go."

So apparently we're not going to discuss this now. Okay, but I'm not going to just let it go. Not long term. Of course some conversations between husband and wife are appropriate in the time it takes to get out the door. Some aren't. I'm giving Remy the benefit of the doubt on this one. I change the subject. "We had a nice time together today, Georgina and I."

"I'm glad." He waits in the laundry room doorway for me.

"Leaving Jojo home was a good idea. We bought Georgina's cell phone and then we went shopping for a few things. Then the grocery store. Did you know she knows how to make eggs Benedict? She can make hollandaise sauce. From scratch." I walk past him.

"I didn't know that. Did you talk?"

I grab my raincoat off a hook and hand him my suede bag so I can put the coat on. "A little. Not really. Not about anything important, just . . . A little bit about what she likes to wear, what she doesn't. She really likes gray." I slip my arm into one sleeve, then the other. "Don't you think that's weird? Aren't teenage girls supposed to like . . . I don't know. Purple?"

Remy grabs the back of my coat at the collar and helps me into it. "Not necessarily. She likes what she likes."

"She's not crazy about the idea of going to family counseling."

He hands me my handbag. "Neither am I."

"Remy. You said you'd go."

"I said I'd go. I didn't say I was crazy about the idea."

I exhale. I've had a pretty good day. I was upset about Remy taking Georgina to temple, but once I got over that, once I had Georgina to myself, I was better. And I feel like we had a decent day. No, Georgina didn't pour her heart out to me, but she did talk a little. More than she has. And she let me buy her some things. That's progress. She got a cute jacket. Gray. But cute.

I open the door, then turn back to Remy.

He's starting to look annoyed with me. I should quit while he's still in a good mood. But I can't. I have to say this one thing because I've been thinking about it all afternoon. Obsessing.

"I asked her if she remembered me." I say it quietly. And suddenly I'm on the verge of tears. It comes out of nowhere and I wonder what on earth is wrong with me. Why can't I just be happy having Georgina home? Having her alive, for heaven's sake. God answered my prayers. The way I wanted them answered. How many people can say that?

Remy exhales. We're standing close enough that I can smell the body wash he uses. He smells good. Manly. Earthy.

"She said she didn't remember us," I tell him. "Not me. Not you. Doesn't that make you sad?"

"She was two years old." He says it softly, meeting my gaze.

I can tell he's trying to see where I'm coming from. But he can't. He doesn't understand why it hurts me. Is it a difference between males and females? Because men can't give birth? I'm Georgina's mother. She came from my body; my blood was once her blood. I breastfed her until I got pregnant with Jojo. It occurred to me today, when I was looking at her while we stood in line to check out at the market, that she must have cried for me when that woman took her. Georgina must have cried for me for days. Months? How long does it take a two-year-old to forget her mother?

"She doesn't remember the house," I go on, even though I know he doesn't want me to. "She doesn't remember Sadie. You would think a little girl would remember her dog, wouldn't you?"

He rests his hand on the doorknob. He won't look at me. "She was a little girl. You can't be angry with her for not remembering. A lot of people can't remember anything from when they were two."

"Did you know that she thought her birthday was in August? She was disappointed when she found out she's younger than she thought. She asked me about driving. Did you know she has a driver's license—not to drive alone, of course. Can you believe that woman—"

"Harper," he interrupts. "Georgina's old enough to have an intermediate license."

I lower my head. "I know, I just—"

"You've got to stop this."

He closes the door. So the girls can't hear us? Or so I can't get away from him. So I have to listen to what he's saying. So I have to admit he's right. Which he is. I know that. Logically I know it, but for so long I've been so scared that it's hard to think of Georgina and even Jojo as more than children. It's so damned hard.

"I know why you are the way you are," Remy says, his hand on the door. "But you've got to back off. It's okay to be afraid, but your fear can't keep our girls from growing up healthy and happy. Last night you said something about Jojo's immaturity. Why do you think she behaves immaturely? She acts like that because you treat her like a child."

"Wow," I say softly. Trying not to be hurt by his words. Still hurt.

"Harper—"

"No, you're right. I need to expect more of her. I need to . . ." I let my sentence go unfinished. There are so many things I need to do better as a parent that I can't even begin the list because I'll feel so overwhelmed. "I'm sorry. I'm trying."

"I know you are."

"I just need to try harder," I say.

He doesn't answer. He just kisses my temple and opens the back door. "Come on. Our girls are waiting."

22

Lilla

Our Lady nursing home smells a little weird, but it doesn't seem like a bad place. I bet it's expensive. The landscaping is pretty fancy. There's a baby grand piano in the foyer. I don't play any musical instruments so I have no expertise in this field, but it looks like a nice one.

I still can't figure out if my parents are rich or not. They have that big old house in that ritzy neighborhood, but Remy inherited it when his dad died. I don't think he pays a mortgage on it. He and Harper Mom both have good jobs, but she doesn't work full time. They only have the one car, but the seats are leather. Harper Mom doesn't wear diamonds; she doesn't even wear a wedding band. Neither of them does. Jojo's got Ugg boots, but they're at least a year old. So maybe they have the fancy house, which has to be expensive to maintain, but they don't have a lot of money. But this place . . . *somebody's* got money to be paying for a room here.

As we walk through the halls, two nurses and a man emptying trash cans say hello to Remy and Harper Mom. Everybody acts like they know each other. I guess the parents come a lot. Which isn't surprising. I'm not an idiot. I know they're nice people. Sharon would say *good people*. Remy and Harper Mom would take care of their parents, even when they were sick . . . or crazy. I don't mean that in a callous way. I just mean that some people might not see the sense in visiting someone who doesn't know you anymore. Who won't remember whether you came to visit or not. Putting them in a nursing home where they'll be fed and kept safe is one thing; driving half an hour in each direction, several times a week, to talk to somebody who doesn't know you is different. It says a lot for Remy in particular because this granddad isn't even his father. I know he came twice last week because Harper Mom didn't. Because of me.

Jojo sulked on the car ride all the way here. She's really pissed at me. Maybe she thinks I'm going to tell on her. Which is dumb because if I was, wouldn't I have already done it? I wonder if I *should* tell, though. Is that what responsible big sisters do? To keep little sisters out of serious trouble? I have no idea. I've never done this before. I've never felt a sense of responsibility for anyone else but Sharon Mom.

My gut instinct tells me to keep my mouth shut. At least this time. Maybe when Jojo's done being mad she didn't get to go to the party, she might be glad I kept her from getting into big trouble when she got caught. Maybe she'll even like me. A little. I don't know how I feel about that, either. I've never cared about what anyone but Sharon Mom thought about me. Now there are three more people in my life that I know I should care about. Even more waiting in the wings, because Remy and Harper both have family I haven't met yet. That's supposed to be sometime soon. We're going to have a *family dinner,* which I hope doesn't resemble our *family meeting.*

The parents didn't seem to notice in the car that Jojo was in a bad mood. There was something going on with the two of them. They were acting weird. They were talking, but their voices were . . . tight. What their disagreement or whatever was about, I don't know. Probably had something to do with me. It seems like it always does.

We keep walking down halls, first one, then another. There are old people walking around. An old lady in a wheelchair wearing plastic Mardi Gras beads waves at us as we go by. The nursing home is a big place. It looks like a cross between a hospital and a college dorm. I've never actually been to either. I wanted to go to a computer coding camp for high schoolers last summer at a college in Alabama. They provided a room and meals and everything. I really wanted to go and I was so angry when Sharon told me I couldn't. Her excuse was lame, something about transportation because she had to work. Looking back, I realize that she gave me plenty of freedom in some ways, but in others she didn't. I was always allowed to do what I wanted alone, but not with other people. I guess she was paranoid about someone getting too close to me and finding out her secret. Which is absurd. How could I tell someone I wasn't her daughter, if I didn't know it? So Sharon was crazy *and* paranoid. Or do they go together and get lumped into one?

Neither of us was ever sick, and we didn't have any close friends, so I was never inside a hospital, either. My experiences are secondhand. I saw dorm rooms in movies like *Liberal Arts* and *Monsters University*. And hospitals on TV. Sharon and I watched *Grey's Anatomy* together for years. Until it got too silly.

We stop at a door with a nameplate that says "Joseph Wolff." That was Harper's maiden name before she married Remy. I saw her undergraduate diploma on the wall in the office in the house. I wonder why she decided to take Remy's name when they got married. A lot of times female doctors don't take their husband's name. If I worked as long as she did to be called doctor, I don't know that I would have changed mine. Of course I don't have the same last name I did three weeks ago so I'm not sure I'm a good person to ask.

Remy knocks on the door. "Joe?" It's open a little. He pushes it in. "Joe, it's Remy, your son-in-law." He walks in. "I brought someone special to see you."

Harper Mom stays in the doorway. "Go on in," she tells me. "Your dad will introduce you. I want to talk with my dad's nurse before she heads home for the day." She cuts her eyes at Jojo. "You too. Go say hi to Granddad. One day he'll be gone and you'll be glad you did."

Jojo doesn't look to me like she's ever going to be glad about anything.

Harper points. "Go on."

"Do I have to?" my sister huffs.

I wonder if Jojo knows what a poor impression she gives people. Her mom and dad are smart and nice. She can't be the total loser she acts like she is most of the time.

"I'm hungry." Now Jojo is whining. "Can I go see what's in the vending machine?"

"We're going out to eat. Go say hello, Josephine."

I step inside. It's a decent-sized room, but it's got a lot of furniture in it. I hear a TV. Loud. There's a single bed that's made with a blue bedspread and a nightstand next to it. Then there's a dresser and a bookcase and something that looks like a huge dish cabinet. There's a big TV on a stand. And a recliner where a little old man sits.

"Look who we've brought, Joe," Remy is saying, loud, so he can be heard above the TV. He picks up the remote from a table next to the chair and uses it to lower the volume.

"Remy?" the old man says. He squints, staring through wire-frame glasses. "My son?"

"Son-in-law. Your daughter Harper's husband." Remy offers his hand and the old man shakes it, but he seems suspicious. Of all of us.

Joe Wolff, my grandfather, is wearing blue pants and a blue flannel plaid shirt with a knit vest over it. He's got a lot of hair for an old man, hair so white that it doesn't look real. He has a nice face, really wrinkly, but nice. I wonder how old he is. Seventy-five? Eighty-five? I'm not good with ages. His eyes are very green. Like Harper Mom's and Jojo's.

"This is your granddaughter, Joe," Remy tells Granddad. "We brought Georgina. Your granddaughter."

"My granddaughter?"

I walk over to him and offer my hand the way Remy did. I feel a little weird. I don't really know any old people. Last year, I had a social studies teacher, Mrs. Benson, who was pretty old. She retired at the end of the school year, which was a shame because she was really good. She wore old-lady shoes, and this guy in my class said she was seventy, but she didn't act old.

"Nice to meet you, sir," I say. His hand is warm and dry and bony. But not creepy. I think we're going to shake the way he and Remy did, and he'll let go, but he holds on to my hand.

Granddad frowns. "Who are you again?" he asks me.

"Remy," Harper Mom calls from the doorway. "I'm going to go down and talk to Maddy. She gets off soon."

"I'll come with," Remy says. He looks at me. "We'll be back in a few minutes." Then he leans and whispers to me. "He's really nice. It doesn't matter if he doesn't remember you. He played with you when you were little. He only lived a few blocks away. He read to you all the time. You adored him."

I nod, looking at the old man again. He's still holding my hand. Staring at my face like he's trying to remember me.

"Stay here," Remy tells Jojo as he walks by her.

"Tell me again. Who are you?" my grandfather asks me again.

I ease my hand from his. "I'm Lilla," I say, half spooked, half mesmerized by him.

Jojo makes a sound of annoyance. "It's Georgina, Granddad. Your granddaughter who got kidnapped. Remember? Somebody took her out of her stroller? Have you got any snacks?"

He points to the dish cabinet that doesn't display any dishes. "Cookies, Cheetos, and red whip licorice." He turns his attention back to me. "I like red whip licorice. You like it?"

Jojo abandons me.

"You like it, Granddaughter?" he says to me.

I'm not sure what whip licorice is, but I nod. "I like red licorice."

"Hey!" Granddad calls to Jojo. "Don't eat all the licorice. Bring us some." He reaches for an upholstered footstool that matches the chair he's sitting in. It takes him so long to pull it closer that I debate whether or not I should help him. But he's getting it done. Sometimes people don't want help. They want to do things themselves.

When he finally gets the footstool where he wants it, he pats it. "Sit," he tells me.

It's a little closer than I want to be to him, but I sit. He doesn't smell bad. In fact, he smells good, like soap and fabric softener. I notice that his clothes are clean and new. And he's wearing expensive sheepskin slippers. Maybe he pays for this fancy place himself.

"So what's your name?" he asks me. Before I can answer, he goes on. "Georgina or Lilla? Which is it?"

I'm surprised he remembers what Remy said and I said. From the way Jojo was talking about him, I figured Granddad was pretty out of it.

"Um . . . both," I say.

He stares at me, adjusting his glasses. "You've got two names?"

I look at Jojo. She's taken a big tin out of the cabinet and she's pulling out bags of chips and cookies and candy. I look at Granddad. "You knew me by Georgina. That's what Harper Mom . . . Mom and Dad called me," I explain. It feels weird calling them that. Not Remy so much because I never had a dad, but calling Harper "Mom" feels like a betrayal of Sharon. Who doesn't have a right to be called Mom anymore, I know that. But I don't have all these ideas set in my head yet; they're still swirling around and I'm waiting for them to settle.

Granddad waits for my explanation.

"I was abducted when I was a baby." I say it quietly, hoping Jojo can't hear me over the sound of the TV. I don't know why I care if she hears me. I just do. "The lady who kidnapped me named me Lilla. So growing up, I thought my name was Lilla. She was Jewish." I have no idea why I say that. It has nothing to do with anything. Maybe I figure I ought to tell him since he's obviously Catholic. A big crucifix, the kind with the dead Jesus, hangs over his bed.

He squints. "You were kidnapped?"

I rip a dry cuticle off my thumb with my teeth. "Yes, sir."

"From my daughter. When you were a baby?"

I nod.

He looks like he's thinking. He thinks for a long time. Jojo is rustling a bag. *Planet Earth* is on the TV. I've seen this episode. It's about grasslands. I like *Planet Earth*.

Granddad speaks again. "You were kidnapped when you were a baby and now you're back."

"Yes . . . I . . . They found me," I say awkwardly.

"And now you're grown-up?"

"I'm sixteen."

He thinks again. "But you're definitely my granddaughter." This isn't a question. He's studying me.

"Yes."

He smiles at me and I smile back. I feel a weird connection to him. It's like . . . he gets me. He gets what it is to be me. I get the sense that he understands what it's like to be in this weird place where people are telling me who I am, but I don't remember. I bet he feels the same way because he doesn't really remember who we are . . . or maybe even who he is anymore.

"So what do you want me to call you?" Granddad asks.

"I . . . I don't know." I press my lips together. I really like this old man and I don't know why. Is it because I feel a connection to how lost he must feel without his memory? Or is it because he read to me when I was little and I love books and somehow, subconsciously, I remember him? It seems far-fetched, but what part of my life doesn't seem far-fetched anymore?

He frowns and his forehead becomes a mass of wrinkles. "What are my choices again?"

I smile. I can't help myself. "They named me Georgina, but I thought I was Lilla."

"Lilla. Like Lilly. Only with an *a*. That how you say it?"

"Yes, sir."

He nods slowly. I study his face. I know we don't have wheels for brains, but I can almost see his turning. It's like he's trying so hard to follow the conversation and figure things out.

"I like Lilla," he says after a moment. "I think I'll call you Lilla."

"Okay." I pick a piece of fuzz off my new jacket. "I'm not sure how your daughter will feel about that. But that's fine with me."

He gives a wave. "She'll get over it." He looks past me. "Hey you, girl. Are you eating my licorice?"

Jojo laughs.

"Bring Lilla and me some red whip licorice." He looks past me at the TV. "You like *Planet Earth*?"

I turn on the footstool so I can see the TV. "I do."

"You want to watch with me and eat red whip licorice, Lilla?"

"I do, Granddad." I reach for the remote and for the first time since the police took me out of our house, I feel a little bit like myself. Not like Lilla Kohen. She's gone. But maybe a little bit like this new girl, Lilla Broussard.

23

Harper

I stand in the kitchen, alone, sipping a cup of coffee in semidarkness. The only light on is the one above the stove. I know I shouldn't be drinking coffee at seven p.m. I'll never sleep. It doesn't matter; I'm not sleeping much anyway. And it's not due to too much caffeine. It's Georgina. It's Remy. It's Jojo.

Me.

Most of all, me.

I know nothing is ever quite as good as you think it's going to be. I'm not naïve. But Georgina's been here three weeks and our household doesn't remotely resemble what I thought it was going to. What I dreamed of, for fourteen years, when I prayed to God to bring her home.

No one is getting along. No one can agree on anything. Except maybe their dislike of me.

No, that's not true. Remy and Georgina are getting along great. She never gives him that dark-eyed stare. She never gets angry with him. Even though I make him be the bad guy whenever I need a bad guy. Remy was the one who told her she had to continue at Ursuline even though after three days she said she wasn't going back. He told her she couldn't get a part-time job. Not yet. And he's the one who's been putting her off for weeks about contacting Sharon. And now we know where she is.

I swear, I feel as if I'm living in an alternate universe. The woman who kidnapped my child, a woman in prison, has actually become a person in my life. Her name actually comes out of my mouth as if she were a neighbor or an acquaintance from church.

The house phone rings. I don't pick it up. No one else does. I think we're going to disconnect it. No one we want to talk to ever calls the house. Just telemarketers. Anyone we want to speak to has our cell numbers.

After the fourth ring, it stops. It's the second or third time it's rung today. I haven't checked the messages in days. And certainly no one else in the house checks them. Last week someone called from a newspaper and left a phone number, making a reference to Georgina's kidnapping. We've been fortunate that we've been able to keep her safe return out of the media. Remy and I had agreed we would give no interviews and we didn't want any of the information released to the public. The fact that Georgina is still a minor helped make that happen. So, obviously I won't be returning the reporter's call.

I sip my coffee and fan myself with a takeout menu. Hot flash.

Friday we had our first family counseling session. It wasn't a disaster, but it certainly wasn't a roaring success. Mostly I talked. Georgina did the same thing she always does. She answered direct questions, but she didn't elaborate. Remy's the only one she will talk to. They're in the living room right now, talking. I don't know what they're talking about, but I can hear their voices. They're watching some awful nineties horror movie together while she does homework and he works on something he brought home from the office.

I don't bring work home. I do my charts as soon after I see my patients as possible. And when I do my charts, I don't want anyone talking to me, I don't want to listen to music, and I certainly don't want to watch anything associated with Wes Craven's name. Jojo doesn't do well with distractions, either. She goes to her room to do her homework. Remy and Georgina laugh and chat while they work, and she comes home with A's.

I've never been a jealous person, but I'm jealous of Remy. I suppose I should give myself a pat on the back for recognizing that. I hate feeling this way. I'm jealous of how easy this transition, having Georgina back in our lives, has been for him. I'm jealous of how much she seems to like him.

This morning she called him "Dad." I had to leave the room so neither of them would hear the green monster in my voice. Or see the tears in my eyes.

I hear footsteps in the hall and then Jojo's voice. Now the three of them are talking.

Ann has suggested, as gently as possible, that I'm being hypersensitive. She's been doing some reading for me, reading I can't do myself. Then she relates what she's read, serving as my buffer. She says it's common for adopted children, when first placed in their new home, to resent the mother in the family. It all has to do with their birth mother abandoning them. I tried to make the argument, loudly, that we didn't adopt Georgina. She was ours to begin with. Ann humored me because she's the best friend a woman could ever have. She also reminded me that Georgina has had, whether I like it or not, a mother figure in her life all this time. She has not had a father.

And I see what she's saying, even though I didn't want to. A child removed from her home where she was happy, even a foster home, has to be angry with someone. And as much as I don't want to think about it, I've pretty much come to the conclusion that Georgina really *was* happy with Sharon. I don't have to take her word for it. She was clearly never abused, physically or emotionally. Georgina acts like a teenager who was well adjusted and happy. *Was* being the operative word. Because I ruined that the day I walked into Perfect Cup.

I'm considering seeing my therapist again. On my own. In addition to the family counseling. Maybe the family doesn't need counseling, maybe it's me. I also wonder if Remy and I need to try marriage counseling again. I felt so close to him when he first moved back in, but now it's beginning to feel as if I was imagining there was more than there is between us. I just don't feel as connected to him as I did those first few days. I keep thinking that maybe it's just the honeymoon is over and that we're back to being a couple who's been married for twenty-plus years. Or twenty-minus years, depending on whether you count the fact that we're not actually married anymore. I want to tell myself I'm just being paranoid or imagining things, but I have the nagging suspicion that's not true.

I hear footsteps from the direction of the living room and turn to see Jojo coming into the kitchen. "What are you doing in here in the dark?" she asks. It's rhetorical. She flips on the overhead lights from the light switch on the wall.

Electricity was added to the house after it was built, so we have those cool little round switch boxes on the walls. They allow for the wiring that runs on the exterior of the walls, rather than through them. You don't see it in the U.S. much anymore, but there are plenty of homes in Europe still wired this way. Years ago, Remy and I discussed having the whole house rewired properly, but the cost was astronomical, and I like it the way it is.

As my eyes adjust to the brighter light, I watch Jojo go to the refrigerator and get out a can of carbonated, flavored water. Then she goes to the pantry and pulls out a box of wheat crackers. She's wearing sweatpants and a tight long-sleeved T-shirt and I realize her body has changed from a child's to a woman's. I'm not sure how I missed that. I was here for buying first bras and tampons and even a discussion on menstrual cups, but I realize that while I might have been here, I wasn't fully present. And it makes me sad. Sad for her and for me.

"What's up?" she asks me.

I smile. I know Jojo is in the throes of teenage self-absorption, but she seems to be the one person in the house who ever asks how I am. At least on occasion.

"I'm making a list of things I have to get done tomorrow. I'm working all day Tuesday. Samantha's going to be out all day. She's got that new vet she hired part time, but she said she'd be more comfortable if I was there."

She sets the can on the counter beside my coffee cup and digs into the box of crackers. "I think that's a good idea. You going back to work." She stuffs several crackers into her mouth.

I sigh. "You're probably right. I wanted . . . I wanted to be here for Georgina." I talk softly so they can't hear me above the female screams on the TV. "I thought maybe we could both take a couple of weeks off, from school and work and . . . get to know each other."

She meets my gaze. Shrugs. "She likes school, maybe not Ursuline, but school in general. I don't get it, but . . ." She pops more crackers into her mouth. "Whatever."

"I know, I just . . ." I just what? I wanted to hang out with her? I wanted her to tell me everything that's happened to her since that last time I saw her in her stroller on Napoleon Avenue?

"You do better when you're busy, Mom. You're happier."

Jojo's embarrassingly right. The less free time I have, the less time I have to overanalyze my life and everyone else's. I reach for my coffee. "I was looking at rentals. What's your vote for our Mardi Gras vacay? Austin, Texas, or Panama City Beach, Florida? Hopefully the weather is going to be good."

Every year, since the first anniversary of Georgina's kidnapping, we've gone away at least part of the week of Mardi Gras. I can't stand Mardi Gras parades; I can't stand any parades. Just the thought of one makes me break out into a sweat. For years, Remy, Jojo, and I did mini vacations. We made our escape from the city, and its traffic and drunks urinating on our sidewalks, fun. One year we even went to Disney World. When Jojo was still into Disney princesses. After the divorce, Remy still went, but Ann and George and Makayla joined us. For the last two years, Jojo's put up a fight about going. She's getting to that age where she likes the parades, or the confusion revolving around them. I brace myself for an argument.

"Whatever. We going for a whole week?"

"Um. Probably not. Your dad doesn't want to miss too much work."

She bobs her head. "Aunt Annie and Uncle George and Makayla coming?"

I'm pleasantly surprised that she doesn't bring up staying in town. I want to hug her, but I don't want to run her off. I should probably take what I can get and be satisfied to stand here and talk with her. Jojo's never been a particularly physical child, but she doesn't freeze when I put my arms around her. Not like Georgina does. Remy suggested I back off and let Georgina be the one to initiate physical contact. I suggested to him that I wasn't certain I would live long enough.

"To be determined," I tell Jojo. "Annie was waiting on George."

"I hope they're coming." She's still munching on the crackers. "Otherwise it's going to be a total drag."

I almost laugh aloud at her choice of words. A *drag?* I wonder where she got that. It's not something you hear often in this decade. "I'll text Ann to see if they know what they're doing yet."

She grabs her drink. "Guess I'll go back upstairs and kill a couple more brain cells trying to do my geometry homework."

I nod and reach for my phone. "Hey, what's going on in the living room?" I lift my chin in that direction.

Jojo arches her eyebrows. They seem thinner than they usually are. And darker. "Dad and Lilla?"

This is why I feel like everyone is against me. Now Jojo is calling her by that name. "What are they talking about?"

"How would I know?"

"You were just in there. I heard you guys talking."

Jojo shakes her head. "Mom, you have to chill. We weren't talking about anything. I mean . . . we were talking, but . . . like about the commercial on TV or whatever. Dad asked me what I was doing upstairs. Lilla said she'd help me with my geometry, if I want."

"You should let her help you. I'm sure she—"

Jojo motions with the box of crackers in one hand, the can in the other, as if she's trying to signal a speeding car to slow down. "Mom, *chill.*"

She walks out of the kitchen.

"I'm just saying that if you need help—" I let it go. She's already gone. "I love you, Josephine!" I holler after her.

"Love you!" she calls back.

Which means my life isn't as terrible as I'm making it out to be, standing here in a dark kitchen, chugging high-test coffee. I have a roof over my head, a good job, a good husband, ex-husband, whatever. I have one daughter who loves me and another who's come back from the dead. How can I complain?

Smiling, I pick up my cell off the counter and text Ann.

Austin?

The little dots appear. Then her text pops up.

G's taking his evening constitutional. Get back to you

I chuckle and set my phone on the counter. I doubt George would appreciate his wife sharing his bathroom habits. I take another sip of coffee, carry it to the sink, and pour out the half cup still in the mug. Jojo's right. I need to chill.

Remy walks into the kitchen, his flip-flops slapping the backs of his heels. "I talked to Lilla about the boxes the movers brought over from her old house," he says, going to the fridge to refill his water glass.

I cross my arms around my waist as if I can somehow protect myself.

"The stuff she said she wanted went up to the attic. She says for me to donate the other things. Sharon's."

My gaze shifts to the leather roll on the counter next to our knife block. It seems to glow radioactively. At least in my mind. Sharon's knives. We made dinner together tonight, noodle bowls. Everyone chopped vegetables. It was actually kind of fun, and we covered family meeting stuff while we did it. But it was hard for me to watch Georgina use Sharon's chef's knife.

Remy comes to stand beside me, drinking the water. "I'm not sure if that's what I should do. I could just pay to put it in storage for now."

"If she says she doesn't want it, shouldn't we respect that?"

"Her feelings for Sharon are pretty up in the air, baby." He finishes the water and sets the glass down. He looks at me. "I think we need to think about letting her talk to her."

I don't have to ask him to clarify what he's talking about. I just stand there.

"Or at least write to her," he adds.

I don't know what to say. Remy knows how I feel about this. I cover his hand, resting on the counter, with mine. "Maybe we need to talk to the family therapist about it. Without the girls."

He doesn't move his hand away from mine, but he doesn't take it, either. "Harper . . ." He stops. Then goes on. "I'm fine with the group therapy thing, but . . ." He exhales. I can tell he's searching for patience. "She's our daughter. Don't you think we know what's best? I know we're just getting to know her, but I feel as if . . ." He looks away, then back at me. "If we want her to trust us, don't we have to trust her? She understands the situation. She knows this is permanent. I think she just needs closure with Sharon."

I take my hand from his. I thought having Georgina home again would bring us closer together, but I'm feeling more distant from Remy with each passing day. "I don't know, Remy." I walk away from him, raising my hands in the air. "I don't know."

He doesn't say anything.

I turn around and we stand there and look at each other. An impasse.

After a moment, he picks up his glass and goes to refill it. "I'm going up to take a shower. I didn't get one after I worked out."

I watch him walk out of the kitchen. Listen to him amble down the hall. Up the stairs. I grab my cell, tuck it into the back pocket of my jeans, and walk out of the kitchen. I take a breath, gird my loins, and walk into the living room. The TV is off. Georgina is sitting on the end of the couch, a pile of books beside her, her laptop on her lap.

"Hey," I say.

She glances up. "Hey." She looks down at her laptop again.

I consider surrendering. Just going to bed and trying again tomorrow. But I'm not a quitter. I'm not. I clear my throat. "I'm going to see Granddad tomorrow. You want to go? I can pick you up after school. Jojo has basketball practice."

She doesn't look up from her laptop. "Sure."

"Okay. Good. He'll be tickled to see you." I stand there trying to think of something to say. Then I remember why I came in to begin with. I really am perimenopausal. "I was talking to Jojo . . . We always go away for Mardi Gras. The city's packed to the gills. There's no place to park . . . And you and Jojo have the whole week off from school. We were thinking about Austin, Texas. Have you ever been there?"

She looks up. A frown. "We're not going to be here for the parades?"

It takes me a second to respond. "No. No, we don't stay in town for Mardi Gras." The reason seems obvious, but she's sitting there looking at me like I'm an idiot. "Georgina . . . After . . . after you went missing, we . . . I couldn't stay in the city. For me, all the revelry, the parades, even the beads, they all . . ." A lump rises in my throat and I fight it. I look down at the floor. The area rug needs vacuuming. *I will not cry. I will not cry.* "They all bring back the painful memories of when you went missing. I just can't handle it."

"So I'm not going to get to see the Mardi Gras parades." She meets my gaze.

I've been looking for emotion from my daughter; well, here it is. *Defiance. Anger.*

"You're not. At least not this year," I add.

"But I've been looking forward to Mardi Gras since we moved here. I got to see a couple of random parades, but I really wanted to see some of the real parades. The Mardi Gras parades. Sharon and I were going to go see one uptown and one downtown."

"I'm sorry, Georgina."

"But I wanted to go." She's speaking slowly now, her lips

tight. "I went to the Mardi Gras Museum. I learned all about the parades. Can't you . . . Maybe you and Jojo can go to Austin. Dad and I will stay here. He'll go to the parades with me."

"We take our vacations as a family."

She closes her laptop abruptly. "What if I don't want to be a part of *the family?*"

"It's too late, Georgina." My voice gets testy. "You already are. You were the day you were born."

She pushes her laptop off her lap onto the pile of books. "I'm not going!"

I walk toward her without even realizing I'm doing it. "What did you want me to do, Georgina?" I say in a voice close to shouting. "When I walked into that coffee shop, and I saw you there. What was I supposed to do?" I demand.

She just sits there staring at me, her face a mask of anger and something that looks very much like hatred.

"Was I supposed to just walk away? And leave you to live your life with Sharon, never knowing you were ours?" My last words are definitely at a volume that could be considered yelling. I don't think I've ever yelled at Jojo in my life. "Never knowing she took you from me?"

"Yes!" Georgina shouts at me. "You should have left me there. Because I was *happy!*"

I take a breath. A strange calm comes over me. "I'm sorry, but I couldn't do that. I couldn't walk away, knowing it was you. And I know you may not be able to understand that, right now. But someday . . . when you're a mother, you will."

We're both still looking at each other. I wait for what she'll say next, but she doesn't say anything. Her eyes are wet, but she isn't crying.

"I'm sorry," I say softly. I start to turn away and then turn back. "But for what it's worth, I love you, Georgina. And even if you don't love me back, I'll still keep"—my voice catches in my throat—"I'll still always love you. You'll still always be mine."

I walk out of the room and down the hall.

Remy meets me halfway between the stairs and the living room. "What's going on?"

"You should probably go talk to her," I say. Tears are running down my cheeks.

He looks at me and then in the direction of the living room.

I lay my hand on his chest. "Just talk to her, Remy," I whisper. And then I make a retreat to my bedroom, hoping maybe I can find a hole to crawl into.

24

Jojo

When I come out of the bathroom, the hall is dark. No light downstairs, except the little one Mom leaves on in the front hall. So thieves don't bust in, thinking no one's home. I flip off the bathroom light and stand there in the dark, listening.

Mom and Lilla had an argument about something. I've never heard Mom yell like that. It scared me. Not because I thought she was going to hit Lilla or anything. I was scared for Mom. Because how upset would she have to be to holler like that?

What were they arguing about?

This whole thing with Lilla being here after all these years is wild. I think Mom thought somebody was going to bring baby Georgina home. I really think she thought she was going to get a two-year-old. Maybe even wearing the same clothes she was wearing when she got snatched. But Lilla's sixteen, and acts like she's twenty-six. Or maybe fifty-six. Sometimes I think she acts more mature than Mom. Georgina's so grown-up and so smart. But she's also weird. She reads a lot. And she's into history. She and Dad talk a lot about things like movies and books and Viking graves in Iceland. Sometimes, I feel like both of them are from another planet.

Or I am.

I creep down the hall toward Mom and Dad's bedroom. Their light is on, but the door's shut. I glance behind me. Lilla's door is shut, too. It's, like, not even nine o'clock yet and everyone is in their rooms. I don't know what went down, but it was something big.

I listen at the door. I can hear Dad talking.

My phone dings and I jump. I grab it out of my back pocket. I don't know how the mute got off. It's Makayla.

I'm bored.

Not boring here, I text back.

Sup?

M & L had a fight. Yelling.

L yeled at your m????

It's funny, Makayla is the smart one of the two of us, but she's always misspelling things in her texts. I don't know if she's a bad speller or a bad texter. It's not something you bring up with your best friend. Not at this point. Not when she's been misspelling things in her texts since we got phones when we were twelve.

Both yelled.

Makayla sends an explosion meme, which makes me smile. Then she texts:

Big bummer here. Not going on vacay this year with you. Dad's work. M say we're staying home to "be supportive."

I roll my eyes. This is bad. *Bad.* Spending a week trapped with Mom, Dad, and the big sister in a condo sounds like a disaster. If Lilla runs away when we're in a different state, how do they think they're going to find her?

B right back, I text.

I slip my phone back into my pocket. I hear Mom's voice. I hear Georgina's name, but these old doors are thick. And Mom and Dad are sneaky. They talk quiet when they don't want me to hear them.

I go back down the hall toward my room. But I stop outside Lilla's door. I can smell the new paint. I wonder if she has a window open for ventilation. Can't smells like that kill you?

I kind of want to see if Lilla's okay. I want to knock on her door. But what will I say that won't make her think I'm an idiot?

Or butting into her business. Am I supposed to check on her? Or am I supposed to leave her alone?

I never thought about what it would be like to have a sister. Or be a sister. Because I never had one. Well . . . I've always had a *dead* sister. I know what that's like. When you have a dead sister, your mom cries a lot and talks about her a lot. And you try to make up for the fact that you're here and she's not. But you know you never can.

The light under Lilla's door goes out.

I stare at the crack in the door. Did she hear me? Now do I have to knock, otherwise she'll think I'm stalking her?

I try to think about what to say. What excuse I can use to knock. Maybe I could ask her about her trip to the bakery yesterday. Mom let her take the streetcar to get bread by herself again. Mom only let her go because Dad said so. And Mom stood at the kitchen island the whole time Lilla was gone, drinking coffee and looking at the clock on the stove.

I could ask Lilla how the ride on the streetcar was. Or maybe . . . tell her thanks for the donuts she got at District Donuts. I love their donuts. She got this kind that had a flower on it and she gave it to me when she got home. She said she got it just for me. It was so pretty I didn't want to eat it. But I did and it was so good.

Before I chicken out, I knock.

There's no answer.

Her light has only been out a minute or two so I know she's not asleep. I knock again and press my mouth to the crack in the door. "Lilla," I murmur. "It's Jojo."

I wait.

Nothing.

I'm standing there trying to decide if I should knock again or just forget it, when I hear her voice. "Come in."

I open the door thinking this is a dumb idea. She doesn't want to talk to me. She doesn't even want to live with me. Which I totally get. Makayla and I were talking the other day and we were imagining what it would be like if this happened to one of us. Like . . . what if the police had come to our door and put Mom and Dad in jail and made me go live with Lilla and Sharon? I'd freak out. I'd probably run away or maybe go on a hunger strike or something.

I push open the door a little farther.

She's lying in her bed, which is still in the middle of the room because she's still painting her walls. Even though there are bags of clothes she bought sitting next to the door, the room is pretty empty. And really clean. There are always clothes all over my floor, and thrown over my chair and my desk and hanging from all the doorknobs. And trash: balls of notebook paper, disposable coffee cups, broken pens, shopping bags.

Lilla's propped up on pillows, her computer on her lap. I wonder if Mom snooped in her laptop when she was at school this week. Mom's a snooper. I know she checks my Facebook page. That's why I don't post there too often. Mom doesn't know how to get into my Snapchat so that's the way my friends and I tell each other stuff, if we don't want to text. Mom used to be able to read my texts from her computer somehow, but Dad and I convinced her that was an invasion of privacy. And it's not like I'm doing drugs or dudes. I don't know why she thought she needed to see what my friends and I were saying. More of the whole "everyone wants to kidnap you" psychodrama, I'm sure.

The light from Lilla's computer illuminates her face. She looks like she's been crying. I feel bad for her.

"I, um . . ." I feel stupid, not knowing what to say. "I wanted to see if you were okay."

She looks at me and I look at her. There's no expression on her face. I can't tell if she thinks I'm a dunce or not.

"I, heard you guys yelling," I add.

She glances at her laptop. "I'm okay."

I hesitate, then ask, "What were you guys fighting about?"

Her expression changes, like she's trying to figure something out. I think she's trying to decide if she should say anything to me. Like she's wondering if I'll run across the hall and tell them everything she told me. I don't do that. Not with Makayla. I'd never tattle on Makayla even if I was in trouble. So I figure the same rule goes for sisters as friends.

"Doesn't matter," she says.

But I can tell by her face that it does. I take another step into the room. If Mom opens her door, I don't want her to be able to see me or hear me. "Mom wouldn't tell me, but . . ." I touch a zit coming up on my chin. "I'm sorry. I know this sucks. All of it."

She looks up at me and kind of smiles. "It does suck." She keeps looking at me and then she says, "I've been looking forward to Mardi Gras for months. To see some of the parades. I've seen them on YouTube, but I really wanted to go to one. When Sharon told me we were moving to New Orleans, even though I'd already started the school year in Baton Rouge, I told her it was okay. Because of the parades."

"Right," I say. "And now Mom wants to go to Austin. Because Mom doesn't do parades because kids get kidnapped during parades. Her kids. Kid," I correct.

Lilla chews on her bottom lip. "It wasn't my fault Sharon kidnapped me."

The way she says it makes me want to cry. I don't know what to say. But for the first time, I feel like she's not just some stranger staying in our spare room. I mean, I don't feel like she's my sister because we didn't grow up together, but . . . she means more to me now than when she was just photographs and Mom's memory.

"I don't think she thinks it's your fault. Mom's just . . . paranoid. Overprotective," I add. "Sometimes a little psycho." I say that part nice, not mean. Since Lilla got here, I've felt like I kind of need to defend Mom. Dad can be harsh on her sometimes.

Lilla doesn't say anything.

"I could talk to them, if you want," I suggest. "I don't want to go this year, anyway. Makayla can't go." I'm quiet for a second. "And it would be kind of fun to see one of the parades. I live in New Orleans and I've never seen a Mardi Gras parade, either. It's whack. You want me to talk to them? I bet Dad would go for staying here and seeing a parade if we like . . . promised to chain ourselves together or something."

She kind of laughs. Which makes me smile. She's right. It really isn't her fault Sharon kidnapped her. Babies can't be held responsible for that kind of stuff. "I'll talk to them. Okay?"

She smiles, but keeps her lips together, so it seems like a sad smile. "Thanks."

"Sure." I back out of the room. "Night."

"Night."

I close her door and I'm in the dark in the hallway again. The walls are covered with pictures, not of the old farts like going down the stairs. These are pictures of me and Lilla, previously known as Georgina. Mostly her, which makes it creepy. Downstairs in the parlor, there's a little place on a marble-top table with a picture of Lilla when she was little and there's a cross there and a candle Mom lights. Like a shrine. Which is *super* creepy.

I check my phone. I'm still not done with my geometry homework. I'm supposed to be able to identify a bunch of shapes for a quiz tomorrow. I can spot a circle, a rectangle, and a square easy enough, obviously, but all those different triangles . . . I can never remember their names. If I fail geometry, Mom's going to kill me. But if I do fail, I'm going to tell her it's her fault. I knew geometry was going to be too hard.

I'm not even supposed to be in the ninth grade, technically. I was homeschooled when I was little and when Dad said it was time for me to go to Ursuline, they had me tested. Mom wanted to have me bumped up so I could be in the same grade as Makayla. So she could be my bodyguard or whatever, I guess. Like fourth graders can protect you. Makayla is only three months older than me, but because my birthday fell after the deadline, and hers didn't, I should have gone to third grade. I think the Broussards have given a lot of money to Ursuline over the years and that's why they let me in. Mom said it wasn't true, but if it was, would she tell me?

I check my cell. Makayla texted me when I was with Lilla.

U their?

It's supposed to be here, not *their*. I laugh and text back. **Hang on**

Mom and Dad's light is still on. I guess this is as good a time as any to tell Mom and Dad that I want to skip the escape–Mardi Gras vacation this year, too.

I push my phone back into the pocket of my sweatpants and go to their door. Knock. "It's Jojo." I say my name because yesterday Dad said that Lilla and I sounded a lot alike. I don't think we do, but he's old so maybe he's already starting to lose his hearing. Granddad wears a hearing aid. Otherwise he has to turn the TV up so loud, it blasts out the lady in the room next to him. There was a big incident in the fall about it. I guess she wasn't into *Planet Earth*.

"Come on in," Dad calls.

I open the door slowly. I'm fine with Dad being here. I mean, it *is* his ancestral home, but it feels weird for him to be in Mom's bed. He's lying on his back on top of the quilt. He's got plaid flannel pajama bottoms on and a black T-shirt. The girls at school think he's hot—for a dad. I bet they'd like it if I took a pic of him right now and Snapchatted it.

I glance at the bathroom door, which is closed. I hear the shower running. I wonder if she's really showering or just hiding. I hope she's okay.

"What's up?" Dad says.

I point at the bathroom door, but don't say anything.

"She's fine," he says, like he knows what I'm thinking.

"Um . . . I don't know if I'm supposed to wait for our next family meeting or if this is something I'm supposed to say when we go to family counseling again, but—" I wrinkle my nose, lowering my voice. "Do I have to go again? To counseling? It seems dumb and I bet it's expensive. I'd take my share in"—I shrug—"I don't know. Gift cards from Lululemon?"

"No." He holds up his finger and smiles at me. "But good try. What did you need?"

I take a breath and just say it. "Mardi Gras."

He makes a face. When I was little, I loved the faces he used to make. I don't love them as much anymore.

"Dad, I'm not, like, taking Lilla's side on purpose, but I don't want to go to Austin, either. I want to stay here. Makayla says they can't go."

"Your mom know the Parkers can't go?"

I shrug. "But serious, Dad. Isn't it kind of dumb that I was born in New Orleans, that I live here, and the only parade I ever saw was when I was three months old?"

"You've seen parades. You and I did the uptown St. Paddy's Day parade last year."

"I want to see the Krewe du Vieux parade." I say it with a French accent. My French isn't too bad. I actually get A's in French. Except when I forget to do my homework. "I don't care if it's downtown and it's crazy. I just want to go once."

He sits up in the bed. "You and Lilla talk about this?"

He's lowered his voice. Which means this is for our ears only. But the shower is still running, so Mom probably can't hear us anyway.

I hesitate, then nod. Which is not tattling. I didn't say what Lilla said. "I just talked to her. She wants to go to a parade. She had to leave Baton Rouge after the school year started, but Sharon promised her she'd be here to see the parades." I rub the zit. I know I'm supposed to leave them alone, but how am I going to go to school tomorrow with a gigantic zit on my chin? "I think you guys are making this out to be a bigger deal than it is. I know it's hard to get around during Mardi Gras because of the traffic and all the tourists, but we could take our bikes downtown. We could borrow Aunt Annie's for Lilla."

I can tell he's thinking.

"Please, Dad? My sister's back. I think I should get to be like other girls now."

"I'll talk to your mom."

I think for a second. "I know parades scare Mom. She wouldn't have to go. Lilla and I could go with you."

"I said I'll talk to your mom."

I nod. "Okay. Thanks." I turn to go.

"Jojo?"

I turn back.

"I'm glad you talked to your sister about this. We've all agreed this is hard for her, but I know it's hard for you, too."

I just stand there because I don't know what to say. Dad's right. This does suck. Having this girl in our house I don't know. Mom being upset. Dad being here pretending they're married. Because I think Lilla thinks they're still married. I don't think they told her that Dad has been gone for years and that he came back because she was coming back.

"Your sister could use a friend right now. Or a sister," he adds.

I think about that for a minute, but I don't say anything about it. "Gotta go finish my homework. Good night."

"Night, Jojo. I love you."

I walk out the door. "Love you, too, Dad."

25

Lilla

"How was your day?"

"It was okay." I stare out the window, watching the buildings we pass. Harper Mom picked me up after school. Jojo had to stay for basketball. It's raining today. Who knew it rained so much here? And cold. Cold for Louisiana. I can't wait to get out of my uniform and put on my new sweatpants. I got some cool stuff at a resale store I went to with Dad. The sweatpants look like no one ever wore them and they were six bucks.

"You talk to Em about walking home with you tomorrow after school?"

I can feel her looking at me. I wish she'd watch the road. You have to pay attention every second. Especially in city traffic. I learned that when I took driver's ed. And Sharon talked about it when she let me drive a little. We had a car when we moved here, an old Jeep. One of the big ones, not the little ones. It was in a shop getting the transmission fixed when this all went down. I wonder what happened to it.

"Your dad or I will be home by six. We can give her a ride home, if she wants."

We stop at a light and I watch a girl my age carrying a bag of groceries. She must go to a school around here. She's wearing a uniform, but she doesn't go to Ursuline. No dorky skirt. I wonder if she's going home to make dinner for her family. I wonder what she's going to make. I think if I was making dinner tonight, I'd make pho, which is a Vietnamese noodle bowl thing. Sharon made great pho.

"I'll ask her tomorrow."

"I can call her mom if you like." The light turns green and Harper Mom eases off the brake.

I made the mistake of telling Dad at dinner last night that there was a girl in my English class who was being super nice to me. She asked me if I wanted to maybe go see a movie Friday or Saturday. Her best friend just moved away at Christmas. Which I know makes me her second string, but I don't mind. She's nice and she likes *The Great Gatsby*. We're reading it in English class. I read it freshman year, on my own, but that's okay.

"You can't call her mom," I say before I catch myself. At that point, I figure I might as well go on. Dad says I need to tell them what I think. What I want. He says that doesn't mean they'll agree with me, or let me do what I want, but I have to learn to speak up. Sharon and I always had the same kind of deal. "You can't set up play dates for me." I sneak a peek at her. I feel like we've both been walking on eggshells. Since we hollered at each other last week. But it's weird . . . a part of me almost feels better since then. Like . . . a little more normal. Like I'm not just standing off to the side, watching myself, hearing what I say.

"You're right," she says, which surprises me. "You're right. I know you are. And . . . if it doesn't work out, you can walk home and . . . text me when you're safely in the house with the door locked. And the alarm's set," she adds.

I smile to myself. Sharon always said that people can't change; they are what they are. But I don't know if I believe that. Harper Mom seems to be trying. I feel like I have to give her credit for that.

"I'll text her later," I say.

"Good." She's quiet for half a block. "Georgina . . ."

When she doesn't say anything, I look at her. "Mmhmm?"

She waits until I make eye contact, then looks at the road

again. There's construction on St. Charles, so she's going the long way around to get home. "We haven't talked about Sunday night."

I stare straight ahead. "I know I apologized the other day, but I am sorry I yelled." And I *am* sorry. I don't like yelling. It doesn't seem like a good way to resolve things.

"I'm sorry, too. I should have handled the conversation better. I'm trying to see things from your perspective." She's quiet for a second. "Georgina, you need to try to see mine, too." She lets that sink in and then goes on. "Your dad thinks we should stay home this year. Skip the vacation."

I look at her. "Stay for Mardi Gras?" I know I sound cheesy getting all excited, but I don't care.

"Jojo wants to stay, too. And the Parkers can't go anyway."

I nod. Look at her hopefully. "So *are* we staying?"

"I don't know."

We're stopped in traffic for no reason at all that I can see.

"But . . ." Harper Mom looks at me. "I understand why you girls want to stay and . . . I know I need to get past my anxiety over your safety. Yours and Jojo's. Because you're home now—" Her voice gets full of emotion like she's about to cry. But she doesn't. "We just . . . Georgina, we need to find a way to . . . we need to talk more. You need to talk to me so I can get to know you better. And you can get to know me. You're . . . almost grown. You're going to college in two years. We have a lot of years to make up for." She takes a breath. "I want you to ask me things. About me. And I need to be able to ask you questions." She gives a little laugh. "I don't even know what your favorite ice cream is."

"Mint chocolate chip."

She smiles and, weirdly enough, she makes me smile. "Mine too. And coffee," she adds.

I nod, looking ahead. We inch forward the length of one car and stop. "I like coffee ice cream, too," I say. "Have you been to that gelato place where you get a little paper cup of espresso and pour it on top of the gelato?"

She shakes her head as we move forward again. "No. Sounds glorious. Where is it?"

"I don't remember exactly. In the Central Business District. Julia Street, maybe? I could Google it." I hesitate. "Maybe we could go sometime?"

"I'd like that. I—"

She slams on her brakes. The lady in front of us in an orange VW bug slammed on her brakes and Harper Mom had to do the same to keep from hitting her. Her bag on the backseat flies off and dumps on the floor.

"Some people," Harper Mom says through gritted teeth.

I turn around in my seat and lean down to pick up her stuff.

"You can leave it. I'll get it when I get home."

"I don't mind." I pick up her purse and put the matching suede wallet back in, then her case with her reading glasses and two lipsticks. I have to feel around on the floor because I can't turn all the way around while in my seat belt and there's no way I'm taking it off with Miss Happy Brakes ahead of us.

I find a pen and a tin of mini mints and add them to her bag. Then my fingertips touch something little on the floor of the car, something cool and smooth. Metal. I pick it up and sit up in my seat. It's a little baby, like a charm, maybe two inches long. "What's this?" I ask, turning it in my hands. It looks old. The creases are tarnished, but the belly and cheeks are shiny silver.

She looks down. "That's a cake baby."

I stare at it. Something feels weird about this little thing. I just can't figure out what. "A *cake* baby?"

"It gets baked into a Mardi Gras king cake. Usually they're plastic, now. Whoever gets the baby is the king for the day, and then has to host the next party. And buy the next cake."

I stare at the little silver charm in my hand and get the strangest feeling. As if I've seen it before. "It's old, isn't it?" I ask.

"It is. From France, I think. My grandmother gave it to me. I grew up in the Philadelphia area because that's where my dad's family was from, but my mother was from Louisiana and so was her mother. My grandmother gave me this crucifix I always wear, too." She pulls the little cross she wears around her neck out to show me. "Someday it will be for—" She lets go of the necklace and puts both hands on the steering wheel again. "Looks like we're moving."

"Is it just supposed to be loose in here?" I hold up the baby charm.

"Goes in the zipper compartment with my lipstick. I guess it wasn't zipped. I don't know how I've held on to that thing all these years."

I put the weird little baby charm into the compartment and zip it up.

We're on St. Charles now. We hit another light.

"Okay, so you like mint chocolate chip ice cream," Harper Mom says. "You answered my question, now you ask me something."

I chew on my lower lip. I have no idea what to ask her. It seems dorky to ask what her favorite color is. And I don't want to turn up the dork any further. I already admitted I'd read American literature when I didn't have to. Maybe her favorite food? I can tell she's waiting. I turn to her, realizing there is a question I want to ask her. "Are you named after Harper Lee? Who wrote *To Kill a Mockingbird*?"

"You've read *To Kill a Mockingbird*?"

I wrinkle my nose. "Of course. It's an American treasure."

She laughs and I like the sound of it. "You sound like your father," she tells me.

"I read *Go Set a Watchman*, too. It was released, like, fifty years later," I point out. "Which I liked better than the first book. Which my friend Ruby said was crazy."

"Ruby. Was she a friend from school where you went in Bayou St. John?"

I shake my head, looking forward. "Atlanta," I say softly. "We were there almost two years before we moved to Baton Rouge. This last time." Thinking about Ruby makes me sad for a minute. But Ruby was an old friend from an old life and now I have to make friends in this new life. "Of course you know Harper Lee wrote *Watchman* first."

"Right. I haven't read it."

"You should," I tell her. "I'm surprised you haven't. It's big with women's book clubs."

"Maybe I should bring it up at book club."

"I didn't know you belonged to a book club."

"Well, I . . . I've been busy at home so I didn't go this month, but . . . I'll suggest it."

I think she means she skipped book club because of me, which sounds silly, but I don't say so. "Ruby and I had our own book club. We made lists of books to read and then we asked each other questions we found on the Internet that were meant for book clubs. Sometimes there are questions in the back you can use for discussion."

She smiles at me as she flips on the signal to turn onto the street that runs behind our house. "So . . . to answer your question, I was *not* named after Harper Lee. People ask me that all the time. I was named after my maternal grandmother. The same one who gave me the cake baby. Harper is a Southern name."

"It's a good name. I like it. Why didn't you name me Harper?" I ask. "Like maybe my middle name?"

She thinks about it for a minute. "Actually your father wanted to, but I don't know." She pulls into the driveway and parks. As she shuts off the engine, she drops her hands to her lap and looks at me. "I suppose I wanted you to be your own person, separate from me."

I hand her her bag that's still on my lap, thinking that's pretty cool that she wanted me to be myself and not like a carbon copy of her. Which is a good thing probably, because I'm not much like her. Except that we both like mint chocolate chip ice cream. And coffee.

We make a run for the house because it's starting to rain harder. We leave our wet coats in the laundry room. And our shoes. In the kitchen, she drops her bag on the counter. "I'm going to run upstairs and take a shower," she says, looking down at her scrub bottoms. "I feel gross. I saw this big mastiff this afternoon. He was sweet, but he drooled all over me."

She worked again today. She dropped Jojo, Makayla, and me off at school and then went to work. But she only worked until school was over. She still doesn't want me walking the twelve blocks or so home, I guess. Which I told her I was fine doing, even in the rain. But Dad said to let it go, that we were making progress. So I'm letting it go. I put my backpack on one of the stools at the center island. "I'm going to get something to eat and start my homework after I change. I've got a paper due Monday."

She stops in the doorway. "What's the topic?"

"Mrs. Dobson gave us a couple of choices. I think I'm going to write about the parallels between Daisy and Zelda Fitzgerald."

She nods. "I can see that. I remember reading *The Great Gatsby*. I think I liked it."

I open the refrigerator door and look in. "Like I said, I've read it before. I like it, though."

She stands there for a second as if she isn't quite ready to go yet. "Well . . . I'll be down in a few minutes."

"You want coffee?" I call as she disappears from my sight.

"Sure."

I get a pear and a yogurt out of the fridge, set them on the island, and then get two mugs from the cabinet for the coffee machine. I get milk. I'm making us both cappuccinos. I might even add a little cocoa with the sugar. Harper Mom likes mocha anythings. When I turn on the coffee machine, it says I need to fill up the water reservoir, so I have to get filtered water from the fridge door, which takes forever. Finally I get the coffee machine going and I'm standing there, waiting while it heats up, when the house phone rings.

Last night Harper Mom was complaining that no one ever answers it.

I go over and pick it up. As I hit the button, I realize I'm not sure what I'm supposed to say. We never had a house phone that I can remember, just Sharon's cell, and I got mine when I turned fourteen. Am I supposed to say, "Broussard residence," like I've seen in movies? I go with "Hello."

"Hello," says a female voice that sounds like a recording. I'm lowering the phone from my ear, thinking it's a telemarketer, when I hear, "This is a collect call from . . . *Sharon Kohen* . . . an inmate at Louisiana Correctional Institute—"

I almost drop the phone. It was my mother's voice that gave her name. Sharon's. The recording is still continuing. "—accept the collect call, please press one. If—"

I don't know what to do. I don't want to talk to her. Not ever again.

But I want to talk to her. I want to talk to her so bad. Tears fill my eyes.

She ruined our lives. Mine and hers. I want to tell her how much I hate her. How much I love her.

I hang up and drop the phone on the counter like it's a piece of dry ice. Sharon once brought some crawfish home in a bag and when I picked up the dry ice packet, it burned like I touched a hot oven rack. It was years ago, but I remember how shocked I was. Almost insulted that ice would burn me like that. You just don't expect ice to feel hot.

And you don't expect the woman who kidnapped you to have the guts to call your real family's house. Collect. From prison.

The coffee machine spits the last of the first cappuccino into the mug and I set it on the counter and slide the other mug onto the little platform to make Harper Mom's.

The phone rings again and I whip around to stare at it like it's an apparition or something.

It keeps ringing.

I keep staring at it.

I want to answer it. I want to holler at her. I want to ask her how she could have kidnapped somebody's baby. I want to ask her about her baby who died. Was her name really Lilla, too? Did she name me after a dead baby?

The phone stops ringing and I suddenly realize I've been holding my breath. I exhale and then inhale deeply. My heart is pounding. My hand is shaking as I carry my cappuccino to the counter.

What am I going to do if she calls again?

26

Harper

Walking out of the bathroom in my robe, I pick up my cell. I'm smiling. I can't stop smiling. I ring Ann.

"Hey," she says.

"Hey." I adjust my microfiber towel on my head with one hand, holding my cell to my ear with the other.

"How was your day?" she asks. It's what we do. When Remy left and he wasn't here in the evening to ask me how my day was, Ann took his place. Funny thing is, he doesn't ask me how my day went anymore. Even now that he's here again. Probably because he doesn't like to hear about cranky clients or bowel obstructions.

My grin widens. "It was good, Annie. It was . . ." I sit down on the edge of the bed. "I think it was my best since Georgina came home."

"Harper, honey, that's great news."

I bob my head, getting a little teary. "She never said a word all the way to school this morning."

"Well, it *is* a five-minute ride from my house to Ursuline's front door," she points out.

"Right, but I had her in the car alone this afternoon. And she talked to me." I wipe under one eye and then the other with the corner of my towel. "Annie, she talked to me. I found out that her favorite ice cream is mint chocolate chip—"

"Like you."

"Like me!" I'm laughing so I don't cry. "And she likes *The Great Gatsby*. The book, not the movie. I don't even know if she's ever seen the movie. I'll have to ask her." I circle back around. "They're reading it in English. She's read it before, but she likes it. She's writing a paper that compares Daisy and Zelda. She's really smart. I think she's really smart."

Now Ann is laughing. "Of course she's smart. How could she not be smart with you two for parents?"

"Funny you should bring that up . . ." I pull the towel off my head and fluff my hair. It's getting thinner. How in heaven's name can it be getting thinner already? My grandmother had thin hair, but she was in her seventies by then. "I read something the other day—*Huffington Post*, I think—that geneticists have found evidence that suggests intelligence may come more from the female than the male."

"I suppose anything is possible."

We both take a breath. Even on the phone, we feel a connection with each other.

"I think maybe we're going to be okay." I whisper the words because I'm afraid to speak them out loud.

Okay seems like such a middle-of-the-road word, but the width and breadth of it is almost overwhelming for me. We're going to be okay; I'm not going to have a nervous breakdown. We're going to be okay; Georgina is home to stay. We're going to be okay; Remy isn't going to leave us for an adjunct professor half my age. We're going to be okay; Jojo isn't going to demand that Ann and George adopt her. Or run away to join the circus or appear on a reality show on MTV.

"Of course you're going to be okay," Ann says firmly. But her voice is kind. "You were always going to be okay, Harper. No matter what happened. Even if she didn't come back, I knew you were going to be okay."

Tears run down my cheeks. "It's the fifty-four-day rosary novena. I told you they work. And I haven't even finished it."

"I don't know about that, but I'm happy for you, Harper. I'm so happy for you."

"I definitely think we've turned a corner." I get off the bed. I need to get dressed and go down and have my coffee with Georgina. Maybe we'll talk some more. Maybe she'll even want some help with her paper, even if it's just to read it for typos. I'm a great proofreader. "Georgina and Jojo have stopped acting like they're strangers. This morning they argued over who got the last of the granola; sisters do that kind of thing. And Georgina has taken a real interest in Dad. She wants to go to the nursing home alone. She wants to Uber." I chuckle without humor. "Like I'm going to let her get in a car alone with a stranger."

"Uber is pretty safe," Ann injects. "Of course if you let her start driving—"

"Okay, enough, Annie. Baby steps. Baby steps."

She laughs. With me, at me, it doesn't matter.

"I better go," I tell her. "She's making me coffee. I just wanted to tell you I had a good day."

As we hang up, Remy comes through the bedroom door. Closes it behind him.

"You're home early." I toss my phone on the bed and go over to give him a kiss.

He stands there, arms at his sides. His pants are wet. He must have ridden his scooter home in the rain. I wonder why he didn't come home in his little Fiat; it's parked at his place. I haven't seen him in it in weeks. He likes the scooter, though. I think it makes him feel young and carefree and not saddled with a wife and two children.

He lets me kiss him, but there's no pucker back. I rest my hand on his chest, looking at him. I know that face. My laid-back husband isn't always laid-back. "Bad day?"

"It was fine." His tone suggests it wasn't.

"Is Peter giving you a hard time about the endowment you—"

"I don't want to talk about it. I just came home because I forgot my gym bag. I'm headed for the gym." He walks away from me. Goes to his giant antique chifforobe, one of the two in the bedroom. His parents once used them and his grandparents before them. The house wasn't built with closets. He pulls open one of the double doors and pokes around. "It's not here, either." He shuts the door. Hard. "I guess I left it at the apartment."

I nod. I didn't even know he'd been to the apartment since Georgina came home. We haven't really discussed what he was going to do with it. The lease isn't up for at least six months, so it hasn't been a priority. And of course we haven't discussed the obvious question of whether or not he's staying here. I've been sticking to the *see how it goes* plan he proposed and praying. I watch him, wondering what he was doing there that he might have left his bag. I sense this isn't the time to ask. "Just grab another pair of shorts and a tee, hon. You'll find it."

"My good sneakers are in the bag. My gym sneakers."

I'm still in my robe. "We could do something else for exercise," I suggest, giving what I hope is a sexy smile.

He just stands there, looking at me. "I really wanted to go to the gym."

Which is a not-so-subtle no-thank-you to my offer of an afternoon quickie. I decide not to let my feelings get hurt. I'm in too good a mood.

He turns back to the chifforobe, staring at it as if the doors are going to fly open and his gym bag is going to fly out.

I pick up the towel from my hair off the bed and walk toward the bathroom. "Maybe it's in my car. You took it to the gym the other day."

He doesn't say anything.

"I had a nice talk with Georgina today, on the ride home from school." I grab a pair of panties out of the top drawer of my dresser and step into them. "I feel as if we're starting to connect. Maybe not the way you two are, but—"

"Harper, we're not going to get into this right now. I feel like we've discussed it ad nauseam. It makes sense that it's more difficult for her to relate to you because she already had a mother. She has no expectations for a father."

And you're so cool, who wouldn't want you for their dad? I want to say. But I don't. Because everything isn't about me in our marriage. It can't be. I know that.

I grab my jeans from the day before and pull them on. Then I turn my back to him to put on a sports bra. I'm not going anywhere else today; no underwires required. I pull on an old long-sleeved T-shirt some drug rep gave me. I'm now a walking billboard for a topical flea-and-tick medication.

"I wasn't complaining, Remy. I was trying to tell you that we had a good conversation."

"I guess I'll check your car." He walks to the door.

I'm disappointed that he doesn't want to talk about my conversation with Georgina. And I genuinely want to know why he's in a bad mood. In the past, I would have persisted at this point. I would have insisted he tell me what was going on. But I know the right thing is to just let Remy go right now. Talk about it later.

"You'll be home for dinner?" I call after him as he goes out the door.

"Yeah. No . . . I don't know. I might go back to the office after I work out. I'll text you," he calls when he's out of sight.

I stand there for a minute wondering if I said something wrong. If I could have been more supportive. When Remy left, that was one of his reasons. He said I was so wrapped up in myself that I was never available emotionally for him. And he was absolutely right. The funny thing is that after he left, my ability to support him actually improved. Which makes no sense.

But I'm not going to worry about it today. I grab my phone and step into my sheepskin slippers. Today I'm going to bask in the joy of the chat I had with my daughter and I'm going to go downstairs and have a cup of coffee with her.

Only she's not in the kitchen when I get there. There are two cups of coffee made, sitting on the counter, but no Georgina.

Maybe she went to the bathroom. Or to change her clothes. I take a sip of coffee. It's good. I go to the refrigerator to dig around to see what I can make for dinner. Maybe noodle bowls. Georgina and Jojo both like that. It's not great heated up, though. I close the refrigerator door. Maybe I'll wait to see if Remy is coming home to eat with us or will be late.

I sit down at the island to wait for Georgina. I'm halfway through my cup of coffee when I begin to wonder where she is. But I don't panic. And my heartbeat doesn't increase. I glance around the kitchen. Her yogurt is sitting on the counter unopened. And a pear. She didn't run away.

But I don't see her backpack.

She didn't run away. I'm being paranoid. She must have gone to her room. But if she left the yogurt out, she must have intended to come back down. I finish my cup of coffee as I wait. When she's still a no-show, I go upstairs.

Her bedroom door is closed.

I knock. "Georgina?" I glance down the hall. The bathroom door is open; the light's off. I tap again, lightly. "Are you coming back down?" I try not to sound needy.

"Doing my homework," comes her muffled voice from behind the door.

Something in her voice doesn't sound right and I debate knocking again and asking if I can come in. I resist. "You okay?" I keep my tone light.

She doesn't answer.

"Georgina?"

"I'm fine. I . . . I have a headache. I might lie down for a few minutes. Then do my homework."

"Okay." I rest my palm on the door as if I can somehow touch her through the solid wood. Something in her voice sounds off. I don't know how . . . almost as if she's afraid. Upset. Something.

I turn away. Did I push her too hard in the car? Did I misinterpret what seemed like a conversation that was going well? I turn back. "I'll call you for dinner when Jojo gets home."

"Okay."

I walk down the stairs slowly. Georgina's a teenage girl, I tell myself. One who's been through a hell of a lot in the last six weeks. She has a right to mood swings. And teenage girls hide in their bedrooms. It's in their DNA.

And it's in a mother's DNA to worry about her cubs.

27

Lilla

I stand alone in the kitchen in the semidarkness. A storm blew in suddenly, just as I left school. It started to rain. This girl in my political science class who has her own car saw me walking so she gave me a ride. Between that transgression and the fact that I lied to Harper Mom, saying Em was coming home with me, I'll probably be grounded for the rest of my life. But I don't care. I had to get home. I have to be here alone.

The storm seemed to come in out of nowhere. The wind is howling. I can hear one of the shutters on the front of the house banging. They actually work. Like if a hurricane was coming, we could close the shutters on the windows on the whole house and latch them. The doors have shutters, too, that work the same way.

Hurricane season is supposed to be over at the end of November, but the wind is blowing so hard that I wonder if there's such a thing as a rogue hurricane.

Or is it really not blowing at all outside? Is it sunny? Is this just all in my mind? Because of why I'm standing here in the kitchen . . .

I stare at the cordless house phone laying on the granite countertop.

I know it's going to ring. I know Sharon. I know she'll call again because she knows I'm home this time of day. Because I answered yesterday. And she'll keep calling until she gets me.

I wonder how Sharon got the number to our house. Then I shake my head because I can be such a dunce sometimes.

It probably wasn't too hard at all, because I know she knew who she kidnapped me from. She must have heard it on the news, read it in the newspaper. For all I know, she kept a newspaper clipping of her crime. She told me we left New Orleans when I was two. Translation: When I kidnapped you, we moved to Alabama. Sharon has known all these years that Dad and Harper Mom were wondering what happened to me.

When the phone rings, I'm not going to answer it. My gaze shifts to Sharon's knife roll on the counter. I used it last night and forgot to put it in the drawer where it lives now. Why should I answer the phone? She effed-up my life. She knew she would have to give me back someday. She had to have known. She had to have known that eventually she would get caught. She knew I would have to go home to my birth parents and I would miss her so much that—

Tears sting my eyes.

Why should I answer the phone? Sharon ruined her own life. *She* did this. And now she'll be in jail for years and years. I Googled it. Sentencing is complicated. The kidnapping sentences vary state to state and it matters whether or not you used a gun when you committed the felony. I wasn't sure if what she did was child abduction or kidnapping, but you can get, like, twenty-five years in prison for abduction. In twenty-five years, she'll be seventy-one years old.

So why should I answer the phone? She didn't just wreck her life and mine. Look at what she did to Harper Mom and Dad and Jojo. And Granddad and Dad's sister, Aunt Lucy, and his brother, Uncle Beau . . . There are more people in the family than I can even name yet. The day Sharon took me out of that stroller, she hurt them all. And it's damage you can never fix. You just have to get to know Harper Mom to know that.

So I shouldn't answer. Even though I know it's going to hurt Sharon. Doesn't she deserve to suffer like I'm suffering now? Like the Broussards suffered all these years?

I walk over to the coffee machine on the counter and get down my favorite mug. The ceramic white one with the little swirly circles on it. My hand is shaking. I slide it under the little stainless-steel spigot and turn on the coffee machine. It hums as it warms up and the display screen lights up.

Maybe I *should* answer the phone. So I can tell Sharon how pissed I am at her. How bewildering this all is to my little sixteen-year-old mind. I fight another wave of tears.

I don't understand my feelings for her. She kidnapped me. I should hate her. But I don't. I don't understand my feelings for the people in the house, either. For Harper Mom and Dad, who are trying so hard. Even for Jojo. Maybe I should answer the phone to tell Sharon how much this all hurts me. Hurts all of us here in this house.

I wish I had someone to talk to who isn't in the middle of this hurricane Sharon created. Someone who could tell me what to do. Maybe I could call the therapist we saw. She seemed okay. She'd know what to do; she went to college to study what to tell sixteen-year-old girls to do when the woman who abducted them calls to say she's sorry. Because I know that's what Sharon is going to say.

But what if the therapist calls Harper Mom and tells her Sharon called? I'll get in trouble for sure. And what will happen to Sharon? Which is kind of dumb to consider because what *are* they going to do to her? She's already in jail till she's old enough to collect Social Security. Are they going to put her in the hole? Solitary confinement. That's what they do to prisoners who don't follow the rules. Ruby and I watched a bunch of documentaries on Netflix about prisons. We loved prison documentaries. We saw all the ones on Netflix, ones about women's prisons, maximum-security prisons, even Russian prisons.

But could the therapist *legally* tell Harper Mom? Isn't there some kind of confidentiality thing? Like with lawyers. Because even if you confess to your lawyer that you killed somebody, they can't tell.

The only other person I can think of to call is my friend Ruby. But I can't call her, either. Because she was friends with Lilla Kohen and that girl is dead.

It's the only way I can make things make sense in my head. To tell myself Lilla Kohen is dead. So she doesn't have any friends anymore because dead people don't have friends.

Of course, that leads to the question of who I am now. Because clearly I'm alive. But I'm certainly not Georgina Broussard. That girl is two years old and loved Madeline books, according to Harper Mom.

Which is actually kind of crazy because when I was Lilla Kohen, *I* loved Madeline when I was little. Mom used to read the books to me all the time. I remember sitting on the leather couch with my floppy Madeline doll.

I suddenly feel dizzy, like the floor has shifted. Like in a fun house. I've never been in a fun house. I don't even know if there is such a thing anymore. But I've seen them on TV.

I definitely remember Mom reading to me about Madeline the little French girl on the leather couch that smelled good . . . only Sharon never had a leather couch. And I never had a Madeline doll. Sharon never bought me dolls, not even when I was little. She thought it was sexist to buy girls dolls. But I know I didn't imagine the Madeline doll . . . which means—I can't catch my breath. I stare at the coffee machine. I reach out and push the button for the double espresso.

I try to think. Hard. I remember how happy I was sitting on that couch, reading book after book. I remember holding my Madeline baby doll. And her voice. Mom's voice. I always associated that memory with Sharon's voice, but now I realize . . . maybe it wasn't hers. Which would mean it was Harper's . . . She's the mother I remember reading those books to me. She's the mother who gave me the doll. And the blanket with the bunnies on it. Tears blur my vision. I remember being little and asking Sharon about the blanket with the bunnies. She got a funny look on her face and just said it was gone.

I watch the espresso spurt out of the machine into the white mug. When it clicks off and the little message goes across the screen saying "Have a Nice Day," I reach for the mug.

Just as I pick it up, the house phone rings. It startles me so badly that I drop the mug. It hits the tile floor in an explosion of hot black coffee and shards of white ceramic.

I stare at the phone on the counter as if my laser gaze could make it combust.

It rings a second time. I hear the wind howling, the rain beating on the windows. I hear the shutter banging.

I'm not going to answer it.

I'm not going to talk to Sharon.

Not ever again.

It rings a third time.

If I don't pick it up now, the recorded greeting will play. *Please leave a message.* And you can't make a collect call that way, so Sharon won't be able to leave a message. She'd give up and she'll never call again.

I grab the phone and hit the "on" button. "Hello?" I whisper.

"Hello," says the female robot voice. "This is—"

I hear Sharon speak her name. The message goes on.

"Yes," I murmur into the phone when it asks if I'll accept the call.

There's a click and then it's like dead air. She doesn't say anything. But I know she's there.

I'm dizzy again. And I feel as if I'm going to throw up.

"Lilla?" Sharon says.

I press my back to the counter. I slide down until I'm seated on the cool tile floor that I can feel through my uniform skirt. I draw up my knees to my chest, hugging them. There's coffee everywhere and the smell is strong. There are little bits and big pieces of white ceramic in the coffee. I see the handle.

"Lilla? *Bubbeleh?*"

A Yiddish endearment, like sweetie. This girl in a Torah class I once took told me my mother was calling me grandma. But Sharon said the word has lots of meanings. Lots of spellings. She said it *could* mean grandma, but it actually means fritter. Like a fried sweet. She wrote it out for me in Yiddish. Sharon could write in Yiddish.

I don't know what to say because I want to call her Mom, but I can't. I can never call her that again. I don't think I can ever call anyone Mom again. "I'm here," I choke.

"Lilla . . ." It's an exhalation. "I'm so sorry. I never meant to—"

"You can't call here," I tell her in an ugly voice. "You can't do this to me and you can't do it to them."

"I know. I know, I just—"

"You just *what?*" I shout the last word.

She doesn't say anything and, for a second, I'm afraid she hung up. She doesn't have a right to hang up on me. I can hang up on her, but she can't hang up on me.

"You need to let me explain, Lilla. I was sick."

"You took me out of my stroller!" My voice is rough and filled with a rage of tears I'm fighting against. I don't want to cry because if I cry, I won't be able to tell her any of the things I've gone over and over in my head for weeks. "You took me from my mother!" Now I'm screaming.

"I know. I know." She's sobbing. "I'm so sorry. But, Lilla, I loved you. I always loved you and I took care of you. I—"

"It doesn't matter," I tell her, still shouting. "None of that matters! Because I wasn't yours to love!" I press the heel of my free hand to my forehead like I can somehow push her out. Erase all memory of her and our happiness.

We're both quiet for a second, but I can hear her crying softly. And I can hear voices in the background. Women talking. Prisoners.

"I just wanted to make sure you were okay," she says. "Are you okay, Lilla?"

"You mean with my *parents?* My *parents* who have loved me all these years and cried for me? They thought some pervert kidnapped me, sexually abused me, and buried me in the bayou! Do you have any idea—" I cut myself off, taking a deep, shuddering breath. Then I whisper, "I'm okay."

"You're okay," she pants, still crying.

"They're . . . good people." The lump rises in my throat again. I stare at the coffee all over the floor. The shattered mug. That's what I feel like. That mug, broken on the floor. How did this happen? Why did this happen? No sixteen-year-old girl should be sitting on a kitchen floor in the dark, talking to the woman who lied to her for fourteen years saying she was her mother.

"They're good people," she repeats, relief in her voice.

I hear a vibration and I look at my backpack on the center island. My cell phone.

"I have to go."

"No, Lilla, please. I—"

"She's calling me on my cell."

"I tried your—"

"Not that cell. I threw it away. I have a new cell, now. It's Georgina Broussard's. That's who I am now. Georgina Elise Broussard." I say it mean.

"I'm just glad you're okay," she tells me. "That's all that matters to me, Lilla. You have to believe me when I say that. I only care about you. I don't care about myself."

I get to my feet. Step over a puddle of coffee. "You can't call me, here, anymore. You'll get in trouble."

"You'll get in trouble?" she asks me, as if they would have no right to object.

I reach my backpack and search for my phone in the front pocket. "I'm saying *you'll* get in trouble if the police find out you're calling me."

"I don't care," she says. "I just wanted to hear your voice."

It's on the tip of my tongue to say, "Yeah, well, I didn't want to hear yours. Ever again." But I don't say it. I look at the screen on my cell. HM called. Harper Mom. It starts to vibrate again in my hand. "I have to go," I tell Sharon Mom. If I don't respond to Harper Mom, I bet she'll send the police, or at the very least come home.

"Can I call you again?" Sharon begs. "Please, *bubbeleh?*"

"No!" I close my eyes. "I don't know," I say with less certainty. I'm so confused.

"Are you home alone every day after school? When they're still at work?"

"No." I'm talking softly now. I feel kind of dreamy. "Not every day. Tuesdays. She's working later on Tuesdays, now. A new schedule." My cell's stopped ringing. I imagine I'll start hearing the SWAT team helicopters overhead at any moment.

"Is it okay if I call you again sometime? Some Tuesday?"

"I have to go." I grip the phone so tightly that my hand cramps. "Take care of yourself."

I move the house phone away from my ear. I hear her voice, but not what she says. I hang up and drop it on the counter. Then I text Harper Mom to tell her I was in the bathroom and not to call the state police or the FBI.

28

Harper

Propped on pillows, sitting up in bed, I take a sip of wine and flip the page in my book on my iPad. I love the weight of a real book in my hand, the feel of the pages as I turn them, but by evening, I find it hard to read a physical book. My eyes are scratchy and tired; I can't get the lighting right in my room. So last year I surrendered to my *advanced age*, downloaded a reader on my iPad, and refused to allow a long day to keep me from losing myself in the pages of a good book. Tonight I started a mystery set in Amish country not far from where I grew up in Pennsylvania.

I read another page and check the time on my phone. It's after nine and Remy's not home yet. He's missed dinner with us two nights in a row. He's missed two nights with the girls and me. He's got some big project going on at work, but I feel as if that's not what's keeping him out late. I think it's me. Of course, rationally, that makes no sense. We haven't even had a real argument. But he *has* seemed distracted for days, seemed emotionally distant. Not just from me but the girls, too. Even from Georgina.

I consider calling him, just to check in. To see how late he'll be. But I already texted him and he texted back that he'd let me know when he was on his way home. I texted him again to ask if I should save him a plate. He never responded. I made a conscious decision not to be suspicious. I refuse to live that way again.

I hear a tap at my open door and I look up. I'm expecting Jojo. She and I had a bit of a thing earlier. She wanted to know if she could go camping at Fountainebleau State Park with a girl from school. Who goes camping in February, even if they *are* staying in a cabin? She begged me to call Olivia's mother and get the details. I said there was no need for me to call because she wasn't going.

"Georgina," I say, setting my iPad down. I stifle my immediate impulse to barrage her with questions. How her day was. How the paper on *The Great Gatsby* is going. If she's made any new friends. I'm trying to take a step back and not *smother* her. That was the word Jojo used this evening when Georgina didn't come down to eat. Jojo said her big sister was hiding from me because I *smother* her. Of course I'd just told Jojo she wouldn't be going camping, so I know I should take her comment with a grain of salt.

Georgina stands in the doorway looking unsure of herself. I can't get over how beautiful she is, or how old she looks. She could easily pass for a Tulane student in Remy's sweatshirt she's wearing. Her beauty isn't cute; it's a mature beauty that I suspect she'll carry her entire life. She glances around my room, seeming to take it in. "How was your day at work?" she asks me. "Any adorable puppies come in?"

I doubt she's come to my room to ask me about puppies, but I'm so happy she's crossed my threshold that I don't care what we talk about. I only care that she's actually initiating a conversation. "Actually I *did* have a cute puppy. A well check." I sit up off my pillows, crossing my legs. "It was a Catahoula Leopard. You know what those are?"

She shakes her head.

"You don't?" I tease. "It's the Louisiana state dog. Look them up. It's a type of hound, well, technically a cur. Slender, spotted, with amazing blue eyes. We used to have one. When you were little."

"We used to have a dog?" She walks into my bedroom.

I pat my bed in invitation. "She was a blue merle. Her name was Sadie." Georgina's looking at me oddly and my first thought is that maybe she remembers our dog. That's something a little girl would remember, isn't it? I want to blurt out, "Do you remember her?" But Jojo's accusation whispers in my ear. "Want to see what they look like?" I ask instead.

I grab my iPad, close my book app, and go to an Internet search screen. My impulse is twofold. I want to show her a picture of what a Catahoula looks like, just in case it does nudge a memory, but I also want her to come closer. Even after having her home for weeks, I crave her: touching her, smelling her. I want so badly to hug her. She's made no indication she wants a hug from me, as of yet. I've resisted the urge to hug her anyway, sometimes having to physically force my arms to my sides. I feed my longing with a touch here or there when I hand her something, or by walking behind her and brushing her lightly on the back as I pass. She doesn't jump anymore, but she certainly hasn't thrown open her arms to me.

I adjust my reading glasses on my nose and type the dog breed into the search bar. I resist looking up when she sits on the edge of my bed, beside me. I want to take her hand. I want to kiss it. I hit the return key.

"I've always wanted a dog," she says. "Sharon wasn't into pets."

"We could—" I catch myself before I offer to run out and buy her one tonight. I've made a promise to myself to start treating her more like I treat Jojo. As if she hasn't left my sight since I gave birth to her. "I've been thinking about getting another dog. Our Buttons died last year."

"Boy or a girl?"

"Boy. He was a Pit-Catahoula mix. A rescue. I brought him home on impulse. Your dad had a fit. Long story, but Buttons turned out to be a good dog. He just didn't live long."

"What did he die of?" she asks.

I look up from the iPad, over the rim of my glasses. I feel as if something is going on with her, but I have no idea what. An issue at school? With Jojo? Or is she just missing Sharon and the life she led with her? Which I'm learning certainly had fewer rules.

When Georgina said she wasn't coming down for dinner tonight, I came up to see if she was sick. She said, through her closed door, that she wasn't. She said she just wasn't hungry and she had a lot of homework. I let it go. So I'm thrilled that she's come to me, now. To me, not Remy. It's the first time she's done it since she arrived.

"Buttons died of cancer. I had to euthanize him." I look down at the screen again, surprised by the emotion bubbling up. It's hard to believe I can get teary over losing a dog. I'm a veterinarian, for heaven's sake. And a mother who, for fourteen years, lived day to day with the horror of having had a child abducted.

I suppose humans have an amazing capacity for sadness. But I like to think that's true of joy, as well. I smile to myself at that thought.

"Do you think we should consider getting a dog?" I ask her. "They're a lot of responsibility. Not just feeding them, but walking them, playing with them."

"That would be nice." She hesitates. "But . . ."

She's glancing around the room again. My mother's radar is singing. Why's she so interested in the room, our dog?

"I don't know," Georgina goes on. "I'm going to college in less than two years. I don't know that I'm the one who should be saying we should get a dog. I won't be here to take care of it."

"Good point. I wish some of my clients were as thoughtful as you." I hand her my iPad. Her fingertips brush mine as I pass it off and I feel a little thrill. "Catahoula Leopard. Catahoula is a native Choctaw word. They're cattle dogs. Fifty to ninety pounds. They come in all sorts of colors and patterns, but they have a very distinct look. They're the only known domesticated North American dog."

She holds the iPad, studying it. I brought up pictures of blue merles.

"Georgina, do you remember Sadie?" I ask quietly.

She's still staring at the pictures. "I've seen these dogs before." She shakes her head. "But I don't remember her. Not here in the house."

But she keeps holding my iPad, staring, as if she wants to say something else. I make myself sit still. Stay quiet. And not touch her.

"Did I—" She closes her eyes. Exhales. "This is silly. I don't know what to call you." She suddenly sounds anxious, as if she's on the verge of tears. "I never call you by name because I don't know what to call you."

The pain in her voice chokes me up. I have to take a second before I speak. "I won't lie to you. I want you to call me Mom. Like Jojo. When you were little you called me 'mama.'" I give a little laugh. "But, Georgina . . . I understand if you can't do that. I do." I take a breath. "What do *you* want to call me?"

She opens her eyes. Now she's holding my iPad tightly against her chest, pressing it into the folds of her father's sweatshirt. "I . . . um . . . in my head, I think of you as . . . Harper Mom." She steals a glance at me.

"Harper Mom?" I slide my bare feet over the edge of the bed so I can sit beside her. Our thighs touch.

"Yeah, you know like . . . Sharon was my mom and now . . ."

"Ah. Sharon Mom. Harper Mom. I get it." I think for a moment. "Okay, so call me Harper Mom. Why not?" I shrug. "You called Remy by his first name for weeks." What I don't say is that she's calling him "Dad" now.

"But I never had a dad," she says softly, "so that's been easier."

I turn my head to look at her and she's looking at me. And I feel this amazing connection that I've dreamed of since she came home to us. Since she was born. I feel overwhelmed with happiness, but I keep it to myself, afraid I'll spook her and end this amazing moment. "Did you need something? When you came in?"

She looks straight ahead, still holding on to the iPad for dear life. "Yeah. I wanted to ask you . . . This is going to sound dumb, but . . . did I have a Madeline doll? From the books about the French girl. Floppy like a Raggedy Ann?"

I freeze. For a moment all I can do is stare at her. She remembers something? Of us? Of who she was before we went to that parade? I check myself. Will myself to stay calm and not burst into tears. Because lots of little girls have Madeline dolls. "You did," I say, watching her.

"And you read me the books?"

Tears spring into my eyes, but I don't cry. "I did." I press my lips together, feeling a little shaky. "'In an old house in Paris that was covered with vines,'" I recite, "'lived twelve little girls in two straight lines.'"

"'And the smallest one was Madeline,'" Georgina finishes.

We're both quiet and then I say, "Do you remember me reading the book to you?"

"I don't know," she murmurs, still not looking at me. "Because Sharon read it to me, too, but . . ." She slowly turns to me. Her voice is barely a whisper. "I think I remember the couch."

"The couch?"

"The leather couch in the parlor. Dad said it was old. Did . . . did you read to me there?"

I grin. We used to read in there all the time. "You remember the parlor?"

She shakes her head slowly as if to rattle the memories loose. "I don't know . . . Not the parlor, exactly, but . . . I remember the smell of the couch. The leather, I guess. And it was slippery."

I cover my mouth with my hand.

"And a bunny blanket." She shifts her gaze. She looks out into the room, but I don't think she's seeing the chifforobe in front of us. "Did I have a blanket with bunnies on it?"

I take a shuddering breath behind my hand. "You did," I say. "You'd had it since you were a newborn. It was just a little cotton blanket like . . . flannel. You wanted to bring it with you that day. To the parade." I stop. "Do you . . . do you want to hear this? Because . . . I don't have to tell you. I don't want to hurt you, Georgina. I don't want to bring up bad memories."

"I don't have any bad memories. I don't remember the parade. I didn't think I remembered you. I thought I only remembered Sharon." She looks at me again. "You said I wanted to take the blanket? That day?"

I nod. "I said no. I was afraid you were going to lose it. You'd lost it in a grocery store the week before. Your dad had to go back for it; luckily it was in the lost and found. Anyway, that day. The day of the parade, you threw a fit about the blanket, wanting to take it with us. I still remember standing by the back door with you in the stroller. You were already cranky and we hadn't left yet. Your dad offered to stay home with you and let me go to the parade, but it was supposed to be a family outing. I gave in and went back into the house for your blanket. I was usually pretty good about not giving in to you, but I was beat that day. Jojo was a fussy baby. She still wasn't sleeping at night. I just wanted you to stop fussing." I laugh though I'm fighting tears. "You were such a stubborn toddler, Georgina. You knew what you wanted and you weren't easily distracted or appeased."

"So I took my blanket to the parade?" She lowers my iPad to her lap.

"You sure did. And when . . . when Sharon took you, she left your blanket." I whisper the last words, the pain still so sharp that I can almost see the blood it draws. "That first night, all I could think of was that you wouldn't be able to sleep without your bunnies. The police used it to get a scent. They tried to use dogs to try to track where you'd been taken, but it didn't work." Now we're both staring at the chifforobe. Neither of us seeing it.

"Did the police keep it?"

"No. I have it. In a box in the attic." I think about offering to get it for her, to show her, but my instinct tells me not to offer. Not to put her in that position. It's too much for her, right now. When she asks, if she asks, that's when I'll find it for her. In the attic where there are boxes of her baby things. Next to boxes from her life with Sharon that Remy had delivered and carried upstairs.

We both sit there, side by side. Neither of us speaks for what seems like a very long time. Then she says very softly, "I'm sorry this happened to you."

When I turn to meet her gaze again, I see that her eyes are full of tears. I sniff. I want to put my arm around her, but I'm afraid to. Instead, I lower my head to her shoulder, just for a moment. And for now, it's enough. "I'm sorry it happened to us both," I whisper.

29

Jojo

"Please, Mom?" I don't want to whine. I know it's obnoxious. It just comes out that way.

"Jojo, could you give it a rest. Five minutes? Ten?" Mom stops in front of the pasta and stares at the shelves. "I'll give you twenty dollars if you just stop talking for five minutes."

Lilla's pushing the cart. She's not paying attention to where she's going and she almost runs into Mom, who did stop kind of short. I'd laugh if I wasn't so mad.

"I told you, Olivia's mom said to call her. She can give you all the details." I'm not giving up. I don't want her twenty dollars. I really want to go with Olivia and I'm tired of never being allowed to do things my friends get to do. I'm tired of being punished because some crazy woman kidnapped my sister. Not my problem. "It's only an hour away. It's like . . . a girls' weekend. Olivia's mom, and her sister who lives in Alabama, do it every year. Olivia's cousin always goes, too. No guys allowed. So you don't have to worry about a perv—"

"Josephine," Mom says sharply. She shakes a box of fettuccine noodles at me. "Is it necessary to talk that way in a public place?" She puts the box in the cart. "Why would you want to go if Olivia's cousin is going? You don't know her."

I put a bag of cookies in the cart that I've been carrying

around. "Mom." I drag the word out. "Would you listen, just for once? I told you, Olivia's cousin can't go this year. She has some kind of band trip. That's why Olivia invited me."

Mom starts walking down the aisle again. "You could invite Olivia to come stay the weekend with us." She adds two cans of crushed tomatoes to the cart. "We could do something fun."

"*Right.*" I look at Lilla. "Could you please talk to her? Please tell her she should let me go. I'm fourteen, for Christ's sake—"

"Josephine!" Mom whips around, somehow managing to holler at me while still speaking under her breath so as to not draw attention to us. "I will *not* have you take the Lord's name in vain. You know better."

I groan. "I'm sorry."

She's got that look on her face like she's about to get really mad at me. And I don't want that because once she gets really mad, there's no sense talking to her.

"I'm sorry," I say again. Then I add a quick, "Blessed be His name."

"Blessed be His name," Mom repeats quietly, crossing herself.

A lady in a blue pantsuit passes us in the aisle, going the other way. She doesn't even look at us so apparently she didn't hear me committing a sin. Or she doesn't care. The three of us just stand there, not saying anything. When the lady's gone, I loop my arm through Mom's and lay my head against her. "Tell me what I have to do to get you to let me go."

She looks down at me. "Makayla's not going?"

I shake my head. "Not invited." I let go of her. "Mom, I'm trying to make friends with girls Makayla isn't friends with. I'm trying to . . . expand my horizons."

Lilla gives this little laugh and I look at her. "You're my sister. You're supposed to be on my side, aren't you?"

Mom walks again.

Lilla pushes the cart. "You want my opinion, Harper Mom?"

I do this, like, double take. I've heard Lilla refer to Mom that way, but I've never heard her say it before. Usually she goes out of her way not to call her anything.

Mom catches the front of the cart and glances over her shoulder. "I'm not sure how many more opinions I can use today, but sure, what do you think?"

I look at Lilla. She looks at me. I nod my head up and down, like saying, "Go on. Tell her."

"She's fourteen years old," Lilla says. "When I was her age, I was walking home from school by myself, letting myself into our apartment, and making myself dinner. I went to the market by myself and did our grocery shopping. I went to summer camp for two weeks. It's what girls do when they're fourteen. Average girls."

Mom's looking at Lilla now, over the grocery cart.

"You want her to be normal, don't you?" Lilla leans on the cart. She's dressed just like me, in an Ursuline uniform. Basketball practice got cancelled so Mom picked us both up after school. I wanted to go home; I asked if Lilla and I could stay home while she went but that was a big, fat no. Then I asked if we could at least change before she made us go, but she said it was going to be a quick trip. Grocery store trips are never quick enough for me. "And you don't want her to go wild when she gets to college."

"Go wild?" Mom arches her eyebrows. But she's listening. Because it's Lilla speaking and not me. I wonder why I didn't think of this sooner. Maybe I can pay Lilla to tell Mom to let me do stuff.

Lilla shrugs, fiddling with two pomegranates in the seat of the cart. "You know, do crazy things when she gets out of the house: drink, skip classes, behave in a way you'd think was promiscuous. You can't control what she does when she goes to college and lives in a dorm."

"Who says I'm letting her go to college?"

Ha ha. Mom's idea of a joke.

"You need to know she can make good decisions," Lilla goes on. "And the only way kids learn to do that is to practice. Jojo isn't a fool. If you let her do some of the things she wants to do, she isn't going to screw up and jeopardize you letting her go somewhere or do something the next time she asks."

Mom's staring at Lilla. An old guy and an old lady go around us. He's all bent over, pushing the cart really slow. They're talking about cat food.

"I mean, has she ever done something wrong? Has she done anything to make you think she can't make good decisions on a family weekend? With someone whose kid goes to an all-girls Catholic school? Jojo said you guys know the family from your parish church."

"She was on that committee with you last year, Mom. Mrs. Birch was."

Mom glances at me, then back at Georgina. I can tell she's thinking. I hope she's considering letting me go.

"You spend a lot of time thinking about how to raise teenagers?" she asks Lilla.

"No. I just—It just makes sense. You give her a little line. If she makes a mistake, you can shorten it. If you trust her, she'll trust you enough to call you if she has a problem. She can always text you. You guys can come up with a password. That's what Sharon and I did. I didn't go to a lot of parties and stuff, but if I got somewhere where I was uncomfortable, I'd just text her the password and she'd call me and tell me I had to come home."

Mom is shaking her head. I can't tell what she's thinking. She probably doesn't like Lilla bringing up Crazy Woman's name. Or suggesting that maybe Crazy Woman wasn't completely crazy, that maybe she was actually a pretty good parent.

Mom turns around and starts walking again. "I'll talk to your dad about it tonight." She turns back. "Either of you hear from him today? He text you?"

We both shake our heads.

Something weird is going on with him. I don't know what. He's acting strange, like he's impatient with Mom. With us. He's getting annoyed about little things like the fact that the cupboard door is squeaking again and he's going to have to take the whole thing off its hinges. And his scooter is making a weird noise. He's been talking about that for a week.

Mom pulls her grocery list and pen out of her bag on her shoulder. "Okay, let's see . . . Got the veggies, the pasta, the lentils." She frowns. "Paper towels. I forgot the paper towels. You two want to go get your yogurt and I'll go back for the paper towels? I think nap-kins, too." She sounds distracted. "I can't keep track of who wants what flavors." She's marking off things on the list. "And I'll meet you up front?"

"Sure," Lilla tells her.

At the end of the aisle, Mom goes one way, we go the other. "Stay together," she calls over her shoulder.

"I'm going to college in Australia," I say under my breath.

Lilla pushes the cart. "Good luck with that."

Then we kind of just walk in silence. We're at the back of the grocery store so we're passing the aisles. We go by the bathroom-stuff aisle. "Need tampsies?" I ask her.

She looks at me like I'm nuts.

"You know," I say. "Tam—"

"I know what you mean," she interrupts. "I'm good. Thanks."

We pass the dog food aisle. I slow down so she can catch up with me. I walk beside her. "You told Mom I'm smart. Do you really think I'm smart, or were you just, you know, saying that?" I ask her. Then I stop and pick up a box of mini donuts. I act like I'm reading the ingredients, just so I don't look like I'm desperate for com-pliments or anything.

"Don't *you* think you're smart?"

Not an answer to my question. Which means she thinks I'm an idiot. Which I guess I am compared to her. I put the donuts in the cart and start walking again.

"Yes, you're smart, Jojo. Of course you're smart. I think some-times that you don't want anyone to know it."

I don't say anything, but I'm kind of happy she thinks I'm smart. Because everybody knows she's super smart. She'd know, wouldn't she?

"You need to pay more attention in class. And do your own

homework," she adds. She's leaning on the cart now, pushing it slowly. "College will be here before you know it. I'm already signed up to take my SATs. You have any idea what you'd like to study . . . in Australia?"

I catch her eye and I see she's joking. I smile, sort of. I want to tell her, but I don't want her to laugh at me. I hesitate and then blurt it out. "I want to be a lawyer. But you have to go to law school to do that. What do you study in college if you want to go to law school?"

She moves her mouth one way and then the other, like she's thinking. We've reached the dairy stuff against the wall. "I don't know. We'd have to Google it."

I nod. That hadn't occurred to me. I use Google all the time, but mostly to find videos of kittens dancing to Beyoncé songs and stuff like that.

"You should talk to Dad. He went to Tulane intending to go to law school. You know, because that's what Broussards do." She stops in front of the yogurt and we both walk over to stand in front of the refrigerator shelves to pick what we want. "But I guess he was really into numbers." She grabs two yogurts. Vanilla. Yuck. "And he just told his dad he didn't want to go into the family business."

"Wow." I look at her. "I didn't know that. His dad must have gone nuts. Because Uncle Beau was already in law school by then. And Aunt Lucy, she was going to be a lawyer, too."

"I don't know." Lilla shrugs and looks at me. "He didn't act like it was a big deal. But I bet everybody in the family would like it if one of the kids wanted to be a lawyer. And you'd have a place to work when you graduated. If you wanted to do the stuff they do like wills and property settlements and such. They don't do much criminal law."

I smile and reach for my favorite yogurt: banana and honey. I like the kind with the sprinkles or chocolate cookie crumbles that go on top, but I know Mom will have something to say about that, so I don't get those. "How about you?" I ask. "What do you want to be?"

She stands there, a yogurt in each hand. "This is going to sound a little spooky, but I always thought I might like to be a lawyer. But maybe like one who does . . . I don't know, immigration stuff. Or maybe ACLU cases."

"Wait." I drop my yogurts into the cart. I'm not even sure what ACLU cases are, but I don't really care this minute. "You wanted to be a lawyer and you didn't know everybody in our family except Dad is a lawyer? That the Broussards have been lawyers in New Orleans for more than a hundred years?"

"Not everybody." She grabs one more yogurt and starts pushing the cart again. "Our mother's a veterinarian."

"I would never want to do that." I make a face of disgust. "I'm not getting near a dog's butt."

Lilla laughs, and even though I know she's laughing at me, I laugh, too.

30

Harper

We manage to get through our Friday family meeting over pizza in the kitchen and the girls scatter afterward. Leaving Remy and me to do what little cleanup is needed, which is okay because we've all been so busy all week that I don't feel as if we've had a moment alone together.

The family meeting, despite the groaning and moaning from all three of them, went pretty well and we had some decent discussions. It's official, we're staying home for Mardi Gras. We decided that Remy will take the girls to uptown parades on Sunday and Lundi Gras, which is the Monday before Fat Tuesday. While I hide at home in a dark room, possibly under my bed. Then they'll make a decision as to whether or not they'll go to the French Quarter for Mardi Gras. Which would be a logistical nightmare, but I agree to stay out of that conversation, should the three of them choose to have it.

In exchange for parade privileges, they've all agreed to go to Mass Ash Wednesday with me. I was surprised Georgina didn't put up an argument. So far, the only time she's been in a church is when she's expected to attend at school. Due to her special circumstances, only her presence there has been required and she's even been allowed to sit in the back.

I've been agreeing to let Georgina go to temple when she

wants. Interestingly enough, she skipped twice, and tomorrow morning she has plans with her new friend Em. Which means she's not going to temple. I'm not sure what's up with that. I've decided not to bring it up for now and see how things unfold. I really want to have her take a confirmation class, at least to educate her on the beliefs she was born into, but I've decided to wait on that. I haven't even brought it up with her yet. Baby steps.

"Wine?" Remy's already gotten a glass down for himself. His tone suggests it may have been the second time he asked me.

"Sure." I'm folding up a pizza box to go into the recycling bin. I make a concerted effort to push aside all the things whirling around in my head and be in the moment. "Want to sit out on the porch? It's a nice evening. You guys might get lucky and have warm weather for Mardi Gras." Secretly I'm hoping it rains. Hail would be nice. Maybe they'll cancel the parades if it hails.

"Still more than a week away." He gets another glass down and opens a drawer. I hear him digging around in it.

"Jojo really wants to do this weekend thing with Olivia," I say. She'd made yet another plea, at the family meeting, providing written information: a physical address and Web site address to the park; cell number for Olivia, her mother, and her aunt; as well as a projected itinerary. I suspect Georgina was in on the prep work. I can't decide if I'm tickled she's siding with her sister or annoyed. Without Georgina, Jojo's presentation might not have been as impressive.

Remy is still digging through the utensil drawer. "Have you seen my opener? The one I like?" He closes the drawer harder than need be.

I walk over, open the drawer he was just in, spot the bottle opener under a spatula, and hand it to him.

"How do you do that?" he asks, without a thank-you. "How do you *always* do that? I can look in the pantry for the peanut butter for five minutes and you walk over and pick it up."

"It was right there."

"Do you hide things?" he asks, sounding serious.

"I do not hide things so I can find them for you." I go to the trash can and pull out the bag. I can't stand the smell of old pizza the next morning. I glance at Remy as I replace the bag. "What do you think about letting her go?"

"What?" He's peeling away the foil on the bottle, his back to me.

"The weekend with Olivia. What do you think?"

He pops the cork. "You already know what I think."

He's been testy with me since he got home. All week. No, it started last week. And I have no idea why. I know he gets frustrated with me, with my anxiety. But I'm trying. I'm trying so hard and I don't feel as if he's giving me credit for that.

"You didn't speak up at dinner. You never said a word about her going camping."

He cuts his eyes at me, picks up the bottle and the two glasses, and walks out of the kitchen.

I stand there looking at the empty doorway. I'm really tempted to skip the wine and cranky Remy and to go to bed and read my book. I've been thinking about the Amish characters all day, trying to figure out who killed the blacksmith. I'm not sure I feel like dealing with Remy tonight. But I know that's not right. I'm the one who suggested he move back in. I'm the one who initiated this whole "try again" thing with our marriage. If he invites me to sit and have a glass of wine with him, I need to do it.

I take out the garbage, leaving it in one of the cans outside. Back in the kitchen, I wash my hands, dry them, and flip the light off on the way out. At the bottom of the staircase, I holler up to the girls, "We're on the front porch."

No one answers. I hear music. Something obnoxious. It has to be Jojo. I've seen Georgina wearing earbuds, connected to her phone, but I don't know what kind of music she's listening to, if she's listening to music at all. For all I know, she might be listening to NPR news. Or a podcast. She and Remy were talking about different podcasts at dinner.

I walk out onto the front porch and take a deep breath of the warm, humid air. I'm in jeans, a long-sleeved Life Is Good T-shirt, and my slippers, and I'm comfortable. It's hard to believe summer is just around the river bend again.

But suddenly the evidence is everywhere. The azaleas in the flowerbeds are beginning to bloom in bright pinks and white. Our neighbor's Chinese fringe tree is popping with blossoms, too. I inhale again, trying to be in the moment and enjoy the last rays of the sun as it sets. Trying to enjoy the pleasure of having my two daughters safe upstairs doing their homework and having wine with my husband.

I had a good day today. I worked in the morning, then came home to do some housecleaning and went for coffee at Ann's. I resisted the urge to walk to Ursuline so I could walk Georgina home. Okay, Ann was the one who suggested I stay put. But then Georgina texted me when she left school and we met on the sidewalk between Ann's and home. We walked together and we talked about her driving my car. Luckily she can't drive alone yet. I'm not sure how we're going to deal with the fact that Lilla Kohen had an intermediate license and already passed the written and driver's exam, but Georgina Broussard was actually not old enough to do so at the time. I may have to have Remy's sister look into that one.

I glance at him. He's taken a seat in one of the rocking chairs. He hasn't poured the wine yet; he's letting it breathe. I gave up years ago telling him I couldn't tell the difference between the taste of wine that has breathed and the wine that hasn't.

I sit in the chair beside him. We both rock and look out at the park. I could sit here for hours and stare at the lush grass that's already turning a brighter green, and the huge grandfather oaks that serve as our front yard. I watch a girl, a college student probably, with her dalmatian, cut between the trees. She's talking on her phone. I can't hear what she's saying, but whomever she's talking to, he or she is getting an earful.

I glance at Remy. "I've missed you this week," I say.

He runs his hand over his face. His hair is looking a little shaggy; he needs a haircut. Which isn't like him. He's always been very attentive to personal hygiene. His beard is always neatly trimmed and he gets his hair cut regularly.

"The job still hasn't posted and Richard hasn't said a word," Remy says. "Maybe he isn't retiring."

He's talking about the comptroller's position at Tulane. He's been eyeing it for years and I think his boss, Richard, has been dangling it like a carrot in front of him. Remy has worked a lot of late nights and Saturdays in the hopes of getting that job someday. "But he mentioned it Fourth of July," I say. "I heard him telling someone. And you said his wife told you they were thinking about moving back to Alabama. When was that? The Christmas party?"

He shrugs.

"So ask Richard if he's planning on retiring."

"I'm not asking him," he grumbles.

I sit there for a moment trying to decide if I should let him just be in a bad mood or if I should try to get him to talk about it. The thing is, Remy has insisted, in the past, that talking things out isn't always the best option. Not for everyone. He prefers to mope in his own funk until he's ready to climb out of it. And in the past, both before and after the divorce, I've usually been willing to go along with that. But this is a new chapter in our lives. And I don't want Remy to be unhappy.

"What's up with you?" I reach over and cover his hand with mine.

He takes it, but not with much enthusiasm.

"Nothing."

"Remy." I exhale. "You worked late three nights this week and even when you were here, you weren't really here. And we haven't had sex in"—I think back—"more than a week."

He picks up the bottle of wine and pours two glasses. I accept the one he offers. Give him a minute. Then another. He sits there silently and watches his cabernet swirl in his glass.

Now he's beginning to tick me off. He says nothing is wrong, yet clearly there is. When he's acting like this, he usually has something to tell me that he doesn't want to tell me. "Did you find your gym bag?" I ask. I've been wanting to ask for days.

"I'm sorry?" He sips his wine.

"Last week, you couldn't find your gym bag. You thought it might be at your apartment." I try to keep my mind from going there, but it goes there anyway. "What made you think your bag might be there?"

He's staring straight ahead. Shadows are falling. I wonder if it's the sun setting or it's only happening on this porch.

"What were you doing at the apartment?" I ask. Then I voice what I really want to know. I know I shouldn't say it, but it comes out as ugliness sometimes does. "Were you there alone, Remy?" I take a sip of the wine, but don't really taste it.

He doesn't say anything.

"Remy, I know we're not married anymore, but if you think you're going to live in this house with our girls . . ." I turn in my chair to face him. "If you think you're going to sleep in my bed and bang some—"

"That was ten years ago," he says quietly, still staring straight ahead. "A mistake. I told you that. I apologized. I confessed, I did all the things I was supposed to do, Harper." He strokes his beard with his thumb and index finger. "I was there alone."

And now I feel guilty for saying it. For thinking it. For suspecting him for even a moment. I love Remy. And I forgave him a long time ago for his infidelity. We went to marriage counseling and we talked with our priest. Forgiveness is essential to a marriage. I know that. And so is trust. And I *do* trust him. I do. I don't know what made me say it. Think it.

Fear?

"Remy, I'm sorry," I say. "I just—" I look down at the floorboards. "I don't have a good excuse."

"I had to let somebody in to fix the hot water heater."

"You don't have to tell me that, Remy." I look at him, feeling guilty as hell. "You really don't have to—"

"And one night, I just went there for a couple of hours to eat a Hot Pocket and read."

Under different circumstances, I would have laughed about the Hot Pocket. I think they're gross, but he likes them. A couple of weeks ago he asked me if I would buy him some and I told him they were bad for his cholesterol. But this isn't about me not buying the snack foods he likes. "You needed to be alone?"

He glances at me and I realize he doesn't just look shaggy, he looks tired. "I needed some down time," he says. "Without anyone needing anything from me. Okay?"

I shift in the chair and sit back. I rock and think that over. I sip my wine. I've always thought of Remy as being so together. A superman. Maybe because so much of my life has been a mess over the years. Maybe because he's been my superman time and time again. "What can I do to help?"

"For one thing, you can make some decisions on your own," he says, surprising me with his eagerness to tell me what I'm doing wrong. "I don't care what kind of pizza we order. I don't care if you wash my shirts today or tomorrow. And you could stop going over and over things. Dissecting Lilla's every sentence. Her every move. Always trying to analyze her motivation." He presses his thumb and index finger to his temples as if he has a migraine. As if I'm causing his migraine. "Harper, if you could stop talking things to death, that would help. Seriously, how many times do we have to talk about Jojo going for a sleepover? It's just one damned night."

He raises his voice. Remy never raises his voice. I want to remind him that it's for two nights, but I don't.

"And this whole religion thing, with Georgina?" He gets to his feet and points toward the front door. "She thinks she's Jewish. She was raised Jewish. You can't take her from the person in her life who loved her most, bring her into a house full of strangers, and then try to introduce her to a man who supposedly died, nailed to a cross for her, two thousand years ago!"

I'm taken aback by the anger in his voice. And hurt by his smart-ass summation of my beliefs. His. "I just wanted to go to Mass as a family." I throw up my hand. "I don't think that's too much to ask, Remy. Do you think that's too much to ask?"

He turns his back to me and rests his hands on the porch railing. He's quiet. "No," he says finally. But he doesn't turn around to look at me. "It's not too much to ask, Harper." He's quiet for a moment and then goes on. "Look, as far as this thing about religion. I don't think this is something we're going to solve overnight, but I don't think there's anything wrong with you asking Lilla to sit in the pew with us once in a while."

I set down my wine and get out of the rocker to go stand beside him. "Remy, what's going on with you?" I reach up to stroke his cheek. "*Really?*"

He presses the heel of his hand to his forehead. "It's me, it's not you." He says it in an exhalation. "You're doing so well, Harper. With the girls. With Lilla. I just—" He halts midsentence, either unable to express himself or unable to tell me what he wants to tell me.

I meet his gaze. "You just what?" I ask softly. "Tell me what you're thinking."

"I'm afraid this isn't working." He scrapes at a chip of paint on the railing with his thumbnail. Something always needs painting on an old house in New Orleans. "I wonder if I should move out."

I stare at him, feeling the tiniest crack in my heart. "What isn't working?" I whisper. "We have our family again. We have our girls and we have each other." I search his handsome face, the face I've loved since I was old enough to love a man. "*Is* it me? Don't you . . . Remy, don't you love me anymore?"

He puts his arm around me and pulls me against him and I exhale with relief.

"Of course I love you. You're the mother of my children."

Not exactly what I was hoping for.

"It's just that . . ." He looks down at me and then out at the park that is now suddenly heavy in shadows. "Harper . . . this is harder than I thought it was going to be. With Georgina. With being here. With trying to do my job, and be a husband, and be a father, and . . ." He sighs loudly.

I press my lips together, willing myself not to start crying because he used Georgina's name. Her real name. "But you're so good with Georgina. She adores you, she . . . I think she already

loves you, Remy. It would break her heart not to have you here."
I hesitate. "She doesn't even know we're divorced."

"Not one of our better parenting decisions," he says, still holding me against his side.

"Maybe not," I agree. "I know we need to tell her. I think she
has a lot to deal with right now, though."

"Right," he says.

I slide my arm around his waist and rest my head against his
chest. I say a silent prayer and then I feel a little better. "We're
going to be okay, Remy," I say softly, thinking about what Ann
had said. About knowing I was going to be okay. "Life isn't supposed to be easy."

"I know." He kisses the top of my head. "I'm sorry."

"For what?" I look up at him.

"I don't know. For not . . . for not being who you need me
to be."

"You're my husband. You're the father of my children. That's
all I need from you."

He looks out into the darkness that's slowly enveloping the
park, the house, our porch. "That's all you need, is it?"

31

Lilla

I sit in the attic on a cardboard box marked "textbooks" in Sharpie. I wonder if there are really textbooks inside, or if there are baby toys from when Jojo and I were little. I remember all the mismarked boxes in the house in Bayou St. John and the thought makes me smile. But it's a sad smile.

I'm studying two photographs in my hands. Baby pictures of me. One of baby Georgina I took out of the family photo album downstairs. One of baby Lilla from a box Dad had brought here from the house in Bayou St. John. He meticulously labeled the boxes; I've only opened one, the one that said "photos," but the contents reflected the label.

I stare at the photographs, one in each hand. I guess I'm not really a baby in them. A toddler would be a more accurate description. The photo of Georgina is dated two days before Sharon kidnapped me. I'm wearing leggings and a long-sleeved green Tulane T-shirt. I'm laughing, a blue balloon in my hands. It looks like it was taken in the back of the house near the crepe jasmine bush. The other photograph is of Lilla, taken two weeks later, according to the date on the back. I can't believe Sharon's gall. She abducted me, took me to another state, and then she dressed me up in what looks like a party dress and snapped a photo of me. Pretended I was hers. I'm not smiling. I look sad.

Why can I not remember her stealing me? How did I grow up to like her so much? To love her. *How did that happen?* Being here now, I realize how small my life with her was. With no family, it was only ever the two of us. We didn't have anyone else, which I suppose made us closer.

She *said* we had no family. The grandparents died in the Holocaust. She said she was an only child and that her parents were, too. She said they died when she was twenty. In a car accident. She always told me, when I asked questions, that she didn't want to talk about them because it made her too sad. Now I wonder if she didn't want to talk about them because everything she told me was a lie. Is she really Jewish? Maybe she has a brother and a sister. Maybe her parents are still alive. Do they know their daughter is in prison for abducting and holding a minor?

I hear footsteps on the attic stairs. "Georgina?" It's Harper Mom. "You up here?" She appears at the top of the stairs, first her head, then her body. "Whatcha doing?"

"Just looking at stuff. Dad said it was okay."

"The things he had brought from the house?" She points to another box; I can't read from where I'm sitting what it says. "Okay if I sit?"

I nod. "I found some pictures Sharon took of me when I was little." I hold the one in my left hand tightly, not sure if I want to show her. Little Lilla looks so sad. It almost seems wrong to invade her privacy this way, to share her sadness. It seems even more wrong to show the baby's mother. I offer it to her.

She studies the photo for a long time. I watch her. Her eyes tear up. She flips it over and I see by the look on her face that the date registers. She flips it back to look at sad Lilla again. "The police said you lived in Alabama first."

"Mobile, I think. Less than three hours away." I say it softly as if that will somehow ease the blow.

"I can't believe you were so close," she muses. "Pretty dress." She hands back the photo, which surprises me a little. I thought there might be a good chance she would rip it up. Or at least confiscate it.

"And me before—before," I say in an exhalation. I hand her the other photo. "I found it downstairs, in one of the family albums."

She smiles, but her smile, like mine had been, is sad. "I remember taking this. Your dad offered to walk with Jojo so I could get out of the house. She'd been screaming bloody murder all day." She gives a little laugh. "You kept putting your hands over your ears and telling me to 'make the sister stop.'"

She presses her lips together. She's pretty, my mother. Her blond hair is sleek and golden and she doesn't have any wrinkles on her face. Shouldn't a woman her age have wrinkles? Sharon had wrinkles. I know Harper Mom wears makeup, but you can't tell. And her green eyes, they're really green. Like Jojo's . . . and Granddad's.

"You and I went outside," she goes on as if it's a bedtime story. "You'd gotten the balloon at a birthday party that Saturday. A little girl from church. I thought for certain you'd pop it before you got home, but you didn't. That day, we batted it around in the garden and you laughed and laughed. I could hear Jojo crying, but it was okay because you were laughing."

I'm staring at her and not the photo. "Why don't I remember?" I whisper.

She keeps looking at the photo. I can tell she's trying not to cry and I feel bad. She's been crying because of me for fourteen years. And now Sharon's crying. In her prison cell. How can I only be sixteen and already have caused so much unhappiness?

"Why don't I remember her taking me from you?" I ask her.

"You were so little, Georgina, and . . ." She meets my gaze and though her eyes are watery, she's not crying. It's weird, but ever since I got here, I've been thinking of Dad as the strong one, but looking at her face, I think she's strong, too. Just a different kind of strong. The kind of strong moms seem to be.

"A lot of people don't remember being two," she goes on.

"But I remember being two with Sharon," I argue.

She does that thing again where she presses her lips together, making them thin lines. "Maybe you didn't remember as a way of . . . protecting yourself. The human brain is an amazing organ, the most complex in the body. I think maybe your mind blocked those memories." She's smiling again, that sad smile. "So you could be happy in the circumstances you found yourself in."

I stare at the photo of Lilla in my hand. "With the woman who kidnapped me from my mother? Who lied to me and told me *she* was my mother?"

Harper Mom doesn't say anything and we're both quiet for what seems like a long time. Then I say, "I think I remember the cake baby." I glance at her. "I think I remember it in my hands. How it felt. I thought it was bigger," I muse. "I liked it. Did you let me play with it?"

"I did. When we were out and you would get restless, I'd pull it out of my handbag and give it to you. In line at the market, the bank, in slow traffic. You'd be in the backseat in your car seat and you'd ask for it and I'd give it to you. My mother kept telling me I shouldn't let you play with it. She said it was a choking hazard. I told her you were smart enough not to try to eat it. She said you would lose it, an antique given to me by my grandmother. But you never did." She hands me back the photo and stands up. "I'd like to see some more pictures of you sometime. If you'd let me." She hesitates. "I won't come up here and look on my own, although I'll admit to you I've thought about it. But I won't do it. I'll respect your privacy. And hope that . . . that someday you will want to share them with me."

I nod. I'm not ready to look at any more photos today. I'm already too upset. I feel like crying. Or screaming. I feel like crying and screaming at the same time. I keep thinking about Sharon. I purposely avoided being home this Tuesday. I don't know if she tried to call. I keep going back and forth between never wanting to speak to her again and feeling like I need to talk to her. Because she owes me an explanation. As stupid as it seems, I think she owes me an apology. But I almost feel as if I want to see her. Need to see her. One last time. Because I know I need to be a Broussard now, become one, but I feel as if there's something holding me back. Like tugging on my sleeve every time I manage to take a step forward. I think she's the one holding me back. My anger toward her is holding me back. My love for her. Because no matter how hard I try to hate her, how many lists I make of the reasons I *should* hate her, I can't do it. Because she really did love me. And I'm reminded of that every time I use one of her knives.

I look up at Harper Mom. "I want to ask you something," I hear myself say. "And . . . I don't want you to answer me right now. I want you to think about it. Talk to Dad."

"Okay." She stands there waiting.

"I want to . . . I feel like . . ." I exhale. Maybe this isn't a good time to bring this up. Maybe I should bring it up with Dad, sometime when we're by ourselves. Or maybe . . . at a family meeting, or maybe when we go together for counseling. We're supposed to go again Friday. Well . . . we *were* supposed to go. That's up in the air now because Jojo finally got Harper Mom to agree to let her go camping for the weekend with her friend and then found out she had the wrong date. They're going this coming weekend, and it turns out they won't be back until Wednesday because they go to avoid Mardi Gras every year.

I look at Harper Mom, then at my old flip-flops on my feet. I found them in one of the boxes Dad packed at the house in Bayou St. John. He did a good job, choosing which things to keep for me.

"I want to see her. I need to see Sharon," I blurt out.

Suddenly she looks pale.

"I . . . I feel like I need, I don't know, closure." I stand. "She and I, we never got to talk about what she did. The police came into our house, asked her if I was really her daughter, and she just . . . confessed. And then they took me out of the house and they never let me speak to her again." I make myself look at her. I'm feeling that anger again. I'm angry at Sharon. At the cops. At Harper Mom and I don't even know why I'm mad at her. "They should have let me talk to her. One last time, at least."

Harper Mom stands there looking at me. "I can't let you go to a prison and see her."

"Why not?" I demand. I open my arms, a photo in each hand. A distinctly different life in each hand. And here I am, stuck in the middle. "Don't you think I have a right to ask for a . . . an explanation from her?"

"I don't think it would be a good idea. I don't . . . I don't know that it would be healthy, Georgina."

"What right do you have to make that decision for *me?*" I'm not hollering at her like I did that day in the living room, but I'm sure she has no doubt I'm pissed.

"What *right* do I have?" she asks me, sounding surprisingly calm. "I'm your mother. That's what *right* I have." She turns around and heads for the staircase. "Your dad asked me to tell you to come down for dinner. It's almost ready."

32

Harper

I run my finger over a rusty brass bin pull, trying to make out its intricate design. "How about this one?" I hold it up to show Ann.

We're at one of my favorite stores in New Orleans. It's an architectural salvage warehouse in Mid-City. Ricca's has been around since the fifties; the family has made a business of going into homes that were scheduled for demolition and taking doors, windows, shutters, and every kind of hardware you can imagine, for resale. I like the idea of being able to keep a little bit of history of an old house when it can't be saved. It's a way of preserving Louisiana's history, too. Whenever I need so much as a hinge for our house, this is the first place I come.

Ann and I shop here regularly. George owns an interior design company and even though Ann doesn't work for him, she likes to shop for him. She enjoys finding interesting pieces of history he can incorporate into old and new homes. She also buys items for herself for her art. You never know what you'll find at Ricca's; our garden water fountain came from here.

Today Ann's looking for drawer pulls and doorknobs to create a piece of artwork for a restaurant, using a door as her canvas. Apparently she's going to attach all these old pieces of hardware onto a massive paneled door she bought here a few weeks ago. I'm having a difficult time imagining this piece of *artwork*, but

I'm always game for a trip to Ricca's. And I'm a little down in the dumps, as I always am around Mardi Gras. I'm hoping our outing will lift my spirits.

Ann studies the drawer pull I'm holding up for her through a pair of wild-looking readers that have faux jewels glued on them. Another piece of her artwork. "Put it in the maybe pile," she instructs.

I go back to digging in the wooden box across from hers. "Jojo texted me as soon as they arrived at the campground last night. Then again this morning. It sounds as if she's having a good time. She actually thanked me for making her take her hoodie."

"Makayla talked to her briefly last night. She said the same thing." Ann glances at me over the top of her wacky glasses. "Olivia's a nice girl. Nice family. You did good, sweetie."

I groan. "I can't believe after the stink Jojo made over not going on vacation, on wanting to go to a parade, she just sashayed out of town." I gesture with a cut-glass doorknob I'm adding to the definitely pile.

Ann laughs. "She's fourteen. I'd expect no less of her." She holds up a tiny knob that looks like some kind of bird. "Too weird?"

"Yes."

She laughs and adds it to the definitely pile. "But Remy and Lilla are still going."

I frown, looking at her. "*Et tu, Brute?*"

She meets my gaze. "She wants to be called Lilla."

"I named her Georgina," I counter firmly.

"You need to decide how important this is to you, sweetie. Because . . ." She holds up a pretty white glass doorknob and then adds it to the pile of yeses on top of an upended cardboard box. "I think you might get a lot of mileage giving in on this one. Couldn't you just pretend it's her nickname? I mean, I'm sure George's mom doesn't particularly like Skeeter, but that's what everyone has always called him."

"I should call Georgina by the name her abductor gave her?" I ask, knowing I shouldn't be annoyed with her, but annoyed anyway.

She sighs and keeps digging. We're both wearing disposable blue gloves I brought from the office. We'll still feel like we need a shower when we get home. While the warehouse certainly isn't dirty, it seems as if there's a thin layer of dust and time over everything. The place has that distinct antique store smell, too. "I suppose I'm saying I think you should pick your battles."

"And I have," I say stubbornly. I hold up a drawer pull, reject it, and dig in again.

"Need any help, ladies?" a young woman asks, walking by us. She's wearing a Ricca's T-shirt.

"No thanks," I say cheerfully.

"*Holler* if you do," she sings, waving her hand over her head.

"So while we're on the subject of Sharon Kohen," I tell Ann when the employee's gone, "listen to this. Georgina wants to go to the prison and see her."

Ann looks up. "You're kidding."

I shake my head. "Indeed not."

"You going to take her?"

I look at her as if she's lost her mind. Which she has. "No!" I don't mean to shout it, but it comes out that way.

A young woman considering a pair of shutters behind us looks at me; she has a tattoo of a python wrapped around her left leg. I force a smile. She walks on without returning the gesture.

"No," I say more quietly. "I'm not taking her to see that woman. That woman is never going to see my daughter again. She's never going to get her hands on her. She's never going to—"

"You're right about that," Ann interrupts. She leans against a glass display case with a sign taped to it reading, *Please do not lean against glass*. "She's never going to get her hands on her because she's not even eligible for parole for what? Twenty? Thirty years?"

I suddenly feel tired. And old. I feel as if everyone thinks I'm crazy. Remy certainly does. My girls do. And I guess Ann, too. But I'm *not* crazy. It's not crazy to want to use the name you gave your child at birth. It's not crazy to want to keep her from the monster that kidnapped her.

"She hasn't been sentenced yet."

"What's Remy say?"

I toss the pull in my hand back into the wooden bin and go to stand beside her. I decide to be a rebel and lean against the glass case. "I haven't talked to him about it," I admit. "I'm sure he'll be all in for it, though." I shouldn't be sarcastic, but I can't help myself. I'm irritated with him. Angry with him. He hasn't been himself and I think, deep down, I'm scared. I keep thinking about our conversation on the porch last week. He brought up moving out and I can't bear to think about the possibility. Not after all we've been through. Not now, now when Georgina's come home to us. I've dreamed of this family, the four of us, for all these years, and now we have it and he wants to bail?

"Remy, he's . . ." I scratch the back of my neck trying to figure out how to express what I'm feeling, which is hard because I'm not sure. Ann knows all about the porch conversation, but she and I haven't talked in a couple of days, except to check kids' schedules and make plans for today. Two ships passing in the night. Much like a long-married couple with teenagers. "I can't figure out what's going on in his head and he won't tell me. All of a sudden he seems, I don't know. Overwhelmed?"

"With work?"

"Yes. No." I raise my blue latex-gloved hands and let them fall. "With me, with the girls. The house. But this is what worries me"—I turn to look at her—"things are better with us. With him and I. Since Georgina came home. Things are good. I'm good. I'm the one who made him nuts all these years and now I'm better. I'm *so* much better. I let Jojo go out of town with a girlfriend. Me."

"You are better," Ann agrees.

"I think about all the things Remy had to put up with all these years," I go on. "How many times he got me through a holiday . . . or just an ordinary day." I gesture with both hands, pleading. "How can he be overwhelmed *now?*"

She's quiet for a moment, then she says softly, "Do you think he's seeing someone?"

I cross my arms over my chest. I stare at a beautiful stained-glass window hanging from wire from the ceiling. It's a bargain at $325. "He said he isn't."

"Do you think he's seeing someone?" she repeats.

"No." I shake my head slowly. "I don't." I give a halfhearted laugh. "He couldn't possibly have time between work and home and now we're doing this family counseling thing and . . ." I sigh.

Ann steps back up to the bin she was looking through. She's quiet. Which worries me.

I move to stand across the wood box from her. "Do you know something I don't?"

She shakes her head.

"Ann?" It's a plea.

She looks up. "I don't know anything about what Remy is doing or not doing."

"But you guys are close."

"Not like we used to be," she says thoughtfully. "Certainly not since Georgina came home. We had pizza together that one night when you guys came over, but I haven't really seen him."

"I suppose we haven't really seen much of each other, have we? As a family. Not like we used to." I think about it for a moment. "I suppose we've just been busier—you know, having Georgina home. Increasing our family by twenty-five percent."

"Technically, you've increased it by fifty percent. Because Remy came home."

"Right." I pick up several pieces of hardware and reject them for different reasons. I think about what Remy said about us needing to tell Georgina about the divorce. I agree that we need to tell her, but how do you have that conversation? "Oh, by the way, honey, your dad doesn't really live here. He and I aren't really married."

I find an interesting little knob that's made of cut glass and add it to the growing pile Ann's purchasing. "I'm thinking about going back to the church choir." Before Georgina came back to us, I was singing in the choir. And I liked it. I liked getting out of the house one night a week for practice. Jojo would always go hang out with Makayla. Once in a while she'd have dinner with Remy. "And book club. I skipped book club twice in a row."

Ann looks up. "That's a good idea. You need to do things for yourself. You can't always be about Remy and the girls and work."

I hold a little metal bar in my hand, not really looking at it. "I have to be there at six, and Remy's not always home by then, but . . . I'm sure Georgina and Jojo would be okay home alone for a little while. Together."

"I'm sure they would be," she says, smiling at me. "You know you're right. What you said about you being good. Because you are, Harper. You're great. And . . . with or without Remy, you can parent your girls. You can be a good parent. A great parent."

I lower my head stubbornly. She and I have had conversations about my faith-related beliefs in marriage, but we're not always on the same page with that. I try a different tack. "I don't want to be a single parent, Ann. The girls deserve two parents. Who live together. You've seen him with them. He's a great parent."

"He is," she agrees, holding my gaze. "I'm just saying I don't want you to think again that you can't do it without him. Because you can."

I touch my fingertips to the crucifix around my neck and pray it doesn't come to that.

33

Lilla

"This is the Krewe of Thoth parade," my dad yells in my ear.

"What?" The band going by is so loud, I can barely hear him. I raise up on my tiptoes to see a bunch of old guys who look like they're wearing high school band uniforms. Old ones. All in different colors. Which is kind of amazing.

"Krewe of Thoth," he hollers, cupping his hand to his mouth. He's wearing this goofy green knit cap with a pompom on top. Green, of course, and it says *Tulane* across the bottom.

"And a krewe is just like a group of people, an organization that puts on parades for Mardi Gras, right?" I ask. When we first moved here, Sharon and I went to the Mardi Gras Museum in the Quarter, but so much has happened since then that it seems like a million years ago.

"A krewe might sponsor a parade or a ball, or ride on a float in a parade. Sometimes they do social stuff during the year or even charity work. Just depends on the krewe," Dad says. "Thoth was the Egyptian god of wisdom and inventor of science or art, or something like that. I don't remember. You'll have to Google it. The krewe was started in the forties," he goes on, "by a bunch of men who wanted to have a parade that people could see who were too sick or too disabled to get downtown where all the parades used to be. When they first started, the parade route went by hospitals and institutions—"

"Whoa," I say as someone bumps hard into me and I almost fall. I grab Dad's arm to steady myself as the guy goes by, laughing. Drunk. At least he says, "Sorry."

The crowd is overwhelming and today isn't even actual Mardi Gras yet. I feel like a sardine in a can. And the sounds are overwhelming, too. Everything is so loud. Music is blasting from floats and band after band marches by and people are shouting and singing and blowing whistles and crap. I was so excited about coming here today. I had Mardi Gras so built up in my head. Now that I'm here at an actual parade, I wish I hadn't made such a fuss. I'm not usually claustrophobic, but I feel short of breath, and even though it's cold, I'm a little sweaty inside my coat.

I thought it was going to be so much fun, especially after I found out that Jojo was going away and just Dad and I were coming to the parade. I'm so much more relaxed with Dad than Harper Mom. I don't know why. He's just so much . . . easier. His expectations of me are less so I don't feel like a big failure with him. I don't feel as if I'm always disappointing him.

Now I'm almost wishing we'd stayed home and played Ticket to Ride or streamed a movie. Dad and I are going through classic horror films. Next on our list is *Dawn of the Dead*. I could be home right now, where it's warm, eating popcorn and watching a movie about zombies without people pushing on me and shouting in my ears.

I can't help wondering if my visceral reaction has to do with the last time I attended a Mardi Gras parade. It seems ridiculous. But I keep thinking about what Harper Mom said about the human brain. About why I can't remember being kidnapped or the fact that I had a different mom before Sharon. Why I don't remember that I had a different life with a dad and a baby sister and a dog named Sadie. I found a photo of Sadie in one of the family albums; I definitely don't remember her.

I glance around, feeling uneasy, inside and out. I steady myself against Dad, my shoulder pressed to his arm. I wonder if this awful feeling I have deep in the pit of my stomach has to do with what happened to me when I was little. Will I never be able to go to a Mardi Gras parade without feeling a little sick to my stomach and totally weird in my skin?

We left the house two hours before the parade was supposed to start and walked along the edge of Audubon Park and then cut onto Magazine Street. We're standing not far from where the parade turns onto Magazine. Dad and I wiggled our way to a spot right on the edge of the sidewalk, but people keep standing in front of us. They're not supposed to be in the street, so they keep getting pushed back by parade officials.

"You okay?" Dad says in my ear, putting his hand on my back to steady me.

I nod and pull my hat down farther over my ears. It's been nice for days, but this morning I woke up to gray skies and it was cold enough for me to wear my North Face jacket. I stole a knit hat off the floor of Jojo's bedroom. I didn't text her and ask her if it was okay. I figured I'd just throw it back into her room. It's such a mess, she'll never know I borrowed it. Besides, that's what sisters are supposed to do, right? Steal each other's clothes. It's what normal sisters do in normal families.

We watch a float turn the corner and come our way behind a band of men in gold uniforms and top hats. There are girls dancing in front of them in booty shorts and sparkly bra tops. I wonder if they're cold. The band is pretty good, but I'm not into marching band music.

The float is a glittery green, gold, and purple and this gigantic clown with a mouth on the front that's opening and closing. The thing is terrifying. It's not a clown, I guess. The face resembles the Mardi Gras masks you see all over town. It looks like it's about to gobble up the band guys marching in front of it. There are men dressed in emerald-green or purple glitter suits on the float, wearing glitter masks that look like the one on the front of the float. They're throwing beads. Everyone is throwing beads.

Dad puts his hand up and somehow manages to catch a string

of glittery purple ones. Because he's so tall. He hands them to me. "Put them on," he tells me, grinning. He returns his attention to the float going by, swaying to the music. Clearly he's enjoying the parade. I just stand there, holding the beads on the end of my finger like they're something gross, like dog drool.

I went to Harper Mom's office with her one day last week. We both agreed silently that we wouldn't stop at Perfect Cup where she found me. Probably ever again. She had to run into her office for a minute. She wanted me to come in and say hi to everyone, but I've only met the vet she works for and the staff twice. Harper Mom doesn't get that it feels awkward to go in and say hi to people who don't really know me. They just know *of* me. I still feel like an act in a side show from the days where there used to be traveling carnivals. Like I should be Monkey Girl or Snake Woman. An exhibition where everyone stares at me and whispers and wonders if I was sexually abused while in captivity.

So instead of putting myself through that stress, I waited in the car. Doors locked, of course, because it was easier than pointing out the unlikelihood that I'd be kidnapped while Harper Mom went in to check blood work results. While I was waiting, I watched a guy lead his Saint Bernard down the sidewalk and in the front door. The dog had this huge river of drool coming out of his mouth. The beads remind me of that.

I look up and there's a little girl in a pink coat, with lots of beads around her neck, sitting in a seat on top of a ladder. She's maybe three; I'm not good with ages with little kids. I don't know any little kids. Dad told me that people build the ladders and put them along parade routes so they can put their kids on top of them. It's supposed to keep the kids safer and allow them to see more of the parades, but it doesn't look all that safe to me.

The little girl is laughing and clapping. I lift up on my tiptoes, being careful not to bump into her ladder because I'm petrified she'll fall and get run over by the float. Or eaten by it.

I hand her the string of purple beads. She takes them and smiles. "What's your name?" I have to shout for her to hear me.

"Becky," she says. Or at least that's what I think she says.

I smile up at her. A lady standing beside the ladder, who I think must be her mom, says thanks and smiles at me. I can't hear her over the sound of drums, but I see her lips move. Both of them turn to watch the parade again. I just stand there, staring at people's backs, not even trying to see the parade.

"That was nice of you," Dad says.

I shrug.

There's a fire truck in front of us now, lights flashing, and it's making that deafening siren sound. There's a little boy to our right on his dad's shoulders. He's got his hands over his ears. I pull Jojo's cap down farther, seriously considering putting my hands over *my* ears.

A group of guys dressed like pirates on horses are next. Some of the horses are wearing pirate hats, too. The men are throwing something from bags they're wearing. Dad jumps up and catches one as they shower over us.

He hands it to me. "A doubloon." It's shiny green. "Has the year and the name of the krewe on it." He points and then hands it to me. "A lot of people collect them."

I'm not into collecting. Never was, even when my friends were collecting Barbie dolls and stuffed unicorns. Maybe because we always moved a lot; the more stuff I had the more I had to pack up. Or leave behind. I think about giving the plastic doubloon to the little girl, too. Instead, I slide it into my jeans pocket. The pirates are still going by. There are a lot of pirates. And there are little boats, too. It sounds like they're built over riding lawnmowers or something like that.

I glance at Dad, who's watching the parade. I wonder if Harper Mom told him I wanted to go see Sharon at the prison. I think about asking him. Maybe he'd at least understand why I want to go. I don't know that he'll agree to it, though. He's definitely more open to what I have to say and more accepting than Harper Mom is that I'm smart enough and old enough to make decisions for myself, but the two of them have this thing. He gives in to her. She gives in to him. Maybe that's how it works in a marriage.

I have no idea because I've never really known married people. I see marriages on TV, but I'm smart enough to know that's probably not what I should base knowledge on.

I grab Dad's arm as yet another person knocks into me. Dad smiles down at me and turns his attention back to the parade. Instead of watching the parade, I study the people. I can't imagine how many are here. Thousands. Tens of thousands. As far as I can see, they're lined up on Magazine Street, ten deep. Only men and women walking the parade route, holding up their hands to get the crowd to back up, keep them all from spilling onto the street. The crowd moves, almost like it's alive. Like it's more than a sum of its parts. I see old adults and young ones, millennials and baby boomers. Teenagers everywhere. And so many kids. How do they not get lost? I suppose that's why parents put their kids up on ladders.

I was in a stroller that day. I can't imagine being a toddler in a stroller with people surrounding me this way. How could a little kid breathe? It would have been so scary, wouldn't it? But maybe not. Maybe little Georgina wasn't the kind of kid who got scared in crowds.

Maybe that came later.

Everyone is cheering. I have no idea why. I wonder how much longer the parade is. I pull my phone out of my back pocket. I feel as if I've been here for hours. Days. But only an hour and fifteen minutes has passed since it started. Dad said it would be three or four hours long, sometimes five. There's no way I can stand here for five hours.

Dad looks down at me. He's got a weird look on his face. "You okay?" He has to shout it because there's a lady standing behind us talking on her cell, really loud.

I don't know what to say. I don't want to wuss out, especially since I threw such a fit about coming. I mean, they cancelled their vacation so I could see this stupid parade. My eyes sting and I feel as if I could cry. I don't know what's wrong with me. I don't cry. I don't stress out about things. I figure things out. I make it work. And I'm happy. I've been a happy person. Where is that girl? I feel like I'm losing her in this tug-of-war between Lilla Kohen and Georgina Broussard.

I force a smile.

He's still watching me. Waiting for an answer. He must sense something because he says, "We can go if you want. Whenever you want."

"Maybe a few more minutes." I lift up on the toes of my sneakers so he can hopefully hear me. "I'm a little cold." *Wimp. Wuss. Loser.*

"It can be pretty overwhelming," Dad says. He looks concerned.

Overwhelming. It's interesting that he chose the same word I did.

I look away from him, pretending to be interested in another float. It's a big, rolling river paddleboat, only with lights flashing green and purple all over it like an old-school video game or a slot machine. I wonder if this is the kind of thing that gives people seizures. I used to know a girl who had to be careful with flashing lights because of that.

A tall dude moves in front of me, blocking my view of the street. I don't even care. I wonder how much time I can wait before I tell Dad I want to go. I wonder if we could go get Vietnamese food. Harper Mom likes it from this place uptown. I know traffic is crazy, but since the parade is headed in the direction of downtown, maybe we could get to the restaurant.

A guy and a girl with their arms linked step out into the street. Some dude is yelling at them. I guess because they can't be on the street. Some of the floats are so wide; it's got to be a safety thing.

The guy is hollering over his shoulder about what he does and doesn't have to do and crap like that. And then he pushes through the crowd and busts right between Dad and me. People holler at him. Someone pushes him. Then the girlfriend walks between us and someone steps on my foot.

I don't know what happens next. The music is so loud coming

off the riverboat float. I get hit in the head with some beads as I look down at my foot. People are touching me. Bumping into me. I can still hear the guy, behind me now. He's cussing. So's the girl. People in the crowd are yelling at them. I see a uniformed police officer moving in the couple's direction. And people keep pushing me, bumping into me. I feel as if I'm moving, even though I'm not really moving my feet. Or maybe I am.

"Dad?"

I look up and he's gone. He was right there. And now he isn't. Only . . . somehow I'm now behind the little girl on the ladder and to the right. Becky is farther away. And so is the street.

"Dad?"

All of a sudden my heart is pounding and I can't catch my breath. I'm looking around, but I can't see him. There are so many people.

I know I shouldn't panic. There's no reason to panic. I have my cell phone. He has his. And I can just walk home if I can't find him. If he doesn't pick up. It won't take me twenty minutes to walk home. I know all of that logically and yet I'm scared. So scared I can't move. I can't think. I reach for my phone in my back pocket, but my hand's shaking. I'm afraid to pull it out of my pocket. What if I drop it?

"Dad?" I say. Only this time I'm not calling out to him. It's a whisper. "Dad?"

I feel someone put their hand on my shoulder from behind me and I go to shove them away, but then I hear Dad's voice.

"Lilla?"

"Dad?" I spin around. People are pushing and bumping into me and I realize I'm crying.

"Lilla."

And there he is. My dad is there, wearing his dumb Tulane hat with the pompom on top. I throw myself against his chest. He closes his arms around me and I slide my hands up to his shoulders. He hugs me and I hug him back, my tears wetting his coat. He feels so good. So safe.

"It's okay," he's saying in my ear.

And it's all I can hear now. Just his voice. Not the marching band, not the clapping, not the shouting. Just my dad's voice.

"It's okay, sweetie. I'm here. You're okay."

"I couldn't find you." I'm trying not to cry. I feel stupid.

My dad just stands there, hugging me. It's the first time he's really hugged me hard. The first time I guess I've wanted him to hug me.

And gradually I stop shaking. My heart doesn't feel like I'm going to barf it up. I'm okay. But I'm embarrassed. So I just stand there, hugging him.

Eventually he says, "You want to get out of here?"

I nod. I step back, sniffing.

He grabs my hand, turns, and starts pushing through the crowd. I hang on tightly to him. Like I'm never going to let go.

34

Harper

I drop down onto the couch beside Remy. It's after nine, my bedtime; I'm hoping to convince him to come upstairs with me. If not for sex, then maybe some cuddling. I could use a hug after today, after surviving allowing Georgina to go to the parade. I used to tell Remy when I needed a hug, but I'm trying not to be needy.

The living room is dark except for the glow of the TV. He's watching a documentary. A black-and-white still photo of Ethel Rosenberg is on the screen.

I tuck my legs under me, leaning against him. I rest my chin on his shoulder. "Jojo texted me to say good night. They're all playing Monopoly. No Wi-Fi, so no streaming. So no movies or twenty-five episodes of *Buffy the Vampire Slayer*." It's a joke. Remy told Jojo he was going to limit her screen time because she was watching too much Buffy.

I wait. He doesn't respond. There are photos of Ethel and Julius on the screen now. Photos I'm familiar with. I wonder why he's watching this. I know he's seen it before because I've seen it before. At least twice. "You listening?" I keep my tone cheerful.

He's staring at the TV, but the volume's low. He can't possibly hear what they're saying. Of course, maybe he could if I'd stop talking.

"Lilla in bed?" he asks me. No eye contact.

"Georgina is," I answer, feeling guilty, as if I'm somehow picking a fight. Which is silly because I think we've agreed to disagree on this subject. I've agreed to disagree with everyone on the matter of her name: Remy, Jojo, Ann, even Georgina. At Ursuline, her teachers call her Georgina, but I noticed her new friend Em calls her Lilla.

I watch the TV for a moment. One of the Rosenbergs' sons is being interviewed. He looks to be in his sixties, but I don't know when this was filmed. I can't imagine what it must have been like for those two boys growing up, even with new last names. Knowing what their parents had been convicted of. I look at Remy. "So what happened today? At the parade? Why didn't you stay?"

I actually had a decent day alone here in the house. I decided that if I could keep busy, I wouldn't think about the parade. Or that horrible day almost fourteen years ago when Georgina went to a Mardi Gras parade. Or worry about Georgina. Or worry about Jojo. I knew Georgina was safe with Remy. And I knew it was irrational to worry about Jojo hanging out in a cabin in a state park with one adult per teen.

I ended up cleaning out my closet and my dresser drawers. I tried on clothes and culled like crazy. It was satisfying to carry two big black garbage bags of clothes to donate downstairs and throw them in the back of my car. I was making a vegetarian baked pasta dish to put into the oven later for dinner when Remy and Georgina walked into the house. They were both subdued. They offered no explanation other than that they'd seen enough and I let it go. For the time being.

Remy's still staring at the screen, but a commercial has come on. The TV blinks to another channel and I realize he's been sitting there with the remote in his hand. So maybe he wasn't watching a documentary about the Rosenbergs; maybe he was just channel surfing. He changes the channel again. Another commercial.

"Remy?" I sit up, reaching out to lay my hand over the remote. "What happened today?"

He finally looks at me. "Nothing happened. It was cold and loud and . . ." He glances back at the TV. A denture commercial. "I think she got a little overwhelmed is all."

"Overwhelmed?" I draw back my hand.

"She wasn't enjoying it. Too many people. Too loud." He shrugs. "So we came home."

All of this upset, weeks of talking about our plans for Mardi Gras. Canceling our vacation. Both girls insisting they wanted to go to the parades and this is how it ends? I'm almost laughing at the thought of it. Next time I get myself worked up over something involving the two of them, I need to remember how fickle teenagers can be. "You going out tomorrow?"

The TV changes channels again. And again. "I don't know," he says. "Maybe. I'll ask her in the morning. She said she didn't want to go down to the Quarter, though. I told her we could take the bikes downtown. She said Uptown parades were enough for her."

I tuck my legs up tighter beneath me, thinking. Trying to guess what would have made Georgina overwhelmed after she'd pushed so hard to get to go. "You think she remembered anything?"

He glances at me, hesitating. I can tell he's mulling it over. Then he shakes his head. "I don't think so," he says.

"Did you ask her?"

He exhales. Not because he needs to expel carbon dioxide. Because he doesn't want to have this conversation. This is what he was talking about on the porch. Remy asked me to start trying to work out some things on my own. Meaning stop thinking out loud. Stop involving him when I'm still in the *working-through-it* stages. Stop dissecting every word that passes Georgina's lips, every step she takes. I get what he was saying, and I'm trying. But this is important. And I'm not going to stop talking to him about important things.

"I'm asking," I tell him, "because she's starting to remember some things. Did she tell you that?"

He looks back at me, his forehead wrinkling. "What kinds of things?"

"Just . . . slivers of memories. Me reading Madeline books to her on the couch in the parlor. My silver cake baby." I smile at the thought. "But if she remembers being taken, we need to—"

"I don't think she remembers being abducted." He sounds annoyed with me. He's staring at the TV screen again.

"Remy, what I'm saying is—" I press my lips together, forcibly making myself stop. Just stop. Georgina told me about Madeline and about the cake baby. If she remembers anything about the abduction, she'll come to me, I tell myself. Our relationship is improving. She'll tell me when she's ready.

Remy has returned to the channel that's featuring the story about the Rosenbergs. I have one more thing I need to ask him. I consider letting it go, at least for tonight. But he's already aggravated with me. I'm already going to bed alone. He'll sit here half the night, staring at the TV, then fall asleep on the couch. So I hold my nose and jump. "I know we agreed you didn't have to share with me every conversation you have with Georgina. I know I'm not supposed to ask, but when you guys were out today . . . did she bring up going to see Sharon?"

He looks at me and it's obvious from his face that this is the first he's heard of it. The tiny lines that crease his forehead get even deeper. "She wants to see her in prison?"

I'm the one who breaks eye contact this time and stares at the TV screen. Newspaper headlines: A Spy Couple Doomed to Die, Supreme Court and Eisenhower Reject Couple's Last Plea, Spies Die in Chair. "Yes. She says she was never allowed to speak to Sharon, after the police came to their house." I try to keep my emotion out of my tone, out of my head. I try to just relay what Georgina said to me. "She feels she needs some sort of . . . explanation."

"What explanation? How can there be one? The woman is clearly mentally unbalanced." He sets down the remote to actually look at me and engage.

"Not according to a psychiatrist," I point out. "According to

Detective Marin, Sharon Kohen's psych evaluation stated she was healthy enough to be charged and enter a plea."

He makes a sound of derision. "She has to be crazy, Harper." He gestures with his hand now free of the remote. "What other explanation can there be for stealing someone's toddler and pretending she's her own? Giving her a dead baby's name, using the dead baby's Social Security number?"

I understand what he's saying, but I also understand what it is to be a mother, to have carried a child in my womb and given birth. The love for that child is love no one who has not given birth can begin to comprehend. In a way, being a mother is a form of insanity. I would do anything for my girls; I really think I would. To protect them. I'd risk my soul to keep them safe. I'd lie, I'd steal. I'd prostitute myself. In the right circumstances, I truly believe I would kill for them.

I brush my crucifix with my fingertips.

So what happens when a love of that intensity gets twisted? I suspect something like that is what happened to us. Sharon loved her little girl so much that she couldn't accept her death. She loved her Lilla so much that she replaced her. I suspect that, most days, she couldn't even remember that the child she was raising wasn't the child of her body.

"You think we should let Lilla see Sharon?" Remy asks me.

I don't even have to think on that one. "Of course not." But then, against my will, I put myself in Sharon's position. And Georgina's. "I don't think so. I don't know. I don't think I can."

He is quiet for a moment. "I suppose we need to talk about this with the therapist, but I have to agree with you. I don't want Lilla near her. I don't want Lilla in a prison visitation room. Maybe when she gets older," he adds, "but not yet."

If I had my choice, Georgina would never, ever see Sharon again. I don't want that woman to ever lay eyes on my daughter again. I just can't get past that. Not right now, at least. The wound is too raw. Of course I know very well that in less than two years Georgina will be eighteen and then I can't prevent her from going to see her.

Another worry for another day.

Remy and I sit there in silence for a moment and then I rub his shoulder and get up. He doesn't seem angry with me now. "You coming soon?"

He looks up at me. "I've been thinking today, and . . . we need to tell Lilla."

I don't think he means to tell her she's never going to see Sharon under our watch. Because even in the semidarkness of the room, with the distortions created by the TV screen, I can see his face. His *difficult subject* face. His mouth gets tight at the corners.

"Tell her what?"

"That you and I aren't married."

Suddenly he's taken an attitude with me. He hasn't raised his voice, but I hear it in his tone. How would I have known what he was talking about? A minute ago the subject was about a prison visit.

"Why now?" I ask, not sure I'm up for this tonight. I take a defensive stance: my feet spread apart, my hands on my hips. "Are you leaving us?" I'm suddenly scared and hurt, but I sound angry.

"I didn't say that."

I press my lips together. "So tell me what you *are* saying."

He gets up off the couch. We're facing each other. "What I said. Which is that we should tell Lilla that you and I are divorced. That I moved in here because you thought it would be better for her if the family dynamic looked like it looked when she left."

I take issue with his word *left* because she didn't leave of her own volition, but I also take issue with him suggesting this was all my idea. "You agreed it was the right thing to do. And . . ." I look away and then back at him. "And we'd talked about giving our marriage another try. Before we knew Georgina was coming home, we talked about it. Remy, you and I were doing well."

He points at me. "You said you were going out with that guy."

"Remy, I never said I had a date," I huff. "I told you I had thought about going out with the drug rep. Mostly because everyone had been telling me it was time to move on. And . . . I don't know. He's nice. And it was coffee." I take a step toward him. "But I didn't go for coffee with him; I hadn't because . . . I still felt as if you were my husband. Even after the divorce . . ." I manage to say it without tearing up. "You're still my husband. We exchanged vows that said we were husband and wife as long as we both shall live. I still love you, and, Remy, I think you love me. . . ."

"I do love you," he says. "You know I do. But this isn't healthy, her thinking we're legally married. We need to tell her. I think—"

"Wait!" Georgina's angry voice startles me.

I turn to see her in the living room doorway.

"You guys are *divorced?*" she shouts at us.

35

Lilla

I sit in the kitchen at the island, my book in front of me, but I'm not reading. I'm looking at the house phone in front of me. Then the time on the kitchen stove, then the phone again.

Everything fell into place today. Jojo is still with her friend; she's not coming home until tomorrow night, Ash Wednesday. Olivia's mom doesn't want to drive in Mardi Gras traffic. Dad went to work this morning. Harper Mom went to work.

Last night, there was a ten-minute discussion over dinner about me staying home alone today. All day. Even though I've stayed home alone several times, it wasn't all day. That was Harper Mom's issue. Dad said it was fine. I think that, in the end, Harper Mom gave in, trying to make up for the blowup Sunday night.

Sunday night . . . I was so mad when I found out they were divorced. I hollered at both of them. What's with that living room? What's with me, shouting at adults? At my parents?

"You're divorced?" I hollered at them.

"Georgina, come in and sit down with us," Harper Mom said.

The lights were out; the TV was on, so the lighting was weird. Shadows kept moving across their faces, making them look creepy.

"Come sit on the couch and let's talk about this," she said. "Let us explain."

"You're not married anymore and you didn't think I should *know* that?" I direct that to Dad, who's just standing there, looking upset. "You lied to me. You both lied to me," I accused.

"We didn't lie," Harper Mom said.

I folded my hands over my chest. I was so angry, I was shaking. It had already been a rough day. The whole parade thing, and then to find out . . . I just lost it. I was so furious, I wanted to walk out of the house.

But where was I going to go? Our house in Bayou St. John has been rented out again. I went last week on the streetcar when I was supposed to be getting my English muffin bread. I saw a flowered wreath hanging on the door and a kid's bike on the porch. Nobody here knew I went there instead of the bakery. I just lied when I got back and told Harper Mom they were out of the bread. So now I have nowhere to live but here because there's no way I'm living under the bridge at Claiborne under I-10. Not even in a tent. I have to make it work here on Exhibition Drive.

"Omission of the truth, it's a lie," I told Dad, because for some reason I was angrier with him than with Harper Mom. She treats me as if I'm a child most of the time, but he treats me like an adult. I expected more from him.

"Georgina, please," Harper Mom said. She looked like she was going to cry.

"Just say it," I told them. "Say you lied to me. Deceived me." I kept shaking my head. "I can't believe you let me think I was coming here to my parents. To this perfect little family." I said it in a mean tone because I was so mad. "When were you going to tell me?" I asked.

Dad just stood there.

Mom took a step toward me. "Georgina, I'm sorry. We're sorry. You're right. We should have told you from the beginning, but . . ."

She waited like I was going to say, "Oh, okay, you were going to tell me. No problem." But when I didn't say that, when I didn't say anything, she went on.

"Our marriage is complicated. Most are, hon. We divorced three years ago because—"

"Because it wasn't working out," Dad said, coming to stand next to his ex-wife. He paused and then went on. "Honestly, Lilla, we don't really owe you an explanation as to why we divorced. It's personal. Between your mom and me. Had you been here, you wouldn't have been consulted; Jojo wasn't. What I *can* tell you is that for us, it actually improved our relationship." He looked at her. "I think, in a lot of ways, I was a better husband. I was certainly a better father to Jojo."

I just stood there, listening. Still not able to wrap my head around what he was saying. Remy and Harper divorced. They weren't married. That's all I could think of. My parents aren't married. And everybody knows it but me.

Mom kept looking at me like she thought I was going to implode . . . or shatter. Did she really think I wouldn't be able to bear this of all things, after all that's happened to me in the last two months? I don't know them well enough to care if they're married or not. I was just pissed that they were dishonest with me.

"We divorced," Harper Mom said, "and your dad moved to an apartment a couple of blocks from here. But we saw him almost every day. He had dinner here, we visited Granddad together. I know it sounds odd but—"

I threw up my hand, interrupting her. "That's where you keep your car," I said to Dad. He showed up with a car a couple of weeks ago and when I asked him where he kept it, his answer didn't really make sense. Now I see why. He hadn't been hiding the fact that he had a car, he'd been hiding the fact that he had an apartment where he kept it. "I'm such an idiot."

Dad ran his hand over his head as if he was tired. Or didn't want to be here. Which made two of us.

"Even before we found you, your dad and I had talked about trying again. Trying to live together, trying to rekindle what we'd lost. And then when we found out you were coming home," Harper Mom said, "we thought it might be easier if the family unit looked the same as it did when you . . ."

"When she took me," I finished for her. "Like you thought I was going to remember you two?"

When I said that, Harper Mom's eyes got teary.

"We're sorry," Dad said quietly. "We screwed up, Lilla, and we're sorry. But we didn't know what we were doing here. We've never done this before, just like you haven't." He paused and then went on. "Parents make decisions every day and sometimes they're the right ones. Sometimes they're not."

I walked out of the living room and went upstairs.

Before they went to bed, they both came in to speak to me. Separately. What they said made sense, I guess. And I get that people screw up. But the idea that they were divorced and hadn't been living together really messed with my head. I didn't ask either of them what the plan for the future was. Were they married now, for good? Was he planning to go back to his apartment? I can't imagine living here without Dad, but I can only handle so many problems at a time, and right now, Sharon's a bigger problem than the state of my parents' marriage. Or divorce. Or whatever.

That night I texted Jojo and asked why she didn't tell me they were divorced. Because I knew she knew. Obviously she knew. She texted back:

Figured you'd figure it out

Then, **Sorry**

I texted her back, **No worries,** because it wasn't her fault. I know they didn't consult her. And she's got her own crap to deal with. Me, for one thing. I keep thinking about the sterling silver framed photo of me in the living room, with the candle. The shrine, Jojo calls it. That had to be hard for her seeing that all those years.

I check the clock on the stove for the one-millionth time. She should be calling soon. This is what time she called both times. I reach for my glass of water. My throat's dry. What am I going to say? I don't know what I'm going to say.

And then it rings. And instead of staring at it like I did before, I snatch up the phone, hit the button, and say, "Hello," all breathless.

"Hello," says the same recorded lady's voice. "This is a collect call from . . . *Sharon Kohen* . . . an inmate at Louisiana Correctional Institute. If you would like to accept the collect call, please press one."

I push the numeral one and put the phone back to my ear.

"Lilla, thank you," my mother gushes. She's crying. "Thank you for picking up. I was so afraid you wouldn't pick up. My attorney said not to contact you, but I just had to—" She takes a shuddering breath. I've never heard her this way. Sobbing like this. But I guess I never really knew her, did I?

"I had to know you were all right," she says.

My eyes fill with tears. I had this whole thing planned. What I was going to say to her. I was going to tell her she ruined my life. I was going to tell her I hated her. I was going to yell at her like I yelled at Dad and at Harper Mom. Because none of this is even their fault and they're the ones I'm yelling at. They're the only ones I have to yell at. And that's not fair. Someone should yell at Sharon for doing this to me. We should all yell at her. But at least me. I should get first dibs.

That was my plan, but now . . .

"Mama Bear?" I say, my voice cracking.

"Lilla, I'm so sorry. *Bubbeleh*, I never meant for this to happen," she cries. "I never meant to hurt you."

I bite down on my lip until it hurts. She never meant to hurt *me?* What about Harper Mom, or Dad, or Jojo? That's what I want to scream at her. Did you not mean to hurt me, but you meant to hurt them? If you lost your baby, if your baby died, wouldn't you understand the pain you were going to bring to the people whose baby you kidnapped?

But I don't say those things. Because those aren't the kinds of things you say over the phone. You need to say things like that in person.

I wasn't sure of this, but now I am. "I . . . I want to come see you," I manage, fighting not to turn into a blubbering mess like her. My nose is running and I reach for the dish towel on the counter and wipe it. I feel as if I'm liquefying, as if I'm just going to melt into a puddle on the pretty hand-painted-tile floor.

"They'll bring you?" Now she's almost laughing.

Doesn't she know what a stupid question that is? Of course they aren't going to bring me to prison to see her!

"How does this work?" I ask, ignoring her question. I've already started coming up with a plan, how to get out of here and get a head start before they know I'm missing. Harper Mom is scheduled to work for a couple of hours in the morning. Dad will go to work. Jojo will still be out of town. I can even text Harper Mom and tell her I went somewhere, to give me some more time. By the time Harper Mom realizes I'm gone, I'll be long gone. "I think I can come tomorrow," I tell Sharon.

"Oh, *bubbeleh*, tomorrow won't work."

I panic. "What do you mean? Tomorrow is when I can come. I . . . there's no school. I—"

"Lilla," she interrupts gently. "There are specific visiting days. Visiting hours. You can only come on weekends. Can you come Saturday? Saturday is the day my block has visiting privileges. I'm in the women's correctional facility in St. Gabriel."

I get up off the stool and pace. "I don't know. I don't know," I tell her, pressing my hand to my forehead. I had it all planned. Tomorrow would be the perfect day: no school, the parents working, Jojo gone. But if tomorrow won't work—"I'll figure out a way," I tell her.

"Oh, *bubbeleh*, I can't wait to see you. Hug you." She gets quiet. "Are they coming? Because . . . I don't know if I can face them. Not yet, at least. I thought maybe they would come when I appeared in court, but they didn't. When I have my actual sentencing hearing, maybe—"

"They're not coming," I say quietly. Then, "I have to go. Before they hear me on the phone." It worries me that I'm beginning to lie like this. I never used to lie about anything. To anyone.

"They don't know you're talking to me? Lilla, I don't know that that's—"

"Saturday," I interrupt. "I'll be there Saturday."

"O . . . okay," she says. Probably because she's sitting in jail and knows she doesn't get to make decisions about me anymore.

"I think visiting is nine to two, but you have to be here by one fifteen. Or they won't process you. And you need a picture ID," she adds.

"Got it." I'm glad she told me that; it wouldn't have occurred to me that I needed an ID. I can use my old driver's license. I still have it because we haven't really discussed me getting a new one. With my real name on it. With everything going on, I just haven't gotten into my driving again. We've only talked about it a little bit.

"Okay," I say. "I have to go."

"I'll see you Saturday." She starts to cry again.

I hang up.

36

Harper

At the restaurant, we order a dozen oysters on the half shell and I wonder if we should have gotten eighteen. I keep reading blurbs in the news about how we shouldn't be eating raw seafood, but I can't help myself. And Remy loves good raw oysters as much as I do. Several of the entrees look amazing, but we end up ordering four small plates. He lets me choose the food; he chooses the wine.

I watch Remy across the table from me. We're against the wall. I'm sitting on a bench. I like this table; it's cozy and seems more intimate than the tables in the middle of the room. I sip my wine.

"What made you decide to make dinner reservations on the Friday after Mardi Gras?" I ask him. I laugh, tickled he'd be so romantic as to make arrangements for a date night. And at Pêche, one of my favorites in town. "How did you get us an eight o'clock reservation?"

"Magic," he says, topping off my wineglass.

I brush my fingertips against his as he passes me my glass. I watch him; he doesn't meet my gaze. He pours another glass for himself. A Côte de Beaune pinot noir. It's good, of course, but my husband knows his wine.

"Reservations by magic?" I tease.

"No." Remy takes a sip. "One of Phil's TAs works here. He

checked the cancellation list for me. Well, for Phil. Phil was the one who made the reservations for all of us at Christmastime."

I nod. Phil has been a casual friend of Remy's for years. They graduated from Tulane together. Phil's now a calculus professor at Tulane. They're on the same flag football team, too. Once in a while they grab a beer together or meet at a bar to watch a game.

"Is the TA here tonight?"

Remy shakes his head. "He only made the reservation."

"Well, then, thank you, Phil." I nod and lift my glass in a toast. It feels nice to be out like this. I can't remember when we went out to dinner alone together like this. My birthday last year, maybe?

When Remy announced Wednesday night that he and I were going for dinner without the girls, I was excited. And I did well with the new parenting skills I'm learning. I didn't put up a single protest. I didn't even suggest that we should drop Georgina and Jojo off at Ann's on our way to dinner. Remy and I talked about letting Georgina start driving again. He thought she should drive his car because it's smaller, and older. He said it wouldn't matter if it got dinged up. I tried to breathe through the idea of Georgina getting into a car accident. And I realized that if she was old enough to drive, even if it's on a graduated license with us still in the car with her, she was old enough to stay home and keep an eye on Jojo.

Tonight, when we got ready to go, I did second-guess leaving the girls. Jojo, at least, because she wasn't feeling well and was running a bit of a fever. But she insisted she was fine. She said she and her sister would go to their own rooms and watch something on their laptops. A part of me wanted to suggest they do something together, but I kept it to myself. I know I can't force a friendship between them. Trying to do so might actually make them less likely to form a bond. So I zipped my lip and told Jojo to call me if she felt worse. I also asked Georgina to check on her sister. Georgina agreed.

I'm a little concerned about her. She's been subdued since Sunday when she and Remy went to the parade. Or maybe since she stood in the living room and yelled at us for lying to her about being married. I see her point. And I think this error in judgment that could be seen as a lie might have to be brought up next time I go to confession. I don't go often enough and I need to get better about it because I do feel better afterward.

My gaze returns to Remy. I want to remark to him that I'm wondering how the girls are making out, but I decided this week that it's time I start focusing more on my marriage. I'm not just a mother, I'm a wife, too. I think maybe that was what Remy was hinting at the night we had the talk on the porch. He doesn't want me talking issues to death. Issues about the girls, the house, work. But I think he wants me to be more present for him, even if he didn't or wasn't able to express that. So instead of saying anything to him about our daughters, I make myself content with a quick check to see if any text messages have come in.

Nothing from our girls, just a message from Ann saying to have a good time. As I slip my cell back into my bag, the waiter brings the oysters.

While we eat our plump, salty little Dauphin Island oysters out of Alabama, and local Hopedales, we talk about Remy's sister. Divorced for the second time, with a child from each marriage, Remy and their brother Beau are concerned, and rightly so. Lucy's working long hours in the family law office, but then instead of going home to her children, she's being seen on a lot of bar stools. Without saying much, I listen to Remy express his concerns. I dominate too many of our conversations and too often they center around me. Even when they've been about Georgina, and so many have been about Georgina in the last two months, I'm realizing that they've also been about me. Too much about me.

Remy loves his sister and he feels responsible for her. But Lucy has a temper and she doesn't like her brothers butting into her business. So we talk about how Remy can approach a conversation with her, making it nonconfrontational. Beau thought they should do it together, but I agree with Remy that it will seem too much like the boys are ganging up on her.

"A dozen wasn't enough," Remy tells the waiter as he takes

away the oyster shells and we make room for the plates he's bringing. There are lamb skewers, spicy ground shrimp over pasta, and catfish with pickled greens, but my favorite is the crawfish-and-jalapeño capellini. And the hush puppies. We order a second plate of hush puppies after Remy loses the last one playing rock-paper-scissors against me. We laugh and I seriously think about ordering the salted peanut pie with bourbon sauce, but I'm so stuffed I resist. It might taste good now, but I'll feel awful later.

"More wine?" Remy asks me when the waiter has cleared away our plates. "You sure you don't want dessert?"

"No. I can't." I laugh and press my hand to my stomach. I'm glad I wore my black skirt that has an elastic band. "I've already eaten too much." I'm actually feeling a little overheated. Too much food and the tannins in the wine, I suspect. I just need some air. We had to park a good eight blocks away, but the walk will be good for me and I'm wearing my tall black boots, so the trek down the less-than-optimal sidewalks will be safe.

"Can you drive home?" Remy asks me.

The waiter is still standing there.

I nod, thinking it's an odd question. Remy never drinks too much. It's been years since I even saw him get tipsy.

Remy looks up at the waiter. He orders a scotch and asks for the check.

"Scotch?" I ask when the waiter walks away. Remy likes scotch, but he doesn't usually order it out and not after having three-quarters of a bottle of wine.

"We need to talk," he says, reaching across the table to take my hand.

I look at him suspiciously. We've been talking all evening. "Okay . . ." I drawl out the word the way Jojo does.

He's wearing a burgundy oxford shirt and a gray wool sports coat. Very scholarly. And hot. I've always been okay-looking, but my Remy is handsome and I like the idea that he's coming home with me tonight and not with any of the beautiful women in this restaurant.

"Harper—" He exhales, dropping his head to stare at the table.

I look at the way he's holding his head and I'm suddenly worried. Something's wrong. I thread my fingers through his, the heels of our hands resting on the table. I wonder if maybe he isn't getting the comptroller job. Maybe his boss has decided not to retire yet. Or what if they're giving it to someone else? But that makes no sense because they haven't even advertised for the job. To my knowledge.

I stare at him. "Hon, what is it?"

He slowly raises his head. "Baby . . . I need to . . . we need to . . ." He hesitates. "Harper, I can't—" He goes quiet as the waiter walks up to the table, setting down a scotch from the Isle of Skye. And the check.

"I'll take it whenever you're ready," the waiter says, walking away. "No hurry."

Remy pulls his hand away from mine, lifts the glass of scotch, and takes a drink. And doesn't look at me.

I feel like I'm going to be sick. Because it hits me what's going on here. I've been set up. The impromptu date? Reservations Remy made instead of getting me to make them? The couple of awkward moments of silence between us that I chalked up to both of us being out of practice going out alone?

I'm an idiot.

I abruptly stand up. "No," I say. "You will not do this to me." I grab my coat and handbag off the bench beside me.

"Harper—"

"No," I repeat, walking away from the table. I know I'm being loud. People are looking at us. I don't care. As I go, out of the corner of my eye, I see Remy stand, then pick up the little black portfolio lying on the table. He hasn't paid the bill yet. He can't leave.

Out on the sidewalk, I pull on my red wool coat that I rarely wear because it's usually too warm in Louisiana for wool. I keep walking. I fumble, trying to push the buttons through the holes and hold on to my little black leather bag at the same time. My date night handbag. I switched bags just for him. Just because it was a special evening.

It's turning out to be pretty special, all right.

At the corner, I turn right on Julia. In my tall black boots with the little heels, I can walk fast. A crowd of twentysomething revelers, leftovers from Mardi Gras, brushes past me. One of them is carrying one of those tall, lime-green plastic-tube drink cups called a hand grenade. You can buy them on Bourbon Street filled with a nasty mixed drink. For a moment I'm afraid I'm going to be sick right here on the street. Totally normal for the Mardi Gras partiers who just passed me. Not so much for Pêche patrons in their forties.

I keep walking. Marching, really. I pass an art gallery. Closed now. On our way to the restaurant, I mentioned to Remy that I'd like to go in there sometime. Maybe on another date night. He didn't say anything. He didn't say there wouldn't be any more date nights.

Behind me, I think I hear Remy calling my name. It's windy. I keep walking. Pick up the pace.

"Harper! Will you wait? Please?" Remy's practically shouting.

I turn onto Tchoupitoulas. I clutch my little black bag. There are tears in my eyes but I'm too angry to cry. I wish I had the car keys. If I had the keys, I'd get in the car and drive away and leave him. As packed as the city is tonight, I bet it would take him at least half an hour to get an Uber. Maybe longer if I was lucky and he wasn't.

I hear footsteps on the pavement behind me. Ordinarily I'd whip around, thinking it was a mugger. But I know it's just my husband. My ex-husband.

"Harper, please," Remy pants.

I don't stop until he grabs my shoulder and then I whip around. There's an old-style gas lamp beside the door of an engineering office where we stop. The lamp makes a familiar hissing sound like the lamps at our front door. The yellow light they cast isn't particularly complimentary. When I look at Remy's face he seems older than he did at the table a few minutes ago.

"When were you going to tell me?" I shout at him. I don't think I've ever shouted at him in public in my life. I don't bother to look up and down the street to see if I'm intruding on someone's evening that's going better than mine. "Dessert? Is that why you wanted me to get the pie? Because you wanted to tell me you were leaving over *pie?*" I emphasize the last word.

He holds up his hand, his palm to me. "Harper, please."

"You thought this was a good idea? To take me out to dinner, so I would think we were on a date? What? Were you going to tell me in the restaurant, so I won't make a fuss? Was that the plan?"

"No," he says quietly. He lifts his hand again, then lets it fall. "Let's get in the car. It's cold out here."

I want to say no. I want to tell him I want to stand here on the dark street and have it out with him. But it is cold. And what's the sense really? He's already made up his mind. I see it on his face; I know that face. He made up his mind days ago. Weeks. Or maybe he never had any intention of staying and I just didn't know it.

In silence, we walk the last two and a half blocks up Tchoupitoulas in silence. He makes no attempt to say anything and neither do I. He uses the key fob to unlock the door before we get to the car. The headlights blink.

"Am I driving or are you?" I ask, meaning, did he down the scotch.

"I'll drive," he says.

I walk around to the passenger's side.

There was a time in our lives when he would walk around the car with me and open the door. Sometimes, before he opened it, I'd lean back against the car and we'd kiss. It was a long time ago, but I wish we were still there. I wish he still felt that way about me. Because I still feel that way about him.

He starts the engine, but cuts the headlights. So we're going to do this here.

"You're moving out," I say softly, suddenly too tired to be loud. Too sad.

"Yes."

I don't respond.

"Harper, I thought . . . going out to dinner. I thought it would be nice. Just the two of us. Not because I thought we wouldn't argue, when I told you, but because I didn't want to do it in front of the girls."

Tears are running down my cheeks. I dig in my bag for tissues but there aren't any. They're in my big everyday suede handbag. I open the glove compartment where I find some napkins, stashed there after a stop at Melba's for po'boys, probably. I think I can faintly smell fried shrimp as I wipe my eyes and then my nose. But maybe the smell is just lingering on my clothes from the seafood restaurant.

I lean my head against the cool glass of the passenger-side window. I was feeling overheated in the restaurant and that prickly sensation is creeping up again. I can't tell if I'm about to have a hot flash or I'm going to be sick. I unbutton my coat. "Why?" I ask him. "Why are you leaving? Now when we're a family again?"

His sigh is long, so long that I find myself irritated by it.

"I know this is a cliché, baby, but it's not you."

I raise my eyebrows. "Meaning?"

"Meaning you haven't done anything wrong. Georgina and Jojo haven't done anything wrong. I just can't . . . I can't do anything right, not—"

"What are you talking about? You're a good husband, Remy. You take care of me, you love me, you've stuck by me all these years when I know I wasn't just making myself crazy, I was making you crazy, too." I turn to him. "And you're an amazing father. Georgina, she—she's bonded with you. I don't . . . I don't think she and I are never going to have a relationship, but right now, you're the one she goes to. You're the one she calls Dad." I point at myself. "She's still calling me by my first name."

He stares out the windshield. "She was so angry that I didn't tell her we were divorced. She felt I betrayed her."

"That's why you're doing this? Because Georgina got angry with you? Welcome to my world. Remy, she's sixteen years old. And she's been to hell and back. Yes, she's angry that we didn't tell her, but sometimes it's okay for our children to be angry with us. And it's okay for us to have made a mistake."

He's shaking his head. "I can't do it, baby. Not every day. Not day in and day out." He says each word slowly as if slogging through mud in his mind. "I can't do it."

"Do what?" I demand.

He looks at me and I see that there are tears in his eyes. "I can't be your husband every day. Not the one I want to be."

I'm loud again. "So you are seeing someone?"

"No." He laughs without humor. "I can't even handle one woman. Three, depending on how you look at it. Exactly how would I have room for another woman in my life?"

I just sit there, looking at him. "I still don't understand. You say you can't be a husband and father every day. What does that mean? For us?"

"It means . . . I don't know. It means . . . I need time to myself when no one expects anything of me. Not you, not the girls." He runs his hand through his hair. He trimmed his beard tonight. He still looks good to me. Even though a part of me wants to rip that facial hair off.

I sigh and close my eyes. "You want to go back to the way things were?"

"Yes," he murmurs.

"Part-time father." My words come out as somewhat of an accusation. This is sort of the same conversation we had four years ago. "Part-time husband."

"If you'll let me be your husband," he says. "Because, Harper"—he takes my hand—"I do love you. You know that, right? And I love Jojo, and I love Lilla. And . . . I don't want anyone else. I just need . . . time when I don't need to be all the things you want me to be." He kisses my hand and lets go of it.

I stare straight ahead. I need time to process this. Time without him sitting beside me. "You should go back to your place tonight," I say.

"Yeah," he agrees.

"Tomorrow we'll find some time to . . . I don't know, come up with a plan." I shake my head. All I can think of is how heartbroken Georgina will be. This is going to be so hard for her. I try to think about the logistics of this. "I'd like to wait and call the therapist Monday when she's in her office and ask her how she suggests we tell the girls. Maybe we should do it there so she can help facilitate. Or just call a family meeting in the kitchen over pizza. I don't know. I'm too upset to think right now."

"Whatever you think is best, baby." Remy sounds utterly dejected.

I know I should feel bad for him right now. He's obviously torn up about this, maybe more than I am. But I can't feel sorry for him. Not right now. Maybe tomorrow. Maybe the next day. But not now. Because right now, I feel sorry for our daughters and for me. But mostly, I think, for our daughters.

"We should go," I say, searching for my cell in my bag. I want to text Georgina and Jojo and let them know we're on our way home. I want to check on Jojo and see if her fever has come down. "Your place. I'll drop you off."

"I can be back in the morning before they get up. Or . . . I could come home tonight. Sleep on the couch? Or we could sleep together. I could use a hug right now," he says miserably.

And then my anger is gone and I'm just sad. Really sad.

37

Jojo

I stand outside Lilla's door for a long time debating whether or not to knock. The hall is dark. Mom and Dad got home about an hour ago; Mom came in to check on me and then I heard her stop at Lilla's door to say good night. Their door is closed now.

I look at Lilla's door. Since I got home from camping, she's been acting weird. Like weirder than her usual weird. I think maybe she's mad at me. Mad that I didn't tell her Mom and Dad are divorced. She texted me when I was with Olivia, asking me why I didn't tell her. I don't really know why. I guess I didn't think it mattered that much, but I've been living with Mom and Dad's weird relationship my whole life. I texted Lilla I was sorry. Maybe she's mad I didn't call her or maybe it's because I didn't say anything about it when I got home.

I can't figure out how to act around her. What to say. I don't know if I bug her too much or not enough. Makayla and I talk about it all the time. She doesn't know what I should do, either. She's an only child. Like I was until two months ago. I don't know what I could do so Lilla would like me better. I don't know if I care if she likes me. Which makes me feel bad for Mom because I know she wants us to be besties.

I don't dislike my sister. We just don't have anything in common other than DNA. We've been talking about DNA in biology class and it's actually really interesting. It's possible for us to come from the same parents and be totally different. It all has to do with the way the chromosomes shake out.

I hesitate and then knock before I chicken out. "It's Jojo," I say. "Yeah?"

I'm not sure that means it's okay for me to come in, but I open the door anyway.

Lilla's lying in bed in pj bottoms and an Ursuline T-shirt, looking at her laptop. The bed's still in the middle of the room even though it's been weeks since she finished painting. Like I said. Weird.

"I . . ." I stand there leaning on the doorknob feeling like a complete idiot. "I wanted to tell you I'm sorry about not saying anything."

I look around her room. It's dark, but there's enough light coming from my room that I can see a little. It's like no one really lives here: no clothes or shoes or anything on the dresser or the chair or the floor. I can't even figure out where her shoes are. We don't have closets; the house is too old. But she has a big dresser thing where you can hang clothes up inside. Mom calls it a chifforobe. Makayla's mom calls it a wardrobe. Maybe Lilla's shoes are in there?

Lilla's just lying there in bed, but now she's looking at me.

"About them not being married. Anymore." I twist my mouth around, bite my lip. "I guess I . . . You know, when he wasn't living with us, I think we hung out more than when he was living here when I was young." I lift one shoulder and drop it. "I don't know if that's true or not, though. I don't think people always remember things the way they really are. You know? Like . . . Makayla remembers going to her great-grandmother's funeral when she was in second grade." I feel like I'm just blabbing on and on. I don't even know what I'm saying. "Like, she remembers the dress she wore and everything. Except she didn't go. She stayed here with us."

"Right," Lilla says. She's got her thinking face on; she seems to spend a lot of time thinking. "Sometimes it's hard to figure out what really happened and what you think happened . . . or wish happened. I always thought I had a happy childhood. That Sharon was good to me and that she loved me." She looks up at me. "But what if that's not true?"

She looks sad. I chew on my lip, thinking about that. "Mom and Dad always loved you. Even when you weren't here."

"Mom and Dad," she says, and she makes a face. "You understand why I'm upset, right? Because they lied to me. Well, technically, I guess they didn't lie, but they deceived me. On *purpose*. They made me think this family was one thing when it was another."

"Right," I say, because I can't think of anything else. I just stand there.

She's just lying there, looking at her computer now.

"Anyway," I tell her as I back out of her room, "I wanted to tell you I wasn't in on it. Not like they didn't ask me what I thought or anything. I guess I didn't realize it would make you feel bad." I hesitate. "I think maybe they did it because they thought it would make you feel better coming home. Safer."

"Maybe," she says. Then she types something on her laptop. I can tell the screen has changed, even though I can't see it, because the light on her face has changed. "Night," she says.

"Good night." I close her door and stand there. I keep thinking things are going to go back to normal here, like they were before Lilla came. I don't like feeling this way all the time. Uncertain. Of what to do, what to say. Uncertain of myself. Having Lilla here, it's like I'm someone I don't know. I used to know what I wanted. I knew who I was. At least I thought I did. Now I wonder if it's like Makayla thinking she went to her great-grandmother's funeral. Did I just think I knew myself? Did I just think I was happy? I don't want to blame everything on Lilla, especially since none of this is her fault. But things were definitely easier before she came home. I don't know if easier is better or not.

I look at her door again and then I go down the hall and stand in front of Mom and Dad's door. I can see that there's a light on. I wait a minute and listen, just to make sure there's no funny business going on in there. I don't hear anything. I knock.

"Come in," Mom calls. She doesn't sound sleepy.

I open the door. "My fever's down." I glance around. Dad's not in bed with Mom. And their bathroom light is out.

"That's good news. If you wake up in the middle of the night, you should take some more ibuprofen." Mom's lying in bed wearing an old flannel shirt that used to be Granddad's. She uses it for a sleep shirt. She's propped up on pillows, her iPad beside her. She's been reading.

"Where's Dad?" I ask. I didn't see any light coming from downstairs.

Mom pats the bed beside me and I get in with her. She's got an old quilt on the end of her bed that some old aunt in her family made. It's some kind of pattern from Pennsylvania. It's been here as long as I have. I lie down beside her, my head on Dad's pillow, and pull the quilt over both of us.

Mom rolls onto her side, propping herself up on her elbow. When I look at her face, I realize she's been crying. "You okay?" I ask her.

She nods and lies down, her head on Dad's pillow beside mine. She puts her arm around me and I don't even mind. It's probably the fever. I was afraid she was going to say I was sick because I went away for the weekend with Olivia. I was afraid she'd use that as an excuse next time I wanted to do something outside her comfort zone. But she didn't blame Olivia or the trip. And I'm so glad because I really had a good time. Makayla's still my bestie, of course; we were baby besties. But it's fun having another friend. And I really like Olivia's mom and her aunt Judy. Everybody was so nice to me and they like to play games. We played lots of games and ate breakfast for dinner and took walks and shot marshmallows out of little plastic guns at each other.

I stare at the ceiling; it's pretty. There are big tin tiles with olive branch circles pushed into them. Mom says it needs to be painted but I kind of like the chippy paint.

Mom rests her arm across my stomach and sighs.

I can almost feel Dad's absence in the room, like it's radiating off her. Then I realize what's going on. "He's not coming home, is he?" I ask her in a whisper.

She's quiet for what seems like a really long time before she says, "No."

"Tomorrow night?"

"Probably not."

I stare at the ceiling trying not to be angry at him because why should I be? I knew he wasn't going to stay. I knew it even if Mom didn't. He loves us, but it's like he doesn't want to love us all the time. I don't get it, but that's how he is. Dad's Dad. "So he's moving out again?"

She doesn't answer.

I turn my head to look at her. "Mom?"

"He's moving back to his apartment. We decided tonight." She says each word like it hurts her. "We wanted to wait to talk to you girls until after I spoke with the family therapist."

I think the part about the therapist is dumb. The whole therapy thing seems dumb to me. Mom knows me. And she's a good mom. I wish she'd trust herself more. "Lilla's going to be really upset," I say.

"Which is why I want to handle this right."

"You should have told her you guys weren't married anymore. I don't think there was anything wrong with Dad being here, sleeping here, whatever. That's your business. But making her think we were this, like . . . neat little, like you see in commercials on TV"—I turn my hands one way and then the other like I'm forming a box—"family." I shake my head. "Not cool, Mom."

She sighs. "In retrospect, we realize that. At the time, we thought this would make things easier for her. We were so excited; I suppose we weren't thinking clearly. And . . . we were hoping we could make it work, Jojo. Your father and I." She lies back to stare at the ceiling with me. "We really were."

I think about telling her I knew Dad wasn't going to stay. That he liked his life the way it was. Easy, simple. We worked around his schedule and what he wanted all the time. I think he thought he was doing what Mom wanted, but that wasn't the way it was. I was here and I could watch, kind of from the outside. It's not that I don't think Dad loves Mom. He does. He loves her a lot more than a lot of dads I see who still live with their wives. But I get why Mom's sad. She's got to wonder what's wrong with her that he doesn't love her enough.

I guess I should feel that way, too, but I don't. If it were Mom, it would be different. I'd cry forever if Mom left and I was here with Dad. And I guess Lilla now. Because even though Mom makes me crazy with her constant wanting to control everything I do, she and I are still a team.

I look at Mom and she's crying. But she's not making any sound. Tears are making wet lines down her face.

A lump comes up in my throat and my eyes sting. I don't usually cry. It must be this virus. "I'm sorry, Mom," I say quietly. "I know you wanted him to stay here with you."

She turns her head and leans to kiss me on my temple.

"I love you, Josephine."

"I love you, too, Mom." I roll over and lay my head on her shoulder. "And I won't ever leave you. I promise."

38

Harper

Remy kept his promise and showed up this morning before the girls got up. I didn't tell him that Jojo had already figured out what was going on. I'm not sure why. I almost feel as if we're drawing battle lines and I know Jojo is on my side. And I can guess whose side Georgina will be on. I'm still mulling over whether or not we need the therapist's help to tell Georgina her father's moving out.

When I finish my coffee and toast, Jojo still isn't up. If she's still not feeling well, she might sleep all day. "I'm going to the grocery store," I tell Georgina. "Want to come with?"

She and Remy are seated, side by side, across from me at the center island in the kitchen. Looking at their phones. Reading the morning news. They do it every morning unless I specifically exclude the use of iPhones at breakfast. This morning I'm happy to enjoy my coffee and not talk.

"Um . . . no thanks." Georgina glances up at me. "I'm going to take the streetcar to the bakery. If that's okay," she adds.

"No temple?"

She shrugs. She's looking at her phone again. "Dad, you see where that Roman bust was found in Scotland?"

"Did," he answers, not looking up from his phone. "Be a while before we know if it's authentic."

"Decided to skip temple," Georgina says to me. "Maybe next week."

"I've got a flag football tournament next Saturday." Remy sips his coffee, never lifting his head. "Probably be okay if you walk over yourself. Right, baby?"

That last bit is for me. It grates on my nerves that after last night he thinks he can call me *baby*. He's acting as if nothing is wrong. As if nothing is about to change. For all of us. "Okay," I say. "If you text me when you get there and when you leave." I get up, taking my coffee mug with me. "You don't want a ride to the bakery?"

"Nah. I'm fine." Georgina.

"She likes the streetcar." Remy.

I hesitate. I've been tiptoeing around my eldest, trying not to upset her, and I'm realizing that might not be the healthiest approach. For either of us. I need to treat her more as if she's the daughter I've always had, not the daughter I'm afraid I'm going to lose again at any moment. If she were Jojo, I'd tell her to get in the car. "Come on, Georgina. You can ride a few blocks with your mother." I walk my mug to the sink. "Ride with me there and take the streetcar home."

Georgina sighs. "Okay. Fine."

It doesn't sound as if it's fine, but it won't hurt her to spend a few minutes alone with me.

She drains her mug and carries it to the sink. "When are you leaving?"

"Ten minutes."

She walks out of the kitchen.

"I'm going to the grocery store," I tell Remy. I think about offering to grab some things for him that he might want for his apartment, but then I decide he's the one who's leaving. He can buy his own damned groceries.

"Okay," he answers, engrossed in something he's reading. "I'm going to check the clothes dryer vent. See if I can find the leak. I'll look at the girls' sink, too. Don't know if we need a new faucet or just some washers or something." He sips his coffee. "Anything else you want me to do?"

Love me enough to want to stay?

I think it, but I don't say it. "The list is on the refrigerator. Pick a repair, any repair," I tell him, headed out of the kitchen.

Georgina and I are in the car fifteen minutes later. It's overcast, but not cold. I ask her a couple of questions about school, but I get monosyllable answers. She got an A on her *Great Gatsby* paper. Her teacher said it was insightful. She likes her new friend Em; Em invited her to come over next week.

"Just drop me off on the corner of Louisiana," she tells me as we hum along St. Charles.

"I can drop you off at the bakery. I'm in no hurry to buy paper goods and lentils."

"I'll walk to Magazine."

She stares straight ahead, seeming preoccupied. Her backpack is on her lap. To carry her loaf of English muffin bread. I'm almost certain she still has a whole loaf at home; she and Remy are the only ones who eat it. I'm trying to go easy on the carbs. But I don't say anything. She can always put it in the freezer. I get that this has become a ritual of sorts; she does it almost every Saturday.

Spotting a place to pull over a block from Louisiana, I concede and swing into the spot. "Text me when you get there?"

She cuts her eyes at me.

I ignore her. "And when you get home. I might as well run errands while I'm out. So I'll be a little while."

The moment the car stops rolling forward, Georgina opens the door and hops out. "Thanks."

"You're welcome." I lean forward so I can see her face as she stands beside the car, swinging her backpack onto her back. She's wearing the North Face jacket I bought her. She seems to like it. "I love you, Georgina."

She stands there for a moment and then leans over so we're eye to eye. She shifts her backpack on her shoulder. She looks so solemn. "I don't know what to say when you say that."

"You don't have to say anything, Georgina." My smile is tight.

A mother's smile that's hopeful but realistic. "See you at home later."

Before I reach the dry cleaners, she texts me she's at the bakery. Less than ten minutes later, she texts that she's headed home. I've picked up the dry cleaning, dropped off a pair of shoes to be re-soled, hit the post office, and am halfway through the grocery store when I text Remy to check the grocery list on the refrigerator for me. We keep a running list, but I forgot it this morning. I have a good idea what's on it—the same things that are on it every week—but I check anyway.

Got the lentils, green apples, almond milk, and spinach fettuc-cine. Check the list on the fridge, I text Remy. **Anything else?**

Spicy mustard, he texts back.

"Spicy mustard, spicy mustard," I say to myself, pushing the cart, backtracking to an aisle I already went down. I locate the mustard and toss it in the cart.

Got it, I text. **Be ten more minutes here in case you think of something else**

K

I check the time on my phone and text, **Georgina home??**

I push the cart back in the direction I've come. My phone in the back pocket of my jeans beeps as I'm trying to decide be-tween two granolas, one organic, one not. Of course the organic is three dollars more a bag. Choosing the organic because it has dried blueberries in it, I toss it in the cart and check my phone.

No, Remy has texted.

I stand there staring at my phone, feeling a little disoriented.

She's not back yet?

N

It's been forty-five minutes since Georgina texted me she was on her way home. Even on a Saturday, it shouldn't take her forty-five minutes to get back to our house. I call Remy.

It rings once. Twice. A third time.

"Really? You're not going to pick up?" I say under my breath. "I know you have your phone. You just texted me."

He picks up just as I'm about to hang up and ring him again.

"Georgina isn't home?" I say.

"No. Which is why I texted you that she wasn't." His tone is equally as cool as mine.

"But she texted me forty-five minutes ago. Forty-eight, and said she was on her way."

"Maybe she had to wait for a streetcar. You know how they are sometimes. Do you know where the plumbing tape is? The white stuff you wrap around the threads of a pipe? I think I figured out why the faucet is dripping."

I think for a second. "Should I call her? Text her?"

He doesn't respond.

"Remy, I'm asking what you think."

I get one of his impatient exhalations. "Harper, it doesn't matter what I think. You're going to do what you want no matter what I say."

I take a breath. I'm not going to get in an argument with him right now. I'm not going to start one. "You're right. Ultimately I do make my own choices, but I respect your opinion, Remy. And whether I like it or not, right now, you're getting along better with her than I am. So I'm asking you. How do you think I should respond to this?"

"Don't call her. Don't text her. Maybe she got off the streetcar early and she's walking the rest of the way home. She had a lot more freedom in her life before she came here. I know she misses it."

"Right," I agree, pushing the cart again. She can text while she's walking though, I think. "You're probably right. She probably just decided to walk part of the way home. She likes walking. I'll give her a little while longer." I grab a box of crackers and head for the registers. "See you shortly. I'm sure she'll be home by the time I get there."

But she isn't.

"Did you call her?" I ask Remy, trying not to panic as I put down three cloth grocery bags on the counter.

He's standing at the island, digging through a little plastic box of screws and nuts and nails. "No."

"She should be home by now." I pull my phone out of my pocket and call her. She doesn't pick up. "Hey, it's Mom," I say when there's a beep in my ear. "Call me back. *Now,* please," I add. I wait a moment and then set the phone down on the counter and start putting groceries away. I try to keep control of my heart rate that's threatening to ratchet up. I practice taking slow, deep breaths. After two trips to the refrigerator, I pick up my phone and text her.

You okay?

I wait. Nothing. I set down the phone and go back to the groceries. When they're put away, and I've still heard nothing, I text again.

Please call or text. I'm getting worried

As I fold the bags, I watch my phone on the counter. It doesn't light up. It doesn't vibrate. "Can you call her?" I ask Remy quietly. "It's been two hours since I dropped her off. She should be home."

He looks at me.

"Please. She should be here."

He pulls his phone out of his pocket and calls. Waits. "Hey, it's Dad. Call me. We're getting worried."

"Jojo talk to her this morning?" I ask when he hangs up.

"I don't think so. She's still asleep."

I go upstairs, knock lightly, and when Jojo doesn't answer, I open the door. Her hurricane of a room is dark and she's asleep in her bed. I close the door behind me. At Georgina's door, I stand there for a moment before I open it. Nothing looks out of place. The room is still very bare. Her bed's still in the middle of the room. I keep offering to help her move it to the wall. I even suggested she ask her dad if she didn't want me to help. She seems to like it in the middle of the room.

I close the door and lean against it. My heart is fluttering. Where can she be? *Where can she be?* She couldn't have been kidnapped. I know that. I know the odds are infinitesimal. I close my eyes, thinking. Has someone taken her against her will, or has she gone somewhere she doesn't want us to know about?

My gut instinct, my mother's instinct, tells me it's the latter. I go back down to the kitchen. "You think she ran away?" I ask him. "Or, is just AWOL? Like when she went to her old house?"

He's holding his phone. Now he looks worried, too. "I don't know," he says. "The place where they were living has been rented out. The landlord contacted me about some stuff they found in the attic. I asked Lilla about it and she said it wasn't theirs. That it had been left from the previous renters. So she knows it's been rented. That she can't go inside anymore." He glances up at me. "It's not like Lilla to not respond to me. We text all the time; she always answers."

I start to pace. Where would she go? I think. Where would she go? Em's? I don't have her number. To see my dad, maybe? She's been asking to go alone.

"Do you think we should call the police?" Remy asks.

In other circumstances, I might have laughed because that's usually my line. I phone our daughter again, this time speaking sharply. "Georgina, call me back *now*. Your dad and I are seriously concerned."

When she doesn't call me back, I text her again.

Your dad wants to call the police. Where are you?

I stare at the screen. No response. I look up at Remy, wondering if he's right. I wonder how long we should wait before we call the police.

Remy's watching me. "Where would she go?" he asks.

My phone lights up and I grab it off the counter.

I'm fine, our daughter has texted back.

My fingers fly over the keyboard. **Where are you?**

I wait a long, agonizing minute before she responds.

I'll tell you when I'm on my way home. It will be a few hours.

"A few hours?" I demand. I hand the phone to Remy so he can see her text. "Now what do we do?"

Jojo walks into the kitchen. She's wearing yoga pants and a sweatshirt and her blond hair is piled on top of her head. She looks as if she's been awake less than five minutes. She opens the fridge and peers in. "What's up?"

"Lilla's gone somewhere," Remy says.

I press the heel of my hand to my forehead, refusing to allow myself to panic. Telling myself that's the old Harper. That's the woman I don't want to be anymore. "We don't know where."

Jojo frowns as she pulls the orange juice from the refrigerator. "You don't know where?"

I take my phone back from Remy. "I dropped her off at the bakery and did my errands. She was supposed to take the streetcar home. She texted me she was headed home and never arrived. She just texted to say she's okay, but she won't tell us where she is."

Jojo sets the jug of orange juice on the counter and reaches for a glass. She seems to be thinking.

"What do you think?" I ask Remy.

Before he can respond, Jojo says, "Don't you think she'll just come home when she's done whatever she's doing? I mean . . . where else is she going to go?"

"We can't just let her leave whenever she feels like it and not tell us where she's going. I'd never leave the house without telling you where I was going."

Jojo pours her juice, watching it glug into the glass. "I guess you could use the location thingy." She lifts one shoulder and lets it fall. "But where would she go? I bet she's just riding the streetcar line from one end to the other. She used to do that all the time before she moved here."

I look at Jojo, confused. "What *location thingy?*"

My daughter sighs as if I ask the most ridiculous questions. "On your phone, *Mom.* I know you turned it on on mine. So you could *spy* on me."

I have to think for a moment to realize what she's talking about. Then I remember that I was chatting with the cell phone guy the last time I took Jojo's phone in to have the screen fixed. While I waited, I was telling him about how the phone had been lost for three days, so having it turn up with just a cracked screen didn't seem so bad. He turned something on on my phone and Jojo's. He said if she lost her phone we could find it. He also told me, when Jojo wandered away to look at new phones, that it was also a way for parents to inconspicuously keep track of their teens. I want to ask Jojo how she knew I had the *location thingy* on, but I'd save that for another conversation. One to take place when my other daughter isn't missing.

The important information in this conversation is that the same guy sold me Georgina's phone. And he remembered me.

I look at Jojo. "I think it is turned on."

"That's really not cool, Mom." She makes a face and then takes a sip of juice. "Spying on your kids."

I hand Jojo my cell phone. "How does it work? How do I find her?"

She makes an event of setting down her glass and taking my phone from me. There's a long sigh, obviously meant to demonstrate boredom. She taps my phone. Swipes. After a long minute, she says, "I-10."

My heart drops to my feet, ready to be kicked. "What?"

Jojo holds up the phone so I can see the screen. I grab my spare readers off the counter and slide them on. I'm staring at a map, a portion of New Orleans. There's a pulsing red dot. If Georgina still has her phone, she's on the interstate, headed west, out of the city.

39

Lilla

I wipe my snotty nose on the sleeve of my new North Face jacket because I don't have a tissue. I'm trying not to cry. I hate crying. It makes me feel as if I have no control of my life. Which I suppose I don't.

They wouldn't let me in at the prison. I made it all the way here without being hit by a car while walking all the way to an I-10 on-ramp or murdered by a psychopath on the highway, and then they wouldn't let me see my mom.

Because I'm under eighteen.

Under eighteen, you have to have a parent or a guardian, the lady at the window told me after I waited in line for, like, twenty minutes. She said she was sorry, but she didn't act like it. I tried to tell her I only needed to see my mom for a minute. She asked me how I got there and I just mumbled "Thank you" and walked away. I was afraid she would call the police if she figured out I came on my own. I don't think they can arrest me for coming here without permission from my parents, but I didn't want to wait to find out.

Now I'm standing outside the prison, near the sign, crying like an idiot. Because I was an idiot to think this would work. That I could just come here by myself, see my mom, and get on with my life. My new life.

And now it's starting to rain. . . . What happened to warm, sunny New Orleans? It seems as if all it does here is rain.

I shift my backpack. I went to the bakery, but I didn't get English muffin bread. I got these café au lait donuts my mom likes. I was going to see if they would let me take one in to her. I have flavored bubbly water, too. We were supposed to get to sit in a room and talk. It's not like you see in movies, where you have to talk on a phone and only see each other through a glass wall.

I look at the country road I'll have to take back to the on-ramp. I know it was dangerous to hitchhike here. But I was so excited about coming that I wasn't really scared. Two women picked me up near the I-10 ramp. Evy and Jerilene. They were headed to Baton Rouge. They talked about Jesus all the way to the exit to the road to St. Gabriel, where the prison is. I didn't tell them where I was going, but I think they figured it out. They were nice enough, but the Jesus talk was a little overwhelming. I told them I'd think about visiting the First African Baptist Church of New Orleans. I doubt Harper Mom will let me, but I didn't tell them that. I've never been to a Baptist church, or to an African American one. I wouldn't mind checking it out. So I wasn't lying to Evy and Jerilene. And they didn't hurt me. Or even scare me.

But now I'm here and I didn't even get to see Sharon Mom and now I'm scared to hitchhike home.

I look back in the direction of the prison. Maybe I should try to get a ride back to New Orleans with someone here visiting a prisoner. There were a lot of people in the line waiting to get in, a lot of people with kids. No one would kidnap a teenager with their kids in the car, would they?

I almost laugh out loud. I've already been kidnapped once in my life. What are the chances it could happen again? Dad's been telling Harper Mom that for two months now.

It starts to rain harder and I pull up my hood. The rain is cold and my jeans are getting wet. And tears are running down my cheeks. I need to do something, but I don't know what.

Call a cab?

If someone would take me all the way to New Orleans, Harper

Mom or Dad would pay for it. They'd give someone a hundred-dollar tip for bringing me home.

Or do I just call them and ask them to come get me?

I texted Harper Mom that I was okay and that I'd be home in a few hours, but I know she's got to be going crazy, worrying about me.

I should just call her. At least tell her I'm safe.

Maybe she'll call a cab for me and give her credit card number or something. Or maybe there's some way for her to order me an Uber and pay for it with her card.

I look up at the sign that says *Louisiana Correctional Institute for Women*. The place doesn't look like what I thought it would. Not like the creepy brick buildings at Sing Sing or Alcatraz that I saw in documentaries on TV. A lot of these buildings look like pole sheds to me.

I watch a car go by on its way out; there are kids in the backseat. I wonder if I should try and flag them down. Then one of the kids sticks her tongue out at me and I decide I wouldn't want to ride for an hour in the car with them, anyway.

I wonder if Sharon Mom has realized I'm not coming. Maybe she even found out they wouldn't let me in because I didn't have an adult with me. Would someone tell her, or is she just sitting there waiting?

I pull my phone out of the back pocket of my jeans, thinking it would be funny, not ha-ha funny, but ironic funny, if I couldn't get a signal. Then I can't call home. But I've got three bars.

I want to talk to Dad. But for some reason, my thumb finds Harper Mom's number and I touch it. I call before I chicken out and walk out to the highway to hitchhike and possibly beat the odds and get kidnapped again.

40

Harper

When my phone rings, I look at the caller ID on the dash of my car. I see Georgina's name and my first response is surprise . . . no, shock. Then I wonder if someone has taken her phone from her, or is using it to make a ransom call.

I hit the "receive" button on the dash. "Georgina?" I try not to sound as afraid for her as I am.

"Harper . . . Mom?"

"Oh, Georgina." I exhale in a long breath, gripping the steering wheel. "Are you all right?" The windshield wipers make a rhythmic sound and it seems as if it takes forever for her to respond.

"I'm all right." Her voice breaks.

And tears immediately spring to my eyes. "Georgina, thank you for calling me. Thank you for letting us know you're okay." My anger that she's taken off is gone. I'm just so relieved, so thankful to hear her voice. "Did you already talk to your dad?"

"No." She sniffs.

I can tell she's trying not to cry, so I try, too.

"I just called you," she says in the smallest voice.

And my heart is breaking as only a mother's heart can break for her child in pain.

"Where are you, honey?"

"Could you . . . could Dad . . . could someone come get me? I'm really sorry. I just want to . . ." Her voice trembles. "I'm sorry."

"Of course I'll come get you. Where are you?" I repeat. I already know, if the *location thingy* on my phone is correct. I've got my phone mounted on my dash so I could watch her little pulsing dot. It's been in the same place for the last ten minutes. I just took the exit off I-10 to the town of St. Gabriel where the Louisiana women's state prison is located.

"I'm sorry," she says again. "I came to see . . . I wanted to see her. My mom. Sharon. But they wouldn't let me in." She's making no attempt to hold back her tears now. "I couldn't go in by myself. Because I'm underage. I need a . . . I have to have a parent to see her."

"Where at the prison?" I ask, thinking she must be in some waiting room. Surely the prison guards wouldn't have let a minor just walk out of the building.

"I'm outside. Sharon doesn't know I'm not coming. She's waiting for me."

Several things pass through my head. None of them charitable, all along the lines of *Sharon Kohen can continue to wait to see my daughter until hell freezes over.* I also wonder how it is that Sharon thinks *my* daughter, who *she* kidnapped, is coming to see her. Were they writing letters to each other? I know e-mails aren't allowed. Were they talking? Did Sharon somehow get Georgina's cell phone number? Our house number?

"Can you text without hanging up?" I ask her.

"Um . . . yeah." She sniffs. "I don't have a tissue."

"I have tissues in my car. I'll be there in five minutes, Georgina." Four, if I don't obey the speed limit signs, which I'm not. "Honey, I need you to text your dad and let him know you're okay and that I'm almost there. I'll stay on the line."

"How did you know where I was?" My daughter who usually seems to have her shit together better than I do sounds lost. She sounds like a little girl. A lost little girl. "Dad's not with you?"

"He stayed home in case you showed up there." I came because I had to. Because sitting at the house, waiting, wasn't an option for me. "So go ahead and text him. I'll be right here. I won't hang up."

"Okay," she says in her little voice.

A series of beeps come out of the speakers of my car. There's a pause, then Georgina's voice. "I texted him."

"Good. Now where are you?" I turn my windshield wipers up.

"Um . . . I'm walking out to the road."

Relief floods every fiber of my being as I spot her up ahead in her gray jacket, her blue backpack on her back.

I pull onto the entrance road to the prison and throw my car in park, and jump out. I'm wearing my Saturday clean-the-house-and-go-to-the-market flannel shirt and no jacket. Rain hits my face. I reach out and grab Georgina, determined to get a hug, even if she fights me.

She doesn't fight me.

She stands there, arms at her sides, letting me hug her. Hug her and her backpack still on her back. Both of us stand there in the rain and I silently thank God for her. I thank the Holy Mother. I thank her Son. For just the briefest moment, Georgina lays her head on my shoulder.

I feel a flood of overwhelming warmth. How long have I waited for her touch?

"I love you, Georgina," I whisper in her ear, basking in the feel of her in my arms, remembering the smell of her hair when she was a baby. "And it's okay if you don't love me back. I have enough for both of us."

She sniffs and takes a step away from me, and I let go of her. I smile at her. "Let's go home," I say.

She throws her backpack into the backseat and gets in the passenger side. I get in, buckle up, turn up the heat, and make a U-turn, headed for the interstate. But not five hundred feet down the road, I slow up.

I'm thinking about Sharon. I don't want to, but I can't stop thinking about her. I'm imagining her sitting in her prison uniform waiting for the girl she thinks . . . *thought* was her child.

Against my will, I imagine what it would be like to be her. Wanting so desperately to see her daughter. Realizing it isn't going to happen.

And then I think of Georgina. The desperation it took for her to come here. The determination. The bravery.

I hit my brakes and swing onto some sort of gravel access road.

"Where are we going?" Georgina presses her hand to the dash to steady herself.

I back onto the road, drive in the direction we just came from, and turn into the prison lot. "When are visiting hours over?" I ask my runaway.

"Two," she says, staring at me. "But you have to check in by one fifteen. Why?"

I look at the clock on the dash. We have eight minutes.

41

Lilla

I stand beside Harper Mom and listen to her give sass right back to the lady at the window who wasn't very nice to me.

"Two minutes," Harper Mom keeps saying. "The handbook says we have until one fifteen to check in and we have *two more minutes*." She shoves my driver's license and hers across the counter to the woman. "We're here to see Sharon Kohen. She's expecting us."

I've never seen my mother like this before, all authoritative and confident. Dad told me she's a really good veterinarian, that she's really amazing at her job. I wonder if this woman standing here now, refusing to take no for an answer from a prison guard with blue sparkly fingernails like claws, is the woman people in her office see. Is this the woman Dad fell in love with when he was in college?

I stand there holding my breath. I can't believe Harper Mom is going to let me see Sharon. She turned the car around so I could see her. I can't believe it.

"Background check?" my mother says. She has this look of indignation on her face. "Well, if you have my daughter's, obviously mine has to be there. I certainly wouldn't submit my daughter's without mine. Check again, please."

Background check? I didn't send in information for a background check. Sharon Mom must have done it. I think that costs money. How she paid for it, I have no idea. But there's no way Sharon Mom submitted a background check on Harper.

The two of them are still arguing. I'm not going to get in. We're going to have to go home and I'm not going to see my mother. And I don't know if I can come back again. I don't know if I can keep living like this, one thread attached to Sharon, trying to loop another around Harper.

All of a sudden I feel sick to my stomach. Light-headed. I've never fainted before, but I'm guessing it feels like this right before it happens.

Then I hear Harper Mom say, "Thank you," and she grabs my hand.

"Thank you so much for your help, Angel," she says. "My daughter and I appreciate this more than you can imagine."

Angel is smiling at Harper Mom like they're buddies as we walk toward the door to the visiting room. I have no idea what Harper Mom said to her or what she promised her to get us in. Free vaccinations for her dog? My sister?

A female guard in uniform who's shorter than Jojo opens a door for us and we're in a big, stark room with tables and chairs. It's half full of people. I stand next to one mom, looking desperately for the other. I don't see her. What if we came to the wrong place? What if they transferred her or something?

I feel Harper Mom tug on my hand. "You need to sit down," she says in my ear. "She'll be out in a moment." Then she lets go of my hand.

I turn back to her, suddenly scared. "Aren't you . . . are you coming with me?"

She half smiles, her lips together. It's her sad smile. "No. You need to do this alone and honestly, honey . . . I'm not ready. Maybe someday." Her eyes tear up, making me feel like I'm going to cry. "But not today. Now go on, sit down at one of the empty tables. I'll sit right here waiting for you." She points to an empty table near the door.

I feel as if I'm walking through mud as I shuffle to the table.

The room is loud and I think everyone is looking at me. But nobody is. Everyone is busy talking in their little groups around the tables. Nobody cares about me and my problems; they have their own jailbirds to deal with. Visitors and prisoners are laughing. There are children playing in one corner of the room. How do you laugh in a place like this? I wonder as I sit down.

I'm so nervous now that I have to pee. I *really* have to pee. But it's already one twenty. There isn't much visiting time left today. And if I go out to use the bathroom, they might not let me back in. I glance over my shoulder at Harper Mom. She's talking to the guard who let us in. They're both smiling. Harper Broussard is making friends with a prison guard. I'm in a prison lounge waiting to talk with the woman who kidnapped me. I feel as if I'm on another planet. Or in a dream. I feel—

"*Bubbeleh.*"

When I hear her voice, I feel as if I'm being sucked back through a big wind tunnel. I'm a little girl again. In a park in some Southern city, flying a kite. At a kitchen counter, cutting vegetables when I'm too young to be using a knife. In a bed, snuggled next to my mother, listening to her read *Harry Potter and the Half-Blood Prince.*

And suddenly there Sharon is, in a light-blue top that looks like one a dental hygienist would wear. And baggy navy pants that have the letters LCIW stenciled down the leg. Louisiana Correctional Institute for Women.

I should stand but my legs feel like jelly. She wraps her arms around me and I close my eyes and breathe in her smell. And even though I know it's not possible, I smell her Calvin Klein perfume and sweet potato biscuits.

"Lilla," she breathes in my ear.

Mama Bear. I move my lips but I'm not sure if I say it out loud.

"Sharon," a male guard in the corner of the room says in a heavy Cajun accent. "Have a seat."

Sharon squeezes my arm, lets go, and plops down in the chair across from me. She reaches for my hand but I keep them on my lap. I look at her and she looks at me. Her eyes are full of tears, but mine aren't now. I had so many things I wanted to say to her. A whole script I wrote in my head. But now that I'm here . . . I can't remember a single one of my lines.

"Lilla, you look so pretty," she says. "And you're taller. Have you gotten taller?"

I look down at the table. I can barely find my voice. I think about the donuts I bought for her this morning. Harper Mom said to leave my backpack in the car. She said we wouldn't have time to take it back if they wouldn't let me take it into the visiting room. She just carried her keys and her wallet. The donuts probably aren't good anymore anyway. They're probably smooshed. And I drank the water earlier when I got thirsty.

"I can't stay long," I hear myself say. "Visiting hours are only a half hour more."

"I thought you would be here earlier," she bubbles. "I've been waiting hours."

"I couldn't get in by myself. My mom had to come in with me." I don't know why I say the word. To hurt her the way she hurt me? Or because I'm beginning to think of Harper as my mother. I don't know which explanation is more upsetting.

Sharon doesn't respond to my dig.

"No one under eighteen is allowed in without a parent," I say. "Harper had to bring me." I don't go into the details. What's the point?

"She's here?" She looks up, scans the room, and then breathes in sharply.

I don't look over my shoulder, but I can guess she's figured out which one Harper is.

"She's so beautiful," Sharon murmurs. "So young. Blond."

She touches her own dark hair, which is a lot grayer than I remember. It's been two months since the police took me from my home and dragged me to the *upside down*. Looking at Sharon, it seems as if it's been three years. Or thirty.

"She doesn't want to talk to you," I say before she asks. "You know, since you abducted me from her and held me captive and all." Those words were definitely meant to be mean, though they weren't in the script.

More tears.

I ignore them. "Have you been sentenced? My dad told me you had an attorney. That even though you pleaded guilty, you'd get a sentencing hearing."

"I'm still waiting. It's . . . next month, I think. My attorney is good. And nice. She . . . she's putting my finances in order. There's money for you. Money I've been saving since you were little. For college. And a little money I inherited from my parents when they died. She'll be contacting your father and making the arrangements."

I nod. So her parents *are* dead. At least that's not a lie. "The landlord rented out the shotgun to someone else," I say. "I got some stuff out of the house before they moved in. Your knives."

That seems to upset her. Her eyes fill with tears and she looks away, but she doesn't seem to be looking at anything in particular. We sit here for a minute not saying anything and I think about getting up and walking out of here. Because I don't know if I'm ready to do this. Before I can make up my mind, she turns her attention to me again. Her eyes focus again.

"*Bubbeleh*, I'm so sorry. I know you can't understand why I did what I did."

"Why you abducted me, you mean."

She sighs as if she's very tired from a long night at work. "I hardly understand myself why I did it. Let me explain to you what happened—"

"I know what happened," I interrupt. "The police told us. Your baby Lilla died and so you took me and made me your Lilla." I pick at one of my cuticles. "What I want to know is did you ever think about them? About my mother who was crying for me the way you must have cried when your baby died." I look up at her. My eyes are wet, and my throat is constricted, but I'm not crying. I'm too angry to cry. Too hurt.

"I was sick, Baby Bear. I actually . . . I thought you were the

Lilla I gave birth to. Most of the time. You have to believe me when I tell you that I didn't go to the parade that day to take someone's baby. I went because . . . I was so sad. I thought it might cheer me up and then I saw you and . . . I thought you were Lilla." She begins to cry loudly.

I glance around to see if anyone is looking at us, but they're not. Except probably Harper Mom, but I don't look over my shoulder at her because if I do, I know I'll lose it.

"Stop," I say in a whisper.

She makes a shuddering sound and reaches into her pocket and pulls out a wad of toilet paper. She wipes her eyes and blows her nose. While she's doing it, I study her. She's lost weight and she looks older. She looks like the mother I grew up with, and yet she doesn't. In a way, she just looks like a woman with the name of a prison stenciled on her pants.

"You have to believe me when I tell you I never meant to hurt anyone," she says when she has control of herself again. "Least of all you."

"Okay, so you made a mistake. Why didn't you give me back? When I was a baby. You could have left me at a police station or a synagogue or . . . a grocery store. At any time." I lift my hand and let it fall to the table. "I get taking me. Sort of. It was an impulse. You were grieving. But *keeping* me? Keeping someone else's child?" I lean across the table, looking her in the eye. "My parents thought some pervert kidnapped me, raped me, and murdered me. Their two-year-old! My sister told her friends I was buried in pieces in the bayou."

That gets the attention of an old lady next to us. I sit back in the plastic chair.

Again, we're both quiet.

Sharon sniffs and looks at me. "I couldn't because I fell in love with you. I loved you too much. And as time passed, the weeks, the months, the years, I . . . pretended. Because I wanted it to be true." She hangs her head for a moment and then lifts it again.

"Our life together was based on untruths, but my love for you was a truth." She hesitates. "And your love for me was a truth, too."

I look into her eyes for a long moment. And I believe her. I believe her love was real. I know mine was.

My lower lip trembles. "So now what?" I whisper. "Now what do I do? Because you're going to be here for at least twenty years."

"What do you do?" She reaches out and takes my hand. When I resist, she clasps it tighter. "You don't allow what I did to ruin your future. You live your life. You be happy. You get past this and you live a good, happy, productive life. That's what you do, *bubbeleh*."

I refuse to meet her gaze, but I don't pull my hand away.

"They're good people, your mother and father. After it happened . . . after I did it, I followed their story in the news. They seemed like good people. And I know they love you. I can't imagine how happy they are to have you home." She's quiet for a second. "Actually I can." She lets go of me.

I leave my hand where it is on the table. "I don't know if I can come back here to see you for a while," I say softly. "It's really hard. Being Lilla and Georgina at the same time."

"I understand."

I take a breath. Let it out. "I don't know when I can come back, but . . . until I can, we could write."

"I would love that." She looks past me. "Will they let you write to me?" She gives a little laugh. "I suppose if they were willing to bring you here, they're willing to let us correspond."

Suddenly I feel overwhelmed and it's hard to breathe. I knew it was going to be difficult to come here. To see her. But I didn't realize how conflicted I would feel. How much I would love and hate this woman at the same time.

"I have to go now." I start to get up.

"No, no, we have a few more minutes," she says desperately. "Please, Lilla—"

I shake my head. "I have to go," I repeat.

She's up now, throwing her arms around me. Someone calls her name. I guess we're not supposed to be hugging. I lift my arms and give her a quick squeeze and then I turn away. I hear her call my name, but I can't look back. Not now. Not today.

And then I see my other mom. Harper's just standing there by the door waiting for me. Waiting to take me home.

42

Harper

"Another family meeting?" Jojo stands at the top of the staircase looking down at me. "Mom," she groans dramatically. "I just took a shower. I have to blow-dry my hair, otherwise it'll get all frizzy." She's wearing yoga pants, a sweatshirt, and a towel twisted and piled high on her head.

"Dinner and family meeting," I say firmly. "Five minutes. In the dining room."

"Dining room?" Another groan. "Must be serious."

"Tell your sister!"

I find Remy in the dining room lining up cartons of takeout. He went to my favorite Thai place. A peace offering. He stayed over last night, mostly because I think he had to keep vigil over me so I wouldn't sit outside Georgina's bedroom door with a shotgun. If we had one. He and I lay in bed most of the night talking. We fell asleep in each other's arms. Tonight he's going back to his place, so it's time to talk to the girls.

I'm overwhelmed. Sad. Tired. But I have the strangest sense that things are going to get better now. Georgina and I actually talked on the way home from the prison yesterday. I think she has a better understanding of my feelings as the woman who gave birth to her. And I understand her better, too. There were no declarations of eternal love. No hugfest. But we both walked into the house, though drained, more aware of where the other was coming from.

Now I just want to get past the Remy detonation. So we can make a plan. So we can figure out what our family is going to look like now because obviously I'm not going to get the nuclear I dreamed of.

"They'll be down in a minute," I tell him.

"I poured wine for you." He points to a glass beside my plate. He's set the table and though we're serving out of takeout containers, he's put out real plates and even dug out cloth napkins. We all have water glasses. There's a glass of orange juice at Jojo's place.

I take a sip of wine and exhale through my mouth as if breathing through a labor contraction. I almost smile at the thought. These last months really have been like labor, the longest labor any mother has had to endure.

"It's going to be okay, baby," Remy reassures me, reaching for his own glass. He holds it by the stem, turning it, watching the wine swirl. He lifts it to his nose and breathes. "We'll make this work."

"She's going to be heartbroken," I whisper.

"Not to be unkind or flip, but she's had a lot of that lately." He sips. "She'll be okay. She's strong. Like her mother."

When he says that, it occurs to me that Sharon is really more responsible for Georgina's strength than I am. If I can ever face her, I think I'd like to thank her for that. She probably shouldn't hold her breath waiting for me in the prison waiting room, though. It's going to be a while before I go back. A while before Georgina is ready to go back again, too, I think.

I hear footsteps on the staircase. Two sets. I grab a lighter from a drawer in the massive china cabinet and light the three candles on the end of the table. I don't know why I decided we should eat in this big room, at this big table, huddled down at one end. Maybe because I feel as if we need to huddle together. That we need to form final bonds before others are severed?

Georgina comes in first: jeans, Tulane T-shirt, flip-flops, and bird's-nest hair. Then Jojo: hair still in a towel, scowl on her face. We all take our seats: Remy at the head of the table, me to his left, the girls to his right and across from me.

I fold my hands, bow my head, and close my eyes. "Bless us, O Lord, and these Thy gifts, which we are about to receive from Thy bounty, through Christ our Lord. Amen."

"Amen," Remy and Jojo echo.

I open my eyes in time to see them both cross themselves as I do the same. Georgina has her hands still clasped in prayer, her eyes closed. I have no idea how we're going to come to terms with her relationship to Judaism, but it makes my heart glad to see her head bowed in prayer. Because He's the same God, isn't He? Father Paul reminded me of that when we chatted after choir practice. He also talked about patience. For a priest, he didn't seem to be that upset by the idea that our daughter doesn't believe in the Holy Catholic Church or its doctrine. But the fact that he wasn't worried took some of the worry from me.

"So . . ." I say, reaching for a plate of spring rolls. "We've got something important to talk about."

"We going to go over the rules about visiting people in prison without permission?" Jojo demands.

I cut my eyes at her but before I can speak, she turns to Georgina.

"Sorry," she says, her tone actually contrite. "That wasn't nice." She lifts her gaze to meet her sister's. "I don't know why I say mean things sometimes."

Georgina lifts her shoulder, lets it fall. "It's okay," she answers quietly. "We're good, Jojo."

"Chili sauce for your spring rolls?" I pass a plastic packet to Georgina because I know she likes it. "We've got pad Thai noodles." I point to two cartons with my chopsticks. "Green curry, seafood preaw wan, oh, and rice. White and brown." I indicate the other cartons.

Remy reaches for one of the boxes of pad Thai. "We're just going to get right down to this, girls."

He takes a breath and I realize he's nervous. I don't know why, but somehow that makes me feel better. Not because he's uncomfortable or in emotional pain, but because I appreciate that he really does understand the ramifications of his actions. And he still believes this is best for our family.

He looks at me, then starts pulling pad Thai noodles out of the carton, onto his plate, with chopsticks. "I've decided to move back to my place."

Georgina is dipping a spring roll into chili sauce she's squeezed onto her plate. She freezes, turning her gaze to him. "You're leaving us?"

"No." He shakes his head. "No, I'm not leaving you." He sets the carton down on the table, glancing at me, then at Georgina. "I—" He exhales. "Honey, this is really between your mother and me. It's difficult to explain—"

"So you're moving out, but you think that's not leaving us?" Georgina practically throws her spring roll onto her plate.

He looks at me.

I sit forward in my chair. She has every right to be angry with him. We all do. "Your dad's not going to sleep here anymore, but he's not leaving us. He's not cutting us out of his life. Georgina, you're going to see plenty of your father. He'll eat here most nights with us, he can still go to temple with you on Saturdays, and . . . he—" I take a breath. "I know this living arrangement sounds unconventional, but you're going to have to trust us. We made this work before."

Jojo's put two spring rolls on her plate and is now munching away, saying nothing. She doesn't look in the least bit upset, but she already knew this was the plan. And she already knows that we really can make it work. And that her father isn't abandoning her.

"It's difficult to explain, honey," Remy says again. "Relationships between husband and wife are complicated."

Georgina shakes her head. "Not good enough, Dad. You want to leave us. Okay, so explain it. I know you-all were doing things this way before I got here, but I don't care about that. You can't just change things up on me and not give me an explanation. Why can't you live here with us?" She glances at me. "Why can't you be married to her? She's a nice person and she tries really hard."

He shifts in his chair and my heart goes out to him, because I know he loves us. And I know this is hard for him. Maybe even harder for him than me because I realize, from talking last night, that he feels like a failure. A failure as a father and as a husband. And maybe he is. But he's doing his best and I love him for that. I'll always love him for that.

He opens his hands and then closes them into fists. Trying to find the right words. "I don't know how to explain it, except to tell you that I can't be a husband to your mother all the time. Not the way she deserves. And I . . . I can't be a father to you girls 24/7." His voice cracks. "I've tried and I can't. I need space. I need time to myself. In order to be who I want to be for you." He looks from one of us to the next. Even Jojo has lifted her head to meet his gaze.

"So, your dad is going to move out and the three of us will stay here, but very little is going to change," I start to explain. "Your father—"

"If he's going, I'm going," Georgina declares.

I stare at her, shocked.

"Lilla," Remy says gently.

Georgina shakes her head. "No . . . no! If you don't have to stay here, I don't have to stay here. I want to go with you, Dad." She looks at me, her eyes filling with tears. "I want to go with him," she tells me.

And I feel as if I'm free falling. I never saw this coming. How did I not see it coming?

I look to Remy, pleading. For what, I don't know. For him to stay. For him to tell her she has to stay. For him to save me.

Jojo just sits there, shaking her head. "You know, it makes sense," she says, her voice stark in the silent room. "The two of them living in one place, us in another."

I look at my youngest daughter, feeling as if she's betrayed me. But the tears in her eyes tell me she hasn't. They're telling me she's being truthful.

"Look," Jojo says. "What's the big shocker here? Dad can't be a full-time husband or dad. Not even for you, Mom. We already know that. So, maybe it's the same thing with Lilla." She reaches for a carton of rice. "You want her to be your full-time daughter, Mom, but a couple of months ago"—she hooks her thumb over her shoulder—"she was someone else's daughter."

I reach for my napkin, fighting tears. "Jojo—"

"No, let her speak," Remy says, covering my hand with his.

"You're asking a lot, Mom. Maybe if Georgina lives with Dad for a while, she can get used to things. Maybe she won't feel so overwhelmed. And she can come here for dinners and stuff, just like Dad did . . . like he does." Jojo meets my gaze, suddenly seeming a lot older than fourteen to me. "Mom, I know you don't want to hear this, but I liked it when Dad lived in his apartment. You and I got along just fine. And things were better. You and he didn't argue. You laughed a lot. You liked each other again."

Now I'm the one shaking my head. "No, absolutely not. You are not leaving here, Georgina." I look to Remy. "You're not taking her from me."

"Dad, don't you want me?" Georgina's voice is raw with emotion.

"Of course I . . . I want you." He looks to me. "But I don't know if . . . I . . ."

Jojo groans. "Come on. It's not like you're going to have to keep an eye on her all the time, Dad. She was practically on her own before she came here."

Remy looks at Georgina. "I do want you to live with me. I think it might be good for both of us," he says, obviously choosing his words carefully. He returns his gaze to me. "But this has to be up to your mother."

I hear Georgina's chair scrape on the hardwood floor. She gets up.

"Lilla," Remy says.

"Georgina," I call after her.

But she's already out of the dining room.

I look to Remy, stunned. "You have to fix this," I say in a small, frightened voice. "You can't take her from me. You can't do it."

He grabs my hand. He's teary, too. "I won't. You know I won't. Not without you agreeing to it. But, baby . . . think about what she's asking. Think about what Jojo is saying."

"I'm going to go see if she's okay," Jojo says and gets up.

I just sit there, feeling the warmth of Remy's hand.

"Just consider it. Temporarily . . . it might be a good idea," he says. "It might be easier for her to make the transition."

"But I want her here with me." Tears run down my cheeks.

He gets out of his chair and comes to me. He squats beside me. "I know you do," he says softly, looking up at me. "But what is our goal here? What's your goal?" When I don't answer, he goes on. "I think our goal is to integrate Lilla into our family. To make her one of us."

I wring my napkin in my hands. "But she is."

"To us she is, but not to her."

I close my eyes. I'm trembling.

"You want to be her mother, but right now, in her head, Sharon is her mother and you're just a . . . usurper."

The word makes me take a shuddering breath. The thing is, Georgina said the same thing in the car yesterday. She just said it with more kindness.

"Maybe you two need some space. So neither of you feels so much pressure," Remy goes on. "Because right now you're struggling to be her mother and she's struggling to be your daughter, Harper. And . . . we have to take into account her being old enough and mature enough to make choices like this. If we were divorcing right now, a judge might ask her who she wanted to live with."

"But how can I let her go when I've waited so long to have her again with me?"

He takes my hand and kisses it. "You wouldn't be letting her go. You'd just be letting her live with her father. Baby, half the kids in this country live with just one biological parent and most of them don't get to live a few blocks from the other parent."

I close my eyes. I want to get down on the floor and curl up in a ball and just . . . disappear.

Remy rests his cheek on my hand. "Harper," he whispers. "I think we need to do this. For our daughter."

43

Lilla

I hear the front door open, but I don't look over my shoulder to see who it is. I'm leaning on the porch rail, looking out into the dark. The oak trees look bigger at night; their branches seem like arms reaching out to wrap us in their embrace. I can't decide if it makes them look more sinister, or kinder.

"I found out Friday night." It's Jojo. "That he's moving out." She comes to lean on the rail with me. "I knew he wouldn't stay, so I wasn't surprised. I was going to tell you, but then you did your disappearing act and that sort of took over."

"It's okay, Jojo," I say. "It wasn't your place to tell me."

We're both quiet for a minute, then Jojo says, "Don't be pissed at him. I know it would be nice if he wanted to live with us, but we're still better off than most kids. Who our age still has their dad around? He's usually on a second family by now with a younger, prettier wife and a baby."

A silence stretches between us, but it's not uncomfortable. I wonder if she sees the trees the same way I do.

"He does love us," my sister goes on. "And . . . I know it sounds whack, but he's not lying when he says he loves Mom. Legally they're divorced, but I don't care what anyone says, they'll always be together. Who knows, maybe after we're gone, Dad'll move back in for good." She sighs. "I just think he can't deal with it right now. With work and Mom and us. I think if you go with him, though, he'll be okay. I mean you're practically an adult already. You don't need him leaning over you, telling you what to do and where to go. And he doesn't feel like he needs to boss you around."

I stare into the darkness. "You don't want me here."

She's quiet. I can smell her berry shampoo. She's so close to me that her sleeve brushes mine and I find it strangely comforting. We're nothing alike, and yet . . . I feel this pull toward her. I wonder if it's the blood tie, or the house, or just because I don't have anybody anymore.

"That's not something I get to choose," Jojo says. "Kids don't get to decide that kind of stuff. When Mom and Dad wanted to have another baby, they didn't ask your permission."

I smile at her observation. Jojo thinks she's dumb, but she's not. She's not book dumb and she's definitely not people dumb. I think she's struggling with teenage hormones and whatever. I seemed pretty dumb sometimes when I was fourteen.

"So it's not fair to ask me if I want you here. Because you're my sister." Jojo stops and then goes on. "But if you're asking me if I want you to leave here to go live with Dad . . . I guess I kind of do. Because I liked how things were before Mom found you." She turns to look at me, the towel still on her head. "But whether you live here with Mom and me or with Dad down the street, things aren't ever going to be the way they were for me and I just have to get over it. You know? Because Mom *did* find you. And I don't think that's a bad thing," she adds.

I meet her gaze in the flickering yellowy light that comes from the old-fashioned gas lamps burning on both sides of the front door. I hear the old roof over the porch creak. It's chilly outside, but I'm not cold. "What you said in there about me going with Dad? Do you think it makes sense? For me, I mean?"

She looks into my eyes and then out at the park again. "If I were you, I'd want some distance between me and Mom. She just . . . what you said. She tries *so* hard that it makes things hard for the rest of us. And she's not totally your mom, not like she's mine. I mean, she is . . . but, you know what I mean. You really do have two moms because . . . just because Sharon did what she did, that doesn't wipe out all those years you had together. When you were happy. When she loved you. I think that's hard for Mom to understand."

I think on that for a moment. "Will she let me go with Dad?"

"I think she will," Jojo says softly, "if she can just be brave enough."

44

Harper

Holding hands, Remy and I stand in the hall at the front door. I can hear our girls talking softly on the porch, but I can't hear what they're saying. I have an impulse to grab them coats; they might be cold. But we're in a bit of a family crisis right now so we'll forgo the coats.

I watch through the door, studying how the light from the gas lamps flickers across their backs. Jojo is still wearing her pink towel on her head.

"You want me to go out with you to talk to her?" Remy asks.

I shake my head. My sense of falling has passed. I've hit solid ground again. Semisolid. Maybe a little boggy. I don't like where I'm standing right now. I wish I weren't here. But I know I have to be thankful for all I have and not covet what I don't. Having Georgina right now on our porch is nothing short of a miracle. And a miracle has to be enough for me. I should have seen that all along.

I squeeze Remy's hand and let go. I open the door and walk out onto the porch, hugging myself for warmth. Where's our spring weather? Last year, we had eighty-degree days by now. I watch my daughters leaning on the rail, looking out over the park. They're quiet now, but they're still standing side by side, arm brushing arm. The sight makes me want to smile and cry at the same time.

I take a step forward, because I have to. Because it's what mothers do. "Jojo, could you give us a minute?" I ask.

My youngest leans against her big sister for just a split second, then turns away. She brushes past me, meeting my gaze, and then she's inside the house, closing the door behind her. Closing us out.

I walk over to the rail and look at Georgina. "I don't want to let you go, you know. Not even eight blocks away."

She turns. Meets my gaze. "You don't want me," she says softly. "Not really. You want Georgina. You want a girl I'm never going to be."

I take a shuddering breath. I want to argue with her but I don't. Because I can't. Not if I'm going to be honest with her. With myself.

"But I love you," I manage, fighting back tears.

She smiles. "I know you do. And I think . . ." She keeps her gaze steady on me, my brave girl. "I'm not saying this so you'll let me go with Dad, but . . . I think someday . . . someday I can—"

She doesn't finish her sentence. She doesn't have to. I know what she's trying to say. That if I'll just back off a little, give her some space and some time, maybe she'll come to love me.

I hear the pain in her voice as she tries to express this to me and I just want to wrap her in my arms. I want to hold her the way I did when she was a baby. I want to soothe her tears with my breasts, with my voice, with the beat of my heart. But she's not a baby anymore. She's not even a girl. She's almost a woman. And Remy's right. This has to be her choice.

I feel light-headed as I reach into my cardigan pocket. "You have to come spend the night with us at least once a week. And I expect dinner together, as a family, four or five nights a week. And we're going to do something fun together, you and I, at least once a week. We can go to museums. We don't have to shop."

She laughs through her tears. "Deal."

"And you have to promise to try to let me in, Georgina." I tug on her sleeve. "You have to talk to me. Even if you don't think I'm going to like what you have to say. You have to say it."

"Yes." She sniffs. "I'll try."

"I have something for you," I whisper. My crucifix is for her, it's always been, but I know now isn't the time. I hope there will be a time, but I know this isn't it. But I have something else for her, something I didn't even realize was meant to be hers. "I want you to keep this with you. And know every time you see it or touch it, how much I love you, Georgina Elise Lilla Broussard."

I take her hand and press the silver king cake baby charm I've taken from my pocket into her palm.

"Your cake baby?" she breathes. She holds it in her palm and touches it delicately with one finger. She looks at me again. "I really *did* remember it. I wasn't making that up. You know, because I thought you wanted me to remember something."

"I know." I slip my arm around her waist, and lean into her, feeling her warmth.

"I can't take it," she tells me, allowing my embrace. "It's yours. It's . . . your special thing."

I breathe in the scent of her, savoring the feel of her. "Which is why I want you to have it."

She hesitates, then murmurs, "Thank you."

She doesn't hug me. She doesn't tell me she loves me. But seeing my silver charm clasped tightly in her hand, I smile through my tears. I'll never have the family I dreamed of all these years, but I found Georgina. We found each other.

FINDING GEORGINA

Colleen Faulkner

ABOUT THIS GUIDE

The suggested questions are included to
enhance your group's reading of
Colleen Faulkner's *Finding Georgina*!

DISCUSSION QUESTIONS

1. Do you think Harper and Remy could have stayed to-gether had Georgina not been kidnapped?

2. What do you think about Harper's response to her daugh-ter's kidnapping? How would you have responded, had Georgina been your child?

3. Was Remy a weak man or a strong one?

4. What's your opinion of Remy and Harper's marriage after the divorce, prior to Georgina's return? After her return?

5. Was Jojo's response to the rescue of her sister to be ex-pected? Why or why not?

6. What kind of relationship do you think will develop be-tween Georgina and Harper? Will they be satisfied with the relationship?

7. Do you think Sharon should ever be allowed to see Lilla again? Would this be for Lilla's good or Sharon's?

8. Do think Harper will be able to give Lilla the freedom she wants?

9. Will Lilla and Jojo ever become friends? Why or why not?

10. What do you think of the decision Remy and Harper made at the end of the book? Do you think they can make it work?

Connect with Us

Visit us online at
KensingtonBooks.com
to read more from your favorite authors, see books
by series, view reading group guides, and more.

for sneak peeks, chances to win books and prize packs,
and to share your thoughts with other readers.

facebook.com/kensingtonpublishing
twitter.com/kensingtonbooks

Tell us what you think!

To share your thoughts, submit a review,
or sign up for our eNewsletters, please visit:
KensingtonBooks.com/TellUs.